Dear Reader,

Last month I asked if you'd like to see more humour, romantic suspense or linked books on our list. Well this month I can offer you all three!

I'm thrilled to bring you the final part of Liz Fielding's critically acclaimed and very popular Beaumont Brides trilogy. But, if we're lucky, maybe Melanie's story won't be the end after all . . .

Two stories which can be classified as suspense, but which are very different in style and plot, are offered by Laura Bradley and Jill Sheldon. These authors have won plaudits from critics and readers alike for their earlier *Scarlet* novels.

And finally, those of you who've asked for more books by Natalie Fox will, we're sure, enjoy reading our exciting new author, Talia Lyon, who brings a delightfully humorous flavour to her story of three gals, three guys and the holiday of a lifetime.

As always, I hope you enjoy the books I've chosen for you this month. Let me have your comments and suggestions, won't you and I'll do all I can to bring you more of the kind of books *you* want to read.

Till next month,

Sally Cooper

SALLY COOPER,
Editor-in-Chief – *Scarlet*

TALIA LYON

GIRLS ON THE RUN

SCARLET

Enquiries to:
Robinson Publishing Ltd
7 Kensington Church Court
London W8 4SP

First published in the UK by Scarlet, 1997

A copy of the British Library Cataloguing in
Publication data is available from the British Library

ISBN 1-85487-976-6

Printed and bound in the EC

10 9 8 7 6 5 4 3 2 1

CHAPTER 1

'I adore you, darling. Would you be terribly disappointed if I told you I couldn't make it this weekend? Something's cropped up that can't be avoided.'

Cathy Peterson, arms linked around her lover's neck, put on a brave face to hide her hurt feelings. They'd planned a weekend down at the coast, away from the grind of London city life. Cathy had already made the booking at a five-star hotel overlooking the beach. A suite with four-poster bed, and nouvelle cuisine in the rooftop restaurant, the sort of place where they turned the beds down at night and left chocolates on the pillow and baskets of toiletries in the en-suite.

Cathy swallowed her sigh of disappointment. Just lately it seemed that Charles had something cropping up every weekend.

'Yes, I am terribly disappointed,' she murmured, smiling up at him. 'I forgive you though. I'll just mope around at home on my own, plan a few bank robberies, call a few Mafia friends, get a little drunk.'

Charles grinned and pecked a kiss on the tip of her nose. 'Good girl. I knew you'd understand.' He turned away from her to gather up a pile of faxes from his desk to hand to her. 'Be a sweetie and sort this lot for me. I've some calls to make.'

Cathy took them and swallowed another huge sigh. Why did he make her feel like a faithful pink labrador puppy instead of his lover at times? Well, Lisa, her flatmate, had warned her that company executives and their secretaries made notoriously bad relationships once they let their hearts and hormones creep into the working day.

It had all started out so wonderfully when Charles had joined the company as executive accountant. She had expected a Machiavellian old lecher like her last boss and had been knocked sideways when Charles Bond had walked in. Obviously the brother of James, she had mused with keen interest as their eyes had locked mesmerically across the room.

Fair-haired, blue-eyed, rugby-thighed, he had walked into the office as if on the final take of a quality beer commercial. Anyone less like an accountant she couldn't have imagined. But she had soon learnt his brain put computer technology to shame. The man was pure genius with figures.

Hers too, Cathy thought reflectively as she closed his executive-suite door after her. Most times he made her feel so very special, but now she was feeling exactly what she was, if she cared to face the truth – an accommodating secretary-cum-surrogate puppy, to be stroked now and then.

Dejectedly Cathy tossed the faxes down on her desk and glared at them as she slid into her chair behind the desk in the front office. She was disappointed, painfully so. This was the third weekend he had put her off. True, he had taken her out to dinner twice this week and had been very attentive, but each time had left her rather early with a promise to make it up to her at a later date.

'He's married,' Lisa had teased her on one of those home-early occasions. 'He's probably on the mobile to his wife this very minute: "Sorry darling, on my way, unavoidably held up by a fall on the Nikkei, alias my gorgeous secretary who hangs on every word I utter."'

Cathy had thrown a cushion at her and coiled on the sofa to glare at Lisa as she sat in the chair by the window of their ground-floor Battersea flat, studiously working out menus for her new venture, 'providing' lunches in executive offices.

'I'm a city girl born and bred and I didn't come down with yesterday's acid rain,' Cathy had told her frostily. 'I can tell a married man at twenty paces. Charles definitely *hasn't* a wife or a live-in partner. He might, just *might*, have a dear old Crimplened mum tucked away in Oxfordshire whom he visits every weekend to mow her lawn, and being the macho sort of guy that he is he doesn't want to come over too soft so early in our relationship. He'll tell me about her soon enough, but I expect he's told *her* all about *me* already, warming the way to introducing me – '

'Blimey, life isn't the coffee ads.' Lisa had yawned lazily, which spurred Cathy to bring up a certain Philip Mainwaring with whom Lisa was making as much progress as she might in trying to climb the mountains of Snowdonia in rubber flip-flops on a wet day – two steps forward and three back.

But being the good friends that they were – friends since primary school in Balham – they were soon guffawing and reprimanding themselves for acting like teenagers when they were not, and for talking

3

as if men were their sole reason for living, which they *definitely* were not. Both had good career prospects and a good social set and enjoyed life to the full.

Though Cathy was beginning to wonder if that was enough these days. She flicked through the faxes Charles had given her, but didn't really see them. She *was* disappointed she wasn't seeing him this weekend. She'd bought a gorgeous new outfit especially with him in mind – an outrageously expensive cream Escada dress and jacket that she was simply dying to show off.

She wished she wasn't feeling so disappointed that it wouldn't get an airing yet; it was certainly too good for the pubs around the flat, but the feeling of being let down yet again couldn't be denied. Charles was beginning to matter greatly in her life. She guessed this was love. And him – how did he really feel about her? On a good day she was almost sure she was very much a part of his life and hopefully his future. Hadn't he just said he adored her?

'I'd like to see Charles, please. It's Patsy, isn't it? Charles has told me so much about you.'

Cathy jerked her head up and stared wide-eyed at the woman standing in front of the desk. Unannounced visitors on this high-security financial floor were unheard off. How had this rather elegant woman with gorgeous strawberry blonde hair sleeked into a long bob got past reception on the ground floor?

'Er . . . excuse me?' she faltered.

The woman smiled. 'Patsy, aren't you? Charles's secretary?'

'Cathy,' Cathy corrected her.

'Oh, yes, of course, Cathy. Well, dear, I'd like to see him.' She raised her finely plucked eyebrows slightly

4

indulgently as if she was humouring a child that had learning difficulties.

Cathy searched for her equilibrium. The woman's suddenly appearing out of nowhere had taken her aback, especially as she had been deep in thought over how much Charles was beginning to matter in her life. She smiled brightly.

'I'm sorry, I was miles away,' she explained. She stood up and looked at the woman properly. She was very lovely, beautifully dressed in a pale pink Chanel suit, and there was something slightly familiar about her. Yes, she looked strikingly like Charles. Gosh, she must be his sister and he had talked about her to his sister, never mind that she had got her name wrong, and that must mean . . .

'You wanted to see Charles. Of course.' She grinned. 'Is he expecting you?'

The woman smiled thinly. 'I hardly think so and, before you ask, I've no intention of making an appointment.' She leaned across the desk, as if about to share a secret. 'I didn't think one was necessary to see one's husband,' she whispered conspiratorially.

Cathy's mouth dropped open rather inelegantly and she felt the blood drain from her face as if someone had accidentally pulled the plug on her left ventricle. Her whole body went into shock, trembling pulse rate and all.

'Julia!' Charles barked from the doorway and Cathy was the one to jump in fright. Julia was obviously well used to it, Cathy thought madly as her blood pressure seemed to right itself, bringing with it a rush of chillingly cold realization — like a slap in the face with a wet J-cloth that had just been used to wipe the freezer out.

5

Julia walked briskly across the outer office towards her husband. 'Cora has pulled out this weekend,' she told him accusingly as if it was his fault, 'and Toby wants to bring Simon instead. You are going to have to talk to your brother and – '

Charles closed the door after them both and Cathy stood fused to the spot with shock. Charles, her beloved Charles, had a *wife*! And a brother, too, by the sound of it. She hadn't known about either. As for Cora and Toby and Simon . . . It appeared Charles had a life she knew nothing about.

Her brow suddenly fevered up and she kneaded it with a tremulous hand. Oh, God, he *was* married and she hadn't known, she hadn't suspected a thing. How could she have allowed herself to be so completely and utterly deceived?

Should she get her coat and leave now? Should she storm in there and cause a scene? Should she put her head in the oven and kick the stool away or whatever it was you did?

Oh, what an idiot she had been! Lisa had been right all along! It was horrible, this feeling curling poisonously inside her. Worse than disappointment, worse than the flu, worse than anything she had ever experienced before. She felt horribly sick as she sat at her desk, staring into space.

'Goodbye, Patsy. Lovely to meet you,' Julia cooed as she swept out of Charles's office barely five minutes later. Five minutes during which Cathy's whole life, past and present, had swum dizzily before her eyes. Her future didn't bear thinking about. 'You must come up to Cambridge one weekend. Darling, don't forget Cora,' she directed over her shoulder to a very sombre Charles, 'she really could do with some advice on this one.'

She swept out of the outer office, leaving the air heady with expensive French perfume which made Cathy feel totally undermined in her simple, flower fragrance which Charles had always claimed turned him on. Traitor! Liar!

Cathy glared at him furiously as he leaned nonchalantly in the doorway watching her, all smiling arrogance without a smidgeon of remorse on his implacable face.

'Before you fly at my throat,' he started softly, 'let me explain.'

'Explain?' Cathy exploded. She picked up the nearest thing to hand, a copy of her *Idiot's Guide to Windows Software*. She flung it furiously at his head, but being Charles Never-caught-with-his-pants-down Bond he ducked easily and it splayed open against the wall beside him. 'There is no explaining to do,' she shrieked at him. 'I'm just wondering how long you would have gone on fooling me? Not that it matters – nothing seems to matter any more! Oh, how could you, Charles! How *could* you?'

'In here,' Charles breathed wearily, nodding to his high tec-style inner sanctum.

Cathy's hands shot up in defence. 'No way. I'll never step into your office again, not ever. Not never.'

'Sacking yourself, are you?' he responded coolly.

Cathy gaped at him. She hadn't got that far in her thinking, actually walking out on him and putting herself out of work. She loved her job, she loved . . . No, she didn't. She did not love this deceiver, this wretched man who had fooled her so utterly.

'Right, get yourself in here and hear me out. We

7

don't want the rest of the floor listening to this argument.'

True. No one knew about her affair with her boss, but they soon would if she didn't keep her cool. She could imagine the sniggers and the behind-the-back remarks if she didn't. *Silly cow. Didn't she know? Everyone else did!*

Cathy strode through his office door determinedly, smoothing down her businesslike black Lycra skirt and hating his wife for wearing Chanel in the daytime. She turned on him as soon as he closed the door after them. 'This is not an argument, Charles,' she insisted, determined not to show him how deeply shocked she was. Act nineties, she told herself. 'How can we argue over such a thing? You are married and – '

'Aren't you going to hear my side of all this?' he interrupted.

Cathy's dark brown eyes widened. 'What's there to hear?' she protested. 'You are married, aren't you?'

'Sort of,' he answered cautiously.

'Sort of!' she echoed, hands on hips. 'Is that like being *slightly* pregnant?'

'You're not pregnant, are you?' he breathed faintly.

It was then it really hit Cathy. She felt it in the pit of her stomach, where a baby might have nestled close by if all was well with the world and she and Charles were married instead of him being already married to the beautiful Julia. Not that she had considered their relationship to the extent of a country cottage and a pile of children, but all the same hormones were hormones and she had been getting there, getting pretty close to considering that she might have a future with Charles.

8

'No, I am not pregnant, Charles,' she told him coldly,' and it is the one saving grace in all this. I don't think I have ever felt so humiliated in my whole life.'

He stepped towards her as if to take her in his arms, but Cathy stepped smartly back out of his reach. 'No, don't touch me and don't try to make excuses. I don't want to hear about how unhappy your marriage is and how she doesn't understand you and all the other *stupid* clichés men who get found out offer to their unsuspecting lovers.'

'I wasn't about to say anything of the sort. You really are quite naïve, aren't you, Cathy?' He smiled benignly. 'I've never had a secretary quite as sweet as you.'

Sweet! This was ridiculous. She was five-nine, dark and sultry rather than fair and demure, she took size six shoes in the mornings, six and a half in the afternoon when her feet swelled like shovels, she had a temper to take cover from when it was inflamed, and by no stretch of the imagination could she be described as *sweet*! As for *naïve*, phuff!

'Don't you mean as *daft* as me?' she grated sarcastically. 'Because that is exactly the way I feel, daft, and angry, and bitter, and . . . and – '

'A teeny-weeny bit cheated?' he added for her, head tilted to one side as if he had made a joke and expected her to fall about laughing.

'Hugely cheated!' she cried, even more angry that he was trivializing it all with that theatrical twinkle in his devious blue eyes.

'Well, don't feel cheated, Cathy, darling,' he implored her, quite serious now. 'My heart is with you and not my wife. I won't bore you with the details, but

9

let's just put it like this – Julia and I have an arrangement. She does her thing and I do mine and it makes
for a well-oiled, trouble-free existence all round.'

Cathy stared at him in astonishment. Why hadn't
she seen this absurdly selfish streak in him before?
What had happened to her to turn her into some silly
blind lovesick fool? At twenty-three was she seeing the
biological clock ticking away and grasping at straws?

Was she hell! She was in life's sweet infancy where
relationships were concerned. Put this one down to
experience, she vowed determinedly, and to hell with
nineties thinking, too. Affairs with married men
wasn't her forte. Never, no, *never* would she have
allowed her heart to rule her head over a married man
if she had known. She lifted her chin and narrowed her
eyes at him.

'You, Charles Bond, are a bastard. You and your
wife deserve each other and I wish you years of merry
fun with your horribly obscene *arrangement*. Yes, I'm
sacking myself – foolhardy, maybe, but deeply satisfying. And I won't serve a month's notice as stated in
my terms of employment. Bloody sue me!'

'Cathy, darling, you are being ridiculous,' Charles
protested, 'and I don't want you to go. You are the
best secretary I've ever had – '

'*Had* being the operative word,' Cathy flamed. 'I
sure was had, Charles, fooled completely.'

And the more she stood here listening to his
pathetic reasoning, the more angry she was becoming. She'd better get out before she did something
bloody she might regret, like impale him on the spiky
cactus plant he lovingly tended first thing every
morning. She turned on her heel and went for the
door.

Charles caught her before she could open it. He swung her around to face him, holding her tenderly but firmly by the shoulders.

'Darling, please, don't go,' he pleaded, eyes soft and persuasive now. 'Let's talk about this.' His hands started to caress her shoulders seductively. 'We'll get a little apartment together, a secret love nest. I'll do anything you say, but don't leave now, not in the middle of the yearly financial rep – oh, my God!' Suddenly he doubled up in pain, his breath knocked from his lungs.

Cathy stepped back, a deep smile of satisfaction on her lovely face, her right knee only throbbing slightly. She thrust him aside, easily done in spite of his size because he was still gagging for breath, and stepped smartly out of his office, slamming the door behind her.

Still she wasn't satisfied. Revenge burned. She took up the pile of faxes he had given her before tearing her world apart. *Be a sweetie and deal with these*, she heard.

'Ye-es, sir!' Cathy hissed through her teeth. Rapturously she fed the lot into the shredder. Still on a high, she circled her desk to face her computer. A few mousy manoeuvres and the spreadsheet for the Belgian metal account she had been working on this past week was deleted from screen and memory.

Oh, the feeling was good. Revenge, sweet revenge. She was hooked on it. How well she understood betrayed wives who cut up their husband, clothes, cut up anything they could get their hands on! But she wasn't a wife, she was the other side of the deception fence, the mistress, but now she knew it was the same, exactly the same.

Anything else? Murderously she looked around her

11

office, but she couldn't bear to do mortal damage to the rubber plant he had bought her for her birthday. It didn't deserve her anger. It would live. Would she, though? she wondered as she scooped up an assortment of spare lipsticks, a dried-up mascara, half a chocolate bar and a buckled hairbrush from her desk drawer, and rammed them into her handbag.

The anger and the need to hit out was receding now and pain knifed through her in its place. For a second Cathy clutched dizzily at the edge of her desk. Curious how you felt when something was snatched from you. You wanted it all the more. Should she rush back into his office and say she was sorry and hold him and beg for forgiveness and yes, yes, yes, they would get a little love nest and . . . and . . .?

'Are you out of your mind? 'she screamed at herself.

Grasping her bag, she flew out of the office, into the lift, down and out and across the marbled reception area, heels rat-tatting a defiant retreat. She even forced out a cheery goodbye to Dickie, the security guard, and then she was out of the cool air-conditioning and into hot bright sunshine, and damn it, damn it, she was shaking from head to toe.

Outside the building she bumped down on to a stone wall because her legs wouldn't carry her any further. If there had been a cigar about she would have lit one up and sat there smoking it to 'Air on a G String'.

Horrors – she was out of a job. Just like that she had walked out of a well-paid job that she loved, and she was out on the street. And all because of him. Charles rotten Bond, married, a cheater, a thief of hearts. And she had loved him and he hadn't loved her one bit – wasn't free to – and it hurt like hell.

And then a strange new feeling washed over her.

12

One she was very well prepared to cling on to for dear life. It was a feeling of total stupidity. He had fooled her, deceived her, and that was why she was hurting so badly and it was nothing to do with love. And the feeling was good. Yes, good because her pride was hurting and not her heart. She was feeling an utter fool for allowing him to deceive her in the worst possible way. She had been blind and gullible and that was why she was so mad. Losing *him* didn't hurt, losing her self-respect did!

But her eyes were hurting now and the feeble attempt to argue with herself that pride mattered more than love was already beginning to pall. Her heart *did* hurt and she didn't want it to. She wanted to cry and she hadn't cried for yonks . . . occasionally a PMT rush of tears, but not a real bawl.

Cathy choked back the lump in her throat and glanced at her watch quickly before she lost her vision to a waterfall of tears. Five o'clock, nearly going-home time anyway. She was meeting Lisa in the wine bar at six as usual before they wended their way home to Battersea. She sniffed decisively. No, she wasn't going to damn well cry over him. She was in shock, that was all. In a matter of a few minutes her world had been rocked, but a leisurely stroll through Mayfair and across Regent Street to Soho would sort her out.

With a sigh, and biting back those treacherous tears, she set off, thinking that a slow boat to China would fit the bill for her at the moment. She felt like running away, leaving it all behind her, hiding herself away to lick her wounds as an injured animal might. But she was out of work and the only place she could run to tomorrow was a job agency. Damn married men, especially the blue-eyed variety called Charles. Damn them all.

'A bottle of white wine, Bruce. The first thing that comes to hand, surgical spirit for all I care.' Lisa perched herself on a bar stool at The Vat wine bar and prepared to drown her sorrows. It had been one helluva day.

'Are you driving?' Bruce, the Aussie barman, asked warningly.

'OK – ' Lisa sighed in resignation ' – half a bottle, then, and a bottle of mineral water too.' She grinned sheepishly at Bruce. 'And thanks for looking out for me – knowing my luck today, anything could happen.'

Bruce decorked a bottle of wine as quick as it took a grin to spread across his bronzed, craggily handsome face. 'Bad day, eh?'

'Disastrous. Any more like this and I'll do a Thelma and Louise off the Hammersmith flyover in my catering van,' she bleated self-pityingly.

'Life's precious, sweetheart.' Bruce laughed, sticking the cork behind his ear for later. Lisa and Cathy wondered what he did with them – smoked them or strung them round his bush hat?

'I was only joking, Bruce.' She sighed again. 'You don't want to buy fifty-one freshly baked, individual sticky toffee puddings, do you?'

Bruce's sun-bleached brow rose as if to say, *you gotta be joking*, and Lisa waved her offer away dismissively with the back of her hand as if she was, in fact, joking. But she wasn't.

Tucking the bottle of water under her arm and taking the wine and the glasses, she headed to the marble table in the corner to wait for Cathy, who appeared to be running late. There was an art-deco mirror on the wall above the table and Lisa scowled at her own reflection. Perhaps she shouldn't have had her long blonde hair cropped short and spiky for the summer; it must have zapped all her strength like Samson when Delilah hacked at his. But at the time it had looked like a good career move – hygienic too, no errant long blonde hairs cropping up in the soufflé. When she had decided to progress from selling sandwiches and home-made patties from trendy gingham-lined baskets round the offices of the West End, to executive lunches – all food freshly prepared that very day, which meant a hellishly early start in the morning – she had thought that with her culinary skills success was guaranteed. But she hadn't taken into account the effect Philip Mainwaring had had on her senses. Instead of gazing at him in rapt adoration, her knees weak with longing, she should have listened to what he was saying. Why, oh, why hadn't she listened properly?

Cathy arrived just as Lisa was taking a first gulp of delicious South African Chenin Blanc.

'Can you credit it!' Cathy huffed as she slumped down in a hard wrought-iron chair. 'I decided to walk and, after the day I've had, I broke a heel on the way here. I've just had to fork out forty quid for a new pair of loafers I didn't need. They were fifty quid, actually, but I got a tenner knocked off because one was faded through being in the window. No one will notice if I cross my legs.'

'Wouldn't it have been cheaper to get the heel repaired en route?' Lisa suggested absently. What was a new pair of loafers compared to her misery?

'Oh, I never thought of that,' Cathy muttered,

wishing she had because she could ill afford such luxuries as shoes any more. 'What's wrong with you?' she asked. 'You look how I feel, pinched and pummelled.'

Lisa braved a small smile. 'You couldn't possibly have had a day like I've had.'

'Oh, no?' Cathy murmured obliquely, helping herself to wine.

'No, you couldn't. Nobody in the world could have gone through what I put myself through today, total, absolutely total, humiliation. And all my own fault. I can't blame anyone else. It was my own doing and – '

'Yeah, I know the feeling,' Cathy moaned. 'Well, are you going to share this total humiliation with me or would you rather hack it on your own?' She added wearily.

'I'm a failure, Cath,' Lisa breathed mournfully, lowering her violet eyes and staring bleakly at a chip in the marble table. 'I'm so stupid I think I ought to be put down. That damned, damned Philip Mainwaring.'

Cathy gulped. Men again, nothing but trouble. But whatever Lisa's problem Cathy bet it didn't involve a wife. Lisa was too sweet a girl, a real poppet, for any man to even think of deceiving her in such a cruel way. The thought that she, the supposedly streetwise Cathy Peterson, had been so effortlessly deceived by a married man, and was therefore not seen as a sweet poppet of a person, in spite of what Charles had said, was a horribly sobering thought.

Lisa leaned across the table to Cathy, her eyes mournful. 'I'm ruined, Cath. My first executive lunch, and what do I do? I blow it. All ruined because I didn't listen properly,' she told her, raising her voice

16

slightly because the noise in the wine bar was reaching ten on the Richter Scale, 'I want to blame Philip, but when it comes down to it it's all my own fault and – '

'Calm down, Lisa,' Cathy implored her. 'Start at the beginning, because I don't know what you are talking about.'

'Philip, Philip Mainwaring. Remember I met him when I was doing the sandwich rounds? Chief executive of RAMS Electronics.'

'Huh, how could I forget! You've been drooling over him for months now. And, yes, I remember now, he was your first executive lunch, today. So what went wrong?'

Lisa sighed and took a sip of water before going on. She lowered her eyes, hardly able to look her friend in the eye because Cathy too would think her an idiot for making such a boob.

'I was so dewy-eyed over wretched Philip Mainwaring I didn't listen properly. He thought it a huge joke, laughed and his very words were, "well, you won't make the same mistake twice, will you?" I thought at the very least he would – '

Cathy gritted her teeth. 'For heaven's sake, Lisa, what exactly did you *do*?'

'Catered for fifty when what he actually said was an executive lunch for fifteen,' Lisa told her in a rush to get it over with.

Cathy stared at her in confusion. 'A gaffe, yes, but I can't see the problem. Surely that's good and not bad? I mean, if it was the other way round – you catering for fifteen when you should have catered for fifty – *then* you would have been in trouble. You would have had to perform a miracle with bread and fishes and all that.'

17

Lisa groaned. 'You don't understand, do you? I *over*-catered. Fifteen executives walked into the boardroom dining-room of RAMS, eight of them Japanese visitors, and there was a spread for sixty.'

'I thought you said fifty.'

'I did extra, just in case,' Lisa muttered sheepishly. 'There it all was, enough food to feed the Philharmonic Orchestra, a bloody banquet for eight Japanese who'd rather have eaten shushi anyway – '

'Sushi,' Cathy corrected.

'And Philip and six of his own directors wearing the expressions of those who would much rather have indulged in a liquid lunch. Oh, it was awful. So embarrassing. I wanted the ground to open up and swallow me. And it was all my own fault. I fancied him so much it clouded my business head and I didn't concentrate on what he was saying. I made a fool of myself and all he did was laugh. Put it down to experience was another thing he said, but he didn't offer me any more work to get that experience *and* he only paid me for the fifteen, said he would be in touch if he needed me again but I know he won't and . . . and what on earth are you laughing about?' she growled at Cathy.

'Oh, Lisa,' Cathy uttered, trying to keep a straight face, 'you must admit it is quite funny. Your first lunch and you getting it hopelessly wrong. Fifty, no, *sixty*, instead of fifteen.' She grinned across the table. 'Come on, Lisa, where's your sense of humour?'

'In the back of the van,' Lisa hissed, not at all amused, 'along with fifty-one individual sticky toffee puddings, a couple of dozen exquisite seafood tarts, about sixty marinaded chicken breasts in cream sauce, a bin bag of exotic salads, fresh fruit salad, all with a

18

consume-by date of approximately two hours hence. Oh, and several boxes of wine, too. In other words, a small fortune-worth of useless food. All my money gone and nothing booked after today . . . and it isn't funny, Cathy,' she finished limply.

No, it wasn't, Cathy thought soberly, knowing how hard Lisa had worked and knowing how excited she had been about this new project of hers. Her hand crept across the table and squeezed Lisa's. 'I'm sorry, Lisa, truly. I shouldn't have laughed. When we get home, we'll freeze what we can and we'll plough through as much as we can and throw a few dinner parties. It isn't the end of the world and . . . and . . . well, tomorrow is another day.'

'Yeah, well, Scarlett O'Hara I ain't, Cathy,' Lisa bleated mournfully. 'I'm ruined. The whole effort cost me a fortune. I had to fork out for all that up front and all I got back was payment for the fifteen.' She sighed heavily. 'Oh, Cath, did I set my sights too high?'

'Well, catering for fifty instead of fifteen was a bit out of this world.'

'I *mean* setting my sights too high with Philip,' Lisa cried. 'The sandwich girl and the company director?'

Cathy shrugged helplessly. What did she know about anything to do with men?

'Let's put it like this. It's his loss and not yours,' she offered as a morsel of comfort.

Lisa managed a small smile. It encouraged Cathy. She hated to see Lisa so down. Normally she was so optimistic about everything, but this Philip must be someone special for him to grind her into the ground so. It was obvious Lisa was feeling the loss of *him* more than anything. No, it wasn't funny, letting men matter so much.

19

But Lisa was shaking her head dismally when Cathy lifted her eyes after concentrating on pouring more wine. 'Thanks for that vote of confidence, Cath – sadly, it doesn't give me much comfort. I really thought I had a chance with him. He flirted with me, you know. The sizzling eye contact, a purposeful innuendo dropped here and there. I read the bloody signs.'

Cathy grinned ruefully. 'Yes, well, you always did take the odd nudge, nudge, wink, wink routine as a lifetime commitment.'

Lisa suddenly grinned back and shrugged. 'Yeah, silly old-fashioned thing that I am,' she joked weakly.

'Old fashioned, *you*?'

The girls grinned at each other and lifted their glasses and clinked them. 'Sod 'em all,' Cathy offered. 'You want to hear something worse than fifty-one, spare-to-requirements, sticky toffee puddings sweating in the back of your van?'

Lisa shook her head. 'It can't get any worse.'

Cathy unloaded her bombshell. 'It can. It did. You were right. Charles is married.'

'Self-raising flour!' Lisa breathed in astonishment.

And over the rest of the wine and the rest of the mineral water and a bowl of tomato and basil pasta between them because suddenly economy was the word at the top of their list of priorities, Cathy told her all that had happened that pretty grisly afternoon.

'So there you have it,' Cathy concluded on a deep sigh. 'I walked out, feeling an absolute nerd for allowing myself to be charmed by him, but in a way that's a good feeling.'

'How do you mean?'

'Well, I'm more concerned for my pride than losing

20

him. That's got to be good, isn't it?'

Lisa giggled. 'I suppose so. Same with me, I guess. I was crazy about Philip, but finding myself grossly out of pocket for my efforts is hurting worse. Couple of mercenary old baggages, aren't we?'

Cathy grinned. 'You speak for yourself,' she joked. Then she sighed again; they might be sitting here making the best of two bad experiences, but she knew how deeply disappointed Lisa was over Philip and she herself was still in a state of shock over Charles's betrayal. 'You know, when I saw her standing in front of my desk I thought how like Charles she was,' she mused. 'I happily jumped to the conclusion she was his sister and because she said Charles had spoken of me my silly little heart leapt like a spawning salmon. I can tell you, it floundered badly when she said she was his wife.'

'Hmm, they say married people get to look like each other,' Lisa mused.

'Yeah, dogs and their owners too.'

They were still giggling, both putting on brave faces, when Cathy looked over Lisa's shoulder. The crowds were thinning in the wine bar, people wending their way home after a busy working day. But someone was just coming in the bar rather than leaving it and Cathy's eyes narrowed. She knew that face – the body that went with it was less familiar, though.

'What's up?' Lisa asked, noting her friend's change of expression.

'Don't look round, but guess who's just walked in?'

Lisa shrugged. 'Philip, Charles?'

'Getting warm. Not exactly royalty, but someone who always gave the impression of being a duchess. We used to call her that behind her back, remember?'

Lisa gasped. 'Not Elaine Morton? Our old flat-mate?'

'The very one. How she dare show her face in our favourite watering hole after what she did to us?' Cathy seethed. 'Walking out owing us three months' rent – '

'To say nothing of the phone bill,' Lisa reminded her. 'All those calls abroad. She nearly bankrupted us. Remember – she just disappeared one morning and we never saw her again. How long ago was that – over a year, wasn't it?'

Cathy nodded and lifted her glass of water to her nose to hide her face. The last thing she wanted was a confrontation with Elaine Morton but, on the other hand, calling in her debts now couldn't be a more convenient time. She was out of a job, and poor Lisa had blown all her money on a banquet no one wanted. If she didn't get a new job first thing in the morning, she would be paying a visit to a friendly bank manager, if she could find one. The mortgage had to be paid and life went on, with or without a job.

Yes, perhaps now was the time to resurrect an old friendship, though neither of the girls had been very close to Elaine. She wasn't that sort of girl and mostly kept herself to herself. She had been a bit of a strange one – too uppity, for one thing, but they hadn't known that at the time when she had come from the letting agency. They had a spare bedroom to let and needed the money to help out with the mortgage. Because she looked so well turned out and arrived in a taxi, which she kept waiting while she viewed the flat, they thought there wouldn't be any problems with the rent and her share of the bills. How wrong could you get?

Cathy and Lisa had often wondered why she had taken up residence with them across the river when she clearly belonged on the posh side. She was well spoken, extremely well dressed, came from a moneyed background – her father a judge or something equally awe-inspiring – and yet she chose to live with them in Battersea. Yes, she had been a mystery, but they had jogged along well enough and then she had disappeared, taking all her expensive clothes and make-up with her, which had at the very least put their minds at rest that she hadn't been abducted or worse.

'Has she seen us?' Lisa whispered.

Cathy parted her lips to say she couldn't help but see us as most of the tables were unoccupied now and there were only a handful of hardened drinkers still bonded to stools at the bar, but the words went unsaid. She had watched Elaine intently from the moment she had walked into the bar. Though she had instantly recognized her, she thought how very different she looked. Elaine had always looked so immaculately sophisticated for her job at the press gallery of the House of Commons and had been so obsessed with her weight, she used to weigh herself before and after going to the loo. Now she looked fuller somehow and was dressed very casually in jeans and a flowing silk shirt, hardly her style at all. She seemed to have lost her severity and her haughty air and looked almost . . . vulnerable was the word that came to Cathy's mind.

'Well, has she seen us or not?' Lisa asked again.

'I'm sure she has, she went a little pink around the ears, but she's not looking this way any more. She's ordering a drink from Bruce and . . . and someone has joined her. Gosh,' Cathy breathed faintly, 'the most gorgeous-looking bloke I've ever clapped eyes on . . .

tall, dark, well, just sort of wow . . . and he has just put
his arm around her shoulder *and* given her a loving
hug, the lucky cow.'

'Oh, I can't bear it any longer,' Lisa said and swung
around in her seat to take a look for herself. And then
she let out a strangled cry and jerked her head back to
face Cathy, her violet eyes wide with disbelief, her
lovely face flushed pink with shock.

'What's wrong?' Cathy squawked, thinking she was
about to throw a wobbly.

Lisa swallowed hard. 'The . . . the gorgeous-looking bloke with her,' she whispered hoarsely, 'it's . . .
it's Philip, *my* Philip!'

CHAPTER 2

'Thanks for coming, Phil,' Elaine smiled as Philip gave her a hug on arrival. 'Though on second thoughts, meeting here doesn't seem such a good idea after all. I've just seen two girls I used to know. Thankfully they haven't seen me.'

'Do you want to move on?' Philip asked.

Elaine, trying to avoid any eye contact with either of them, said on a sigh, 'Only if they see me and come across. With all my troubles at the moment, I couldn't face two more.'

She declined to elaborate to Philip the nature of those two more troubles. Cathy and Lisa were history now, though she still suffered pangs of guilt over what she had done to them, walking out owing rent and unpaid bills. But at the time she had been in such a turmoil, to cut and run had been the easiest option. And nothing much had changed since – her life seemed perpetual turmoil. Chaos followed her around like hungry gulls following the wake of a fishing boat.

Philip perched on a stool next to her and ordered himself a drink, a whisky and soda in a tall glass rather than wine. He'd had a terrible day with some important clients: a disastrous lunch brought by a crazy little blonde who was an amazing cook but couldn't count. She'd made him the laughing stock of the boardroom.

'So give,' he asked on a sigh. 'What are the latest developments in your turbulent life? A nine o'clock curfew this time?'

Elaine grinned ruefully, though there was nothing amusing about her latest predicament. But Philip never had taken her and her father's fiery relationship too seriously. He'd told her years back to stand on her own two feet and get out from under his draconian life style. But she hadn't Philip's strength of character. She had needed her father. But she was getting stronger and now, after her recent discovery, she was determined to break away and make her own life – as she had tried to do once before, and failed miserably. This time was going to be different, though.

'If Daddy thought he might get away with it, he'd try and impose that sort of curtailment on my life, but things have changed. His possessiveness has gone too far this time.'

Philip grinned ruefully and took a swig of his drink before speaking. 'Old bear,' he growled. 'I'm just glad he's not my father any more. So go on, what are the latest trials and tribulations between you two?'

Elaine took a big breath. 'Several. For one thing – and it's really a minor thing considering the rest, but the final straw that is breaking the camel's back – he's trying to marry me off to Philip Simmons-Black-shaw.'

Philip's head went back and he roared with laughter.

26

'Phil, this is not funny,' Elaine hissed at him under her breath.

'It's bloody hilarious! The man is a total wimp. True, rich as Croesus with old money, but a total idiot.'

'He adores me,' Elaine offered defensively, but then bit her lip because it had sounded as if she was considering marriage to him. And *nothing* could be further from the truth. 'Anyway, it's getting quite serious. He has Daddy's approval and he is bombarding me with flowers and gifts from Harrods and it's all getting dreadfully embarrassing.'

'Is this why you asked me to meet you here? You want me to intervene and save you from a fate worse than death, marriage to Philip Simmons-Blackshaw?' He started to laugh again and Elaine jabbed him in the side. 'Actually,' he went on, serious now, 'he might be a buffoon but he has some damned good connections. Simmons-Blackshaw could be a very useful addition to the family.'

'You don't choose to be a part of the family any more,' Elaine reminded him. 'When you walked out five years ago after that fearful row with Daddy, you said you would never darken his Knightsbridge doorstep again.'

'And I haven't,' Philip said darkly and took a long swig of his drink before placing it carefully back on the bar top. 'I always seemed to rub my stepfather up the wrong way. I wonder if things would be different if our mother were still alive.'

Elaine stared bleakly at a spot of wine next to her glass. Any reminder of the death of their mother blanketed her in sadness. She had been fifteen at the time, Philip twenty-five when Ruth had died in a light aircraft crash over France in thick fog.

Philip had been ten when Ruth, his mother, had married John Morton after divorcing Philip's father, Peter Mainwaring, for serial adultery; shortly after, Elaine had been born and was much loved and spoilt to distraction. Elaine in her adult years had often thought that if anyone's life was to go badly wrong, by the law of averages, it should have been her adorable half-brother's instead of her own. She had had everything showered upon her, love and affection and all things material. But her father kept a tight leash on Philip, his stepson. And Philip had always rebelled and made it all worse and then, a few years after their mother's death, he had left, though always keeping in contact with Elaine. Life had been a terrible strain after Ruth's death, for all of them, and after Philip left, her father's possessive grasp on his only daughter had tightened even more.

'Sorry, darling,' Philip breathed regretfully and slid his arm around Elaine and pulled her tightly to him. He kissed her cheek warmly. 'I shouldn't have brought that up.'

Elaine smiled and swallowed; as Philip released her, she looked over his shoulder to see Cathy and Lisa standing up from their table rather hastily, Lisa looking as if she was about to faint. Perhaps they had seen her after all. Elaine leaned her elbow on the bar and shielded the side of her face with her hand. Mercifully they were heading towards another exit from the bar, a fire-escape exit at the back that was always open in hot weather. It led to a small cobbled passageway into the street.

'G'day, girls,' Bruce called out as he topped up Elaine's wine glass.

Elaine shrank. Cathy and Lisa couldn't get out fast enough. Philip turned to look in the direction Bruce was saying his cheery farewell too.

'I'm sure I know that girl,' he muttered vaguely.

'I expect you know every girl in the world,' Elaine remonstrated, relieved her old flatmates had gone without incident. 'Now forget your libido for a while and concentrate on what I'm about to tell you.' She was fine now, more at ease and eager to tell Philip her plan.

'I've decided enough is enough,' she told him. 'I haven't told you what happened last week. I'll start there because it's all relevant. I was looking for stamps in Daddy's bureau and found some old letters.' She looked at Philip to make sure he was listening properly and not eyeing every girl left in the bar – he was a world-champion flirt. Satisfied that she had his full attention, she went on. 'They were from Marcus in Marbella, written last year.'

Philip lifted his hand and raked it through his dark springy hair. Suddenly he couldn't look her in the eye and Elaine knew why. The traumas of what had happened last year had been gone over before; Philip's advice then had been to put it behind her – a mistake was a mistake, and life went on. It had been her father's advice too at the time, though his had been dealt out in a fury whereas Philip's had been far more considerate for her feelings. She knew what Philip was thinking now, though: why resurrect her affair with a Marbella bar owner and its disastrous consequences when it was best to let sleeping dogs lie?

'I don't know how Marcus found my address,' Elaine went on in a hot rush, 'because I only ever gave him the address of the flat I was sharing in

29

Battersea at the time. My flatmates didn't know my home address anyway, so they couldn't have passed it on. His first letter to Knightsbridge said how distraught he was that he was unable to get in touch with me any more – in Battersea we had been on the phone to each other every five minutes and – '

'Elaine, will you get to the point you are trying to make?' Philip interjected. 'I really did think all this was behind you.'

'Yes, but you see, it isn't,' Elaine persisted. 'Marcus really did love me, he said in the letters, said he wanted me to go down there to live with him, and – '

'It was a holiday romance, Elaine,' Philip insisted crossly. 'They happen all the time. I've had a few myself. They don't mean anything. A few nights of passion in a heady holiday environment is par for the course. You did the right thing at the time and put it down to experience and got on with your life.'

'But if I had known about those letters, my life wouldn't be the hell it is now,' Elaine bit back angrily. 'Daddy hid them from me. I confronted him with them and we had a huge row. He said the man couldn't be any good, said he must have criminal connections because no one can find the private address of a high-court judge, or his telephone number – apparently he had rung from Marbella too. Daddy told him to take a flyer, said I wasn't available and never would be.'

'He has a point, Elaine,' Philip said thoughtfully. 'How the hell did he get your address and telephone number?'

'Whose side are you on, Philip?' Elaine flashed.

'Yours, of course, I always have had your best interests at heart.'

'Yes, well, support me on this one.'

'Support you on what?' he questioned her in amazement.

Elaine ran the tip of her tongue over her lower lip and then she lifted her chin bravely. 'I'm leaving the country, Philip. As soon as I've made the arrangements, I'm going down to Marbella to be with Marcus.'

Philip stared at her, stupefied.

Elaine lowered her dark lashes and refused to look him in the eye. 'I am, Philip. I'm going on the run down to Marbella and – '

'Just a minute.' Philip breathed tightly, lifting the palm of his right hand to quieten her. 'Have you gone out of your mind? *On the run*! What sort of talk is that? Are you sure this Marcus isn't a criminal?'

'Honestly!' Elaine pouted. 'You sound just like Father. He thinks Marbella is the Costa del Crime.'

'Well, being a judge, he probably knows more about where crooks hang out than anyone else.'

'Don't be absurd, Philip. Marcus runs a perfectly legitimate cocktail bar on the coast. And it just goes to show how far Daddy's paranoia has gone with me. Judges are supposed to be impartial. He shouldn't make judgements like that, think bad things about people just because they live somewhere where a few bank robbers hang out. Anyway, that isn't the point,' Elaine went on. 'The point is that if I tell Daddy my intentions he will try and stop me. He'll block the airports and the ferries, he'll do all it takes to stop me getting away. That's what I meant when I said I'm going on the run – on the run from *him*.'

Philip let out a long worried sigh. 'Elaine, I think you are going over the top here. You found a few old letters, you're cross with John for trying to push you

31

into marriage with Blackshaw, you are looking for reasons to – '

'Marcus loves me,' Elaine insisted, feeling she was losing his support and vaguely wondering if she ever had it in the first place. 'And you and Daddy persuaded me into thinking it was nothing but a holiday fling; because of the shocked state I was in at the time, I let myself be persuaded. Now my hormones are OK and I know differently because of those letters. He really did love me and – '

'And what about Sophie?' Philip delivered lethally.

Elaine's grey eyes widened and a very slight chill ran down her spine. 'I shall take her with me, of course,' Elaine argued. 'Did you think that I wouldn't?'

Philip gulped the last of his Scotch and then rubbed his forehead worriedly. Elaine never had had a very strong grip on reality. He'd watch her grow up, pampered and indulged and then tragically losing her mother in her teens. Was it any surprise she had got herself into so much trouble? He'd always been there for her, though, but he couldn't condone this latest madness of hers.

'Elaine,' he started gently, 'things have changed in the last year. Marcus might well have been in the throes of love after your holiday affair a year ago, but – '

'It was more than a holiday affair,' Elaine protested hotly. 'We really loved each other.'

'Maybe you did *then*, but things have happened since. Sophie for one. Marcus doesn't even know about her. What are you going to do, walk into the bar during the happy hour and and bounce her on the counter in her carry cot, announcing, "Hello Marcus, this is your love child from our fling last year!" '

Elaine's eyes suddenly filled with tears. Oh, it wouldn't be like that at all. Darling Sophie might be a shock to him at first, but he loved her mother, didn't he? And the baby was adorable, he couldn't fail to be enraptured with her. Oh, if only she had been brave enough at the time to face Marcus with her pregnancy. But she hadn't. So shocked at finding herself in that condition, she had allowed her father to take over her life once again. She had been so weak and vulnerable at the time, with her hormones and her emotions all over the place. Her father, ogre that he was most of the time, had stood by her, convincing her that nothing good could be gained from telling Marcus she was carrying his child. Yes, because of the stress of it all at the time she had weakly allowed herself to be convinced that it had been a holiday romance, though her heart strove to tell her otherwise. Her father was usually right, though she was loathe to admit it at times.

Like her first attempt at breaking away from him. The job her father had fixed her up with at the press gallery – he knew everyone in Parliament – had been a disaster. She hadn't known if she was coming or going and the place was so noisy, everyone shouting at each other.

She hadn't really been brought up to make a living for herself. Cosseted as a child and educated in a Dickensian all-girls school for the daughters of the upper class, in adulthood all she was expected to do was to make a good marriage. Till the day she had rebelled and *wanted* to make a life for herself. True, Daddy had met her halfway with the job opportunity, but he had been appalled when she had decided to move into a flat across the river. Across the river of all things!

'Battersea!' he had bellowed. 'No one who is anyone lives in Battersea! You won't survive, Elaine,' he had told her sternly. 'You have a comfortable lifestyle with me, a huge allowance, everything you want. Come to your senses, child!'

'I don't have a life though, Daddy,' she implored, half-understanding why he wanted to keep her safe and secure with him. She was all he had left. Mummy was gone, Philip too. 'I'm not your baby girl any more. You're suffocating me.'

And so their row had raged on for five days and nights until finally, coupled with the stress of the lengthy fraud case he was presiding over, involving zillions of pounds and several thousand distraught pension fund holders, John Morton had finally given in, reached for his umpteenth bottle of malt whisky and released her from purgatory.

But he hadn't been that stressed out that he had lost his marbles completely. If she was to go it alone, alone it would have to be. He had slashed her allowance, fully expecting her to come crawling back in twenty-four hours, a stone lighter in weight, her clothes rags on her back and dragging her pride behind her in a supermarket plastic carrier bag and begging for mercy.

And so it nearly was. Not even the most expensive finishing school in the world had prepared her to budget. She was used to buying good clothes and nice things and suddenly she was swamped with taxi fares to work – she hated public transport – and the rent and the bills she had to share with Cathy and Lisa. Of course, it had been fun at first, quite exciting. She had so longed to be a part of their lives. They laughed such a lot and went to pubs and wine bars and always had a string of boyfriends. But she had never quite slotted comfortably into their lives. She knew they thought her a bit uppity. Once she had heard Cathy call her the duchess behind her back – only in fun, she guessed, but there had been a barrier between them. A class barrier, she suspected.

And her father was right She couldn't survive. Soon she was in debt. Philip had offered to help financially but she had obstinately refused, ashamed of herself for not being able to manage her own affairs. But she had become so depressed at her own inability to cope that she had rather rashly overdrawn at the bank to escape to a holiday in Marbella to get her head together. And met Marcus and fallen in love for the very first time and it had been wonderful. Then disaster when she returned to find herself pregnant.

'I have to go, Philip,' she told him mournfully, twirling her wine glass between her fingers. 'Daddy was wonderful to take me back and look after me through my pregnancy. You, too, you gave me your moral support. I know I was a fool to get myself into such trouble and I've been so lucky, but when I look at my baby I see Marcus. I've tried to forget him and it's been hopeless and when I found those letters and realized how deeply he loves me, well, it all welled up again. I understand what you are saying about springing a baby on him, but I have to try. I can't marry Philip Simmons-Blackshaw. He might be rich, but I don't love him. I want Marcus and – '

'Has it occurred to you that he might well have someone else now?' Philip interjected, not wanting to be cruel, but facts had to be put bluntly at times.

'If his letters are anything to go by, he'll still be free, Philip,' she whispered faintly. 'My love has never died, so why should his?'

'Because he's a man, Elaine darling, a *man*,' Philip insisted. 'He must meet a million gorgeous girls through the season down there. You won't have been the only one, I promise you. Didn't you see the film *Shirley Valentine*? Tom Conti, the Greek bar owner, was chatting up a new bird as soon as Pauline Collins was charabancing back to the airport.'

Elaine sighed mournfully. It was one of her favourite films, a bored housewife breaking away from her humdrum existence to take a holiday in Greece and meeting a gorgeous Greek who changed the direction of her life. She'd ended up cooking chips and eggs in his bar for the British tourists. Well she could do that down in Marbella with Marcus. Not that she had ever cooked chips and eggs, but she could learn.

'Marcus is English, not Greek,' she muttered. 'And I wanted your support on this, not your cynical condemnation. Trouble with you is you know nothing about love. You have a million girlfriends yourself and think all men are the same as you: chauvinists.'

Philip sighed. 'I know how men think and act, darling. Believe me, the guy will have a heart attack if you turn up with his love child, but if he doesn't drop dead with shock he'll break your heart at the very least. I don't want to see you hurt, Elaine.'

'So . . . so you won't come down there with me?' she said weakly, realizing that Philip wasn't with her on this one.

'Is that what this is all about? You want me to go to Marbella with you?' he asked in astonishment.

'I . . . I thought you might be ready for a break, that you might want to come. I thought . . .'

'You thought I'd be there for you to help pick up the pieces if it all went wrong,' he finished for her.

Not altogether, she thought ruefully. Philip worked far too hard. A holiday in the sun would do him the power of good. But in a way he was right. He would be there for her if it did go wrong, just as he had always been there for her in the past. In spite of his attitude now, dead against her going to Marbella to be with her love, he cared for her welfare. Although she was confident that Marcus would welcome her back with open arms, there was a tiny fear pocketed away inside her, one she refused to give too much thought to. A year was a long time. People's feelings changed, though hers hadn't. Her love had endured but . . . No, she wasn't even going to consider that Marcus might not feel the same. She was determined to go.

She lifted her chin. 'I'm still going, Philip,' she told him strongly. 'I've been such a spoilt little rich girl all my life. I've let Daddy pick up the pieces for me every time, but I've changed since having Sophie. I'm a mother now and it's time I started making decisions for us both. Marcus is her father – you only have to look at her to know – and I want to give her the chance to know her father and for her father to know her. It's only right.'

She pushed her glass aside, pulled her Enny bag over her shoulder and slid off the barstool and faced her brother. 'I'll ask just one thing of you, Philip. You've made it quite clear you don't agree with me and won't help, but at least keep quiet about this conversation. Don't tell Daddy where I've gone.'

Philip put some money down on the bar for drinks,

muttering, 'As I haven't spoken to him for years it's hardly likely. Come on, I'll put you in a taxi.'

Outside the wine bar, waiting for a cruising black cab, Philip turned Elaine to him and held her by her shoulders. 'I can't support you on this, Elaine. I wish I could, but I can't. I think you're making a big mistake and I want you to reconsider it. Just one more thing, and forgive me for even bringing it up, but have you considered that if this Marcus was indeed besotted as you are with him, that he would have come over to England to find you?'

Elaine licked her dry lips and swallowed hard; her voice was small and tremulous when she spoke. 'Yes, Philip, I thought of that too. But I will never know if he did or not. I'll only know when I see him and ask him. For all I know, he did come and I wasn't there and Daddy sent him away with a flea in his ear. For all I know, Daddy instructed Karen, the nanny, and the rest of the staff to do likewise as well. The point is, I don't know anything for sure and I *have* to find out.'

Philip shook his head in exasperation. Women's reasoning always flummoxed him. He didn't understand them at all, though he adored them, each and every one.

Elaine resolutely shook her head in return, her throat choked with disappointment that he wasn't giving her the support she needed so badly. Here she was claiming she was trying to take control of her life and yet now she shivered with fear at the thought of travelling alone down to Spain with a small baby and facing Sophie's father. And it was all Philip's fault. She had walked in the wine bar to meet him and tell him her plan and to ask for his help, determined that she was doing the right thing, positive that

Marcus would greet her with open arms and a heart full of love for her. But then Philip had come up with all the points she had refused to think about, reviving the doubts she had crushed because, really, when it came down to it, she was quite useless at anything, Marcus might not want her any more . . . No, she wouldn't think about it. She was going, she really was.

'Hans Crescent,' Philip told the cab driver as he opened the door for Elaine. He hugged her and kissed her cheek before she got in. 'Chin up, darling. Think hard on all this and I'll call you tomorrow when the old bear has left for the Bailey or wherever he does his business these days. You know, this is the first time I've considered closing the rift between me and John. I hate to admit it, but he's right on this one. If I thought it would do any good, I'd call him and maybe together we could talk you out of this crazy idea of yours.'

Elaine slammed the door on him and buzzed down the window to speak to him. Her throat was raw and her eyes stinging, but she managed to sound cool. 'Much as I want you to be reconciled with Daddy, it mustn't be this way, Philip. I wish I hadn't told you now. Best you forget everything I've said. Forget it all.'

'So you'll reconsider?' Philip asked hopefully.

Elaine couldn't say another word. She blew a kiss to Philip and buzzed up the window, as the cab drew away from the kerb, she sank back in her seat and closed her eyes.

She *was* a wimp. Floundering again, just as she had floundered last year when she found she was pregnant. Her father had been wonderful to her after the initial fury had died down, but recently she had felt

39

the net of his over-protection closing in on her once again. He was throwing Blackshaw at her – full on, too, not in the least bit subtly – and talking of a wedding at some cathedral or other and what a good chap he was. But she couldn't bear the thought of spending the rest of her days with him. Philip Simmons-Blackshaw was so *county*, compared to the excitement of Marcus, who could mix a cocktail with such devilish aplomb that people applauded, how could she think of it?

No, not even the thought of Philip's old wealth and that Gothic mansion in the country with seventeen bedrooms, fifteen of them with en-suites, was a temptation. Yes, that was how much Marcus had opened her eyes to the real world – not that he was exactly poor. His bar was the most swinging place on the Costa, packed to the gunnels with beautiful people. Oh, how overwhelmed she had been when he had made a pitch for her amongst all that Marbella glitterati.

She remembered the first time she had gone to his bar. It had taken nerve, all she could summon, which was quite a fair amount when it came down to it, but after three days in the most luxurious hotel on the Costa loneliness was beginning to claw at her very bones. Everyone had a partner, everyone was having fun and she was getting more and more depressed and isolated. Then, one night, after a couple of fortifying cocktails in the hotel bar, she had taken her courage in both hands and swayed out on to the esplanade and, well . . . well, just followed the glitterati, wherever they were heading. Of course she had been horribly ill later on in the evening. Her head was all swimmy and her legs seemed to have a will of their own, but Marcus had been there for her, helping her back to the hotel,

40

ordering gallons of black coffee from room service and stripping her off and tucking her up in bed. Dazed as she was, one overwhelming thought stood out from all the others. He had made no move to climb into bed with her. How sweet, she had thought as she had drifted off.

And the following day it had all begun. He called round the next morning to see how she was, concerned for her, bringing her a huge bunch of pink carnations, and it had gone on from there. He had driven her up into the mountains and they had strolled through the olive groves and picnicked by mountain streams. It had all been so different from London life. And what a lover he had been.

That first time in his lovely apartment over the bar she could still recall in the minutest detail, because it had been so wondrous. Kicking shut the door behind him, he had gathered her into his arms, his warm sexy mouth seeking hers so ardently her head had swum. She'd run her tremulous fingers through his shoulder-length black curly hair, which was free from the leather cord he usually wore to hold it back from his face when he was mixing cocktails in the bar. It was soft and silky and smelt of almonds and ylang ylang, and made her senses swim. Dizzy with love, she had touched his bronze face tenderly, marvelling at his taut skin and his perfect features. He was easily the most beautiful man she had ever touched so intimately. He'd had groaned softly into her hair, trembled against her slim body as the length of his strained against the fine silk of her strappy dress. And she had known then that she was someone special for him as he was for her. He had scooped her up into his arms and smiled down at her as she clung to him and he had lowered her to his sumptous bed and rained kisses over her face and mouth till every cell in her body was crying out for him. So, so tenderly had he slid off her dress and then bent his head to kiss her tiny silk briefs. And when he had stood back to oh, so slowly and erotically strip off his own clothes, she thought she had never been happier in her life. His body was perfect, not horribly beefy like some of the men on the beach but just perfectly proportioned, narrow-hipped, smooth and tanned. None of that ghastly chest hair that was so off-putting for her, though she had thought at the time that if he had been all macho and hairy she would have loved him all the same. But that decision hadn't needed to be made. He had the body of a young Greek god, sleek and golden.

Her whole body had sprung alive when he had lowered himself over her and pushed aside her lacy bra and dispensed with her matching briefs as if he was plucking exotic blooms. His mouth was warm and sensuous as he kissed each new part of her he exposed. And as his exploration of her deepened she became aware of how little she knew, how innocent she was, and he had laughed softly and then proceeded to teach her everything she didn't know about her own body and ought to know.

It had all been a miracle and his eventual deep penetration of her, a first for her, heightened by the eroticism of their gasping breath, the heat of their bodies trembling against each other in expectation, had remained in her heart and soul ever since. He had moved so rhythmically, so perfectly, each thrust honed to heighten her pleasure, each of his murmured encouragements directing her to heighten his till it was impossible to hold back from the fury of fire and liquid gold that enveloped them both, drowning them, engulfing them till they were lost in love and lust.

Yes, Marcus had opened up her life and her heart and their affair had been sublime. When she had returned home she called him several times a day and he said how much he adored her and was missing her and then . . . then . . . Yes, how naïve she had been. She was pregnant and she hadn't known what to do or even how to make a decision for herself. She had simply packed up her stuff and left Battersea to return home with her tail between her legs and let her father take over.

But she wasn't the weak-willed girl now she had been then, and finding the letters her father had hidden from her had changed her life. Well, nearly, she thought despondently. Because now that weak-willed girl of yesteryear seemed to be surfacing again.

Philip had been her last resort for help and support and there was no one else. Her Knightsbridge friends were useless, all socializing and shopping. And she was no different, she supposed despondently

But she was different, she argued with herself. She was a mother now, a single parent, and she wanted her adorable daughter to have a father and she loved Marcus. She had wept uncontrollably when she had found those old letters and realized how stupid she had been in not getting in touch with him immediately she knew she was pregnant. He had loved her and a love like that just couldn't die.

But did she have the courage to go down to southern Spain on her own to face her lover with his child, because alone it would have to be now that Philip

43

didn't want to know? Was that asking too much of herself? She had already decided not to take her daughter's nanny, Karen, with her. Karen, Norland-trained, always took her duties seriously. She had been employed by John Morton and always referred back to him if there were any problems. Her loyalties were strongly with the head of the household who paid her salary; she couldn't be trusted to keep their destination a secret.

No, Philip, her brother, was the only one she could have turned to. It would have been so much easier with Philip beside her to give her strength, someone to lean on. But he was adamant he wouldn't support her in her decision. She wished she hadn't told him now. She had handled it all wrong. What she should have done was simply suggested a holiday together, in Marbella, and he would have accompanied her and been none the wiser. He would have quickly found some gorgeous girl to charm and she could have gone off and done her own thing with Marcus. Too late now – once again she had made a pig's ear of everything. Philip now knew her plan, so perhaps haste was the best policy. Just go and quickly, too.

She bit her lip and gazed out of the cab window as they cruised down Regent Street towards Piccadilly Circus. She was suddenly so afraid and felt so totally alone. There was no one to turn to any more. If only . . .

Suddenly she sat forward in her seat. 'Um, could you . . . I mean, could you do a detour, please?'

'Where to, luv?' the cabbie asked, breaking slightly.

'Er . . . well, Battersea, actually. Bournville Terrace, just round the corner from the Nag's Head.'

'Yeah, I know it. I grew up in Battersea. It ain't like it used to be. Bleedin' yuppies creeping in now and converting all the terraces into flats. The Nag's Head used to have Morrison shelters in the beer cellar during the war; when that siren went off, us kids used to pelt down there and make a right old game of it. Those were the days . . . you know, I never saw a banana till I was six and – '

'Nice,' Elaine murmured, falling back in her seat and closing her eyes. She didn't hear any more. Her head was buzzing with an idea that was forming in her mind. A crazy idea, but she was desperate and desperate measures were needed.

'What number, luv?' the cabbie asked, jolting Elaine into opening her eyes a while later.

'Er, just pull in here, behind that . . . that . . . what do you call it? Skip,' she said quickly. Her heart was suddenly pounding, her palms clammy. Further up Bournville Terrace, Elaine could see Cathy and Lisa unpacking boxes from the side of a white camper van. She hadn't even considered that they might not live here any more – all the same, she was glad that they did.

The cabbie leaned his arm out of the window to open the door from the outside for her.

'Just a minute,' she said. 'I . . . I'm not sure. Can I just sit here for a minute?'

'Anything you say, duck. My time is yours,' he told her, happily glancing at the meter ticking over.

Suddenly Elaine's idea didn't seem such a good one. After all this time, how could she drop into their lives and ask them for help? She needed more time to think about it. She clasped her hands tightly in her lap and watched the two girls. She remembered Lisa used to sell sandwiches in the offices of the West End, from dinky covered baskets. She used to be up at the crack of dawn to make them, delicious great doorsteps of chunky ham and pickles, slabs of cheese with grated onion that used to make her mouth water though she never dared try them – she would have ballooned in size if she had. How she had envied Lisa's nerve, just bustling in to strange offices and selling her sandwiches. Elaine couldn't have done that if her life had depended on it.

And Cathy had been a secretary, she recalled. She and Lisa used to go into fits of laughter over her boss, an old Etonian who Cathy couldn't trust to keep his hands to himself if they were ever alone together. But Cathy was no fool, she knew how to handle him. Cathy was so streetwise she could have put Casanova in his place with just one glance of her sultry dark eyes.

Elaine suppressed a sigh of longing to be back there with them, sharing the flat and gradually being drawn into their happy carefree lives. Given time they might have accepted her . . . though they had tried, she remembered. They had taken her to the Nag's Head once, the dreadful pub on the corner, all beery smells, torn plastic seats and karaoke. Cathy had asked her what she wanted to drink and she had asked for a Pimms and somehow the night had gone flat after that. Lisa had introduced her to their friends, mostly men from a nearby market, but they had been so loud that eventually she had pleaded a headache and gone home. It was later that night, when Cathy and Lisa had come home, knocking into furniture and shushing between giggles, that she had overheard the duchess remark.

Yes, those two hadn't a care in the world. They didn't know what it was like to have chaos and turmoil rule their lives. They knew how to handle men. They were streetwise. They wouldn't let any man get them down.

Though they didn't look too happy at the moment, Elaine observed. Lisa looked as pale and wan as she had in the wine bar. And Cathy looked a trifle washed out, too. But then it was the end of a hot July day and they were probably tired.

And because she was too exhausted after trying to persuade her brother to support her plan, her courage failed her completely. She just couldn't get out of the cab and approach Cathy and Lisa. Anyway, they probably hated her for what she had done last year, leaving them to pay her bills. They wouldn't understand that she had no choice but to run and they wouldn't understand why she was trying to make amends now. No, the idea was out of order and she had no right to even consider it.

'Er . . . I've changed my mind again,' she murmured to the cabbie. 'Knightsbridge, please.'

Elaine closed her eyes again as the cab spun around in the road and headed back towards the river. She longed to get home and hold her daughter close to her. She wistfully wished for Marcus to be waiting too, to gather her into his arms and tell her how much he had missed her and how much he adored his wonderful surprise daughter.

And it was the thought of Marcus's arms enfolding her, his wonderful mouth closing over hers, his wanting her so much spiralling their heated passion to dizzy heights she had never soared to before, that spurred her decision to go ahead with her plan.

47

She *had* to go. She *would* go. After all, tomorrow was another day, and tomorrow she might have more courage and strength. But for now she wanted to hold her small daughter close to her heart and forget for a while how totally incompetent she was.

CHAPTER 3

'Any luck?' Lisa asked brightly as Cathy came into the kitchen, tossing her keys on the kitchen table with such hopeless dejection that Lisa wished she'd never asked. And perhaps asking the boys from upstairs to dinner tonight wasn't such a good idea after all. Cathy looked exhausted and it was getting harder every day to lift her spirits.

With grim determination to make the evening go with a swing, Lisa carried on slicing peppers for a salad to go with yet another couple of defrosted seafood tarts. Most of the food from when she had over-catered for Philip's lunch had had to be binned and what was left she and Cathy were sick of the sight of. And she was pushing her luck defrosting yet more. If they didn't all go down with food poisoning it would be divine intervention. But the boys' stomachs were indestructible and theirs had grown used to eating these defrosted offerings, so all should be well, she thought optimistically.

Yes, they deserved a bit of light relief tonight and the boys were a barrel of laughs. John and Gerry were both hairdressers and worked in South Molton Street in the West End. Cathy had nicknamed them Tom

49

and Jerry because of some of the thuds that came from upstairs. Who was chasing whom around the Conran coffee table was anyone's guess.

'Four agencies I've tried this afternoon and they all said the same thing,' Cathy moaned exaggeratedly. "Why did you leave your last employment?" Huh, I could hardly tell the truth, could I? That I'd been having an affair with my boss only to find out he was married. Hardly the thing you want to boast on your curriculum vitae, is it? I heard myself gibbering that I left because the work wasn't pushing my brain cells enough. Crumbs, I haven't any left after what that creep did to me, shocked them out of my system. Anyway, there's nothing about. A bit of temp work I might have to take if nothing else comes up. Money's lousy, though,' she finished dejectedly.

'Something will crop up,' Lisa said keenly. 'And you should get replies from those ads you answered last night. I'll make you a coffee, or would you prefer a glass of wine, seeing as we have oodles of it? The boys upstairs are coming to dinner, that should cheer you up.'

Cathy groaned melodramatically. 'That's all we need, a night of "Men Behaving Girly" right here in our own sitting-room.'

'Oh, they're all right, Cath, and great fun when they've had a few; besides, we owe them for shifting the dresser on to the other wall, *and* for mending the washing machine, *and* sealing the windows when the rain came in in April. I was amazed a couple of hairdressers had such macho skills, but I suppose the male ego, faced with a couple of useless females, will surface.' She giggled.

'Yeah, I suppose,' Cathy said absently, adding,

'Wine, please. Might as well fuzz it all away. I hadn't realized how hard it would be to get another good job. It's a desert out there in the job market.'

With a frown Cathy moved through to the sitting-room at the front of the house. The house had been divided into two flats with separate entrances on the ground floor. Their flat was on the ground floor and the kitchen and sitting-room were open plan. The three bedrooms and the bathroom were at the back of the terraced house and they had a small patio garden. They were sharing the mortgage; if either wanted to go her own way, they had agreed to sell and divide the profits, which hopefully would be generous as it was an up-and-coming area.

They had moved in eighteen months before and had made it as cosy and comfortable as they could on a limited budget. Lisa was good at soft furnishings; she had brightened the place with cushions and swag curtains and stencilled a border around the ceilings. Cathy's contribution had been some interesting small pieces of furniture and rugs, nothing expensive, from her Aunt Laura's bric-a-brac shop down in Somerset. Yes, their home was a haven, with framed photos of both their families displayed on the stripped-pine mantlepiece: Cathy's two married brothers on their wedding days, Lisa's younger sister, Gayle, who had blossomed from a scrawny teenager to a model on the catwalk in a French fashion house. Lisa was so proud of her.

Yes, their home was a testament to their own particular success, and a reminder of happy, uncomplicated, childhoods. Nothing like this had rocked their lives before. God, her mother would throw a fit if she knew she had been romantically involved with a married man. And now they were both out of work and life wasn't sunny or funny any more.

She gazed around the room they had so enthusiastically made their haven. But how long could they go on living here with neither of them employed?

Cathy sighed and moved the draped curtains of the front window aside to look out into the street. And, on top of all this worry about their future, a stalker. Yes, the car was still there.

By now they knew all the cars and their owners in the street and were used to a succession of skips parked outside during conversion work on the old Edwardian houses. But the dark blue Rover tucked behind a half-skip further down the road was alien to Cathy. She was sure it was the same car that had slowly overtaken the bus she was travelling home on. It had overtaken down on the Embankment and then several times more, as if it was checking to see if she had got off or not. Then, when she had alighted, it had been there, keeping a safe distance behind as she walked round the corner to the flat.

The only reason she had noticed it in the first place was because the digits of the number plate added up to her age. She was always doing it, adding and subtracting number plates and coming up with fantastically coincidental combinations, like the ages and house numbers and years of birth of her family. Once she saw three cars parked side by side and the numbers miraculously matched her passport number.

It drove Lisa up the wall.

'If you're so smart at juggling figures to suit yourself why don't you juggle up the winning line of the lottery!' she had snapped at her while they were driving home from the wine bar the other evening, her horror at seeing her beloved Philip with their old flatmate Elaine Morton making her noticeably irritable, while Cathy was doing her adding and subtracting to pass the boring time in traffic hold-ups.

And they could do with a win on the lottery, Cathy mused as she let the curtain drop and went back to the kitchen area to join Lisa. Only three days after walking out on Charles she was already feeling the shroud of permanant unemployment wrapping itself around her – bloody throttling her, to be more precise. Obviously sending her paranoid, too, because she was imagining she was being followed.

'I think I'm being followed,' she told Lisa. She perched on the breakfast barstool, sipping the wine Lisa had poured and watching her preparing the salad.

After Cathy told her about the blue Rover with the number plate that added up to her age, Lisa laughed dismissively.

'Who'd follow you, for goodness' sake? Certainly no one who was allowed a driving licence,' she teased her with a grin.

'Ha, ha! I just thought it a bit strange that the same car kept overtaking the bus.'

'It happens all the time in London,' Lisa reasoned. 'Traffic gets snarled up, cars creep round buses, buses creep alongside cars and taxis leave the lot standing. What was the driver like anyway?'

'I didn't look.'

Lisa laughed again. 'Fat lot of good you'd be on *Crimewatch*.'

'Well, it was a man anyway, but I couldn't see his face from the top of a double decker, could I? I could see he had a hairy arm as he was leaning on the open window, thrumming his fingers on the edge of the door, and a couple of times he adjusted his wing mirror.'

'Could have been a woman with hairy arms.' Lisa giggled, but Cathy wasn't amused. 'Anyway, sounds like he was impatient in the snarl-ups, and if he was following you he wouldn't be *impatient*.'

'No, just tense as to how he was going to have his evil way with me when the time came,' Cathy persisted.

'You're going mad, Cathy,' Lisa told her, pausing from slicing the peppers and looking at her anxiously. 'I've never seen you like this, imagining being followed. It's not like you at all. It's that Charles that has made you so peculiar. He phoned again, by the way. Said to pass on the same message as the last one. You go back to work and he'll forget the whole thing, but if you don't he'll come round to get you. He's giving you a couple more days to come to your senses and then all hell is going to break loose, he warned.'

Cathy suppressed a shiver of disgust that she had felt so deeply for such a cold hard man. Every time he had called her since she had walked out on him and her job the conversation had gone along the same lines of orders and threats: she had broken her employment contract, she *owed* him to resume her job, she was failing him and the company in leaving at such an inopportune time, etcetera, etcetera.

Where had her lover gone? Nothing to say how sorry he was and how deeply he cared for her and how much he missed her – not that it would have made one iota of difference. It hurt, though, and she was angry with herself for allowing it to hurt. She didn't want to think back on those good times with him, the loving times, the times he took her in his arms and melted her bones, the times he made love to her with such passion and feeling she had been convinced their relationship would be for life. But she supposed it was inevitable. The healing process had to include the walk down memory lane now and then, but it was more like a walk down the tunnel of hellfire and brimstone than anything else. How she wished she could zap out the memory of him from her internal filing system as easily as she had deleted that Belgian metal account from the computer. Why hadn't some smart alec invented Bandaid software for the heart, for goodness' sake?

'How much more hell can he put me through?' Cathy uttered miserably, the thought of him coming round to the flat abhorrent to her. How would she feel face to face with him again, knowing she'd had an affair with a married man? It sent shudders down her spine.

'He must think an awful lot of you, Cath. He's very persistent.'

'He's missing a damned good secretary, that's all.'

'Surely good secretaries are in abundance out there. I mean, I'm not trying to put you down or anything, but it took you forever to get the hang of that new software and well . . . well . . .'

'Well what?' Cathy said sharply, 'Are you implying I only kept the job down because we had a relationship going?'

Lisa tossed a handful of red peppers into the salad bowl and wiped her hands on a sheet of kitchen paper.

'Don't be so touchy,' Lisa soothed her softly. 'I'm just saying I think he's more than just missing your secretary skills. I think he misses *you*.'

Cathy sighed. 'Only because I was such a pushover, which says it all really. Yes, you're right, I'm a rubbish secretary and he only wanted my body and – '

'I wish I'd never started this,' Lisa sighed. 'Cheer up, will you! It's not like you to be so depressed over all this. He's trying to make amends and he wants you back and – '

'I couldn't go back.' Cathy breathed heatedly. 'Even if he said he'd divorce his wife for me, I couldn't. I couldn't live with my conscience.'

'You can't break up a happy marriage,' Lisa told her sagely. 'He must have been unhappy with her to get involved with you.'

'My God, Lisa, you live in an idealistic world, don't you? You never see bad in people. Charles had it both ways – a beautiful wife at home to arrange his social life, me at work to arrange his business life, the common denominator being that he was bedding us both. Unhappiness doesn't come into it. He had it all, the bastard, and he wants to go on having it all.'

'But he keeps ringing you up and – '

'Lisa, will you leave it alone?' Cathy said sharply. 'You don't know what you're saying.'

'I'm saying that you are unhappy and he is unhappy, so why don't you go back to your old job and – ?'

'And carry on where I left off?' Cathy let out a strangled laugh. 'Never. I was taken for a fool and I've got some pride left.'

'I wasn't suggesting you go back and resume your affair, just the job. Pride doesn't pay the bills,' Lisa muttered under her breath and reached for a beef tomato to chop to death and back.

'I heard that!' Cathy snapped and leaned across the breakfast bar towards Lisa. 'If you are so worried about our financial crisis, why don't *you* swallow your pride and get on the phone and tout for some more executive lunch business. You've let it all hang fire since your disaster with Philip Mainwaring. Or at the very least go back to your baskets and the sandwiches – you were earning a fortune with that.'

Lisa concentrated on her chopping and bit her lip before taking a huge breath and slapping the knife down on the work surface. 'Do you think I sit around here all day nursing my battered pride? I've tried, Cathy. I didn't tell you before because two of us moping around here looking glum is one too many. I *have* done some ringing around, and do you know what? I got laughed at – yes, laughed at. Philip damned Mainwaring has done his worst, spreading the word that I'm a walking disaster where executive lunches are concerned, and I can't get any more work for love or money. He's betrayed me in the work market and in my heart and it hurts, it really hurts!'

'Oh, gosh, Lisa,' Cathy moaned, sliding off the stool to hug her friend close. 'I didn't know and I feel so bad now, so selfish. You're having it as rough as me, so why are we rowing like this? We never have done before. Oh, I hate being out of work. It's so depressing.'

'Gerrof.' Lisa laughed, giving her a shove. 'If you want to make amends, give me a hand with this meal. No, second thoughts, sit there and get drunk for the two of us, it might bring your usual cheerfulness back.'

Cathy perched back on her stool and took a huge fortifying swig of wine. Yes, she was being a wet blanket and Lisa didn't deserve Cathy's misery on top of her own. What a cad that Philip was for scuppering her new venture. And what a clot he was for not snapping Lisa up, for her heart as well as her culinary talents. Some men were born stupid.

'I've something else to tell you concerning why I haven't done anything about earning some dosh,' Lisa went on.

'Do I want to hear this?' Cathy moaned exaggeratedly.

'Well, you're going to whether you like it or not – you can call me all the fools I know I am and it won't make any difference.' She took a big breath. 'I can't go back to the sandwich rounds either.'

Cathy's mouth dropped open.'

'I haven't any customers left,' Lisa admitted on a sigh. 'I didn't tell you before because I thought you'd think I was a bigger drip than ever, but when I left the sandwich round I gave my list of clients to a girl I met in one of the offices. She wasn't happy in her job and we used to chat and she always said what a lovely job I had, my own boss and all that, and she has a kid to bring up on her own and . . . and I gave her my baskets, too, and . . .'

'Oh, Lisa.' Cathy moaned, abandoning her wine and putting her elbows on the bar and holding her head in sufferance. 'You are an old softy and I'm such a bitch for having a go at you. Forgive me.'

Lisa sniffed. 'I'm an idiot, I know, but I can't go back and work in opposition to that girl. It wouldn't be fair. I've heard she's doing well too. No, it just wouldn't be fair.'

'You're right,' Cathy agreed and lifted her head and grinned sheepishly. She topped up their wine glasses.

'Nothing for it but to get outrageously drunk and . . .' She gulped suddenly. 'Oh, Lisa, what the hell are we going to do? I can't get a job and – '

'And I've been to a couple of agencies as well and there just isn't anything about.' Lisa sighed and tossed the last of the chopped tomatoes into the bowl. 'The mortgage has to be paid and the bills . . . I suppose we could take in another lodger – '

'Huh, after the last one my butt and my overdraft facility are still stinging, thank you very much. That damned Elaine cost us dearly. We had to go without a holiday this year because of her. We should have seen that coming, you know. A right couple of gorms we were. She took us for a ride and a half.'

Lisa didn't wanted to be reminded of it and went back to the other alternative she was about to suggest before Cathy completely crumbled under the pressure.

'I suppose I could ask my dad for a loan and . . .'

'No way,' Cathy stated firmly, raking her hair from her face and wandering over to the window again. Borrowing was no answer. Lisa's parents weren't well off, her own neither. Both families had been sceptical about them buying their own property. They would have rather seen them both married by now, if not sooner.

The girls had been friends all their lives and they had wanted independence, careers and a certain lifestyle, not husbands to drag home every Sunday for a roast dinner with all the trimmings and the Grand Prix in front of the telly after, nice as that was now and then. Being out of work in London wasn't a prospect that either of them had foreseen, but asking parents for a loan to tide them over was a fate worse than death. Pride paid a heavy price.

Cathy sighed heavily. The blue Rover was still parked down the road, but she couldn't see if there was anyone sitting in it or not because the last of the sun was gilding the windows and the windscreen. Was she heading for some sort of breakdown after her break-up with Charles? Or was it just a coincidence that the car had overtaken *her* bus more than once?

She sighed again and drained the last of her wine. Perhaps she was just being hypersensitive lately, not really coming to terms with Charles's betrayal as easily as she thought she ought to be.

Suddenly she jumped three feet in the air as the phone ringing shrieked in her eardrums. Oh, boy, she *was* in a state, her nerves raw to the edge.

'I'll get it,' she called out to Lisa as she was wiping her hands to answer it.

'Hello,' Cathy said breathily as she lifted the phone and crashed on to the sofa, kicking of the odd loafers and eyeing them critically as they lay on the carpet. Did they look two different shades of blue? Not in this light.

'Cathy, darling. At last you're speaking to me. Your flatmate has been answering my calls lately. Does that mean all is forgiven?' came Charles's silken tones.

Cathy's eyes went ceilingward as she nearly strangled the receiver with one hand while the other sprang to her hair and started madly twirling a strand, a childhood habit that had started during times of stress, usually chemistry lessons which completely freaked her out.

'I hardly think a "hello" is speaking or forgiving, Charles,' she said stiffly, making eye contact with Lisa and pulling a face.

'You're still mad with me?' came Charles's persuasive questioning tone as if, after a while, she would have forgiven him and was just waiting in the wings to stroll back into his life, as if nothing like a wife had strolled between them in the first place.

'Are you quite mad, as in certifiably mad, Charles?' Cathy ricocheted back at him. 'I should think it quite obvious by now that I have nothing more to say to you that hasn't already been said and – '

'Listen, darling, I'm missing you like crazy,' he interrupted and to Cathy's attuned ear, rather desperately. Perhaps Lisa was right and he really did love her. Come to think of it, it was rather a nice feeling that she might have made a tiny impact on his life. It didn't change a thing, though, just made her feel a little less of a gullible fool.

'I mean it, Cathy. I miss you so very much and I do love you and want you back and I'm sure we can work something out. I've been looking around South Kensington for a little *pied-à-terre* for the two of us – '

'Listen, Charles, not even a socking great penthouse on Piccadilly with a faithful handmaiden at my beck and call would make any difference to me,' Cathy shot down the phone flintily. 'I don't do affairs with married men!'

'But everything was wonderful between us before – '

'Yes, before I knew!' Cathy reasoned, pulling another face at Lisa who was hovering with a bunch of spring onions twisting in her hands. 'And knowing makes all the difference, Charles, all the difference in the world. I'm not coming back to you or the job, not now, not ever, and I would appreciate it if you didn't call this number again because if you do – '

'You *stupid* little bitch!'

In alarm Cathy wrenched the phone from her ear and stared at it as if it had just bitten off her ear lobe. Very slowly, with a deep frown of concern furrowing her brow that had Lisa rushing forward as if about to administer first aid, Cathy put the receiver back to her ear.

By now Lisa was perched on the arm of the sofa and had her own ear pressed to the phone and together they listened to the furious tirade which Charles was spouting as if his personal dam had burst its banks. Damn wasn't one of the words that poured over the line though. Cathy was glad Lisa was hearing it all, because to repeat the language would have stretched her embarrassment to its limits. A damn and a bloody here and there was fair comment in day-to-day life, but purple prose was something else

Cathy and Lisa's eyes widened till they nearly popped out of their aghast faces. On and on it went. What it all boiled down to was that she, Cathy Peterson, of all the stupidest women in the world, was the most brainless of them all, was letting him down so badly he might never recover, and did she have a death wish or what, because when the feathers hit the fan her helping would stuff a king-size duvet. Well, words to that effect.

Visibly shaking now, Cathy opened her mouth to try and interrupt, but her vocal cords were round her ankles by now and nothing but a feeble croak came out.

'And you won't have heard the last of this, Miss Prim Peterson, not by a long chalk. No one makes a fool of me and puts my future on the line. You are up to your pretty little neck in this and if you don't think again and come to your senses – '

And it was then that Cathy did indeed come to her senses. She slammed the phone down on its cradle as if it was red hot.

For a good ten seconds Cathy and Lisa stared at each other, neither able to utter a word. Cathy's heart was pounding so fearfully she thought it would pop.

Lisa was the first to move. She leapt to her feet and beat hell out of the phone with her bunch of spring onions.

'That was intolerable!' she cried. 'People pay good money to hear that sort of a thing on the tabloid back-page hotlines. Oh, it was disgusting and we got it for free. I'm going to call BT, have all our calls vetted, go ex-directory, go fax. We shouldn't have to be subjected to that! Oh, I'm so mad I could be sick!'

Stunned, Cathy just lay where she had been sprawling all through that astonishing tirade. She was stiff with shock. Never in her life had she felt so stung. Charles had said such horrible things to her and a man in love, or even supposedly in love, would never use such gutter language. What an earth had she done to deserve that?

Briefly the Belgian account she had deleted from the computer came to mind and the faxes she had shredded, but he hadn't mentioned them before and he must have known about them before today – in fact, he'd never mentioned them at all. Funny, that.

'Are you all right.' Lisa asked weakly.

Cathy inwardly shook herself down and outwardly moved off the sofa to stand up. Lisa was looking so worried she felt she ought to make light of what they had just heard.

'I expect he's just had words with his wife. Men are such cowards where wives are concerned that they usually take it out on their secretaries.'

'But you're not his secretary any more. Honestly, Cath, that was awful. I think you ought to make a complaint about it. He was so abusive. How could you have fallen for a rat like that?'

'I didn't fall for a rat,' Cathy told her thoughtfully. 'I fell for a very clever, good-looking, charming executive accountant who made my blood sing when he walked into the room. That wasn't the same man,' she said, nodding towards the phone. 'That sounded like a man who is in the sh – mire.'

Cathy rubbed her head and went on as if she was talking to herself, almost muttering under her breath. 'Why, why turn on me like that? Was I so indispensable to him, was I a better secretary than I ever imagined? Has he suddenly realized he cares about me? No, I think he's got the office in a mess and he's mad at me for leaving and . . . and none of it makes sense,' she finished dismally.

She lifted her head and Lisa was still standing there, holding the frayed spring onions, looking so worried she knew she had to put her at ease.

'Rat.' She grinned. 'If he ever does that again, I will get BT to vet the calls. Talk about a man scorned. Phew! That was something else. Right, have I time for a bath before the boys come down?'

Lisa nodded and smiled at her. 'Sure, and make sure you clean your ears out after all that.' She eyed the massacred onions in her hand. 'I did for those all right, didn't I?'

Cathy laughed. 'Thanks for the support. If he ever takes it into his thick head to call round here, you can hammer him in person with an aubergine. Right, half an hour and I'll be back on form.'

'Yeah,' Lisa breathed after Cathy had gathered up her faded loafers and lightly stepped out of the room. 'And you don't fool me, mate,' she whispered to herself as she went back to the kitchen end and picked up a lethal-looking carving knife and glowered at it. Cathy was cut to the quick by that dreadful phone call and just trying to shrug it off. Charles Bond had sounded like a man possessed and not one possessed by love either. She shivered slightly and dropped the knife and pulled a lettuce out of the fridge. She was well shot of him, job and all.

And as Lisa pulled the crisp lettuce apart, she couldn't help but think of Philip Mainwaring and her own loss. She wouldn't have put him down as a vindictive man either, but he certainly hadn't done her any favours by making a mockery of her lunch effort to other executives. Perhaps he hadn't known what he was doing, effectively putting paid to her career prospects. Perhaps he'd just lightly made a joke of it to someone and the rumour had blossomed as rumours did and no one wanted to risk her.

She sighed as she washed the lettuce under a running tap. But what really hurt was seeing him with Elaine. They were an item and she and Philip weren't. Elaine of all people, too. But probably more his style than a mere sandwich girl. Elaine came from a good background and hers was South London and . . .

To hell with them all, she thought decisively, wiping a drop of water from her chin. Men were a pain. If only they could both get away for a while, but because of this mess they were in they couldn't. Both out of work and only just recovering from Elaine and the debts she had incurred which she and Cathy had had to cough up for. No, a holiday was out of the question, but it was what they both needed, a break away from city life, a bit of sun on their bodies and a few Tequila Sunrises to end the day. But they were broke, damn it.

'My God, Elaine Morton, you have a lot to answer for with me, on two counts, you damned duchess, you,' she scorned. 'Money and men!'

'Oh, that feels better,' Cathy said breezily as she came back into the kitchen in black silky pants and a matching silk vest top. 'I'll set the table while you take a break till they arrive. What time did you invite the boys down?'

'They'll be here any minute,' Lisa told her, adjusting the timer on the cooker. 'They wanted to eat early as they're going on to a club later.'

'Cheek,' Cathy commented as she went to the front window sill for the candelabra which lived there when they weren't entertaining.

'Not really. Gerry is meeting some television guy there and there's talk of some work on a costume drama in the pipeline for next year. Should suit them, powdered wigs and all that. Cathy – ' Lisa sighed and turned to her, concern on her face ' – are you sure you're all right? I mean, I was thinking while you were taking your bath – that was a dreadful phone call and you tried to be brave for my sake, but it must have shaken you up.'

Cathy gave her a reassuring grin. 'Yes, I really am fine, Lisa. I just wish you hadn't heard it too. You are far too sensitive and it probably upset you more than it

66

did me. I went over it all while I soaked and . . .' she gave a small shrug '. . . it helped more in a way. Charles Bond really is dead and buried for me now. That was a part of him that I'd never encountered before and I reckon I've had a lucky escape. If he phones again, I'll just put the phone down on him and you do likewise. OK, let's forget it now and have a laugh this evening. I'd better set the video, don't want to miss *EastEnders*.'

Lisa gave a small sigh of relief that Cathy had taken it so well. Yes, it was best forgotten. She turned back to the table she was about to attend too. 'Oh, tape *One Foot in the Grave* as well, Cath. I know they're repeats, but – '

'*I don't believe it*!' Cathy screeched at the window.

Lisa, getting a crisp freshly laundered tablecloth out of the dresser drawer, laughed. 'Victor's a hoot, isn't he?'

'I'm not mimicking Meldrew.' Cathy squeaked. 'Come here. Take a peek. Blimey, guess who else is coming to dinner tonight?' she cried.

Lisa was at her side like a shot. 'No way!' she shrieked when she saw who was getting out of a taxi in the middle of the road and fumbling in her bag for money and juggling a cellophane-covered bouquet of flowers in her arms. 'There is no way I would give that bitch the . . . the skin off one of my rice puddings!'

They both flattened themselves each side of the bay window in case they were seen, Cathy clutching the silver candelabra to her chest, Lisa clutching the damask tablecloth to her mouth in case she screeched some more and Elaine Morton actually heard them.

'Perhaps she's not coming her at all,' Cathy whispered hopefully. 'Perhaps she's visiting a sick friend instead.'

'Huh, she never made any friends round here, sick or otherwise. She *must* be coming here. Don't answer the door, Cath,' Lisa pleaded in a hoarse whisper, her violet eyes wide with panic. 'Pretend we're not in. I can't face her, knowing . . . you know, knowing she's with . . . you know . . . Philip.'

Cathy closed her eyes and held her breath and did some on-the-spot quick thinking which she quickly transfered verbally to Lisa.

'Listen, Lisa,' she whispered. 'We don't know what she wants yet. For sure she didn't leave her Reger underwear behind to collect, so the only reason she's here must be her conscience.'

'She hasn't got one!' Lisa argued huskily. 'She left owing us six hundred pounds on the phone bill, three months' rent, to say nothing of the electricity bill. She had the central heating blasting out morning, noon and night, not satisfied with one bath a day, she took hundreds *and* she used to sleep with the light on all night. She left owing us a fortune and only a fool would turn up a year later with a bunch of flowers as if it had never happened.'

'Well, she always was a bit flaky, Lisa.'

'Fat, too, now,' Lisa snorted, uncharacteristically bitchy, after taking a sly peek around the drapes. 'She wouldn't get into that gorgeous underwear now if she used a fork and spoon. Crumbs, she *is* coming here. Of all the nerve! I won't let her in. I just won't!'

'Think for a minute, Lisa,' Cathy hissed urgently from her side of the drapes. 'I know how you feel and not answering the door isn't a good idea at the moment. For all we know, she *has* come to pay her debts. She's got flowers, too. Could be a peace offering. We don't know till we give her a chance to explain. And another thing, she's an item with your Philip – '

'Which makes it all twice as bad,' Lisa moaned, twisting the tablecloth in her hands.

'Put aside your broken heart, Lisa,' Cathy sniped, not meaning to be cruel but she was talking serious money now. Lisa had said it all – Elaine owed them a small fortune, but that could be the tip of the iceberg if she could persuade Lisa to see it the same way. '*You* need to get back on chummy terms with Philip Mainwaring, chief executive of RAMS Electronics. The man has influence in town.'

'What an earth do you mean?' Lisa whispered hoarsely, eyes nearly popping out of her head now.

'Executive lunches of course,' Cathy breathed in exasperation. Couldn't Lisa see what she was getting at? 'Be ratty with Elaine and you are definitely out of it all, but with Elaine on your side she can work her feminine wiles on the boyfriend and get you back in business. Crumbs, this is a golden opportunity to put your whole career on line again, Lisa.'

'Smarm up to Elaine, you mean, so she can smarm up to Philip on my behalf?' Lisa gasped indignantly. 'How could you think so mercenarily?'

There was a ring at the door and both girls jumped in alarm.

'A while ago you were trying to persuade me to go back to hateful Charles and my lucrative job, Lisa,' Cathy urged quickly. '*You* can talk about mercenary!'

Lisa's shoulders sagged. 'That . . . that was different.'

'We'll argue the toss later,' Cathy hissed at her. 'Go out there and answer the door and clasp her to your bosom and gush all over her, long-lost friends and all that,' Cathy urged her.

'Oh, I couldn't.'

'Well, I jolly well can,' Cathy snorted, plonked the candelabra down on the top of the telly and came out of hiding from behind the drapes. "Needs must when the devil drives," she quoted forcefully, 'or is it "when the devil rides"?' She shrugged. 'Whatever, we could be on a winner here.'

They heard the front door next to theirs slam and Lisa groaned and nearly crumbled to the floor with the vapours. 'That's the boys,' she moaned as if it was the last straw to break her back. 'They'll all be on the doorstep together and you'll *have* to ask her in and I'm not going to be able to cope, knowing she and Philip are lovers and – '

'For Pete's sake, get a grip on yourself, Lisa,' Cathy ordered schoolmarmishly. 'This could be the turning point we've been waiting for.'

Later she would have quiet sympathetic words with Lisa, say something that would help her heal the wound Philip had inflicted on her, but this was a golden opportunity for her if she put aside her aching heart and thought sensibly. It wasn't as if she had ever had anything going with Philip to speak of, just a few interested glances and a few dropped innuendoes, nothing to build her hopes on, really.

If she could cope with losing Charles, and that had been a real relationship, then Lisa could cope too and be nice to Elaine and hopefully get herself back into business.

So with a bright, cheery, welcoming smile on her face, Cathy confidently opened the front door to greet her guests.

All four of them.

Cathy reeled back with shock. Her mouth dropped open wide and her eyes registered sheer panic at the sight of John and Gerry both clutching bunches of flowers, a very red-faced, twitching Elaine clutching more flowers and . . . and Charles Bond, smiling apologetically and sheepishly clutching the hugest bunch of red roses Cathy had ever seen in her life.

'Blimey, has somebody died?' Lisa giggled nervously behind her.

And Cathy decided *she* was about to.

CHAPTER 4

Wrong again, Elaine! Elaine thought hopelessly. She couldn't even get her timing right. Trust her to pick a night when the girls were throwing a party. Oh, she should have phoned! She almost had, but decided that her request was far too serious to be dealt with over the phone; besides, it was the coward's way out and she had vowed to be stronger in future and not the same ninny of the past.

But now that new-found courage was shimmering away from her at a rate of knots. She twisted her feet in embarrassment and knew she was going scarlet, about as scarlet as Lisa and Cathy were looking now in the doorway. Lisa was giggling nervously and Cathy looked sort of wild around the eyes and was almost frothing at the mouth.

Then it seemed everyone was speaking at once.

'Gosh, Elaine, how nice to see you.'

'Dahlings, a party, you should have said and we would have ditched the TV producer!'

'Ch-Charles, you've got a damned nerve!'

'Cathy, darling, my sincerest apologies.'

Elaine wanted to cover her ears but her hands weren't free. It reminded her of Parliament, everyone talking across each other. Oh, she wished she hadn't come. It was all so embarrassing.

She tried to turn away, to take flight but a huge bulk was blocking her way. Her nose came up against a huge bunch of fragrant red roses above her own bouquet; the giver snatched them away and Elaine blinked her eyes in recognition.

'Charles – Charles Bond, isn't it? she breathed, momentarily relieved that she knew someone other than the girls. 'Gosh, I haven't seen you since your wedding day.' She giggled nervously when Charles showed no sign of having a clue who she was. 'But you won't remember me, I was a gauche teenager at the time.'

Charles still looked at her blankly and Elaine was sure Cathy had let out what sounded like a strangled whimper.

'Is this a dry house or what?' one of the other two men tinkled. 'We've been on this doorstep all of thirty seconds and no one has offered us a drink yet.'

His friend playfully dug him in the ribs and, like Siamese twins joined at the hip, they shouldered their way into the hallway, thrusting the flowers at Lisa and kissing both girls warmly on each cheek and then kissing each other on each cheek and immediately going into hoots of laughter, which seemed to break the ice. The girls were suddenly making welcoming noises and ushering the boys out of the hallway and into the sitting-room beyond.

Elaine hung back, wondering if she and Charles Bond were going to have the door slammed in their faces because Lisa hadn't looked pleased to see her and Cathy certainly hadn't looked charmed to see Charles.

The boys had been the only two getting a warm welcome.

'Come in, all of you,' Lisa suddenly chirruped and reached for Elaine's arm to haul her in.

'So you are Charles,' she breathed, the smile dropping from her lips and a filthy look taking its place, 'complete with material apology too,' she said, glaring at the roses. 'Well, if you think you can come here and – '

'I'll deal with this, Lisa,' Cathy cut in.

The four of them were standing in the small hallway now, the girls taking wary glances at each other and their guests. Awkward atmosphere was bouncing off the walls. Charles was looking rather sheepish, which surprised Elaine because from what she could remember of him at his wedding he had come across as rather pompous and vain. He'd strutted around his wedding reception as if he had just landed the catch of the century, which her father said he had. Julia Witherspoon of the Cambridgeshire Witherspoons was a very wealthy heiress and Bond, apparently, was a penniless pen-pusher with delusions of grandeur beyond his means.

How on earth did Cathy and Lisa know him?

From the kitchen came the clink of bottles and glasses and a sudden roar of laughter from the boys, which urged Lisa to urge *her* into the sitting-room. Chummily she took her arm.

'Come on, let me pour you a drink. You obviously know Charles, so no introductions needed there. *If* he's staying,' she added pointedly, 'you can reminisce some more later.'

'He's not staying,' Cathy interjected icily, eyes narrowed.

'Um . . . excuse me,' Charles suddenly said before they disappeared from the hallway. He grinned widely as Elaine turned back towards him. 'But for the minute I can't quite place you and I do apologize. It's so unlike me to forget a beautiful woman.'

Cathy shot him a look of pure venom, which Elaine didn't understand and didn't try to.

'Elaine Morton,' she told him with a smile, not at all offended that he hadn't remembered her. As she had just said, she'd been a gauche teenager at the time, marvellously slim, but she recalled a slight hormonal problem which had resulted in an unsightly rash of spots around her chin. She remembered her hysterics at the time and her father promising her the complete range of Estee Lauder products if she promised to shut up. Yes, there had been a lot of water under the bridge since Charles's wedding day. She wasn't so marvellously slim any more and her skin was peaches and cream after the birth of Sophie – who would recognize that skinny, spotty teenager now?

'You must remember my father, though, he's a good friend of your father-in-law.'

Charles's blue eyes widened. 'I'm sorry. I'm still in the dark here.'

'John Morton.' Elaine smiled. 'My father is a judge and – '

Charles blanched and then colour rapidly infused his face and he started to splutter and then turned it into a laugh of remembrance. 'Ah! Yes . . . yes . . . of course. Oh, how very nice to meet up with you again, and how is – '

'OK, that's quiet enough of Happy Families for the time being,' Cathy interrupted snappily. 'Lisa, get Elaine a drink.' She swung on Charles with teeth

75

almost bared and started hurling a stream of accusations that Elaine didn't quite latch on to because Lisa had almost physically thrown her into the sitting-room and closed the door behind her. The other two guests were sprawled on the sofa watching Sky Sport and enthusiastically marvelling at muscular thighs under cricket whites. Elaine suddenly caught on and felt herself go pink.

Lisa quickly introduced everyone and the boys shot up from the sofa and kissed Elaine warmly on both cheeks and did the kissing-each-other routine, which they must have picked up at a pantomime and which only seemed to amuse themselves. Lisa's sparkling violet eyes went skyward.

John and Gerry gushed rapturously over Elaine's Cappalia silk blouse, admired the bounce and condition of her Titian hair, pronounced the French perfume she wore as divinely delectable, and then, satisfied that they hadn't missed anything out, they flopped back on to the sofa to watch cricket again.

'I'm really sorry for this intrusion, Lisa,' Elaine whispered, twisting the bouquet of flowers in her arms and flicking her wide grey eyes from the boys to the table prettily set for four at the other end of the room. 'I seem to have come at an inopportune moment, you're entertaining and – '

'And you are most welcome, Elaine,' Lisa assured her and looked as if she meant it, but Elaine couldn't be sure. How could she be sure about anything in her life?

This wasn't a good idea. She shouldn't have come and this was all so embarrassing. How could she try and persuade the girls to help her out of a spot with all these peculiar people here?

She shoved the bouquet of flowers at Lisa with a

76

nervous laugh. 'Here, I bought you both these, a . . . a sort of peace offering.'

Lisa flashed her a look that said it would take more than a bunch of flowers to make amends for what she had done to them but then she forced a sweet smile and took the flowers. 'They're lovely, how nice,' she remarked thinly. 'And you must stay to dinner, of course. We have plenty, thanks to your Ph – yes, plenty to go around.'

Elaine smiled hesitantly. Lisa looked a little pink. Though Lisa was making all the right let-bygones-be-bygones sounds, Elaine wasn't convinced they came from the heart. But what else could she expect? She had rather badly let them down in the past. But if only they would give her the chance to make amends, she would.

At least Lisa was *trying* to make her feel welcome. She had been the nicer of the two girls, more sensitive and sort of sweet. Cathy had always frightened her more than anything. She was the stronger of the two and didn't take any nonsense from anyone. It didn't sound as if she was taking any nonsense now. They could all hear raised voices out in the hall, Cathy's the more dominant.

One of the boys remote-controlled the cricket commentary up, which drowned her out. Lisa took Elaine's arm once again and guided her down the kitchen end to the drinks on the work surface. She plonked the flowers next to the boys' flowers in the sink and then turned her full attention back to Elaine, seeming to be making more of an effort to make her feel at ease. Her smile wasn't quite so transparent.

'What would you like, Elaine? Sorry, no Pimms, will Chablis do? Fancy you knowing Charles. Isn't life amazing, both of you turning up so unexpectedly and actually knowing each other? He's Cathy's boss – well, ex-boss really. That was what the atmosphere out there was about. You must have picked up on it and of course you can just about hear Cathy sounding off this very minute.' She laughed lightly. 'To cut a long story short, Cathy left and Charles isn't pleased. She's rather left him in the lurch and he wants her back on the job . . . I mean, back at work and I expect they are talking terms at the moment and hopefully it will all be resolved in a minute.' She took a deep breath as she handed Elaine a glass of cool white wine. 'So, Elaine, how are you keeping these days?' She smiled again, warmly.' I must say you are looking very well.'

Elaine didn't know what to say. She hadn't really expected such a gushing welcome. In fact, she wouldn't have been surprised if they *had* slammed the door in her face. At first she was creased with embarrassment when people had started to arrive on the doorstep with her, but now she could see it as an advantage. Cathy was well occupied in the hallway negotiating with her boss and John and Gerry were obviously used to entertaining themselves and she had Lisa to herself and Lisa had just invited her to stay for dinner. It was beginning to look good.

'That's very kind of you, Lisa – yes, I would like to stay if you are sure it's all right. I must say, it all looks very lovely.' She nodded to the table as Lisa laid another place, shifting everyone around a bit to get her in. 'And I remember you were always such a good cook. You were doing sandwich rounds then, are . . . are you still doing it?' She bit her lip as Lisa looked at her slightly frostily.

'No, actually, I'm not,' Lisa told her through tight

lips. 'I'm resting at the moment. Not my intention, actually, but forced upon me by . . . by . . .' her voice faltered but then came back stirringly '. . . unforeseen circumstances. And I must say, Elaine, you are a bit of an unforeseen circumstance yourself.' She took a long drink of her wine as if she needed it and gazed enquiringly over the rim of the glass at Elaine.

Elaine gulped her own wine hastily. Alcohol always gave her extra courage, that little bit of extra oomph to get her over her inadequacies. Lisa knew she was here for a reason and was waiting to hear it. There was one, of course, but for the life of her Elaine couldn't bring herself to explain just yet. She gulped some more and then she put the glass down on the edge of the table and rummaged in her bag like a nervous squirrel looking for its hoard of nuts and not quite sure if it was scrabbling in the place it had left them earlier.

'Lisa, I expect . . . well I expect you expect some sort of explanation,' she gabbled nervously, head bent over the bulging soft leather. 'And . . . and well things were very . . . oh, you know, difficult last year and . . . Oh, *where* is that envelope? Please God I didn't leave it in the taxi – oh, joy, here it is.'

Elaine, flushed with relief and pleasure, thrust the fat pink envelope, monogrammed with her initials, into Lisa's hand.

Lisa's hand was at her side at the time and she gazed down at it in astonishment and then let out a squeak of surprise as the flap came undone and a pile of twenty-pound notes fluttered to the floor.

'Blimey,' she exhaled as she quickly squatted to the pine-stripped floor to gather them up.

'A . . . a thousand pounds. I . . . I hope it covers what I owe you, Lisa,' Elaine whispered, taking a quick glance over her shoulder to make sure John and Gerry weren't watching. 'I really am sorry for what I did and there is more. I mean to say, I want to make it up to you more and I realize this isn't quite the time but perhaps . . . perhaps we can talk about it some time, though, well, there isn't much time and I would rather like to get it all sorted out and . . . Oh, gosh, Lisa, I do so need your and Cathy's help. I'm in such trouble and you and Cathy are all I have and I'm so desperate and – '

The ping of the cooker timer cut Elaine off in mid-sentence. She stood, biting her lower lip hard, horribly nervous again, trying to gauge Lisa's reaction, which for the time being looked thoroughly aghast. She was gaping at her peculiarly and then she tried to smile but nothing much happened to her lips and Elaine guessed she had shocked her with her fervent outburst, and the money, of course.

Lisa said nothing, not so much as a thank-you, but quickly stuffed the money and the envelope into the dresser drawer and slammed it shut as the boys leapt up from the sofa, zapped off the cricket and bustled into the kitchen area to see what they were about to eat.

Lisa playfully slapped away Gerry's hand as he reached out to scoop a fingerful of homemade mayonnaise out of a bowl on the table.

'Gerry, manners!' she cried.

'He hasn't any,' John simpered, 'it's why I love him so. He's the bit of rough in my life. Oh, Lisa, luvvie, everything smells divine. You know, with your looks and talent, you should have your own television programme. We'll put in a word for you later, won't we, Gerry? Now that we are shifting into television, the world is our oyster.'

'Hardly think a producer of costume drama will help me – ' Lisa laughed '– different kettle of fish altogether.'

'Yes, but contacts, darling,' John enthused. 'It's what it's all about these days, who you know in the right places. Don't you agree, Elaine? And what do you do for a crust, luvvie?'

Elaine gulped some more wine. She'd never done very much at all for a crust, so to speak.

'Well, I'm sort of resting at the moment.'

She caught Lisa's eye and the look Lisa gave her was one of interest, as if she was wondering what in fact Elaine was doing with her life lately. Elaine couldn't tell her, of course, that her life had gone so hopelessly haywire lately – well, all her life really. What on earth would they think of her if she told them she had a beautiful daughter now and one without a father – well, not a legitimate father, that is? For all Cathy and Lisa were what she would describe as good-time girls, she suspected they would be rather appalled that she now had an illegitimate child by a Marbella bar owner. But once they met him – which, if all went according to plan, they would eventually – then perhaps they would understand.

But for the time being she must stick to her original plan. Time enough to spring Sophie on them.

'An actress, dahling?' Gerry presumed with a twinkle. 'Oh, perhaps we can put a word in for you too. I can see your sophisticated looks are ideal for period drama. Yes, I rather fancy you as a Jane Austen heroine. What have you been in so far, dear? Anything we might have seen?'

'I . . . er . . .'

'Elaine has been working abroad lately, haven't

81

you, Elaine?' Lisa cut in, helping her out of a situation that was thoroughly flummoxing her.

Dear sweet Lisa. Elaine gulped some more wine from the glass Lisa had just topped up.

'Come on, sit down, all of you. We'll start without Cathy. I think I heard the front door slam just now.'

'You did indeed,' John offered brightly. 'He was gorgeous, by the way. Anyone I should know?'

He received a kick under the table from Gerry and Lisa gave much the same explanation as she had given to Elaine: Cathy's ex-boss etcetera, etcetera.

And as more wine flowed and plate after plate of sumptuous food was loaded on to the table, Elaine began to relax and enjoy the company. Hopefully later she would have Cathy and Lisa to herself and she could outline her plan to them. For the time being, though, she was Elaine Morton, resting actress who had just come back from South America after a very successful tour of a Shakespeare play called *For Whom the Bell Tolls*, in which she played the part of Virginia Woolf's sister, Betty.

And when everyone fell about laughing after she blurted it all out, she drank some more wine and helped herself to yet another individual sticky toffee pudding and was rather glad she had come. She was enjoying herself hugely.

After Lisa had slammed the door after her, safely ensconcing their guests in the sitting-room, Cathy launched into Charles. She was so livid with him for turning up like this, she was close to GBH.

'What on earth do you think you are doing, coming here like this?' she raged. 'After that disgusting phone call I wonder you have the nerve to show your face to me again!'

'Darling. I was out of my mind with lust for you – '

'Oh, no, Charles, pull the other one, it's got bells on! Lust had nothing to do with anything. You are just mad with me because I refuse to go back to you and your job and subject myself to more pride bashing. It's over, Charles, and even if I had been considering coming back, which I wasn't, after that phone call I wouldn't dream of it!'

'I brought you these, Cathy darling.' He thrust the roses forward and Cathy was so heated she took a swipe at them and then cried out and sucked her fingers.

'You might have bought thornless ones!'

'They cost a fortune,' Charles blustered, peering at them as if he had been ripped off.

'Well, there goes a fortune, then,' Cathy blurted out and snatched them again and flung them down in the corner of the hall. 'How dare you insult my intelligence by thinking a stingy bunch of roses will have me slobbering at your feet again.'

'I hardly call three dozen red roses, especially flown in from Kenya, stingy, darling.'

Cathy glowered at him so fiercely Charles hastily reached into his pocket and pulled out a long leather box, which he proudly snapped open for her to see its contents: a stunning, glittering, madly expensive bracelet nestling on black velvet.

'Diamonds, then, darling, that's how highly I think of you, Cathy darling,' he gushed deeply and movingly.

Sight of the gorgeous snake of diamonds and tiny pearls set in a band of plaited gold completely took the wind out of Cathy's sails. She stared at it, mesmerized. No one had ever offered her such a beautiful and expensive gift.

'Now will you reconsider, Cathy?' Charles breathed. 'I can't bear the thought of losing you. Forget the phone call – I'd had a bad day and Julia is giving me a hard time and everything just sort of got on top of me.'

Cathy caught her breath. So she *was* right – the wife was giving him a bad time so why not take it out on the mistress with an abusive phone call? Except she wasn't a mistress any more, had never intended being one anyway, it had all happened by default, his conniving default.

She shook her head determinedly. 'I'm sorry, Charles, your gifts, your remorse, your pleadings are all landing on deaf ears – '

'So what more can I offer?' he pleaded. 'I'll double your salary, back-date it to when our affair started. Remember how we felt about each other, the chemistry between us – we couldn't keep our hands off each other. Cathy, darling,' he pleaded persuasively, 'we can't let it all slip away like this.' He moved towards her as if to take her in his arms and physically show her just what she had given up.

Cathy jerked back out of his reach and backed up against the front door as if she was facing a madman. If he touched her, she didn't know how she would react. She thought she had dealt with all this, had it under control, but with him so close in this small space . . . This was ridiculous. He was married and she had no feelings left for him. She had been fooled and cheated and no way was she open to persuasion. Gifts, a promise of a salary rise that took her breath away

. . . No, she wasn't open to persuasion, but she was suddenly open to suspicion. Never before had he pleaded so passionately. He was more gushing now than he ever had been.

In sudden confusion she brought to mind their affair as he was reminding her to do. The times when, as he said, they couldn't keep their hands off each other. It had happened so quickly, too – the looks first, eyeing each other warily, neither sure and then the certainty for her when their hands brushed and she felt the frisson as if she had been stung, and when he had leaned over the back of her chair to view the computer screen over her shoulder and she felt his warm breath on the back of her neck, her blood had raced and her skin felt seared. And then the time when it had all erupted. She had brought his morning coffee as usual and sat with him as they were going over some lists. There was a slight difference of opinion over the company accounts – her figures didn't tally with his and she was sure she was right. They had argued quite heatedly because, of course, the sexual tension had begun to build by then. Suddenly he had snatched at her in anger and then his eyes had softened and the snatch turned into a caress and then all hell had been let loose. Mouths had bonded frantically, bodies had ground together and then the gasps of shock and the pulling back from each other to gaze into each other's eyes. Not wanting it to happen and yet wanting to die if it didn't.

Oh, yes, how could she forget the bittersweet torture of wanting each other during office hours, watching the clock till the working day was over and they could give vent to their passion? In the office at first, behind closed doors, lost in their desire. Then

there were conferences, the delicious freedom of a
hotel suite with no fear of any of the other staff
interrupting. Lying in bed with him, watching late-
night films, making love and making mugs of hot
sweet chocolate and curling naked under the sheets
to drink it together.

And then the lovely weekend they had planned
together at a luxurious hotel on the coast. No con-
ference this time and it had raised Cathy's hopes that
he might suggest, . . . well, . . . an engagement for
starters.

And then the wife.

'Yes, I remember,' she told him levelly, her head
sorted now. 'I also remember the times you made
excuses, like the last one, *something's* cropped up and
can't be avoided and suddenly that *something* materi-
alized and it was a wife. Well, you can't just sweep a
wife under the carpet, Charles. She exists.'

'And so do we, darling, and we matter too. It's been
hell in the office without you and – '

'And, yes, I'm getting the drift,' Cathy interrupted
shortly. 'You're in trouble, aren't you?'

'T-trouble?' His face was suddenly pale.

'Yes, trouble,' Cathy repeated, folding her arms
knowingly across her breasts. 'You might be a whizz at
figures but as far as office procedure is concerned
you're a no-no. I expect you can't find a thing without
me at your beck and call.'

Charles let out a long breath of relief. His hand went
to his forehead and rubbed it anxiously. Cathy
watched worriedly. She'd never seen Charles like
this, so stressed out. He was usually so on top of
everything. Had she hit the nail on the head? Without
her secretarial skills was he feeling the pressure? She

86

almost felt sorry for him, but then a new thought struck her.

'I'm not indispensable, Charles. I was a good secretary to you, but there are plenty more capable ones around. Why haven't you fixed yourself up with a replacement, for goodness' sake?'

Still he was pummelling his forehead. 'God, I need a drink,' he said plaintively.

Cathy bit her lower lip with concern. He sure did look as if he needed one. She steeled herself, though.

'Well, you're not going to get one offered here,' she told him decisively. 'We have guests and this conversation isn't for my friends' ears.'

His hand dropped to his side and he lifted his head and looked at her, blue eyes pleading with her. 'Is there a wine bar around here? We have to talk this out, Cathy. I can't just let you go like this. You are indispensable. I can't think of another secretary. It would be impossible. Just when everything was going to plan . . . I mean, we made a good team, the best, and – '

Cathy turned and opened the front door – suddenly the need for fresh air was urgent. Charles was suddenly proving to be a mystery to her. First the abusive phone call and now the gifts and declarations of need and this pleading with her, almost begging her to go back to him. No, it wasn't the Charles she had been so besotted with, but perhaps love was blind after all. She had only seen what she had wanted to. But the wife had cleared the rose-tinted mist from her silly eyes.

Nevertheless, she wasn't a cold-hearted sort of person. He had cheated and hurt her, but he did seem to be suffering himself and whether it was because of his personal feelings for her or his loss over her secretarial worth didn't much matter. He was getting neither back, but perhaps she could make it easier on them both with a sensible chat over a pint.

'There's a pub on the corner,' she told him gently. But don't hold out any hopes that you can smooth my way back into your personal and working life because that will be a lost cause, she told herself stoically. And she knew she would stick to that decision. She didn't even like this Charles she was seeing for the first time.

They stepped out into the warm evening air and Cathy breathed with relief as she closed the front door after her. They were out rather than in and that felt a good deal safer. Let Lisa get on with the dinner party and hopefully make Elaine feel welcome and perhaps there might be a light at the end of Lisa's career tunnel at the very least.

Hers had no chance. She was finished with Charles, but he didn't know that yet in spite of them waltzing off down to the pub together.

Charles smiled at her and linked his arm around her shoulder as they walked down the road and Cathy didn't even shake it away. It was peculiar, but she almost felt sorry for him. Perhaps he truly had a bad marriage? That, of course, could be affecting his work. He'd said Julia was giving him a hard time . . . but . . . but why should she care?

'That's better,' Charles breathed and gave her shoulder an affectionate squeeze. 'Fresh air and my darling Cathy back in my arms. A man couldn't want for anything more. Once back into the old routine we'll get away for that weekend we promised ourselves. Meanwhile, we have a lot of work to catch up on in the office. You're right, darling, I have let things get in a mess. I need your signature on several documents and cheques and it won't take long for you to get it all shipshape once again.'

His presumption that already she had given in riled Cathy's temper. Roses, diamonds? She was beginning to think Charles was having some sort of breakdown. He sounded so mixed up, but the overwhelming point he was trying to get at was that he needed her back in his working life rather than his personal life. His office was indeed in a turmoil as she had suspected and he was taking it for granted she would sort it for him. What a rat!

She didn't want another stand-up row in the street, but it was hard to hold back her temper.

Suddenly they were alongside the dark blue Rover that had stalked her home. And the creep *was* in the car. He was reading a newspaper and it was held up covering his face, which was decidedly suspicious.

Impulsively Cathy banged on the passenger window, but apart from the sudden jerk of the newspaper he didn't reveal himself.

'Pervert!' she cried. 'Haven't you got a home to go to?'

She'd needed that, to give vent to her fury with Charles because giving vent to him was proving to be a dead end. She marched on furiously – furious with Charles for taking so much for granted and furious with that idiot for still being parked in her street. Charles lost his grip on her shoulder as she strode away so tempestuously.

'What was that all about?' he asked as he caught her up.

Cathy stopped dead on the pavement. Well, here was a test of his caring if she really needed to strike it home once and for all. She lifted her chin and widened her eyes fearlessly.

'A stalker, actually, Charles,' she told him bluntly. 'He followed me home earlier and is still in the street and isn't it a good job I have you by my side to protect me?'

Charle's mouth dropped open and she saw real fear in his eyes as they flickered between her and the car she had just thumped. And she wasn't really surprised. Then, when he caught her arm and urged her hastily down the road to the pub, as fast as his rugby-thighed legs could carry him, she knew it all. He hadn't a smidgeon of caring for her in his bones, because a man who really cared for his woman would have dragged that man out of his car and socked him in the jaw.

You'll only get lip service from me, Charles Bond, she vowed inwardly as they pushed open the doors of the pub. I'll listen to your marriage problems if you want to discuss them and I'll make 'maybe' sounds when you offer me another million pounds a year to come back as your secretary, and that's as far as you go and then you are on your bike, sunshine. He wasn't the man she once thought him to be and she wasn't going to be the woman he thought her to be, a pushover as usual.

Pensively Lisa started to wash the dishes. What a night! Thankfully the boys had gone and all was peace and quiet. As for Elaine . . .

Lisa turned from the sink and glanced worriedly at the sofa where she was sprawled, sound asleep, her face slightly flushed by too much wine. Surprisingly she had been the life and the soul of the party – that was a side of Elaine Lisa had never seen before. How she had changed.

A sigh of relief escaped her lips as Lisa heard the front door go. It was still fairly early, just gone half-ten, but she had been worried about Cathy.

'Where on earth have you been?' Lisa fretted as Cathy came in, frowning down at Elaine on the sofa. Lisa beckoned her down to the kitchen end, her index finger to her lips so as not to awaken Elaine.

'Down at the pub with Charles,' Cathy told her in a whisper. 'And I'm starving,' she moaned, helping herself to a huge slice of oozing Pavlova. 'I've just spent hours listening to Charles's marriage problems and I was right, he's got himself into a mess in the office and . . .'

And she didn't want to burden Lisa with any of this, this nagging feeling inside her that Charles was having some sort of mental breakdown. She'd left him in the pub drowning his sorrows and walked home thought-fully, after promising to get in touch with him after thinking things over. She'd only said it to cheer him up. She had no intention of calling him, but he'd been in such a state she had felt sorry for him. The only good thing about the evening was that the stalker had disappeared.

Through a mouthful of raspberries and cream she nodded to Elaine and mumbled, 'What's with the duchess?'

'Don't call her that, Cathy. Poor love seems to be in a bit of a state,' Lisa whispered worriedly. 'She's really changed. The boys thought her great. She's had a bit to drink and just flopped out on the sofa after they left.'

'Well, she's not stopping,' Cathy whispered flatly.

91

'After what she did to us she can . . . 'Struth, what's that?'

Lisa had opened the dresser drawer and taken out the pink envelope and tossed it down in front of Cathy.

'A thousand pounds,' Lisa whispered. 'Elaine gave it to me, said she was sorry for everything and she needed our help.'

Cathy's eyes widened in astonishment. 'Wh . . . what sort of help?' she faltered.

A small moan came from the other end of the room and Cathy and Lisa turned quickly.

'Oh, my head,' Elaine groaned as she struggled to get to her feet. 'Oops,' she giggled as she fell back against the squashy cushions. 'Oh, I'd better go.'

'Have some black coffee first,' Lisa suggested, giving Cathy a warning frown and nodding towards the kettle. Lisa went to Elaine. 'Or you can stay the night if you like? Your room is still here,' she grinned.

At Cathy's horrified exclamation, Lisa gave her friend another warning frown.

'Oh, I couldn't stay,' Elaine said quickly and finally managed to get to her feet, swaying slightly. She grinned rather lopsidedly at Lisa. 'I must get home and you've done enough for me tonight.' Suddenly she flung her arms around Lisa. 'Oh, I'm so glad we are friends again, Lisha, and I just knew you would help and understand. And your idea to drive down is just too kind. I . . . I'll call tomorrow and we'll finalize . . . Oh, my head.'

Lisa eased her back down onto the sofa. 'I'll make the bed up for you. I can't let you go home in this state.'

'No, honestly, I must go home. I'm not allowed to stay out all night. Could you call me a cab?' She was on her feet again like a jack in a box. 'Oh, Cathy, you're back.'

'Yes, and I'd like to know what is going on here,' Cathy said through tight lips.

Elaine looked at her hesitantly and then appealed to Lisa with grey eyes wide and dejected.

'Don't worry, Elaine,' Lisa said soothingly, giving her a hug. 'I'll explain everything to Cathy after you've gone. Could you call a cab, Cathy?'

Dumbly Cathy went to the phone as Lisa and Elaine whispered to each other behind her back. She'd had enough for one night. What with Charles and a stalker and now an inebriated Elaine and her best friend acting as if Elaine had never done either of them an injustice in their lives – the whole world was going mad.

'So what was that all about?' Cathy demanded to know after they had folded a giggling Elaine into a taxi, Lisa handing the cab driver a twenty-pound note out of the pink envelope as Elaine seemed to have difficulty in coordinating herself properly

Exhausted, Lisa let out a sigh. 'I'll make coffee and tell you everything.'

'You've got to be joking! *She*'s got to be joking!' Cathy breathed incredulously five minutes later as they sat hunched over coffees at the breakfast bar. 'That just doesn't happen these days!'

Lisa shrugged. 'Well, it's happening to Elaine, an arranged marriage, as I said. Next week, actually, hence the haste. Her father has arranged it all. Apparently he's been an ogre since Elaine's mother died. He totally dominates her life and he's insisting on this marriage. She's supposed to be marrying

Ph-Philip . . .' Lisa paused to bite her lip . . . 'and
. . . and she doesn't want to, she can't stand him.
From what I gather, he doesn't love her anyway, but
she is a judge's daughter and they have loads of dosh
and, well, that is the way it is with those sort of
moneyed people, nothing to do with love and all
that.

'But Elaine isn't like that,' Lisa went on. 'She's
rather sweet actually. She just can't marry a man she
doesn't love, so she's going to run away, keep out of
the way till the wedding day is past, just a couple of
weeks. Hopefully, by then her father will realize that
Elaine is not to be pushed around any longer. That's
where we come in. Elaine reckons that when she
disappears her father will leave no stone unturned
to find her. But three girls on the run won't arouse
suspicion and – '

'Just a minute!' Cathy nearly screamed. 'On the
run! To where, for goodness' sake?'

'Marbella.'

'Marbella!' Cathy screeched.

'And why not Marbella?' Lisa argued. 'Elaine's says
it's wonderful and we'll have a good time.'

'Anyone would think you agree with all this!' Cathy
blurted out incredulously. 'It sounds to me as if you
and Elaine have it all worked out already. Gosh, I was
only out of the house a couple of hours and all of a
sudden you and she are bosom pals and planning some
harebrained scheme to get her out of a marriage she
doesn't want!'

'She doesn't love him, Cath,' Lisa wailed.

'And you do!' Cathy accused bluntly. 'You are so in
love with Philip damned Mainwaring yourself you'll
help Elaine run away from him, leaving the way clear

94

for yourself. My God, Lisa how low can you sink?'

'It's not like that at all,' Lisa protested, twisting her hands in her lap. 'I know there's no chance with him. I knew it when I saw him with Elaine in the wine bar, but now I know it even more because *now* I know that all that lovey-dovey stuff with her was just a pretence. He doesn't even love her and is marrying her because she is a good catch.'

Lisa took a deep breath and went on hurriedly before Cathy protested yet again. 'I want to help Elaine for two reasons. Firstly, it isn't right that she should marry someone she doesn't love and, secondly, I'm fired by something you should understand. Remember what fired you when you found out Charles was married? Revenge! Well, you aren't the only one. Philip was beastly to me after my disastrous lunch, spreading the rumour that I was untrustworthy and spoiling my chances of ever getting work again. I hate him for that and what better way to get back at him than by whisking his fiancée out from under his feet!'

Cathy stared at her friend in astonishment, all powers of speech suddenly frozen. This wasn't dear sweet Lisa talking of revenge! What on earth had happened to them both lately?

'Elaine has changed,' Lisa pleaded plaintively. 'She needs our help and besides . . . well, besides . . .' She sighed dramatically. 'We haven't anything better to do for the time being and a free holiday in Marbella might just be what we need.'

She lifted her chin suddenly. 'I've made the decision anyway, even offered to drive us all down there in the van because, if her father has any suspicions, he'll look for her at airports, not on the road. And if you've any sense you'll come along as well. Elaine is paying for it all – the ferry, the petrol, all expenses on her. We'll have a jolly good holiday, some sun on our cheeks and, when we come back, we'll be rejuvenated. Charles will have given up on you and – '

The phone started to ring and Cathy jerked and stared at the phone, knowing, just knowing that Charles wouldn't let up on her. Suddenly she was seized with exhaustion. What a night, and now this crazy scheme of Elaine's and Lisa wanting to go along with it. Her head was bursting.

The phone rang and rang and Cathy and Lisa stared at each other till finally it stopped.

Cathy let out a long sigh and dragged her heavy hair back from her face. And why not let Elaine compensate them for all the mess she had put them in last year? She could afford to make amends. Yes, why not? She'd considered a slow boat to China to escape from heartbreak over Charles and his deception and Marbella sounded a fair enough runner-up and the closest thing to escape she was going to be offered. Yes, that last persistent phone ringing tipped her over the fence.

'OK,' she breathed at last. 'Let's do it. Let's go and have a whale of time and to blazes with all men.'

Grinning madly at each other, they clinked their coffee cups and toasted Elaine and her mad, mad, mad idea.

CHAPTER 5

'Friends? What friends?' Philip demanded to know over the phone.

Elaine wished she had never called him now to tell him her plans, but she had got rather confused over ports and ferries and her brother knew everything and she needed help.

'I do have friends, Philip,' she retorted tartly at the same time glancing anxiously at Karen, the nanny, who was thankfully busy preparing Sophie's lunch of pureed vegetables on the other side of the kitchen. She'd called her brother at his office from the secrecy of her bedroom, but he hadn't been available and then he had called her back just as Karen was doing the lunch, so this conversation so far had been rather stilted.

Karen, always so deeply embroiled in her nannying duties, switched on the blender, which mercifully drowned out Elaine's conversation.

'I can't talk properly now, Philip. Suffice it to say that I'm going with friends and all I needed from you is some information on ferries. We are going by – Karen, more blender, I don't want Sophie choking on lumps of carrot, thank you very much,' she told the nanny sternly. Karen immediately set the blender in motion again. Elaine, very hot and bothered now, whispered down the phone, 'We're going by road and it's all arranged and nothing but nothing is going to stop me.'

'*I'll* do my best to stop you,' Philip seethed down the phone. 'Come to your senses, Elaine, this is ridiculous.'

Elaine slammed down the phone. Damn Philip. She shouldn't have called him in the first place. She could do this on her own. She didn't need him.

Checking to make sure the food Karen had prepared for her adorable daughter was edible, she nodded her approval – which always riled Karen – planted a tender kiss on Sophie's warm forehead as she lay in her carrycot gurgling for her dinner, and then dashed into her father's study to attack the *Yellow Pages* for travel agents because Philip hadn't been any help at all.

The phone was ringing as she stepped into the oak-panelled room and when she picked it up she was astonished to hear it was Charles Bond calling her.

'Oh, Charles, this is a surprise.' Quite a shock, as it happened – he was the last person on earth she expected to hear from. 'What can I do for you?'

'A lot, I hope, Elaine. It was a very pleasant surprise running into you the other night. I had no idea you were a friend of Cathy's.' He cleared his throat. 'Cathy is the reason I'm calling, actually. I don't know how much you know, but she's my secretary. Unfortunately, we have had a few misunderstandings and she left and I would rather like her back on board and I just wondered . . . well it's a bit of a nerve asking you, but I wondered if you could have a word with her, seeing as we are old friends.'

Old friends! Elaine could hardly believe her ears. Apart from the other night, she hadn't seen him since his wedding years ago. She bit her lip, wondering what to say and thinking that she had better be careful here. To acknowledge a close friendship with Cathy at the moment might put her in a tricky position. They were all off to Marbella as soon as she could sort things out and secrecy was of the uppermost importance.

'I'm sorry, Charles, but I'm not that close to Cathy. I'm more of a friend of Lisa's, and anyway I don't see her very much either and well . . . I'm sorry, but – '

The phone went dead on her and Elaine gaped at it. Gosh, Cathy must be some marvellous secretary for a man like Charles to pursue her so ardently. She shrugged and breathed a sigh of relief that she had got herself out of that one without giving herself away. Charles Bond's father-in-law was a friend of her father's and she could do without any connection there for the time being.

Grabbing the *Yellow Pages*, she hurtled back to her bedroom and then went dreadfully hot all over. Suppose he called Cathy again and Cathy said, 'Pooh to your job, I'm off to Marbella with Elaine Morton whose on the run from an arranged marriage?' It might get back to her father and he'd know exactly why they were heading for Marbella and all would be lost. She'd never escape to see Marcus again because her father would manacle her to the bedpost.

Elaine sat on the edge of the bed and hugged that bedpost and tried not to panic. She had stressed the secrecy to Lisa when she had made up her story about an arranged marriage and she trusted Lisa so, hopefully, she would have transferred the urgency of the situation to Cathy and Cathy would keep quiet too. Oh, it was all so stressful. If only she'd had the nerve to go it alone without having to involve all these people.

Determinedly she flicked through the *Yellow Pages*. Ten minutes later, she rather proudly did a twirl around her elegant pale-green bedroom. The travel agent had been so helpful and, in spite of the fact that it was slap bang in the middle of the season for bookings, he had managed to secure a cancellation, two double cabins on the Portsmouth–Santander ferry, one for Cathy and Lisa and the other for her and Sophie. Elaine had delightedly paid by gold credit card over the phone. Confirmation and the tickets would be sent to Lisa in Battersea by courier immediately – Elaine thought that safer than any correspondence coming here for her father to peruse. The day after tomorrow they would all be off and it couldn't have worked out better – it was Karen's day off and her father was going away, presiding at Chester Crown Court. No one would miss her and Sophie till the next day and then it would be too late. Already her heart was thumping with excitement at the thought of being in Marcus's arms once again.

Sophie. She hadn't told Lisa about Sophie yet. Elaine's euphoria wavered. One step at a time, though. She'd explain when they were on the ferry. The girls could drive down on their own and she'd take a taxi down and meet them there and then it would be too late for them to object to travelling with a baby on board. Not that they would once they saw the heavenly child but . . . oh, Lord, how was she going to explain her? Perhaps then would be the time to tell them the truth, that there wasn't an arranged marriage

100

after all and she was on her way to meet her lover, the father of her child? Yes, time enough to worry about that. For now, what on earth was she going to take with her? She so wanted to look special for Marcus and was there time to shed a few pounds before she left? She dashed into the en-suite bathroom to weigh herself.

'Look, who exactly are these friends you're planning to drive down with?' Philip insisted on knowing later, picking up the conversation that Elaine had previously ended so abruptly

Elaine sat on the bed amongst piles of designer clothes and clutched the phone to her ear with one hand while she held up a Monsigno silk blouse and wondered if the colour would still suit her once her skin took on a tan.

'They are the two girls I shared a house with in Battersea, Cathy and Lisa,' Elaine told him confidently. 'And before you throw a fistful of objections at me, they are good, trustworthy friends. In fact, one of them, Cathy, worked for Charles Bond. Remember we went to his wedding years ago? His wife's father is a friend of Daddy's.'

Yes, that should put Philip's mind at rest. Anyone who had worked for someone who knew her father was A-OK. Elaine opened her mouth to further extol her friends' virtues, but Philip's voice exploded in her ear.

'Charles Bond! That schemer! He married for money and has practically drained his wife's inheritance over the years. So what's he doing now? No doubt bleeding someone else dry. And this friend of yours works for him? Doesn't say much for her – '

'Listen, Philip,' Elaine hissed down the phone,

101

wishing she had never mentioned the man. She'd only used his name to put Philip's mind at rest, but apparently she'd got it wrong yet again. It seemed Charles Bond wasn't the pacifying icon she had expected him to be. 'Look, I know you are only trying to protect me, but it's all right. Cathy doesn't work for him any more anyway. They really are good friends of mine and we are all going together because . . . well, they are due for a holiday anyway and we thought it would be an adventure driving down – '

'You don't drive!'

Elaine's eyes went skywards. This was the biggest mistake she had made, involving her brother in her plans. He was putting every petty obstacle in her way.

'No, but they do and it isn't a problem,' she insisted. 'We're taking the ferry the day after tomorrow – the night ferry, so hopefully Sophie will sleep and – '

'What port are you going from?' Philip demanded to know.

'Portsmouth,' Elaine told him, immediately biting her tongue. Another mistake. Now Philip would do something drastic to stop them, just as her father would do if he knew what was going on behind his back. 'And don't even think about doing anything to stop me, Philip,' she warned him tightly. 'If anything happens to prevent me making this trip, I'll hold you responsible and I will never, never speak to you again as long as I live. And I mean it!'

There was a long protracted sigh of resignation. 'Have it your own way and be it on your own head. If anything goes wrong, don't say I didn't warn you.'

'Clichés, Clichés.' Elaine laughed, feeling she had won a reprieve from this inquisition. 'What can possibly go wrong, Philip?'

'Huh! Everything, knowing you. Now give me an address so I can get in touch with you when you arrive.'

'Er . . . what?'

'The hotel you're going too.'

'Er . . .' Elaine felt another hot rush coming on. She hadn't given hotels a thought what with everything else to think about, and in the middle of the season . . .

'Oh, no, Elaine.' Philip groaned. 'You really are a fluff head. Is it any wonder I worry about you so? OK, leave this part of your already ill-fated trip to me. It's the very least I can do if you are so determined. I've a friend who owns a villa down that way. He only uses it for himself and he's in Hong Kong at the moment so it will be free. I'll call him and make the arrangements and call you back.'

Tears brimming in her eyes, a hand clutched to her throat, Elaine croaked, 'Oh, Phil, I really am a goose and you are so wonderful to me. What would I do without you?'

'I dread to think.' Philip sighed. 'Now get back to your packing and I'll call you back.'

'How did you know I was packing?' Elaine giggled.

'How did I know . . .' Philip drawled sarcastically on a sigh and put down the phone.

Elaine did another twirl of excitement around her bedroom. Dear, dear Philip. Now they had a villa to stay in. Cathy and Lisa would be thrilled to bits; if they had had any doubts about this trip, they would soon be quashed. And she had no doubts now. Not a single one. They were going to Marbella and darling Marcus would be there and everything, but everything, was going to work out. She could hardly contain her excitement. Soon, very soon she would be in Marcus's arms and he would adore Sophie and all would work out beautifully.

'How many noughts to a million?' Cathy asked Lisa pensively as they collected factor five sun oil, a huge tub of moisturizer and UV block lip salve from the supermarket shelf.

'You're asking me? You're the whizz at figures. Work it out for yourself,' Lisa murmured. 'I think with my fair skin I ought to go for a factor eight. What do you think?'

'I think the bank must have made a mistake,' Cathy mumbled, popping a packet of cotton wool pads into the trolley.

'What an earth are you mumbling about, Cath? Forget money for a while, we're leaving after lunch and we have all the dosh we need. Thanks to Elaine,' she chortled. 'Oh, I'm so excited. A free holiday. I bet the villa we're going to is out of this world if it belongs to a friend of hers. Elaine might be a bit flaky, but she has good connections and seems to have loads of money now.'

'So have I, according to the cashpoint machine.'

Lisa turned to Cathy. Cathy looked worried out of her mind instead of excited at the prospect of a couple of free weeks in the Spanish sunshine. Cathy met Lisa's enquiring gaze and shrugged her shoulders. 'I went to draw out some more cash, just in case we need it and, according to the account standing – you know that strip of read-out on the machine – I have more than a million pounds in my account. Of course the more bit is my own.'

Lisa laughed lightly. 'It's a mistake. Banks are

104

always making them. You just try drawing it out and the bank will soon discover it's made a boob.'

'Yeah, you're right,' Cathy breathed. 'I wonder what the legalities of that are? I mean, supposing I bowled into the bank and demanded the million and they hadn't discovered the mistake. Would I be entitled to that money when they did find out?'

'Don't be daft. You probably read it wrong, the sun shining on it or something. Pull yourself together, Cathy,' Lisa warned, suddenly fed up with Cathy's paranoia lately. 'You're seeing things. Millions in your account, stalkers in dark blue Rovers. Charles is doing this to you since you walked out on him, sending you crazy. Thank goodness we are getting away. You'll crack up if we don't. Now, come on and let's finish this shopping. We have to leave soon if we are going to catch this ferry on time.'

Lisa was right, Cathy conceded. She was going round the bend, but not without help. Charles was still pestering her by phone – he'd even called Elaine, she had been disturbed to hear from Elaine herself when she had excitedly called to tell them their travelling arrangements. And there *was* a stalker, that secret faceless person who drove a blue Rover and seemed forever parked down their street with a newspaper up to his face.

She wished she hadn't told Lisa about it now because Lisa always looked on the bright side and saw no evil in the world and was now thinking she was mad. Cathy was a bit more cynical about life since finding Charles had a wife. She supposed all her worries had stemmed from that. But perhaps the guy in the Rover was simply a private eye, following someone else on the street, gathering evidence for a divorce case, possibly, and not interested in her at all.

But Charles's persistence couldn't be denied and that worried the hell out of Cathy. Every time he called, it messed up her emotions. Once she'd had strong feelings for the guy, till she'd met the wife. And now she was beginning to feel more and more sorry for him and it was wearing her down. His persistence was indeed a worry, because she had never realized just how deeply he had felt for her until she had walked out on him and it made her feel uncomfortable.

Cathy and Lisa loaded the van with their supermarket purchases, Lisa chattering excitedly all the time and Cathy trying very hard to put everything behind her. They were off to Marbella and Elaine was footing the bill and what could be a better way to get back on her feet? They'd soak up the sun for a couple of weeks and by the time they came back they'd both be refreshed enough to take stock of their futures and get back to some sort of normality. Both would get jobs, Elaine would have wriggled out of her marriage arrangement and made the point to her father and her intended that she wasn't to be pushed around any more.

Yes, the holiday would be fun. Just what they all needed. She would forget Charles and hopefully he would forget her and stop his pestering. Lisa would get Philip Mainwaring out of her system. How better to do it than spending a couple of weeks with his fiancée and thwarting his marriage to Elaine? To Cathy's way reasoning, it was a weird way of going about an exorcism, but already Lisa was coming to despise him all the more, so who was she to judge? He'd wrecked her career prospects and was making Elaine's life a misery – Lisa was beginning to see that he wasn't a nice person to know at all.

The last thing they did as John and Gerry hugged them goodbye in the street and chortled their *bon voyages* hysterically was to give them the key to their maisonette just in case of an emergency, flood, fire or burglary.

'And no wild parties in our flat while we're away,' Cathy warned from the passenger seat as she buckled up and Lisa revved the engine.

Gerry, pocketing the key, grinned widely. 'Wouldn't dream of it, darling. Have fun and be careful, you two. Bring us a stick of rock back.'

'We're going to Marbella, not Blackpool.' Cathy laughed, immensely glad they were going now. Already she could feel the weight lifting from her and holiday fever building up.

'Same thing, luvvie,' John teased and waved theatrically as they pulled away from the kerb.

Cathy relaxed back in her seat and breathed happily. Then suddenly she shot forward and in a wild moment of daring she leaned on the car horn as Lisa drove down the street. She gave the occupant of the dark blue Rover, still with a newspaper up to shield his face, an exaggerated royal wave quickly followed by a naughty gesture.

'That will teach him. I'm sure he must have a couple of slits in the paper to see through. If he follows, we'll lose him on the motorway – '

'Will you shut up!' Lisa laughed as she signalled to turn left, glancing in the rear-view mirror. 'No one is going to follow, no one ever was following you in the first place, so drop it before I get really mad. OK?'

'OK.' Cathy grinned, totally relaxed now.

Lisa wasn't quite so relaxed now, though. What she couldn't tell Cathy was that in the rear-view mirror she had just seen the occupant of the dark blue Rover get out of the car and cross the road to John and Gerry, who were still waving them off. It was only a brief glimpse, but enough to know that if he had been following and watching Cathy these past few days, Cathy should feel priviliged. The stalker was gorgeous. Tall and muscular, casually dressed in jeans and trainers, with fair hair bleached by the sun.

As Lisa waited at the junction for a gap in the traffic, she tried to look harder, but it was difficult as they were quite far away now. She couldn't see the features clearly but the overhaul effect was enough. No danger there. A secret admirer, no doubt. Pity they were going away – Cathy could do with a new man in her life to get over Charles. She watched as John and Gerry and the stranger laughed and then they all went into the boys' flat.

Lisa grinned to herself as she pulled out into the main road. But perhaps he hadn't been shadowing Cathy at all. Perhaps he was more interested in a couple of good fun hairdressers who lived upstairs from them!

'Where the devil has Elaine got to?' Cathy sighed, pushing her thick hair back from her forehead. The journey down from London had been smooth and uneventful, but now they were here on the quayside she was beginning to fret. 'If she's starting her tricks already on this trip, I've a good mind to – '

'She'll be here,' Lisa interjected quickly. 'She's coming by taxi and if she's running late the cabbie will put his foot down.' She poured hot water into two

108

mugs and dipped a tea bag in both. 'We're all right for time anyway. We can't drive on yet and there's a queue anyway. We'll have this cuppa while we wait.'

The van had been equipped for camping when Lisa bought it, with a small two-ring cooker run on bottled gas and a round stainless steel sink next to it with a tap. Water was pumped from a container under the sink. There was even a small fridge, which ran off gas too.

Though Lisa used it for work she hadn't wanted to strip it down. There was plenty of room for all her catering equipment and the sink and fridge had come in handy at times. The upholstered bench seats were comfortable, too, with extra storage underneath. It was ideal for their trip through Spain and at a squeeze the three of them could bed down in it, though Lisa wondered if Elaine was up to roughing it a bit at night. It would save money on hotels, though.

She handed a mug of tea to Cathy who was anxiously peering out of the side window looking for Elaine, her long floaty cotton skirt bunched up around her thighs as it was hot in the van. They were parked up on the quayside and there were crowds of holidaymakers swarming everywhere. It was a warm balmy evening and the sea was calm which promised an uneventful crossing. Lisa wasn't sure if she suffered sea-sickness or not as she had never been on a ferry before and she was slightly nervous.

'Watch that gate over there.' Lisa nodded towards it as she sat on the seat across from Cathy, careful not to spill her tea. 'She'll have to come in that way. Wow, look at that chauffeur-driven Roller coming in. Aren't people funny? If I could afford a a car like that and a chauffeur, I'm sure I'd fly rather than ferry.' She swallowed a couple of Diacalms with her tea.

109

'He probably owns the ferry.' Cathy grinned. 'Come to collect the takings. Oh, look, there's a black cab. Is it her? Yeah. Sorry, Elaine, I take back all I was thinking.' She slid open the side door and jumped out and started to wave her hands frantically at Elaine, who was half-hanging out of the taxi window looking for them.

'Fancy coming all this way from London in a cab,' Lisa said in awed tones, as she joined Cathy on the tarmac. 'The girl's got style, whatever you think of her, Cath.'

'More money than sense if you ask me. Silly cow – look, she's asked the cabby to pull up alongside that Roller. Does she think it's us and we're all going down in that?'

'Oh, no!' Lisa let out a strangled cry and her hand went to her mouth.

'What's up?'

'Look who's just got out of the limo! That's it, then! The trip's off. She's been rumbled.'

'What an earth are you going on about?' Cathy craned her neck to see over the crowds and parked cars. 'Crikey!' she breathed. 'It's the guy in the wine bar. Your Philip, Elaine's fiancé. He's caught her. Look, they're rowing like mad.'

They were too far away to hear what was going on, but people closer to them were looking at the furious Elaine curiously.

'Philip, how could you?' Elaine screamed as she leapt out of the taxi. The first thing she had seen on entering the port was her damned brother's black Rolls Royce. 'You're not stopping me from going. You've no right. You're not Daddy, though you are acting like him lately. How dare you come here? How dare you try to spoil things for me? You're beastly, absolutely rotten!'

Philip ignored her for a moment as he took a bulky hold-all from his chauffeur and spoke to him quietly before the chauffeur got back into the driving seat and backed the car out of the parking bay.

Elaine, fists clenched tightly at her side, springy Titian hair billowing in the breeze, gaped at the leaving car, confusion running riot in her head. She had expected Philip to bundle her in the back and whip her back to Knightsbridge, not send his driver off with the car without either of them in it.

Philip turned to her and grasped her by the shoulders to steady her.

'Calm down, Elaine,' he said smoothly. 'I'm not trying to stop you. All common sense says I should, but I'm not.'

'You're not?' Elaine gasped in amazement.

Philip smiled and lifted a hand to close her mouth for her. 'I'm coming with you.'

Elaine's mouth gaped open again.

'I can't let you do this with just a couple of girlfriends. Not with the responsibility of baby Sophie, too. Three girls on the run can get into all sorts of trouble. It's my duty as your brother to make sure you are safe, so I'm coming with you. It's a long drive down and I can help with the driving. One more in the car won't make any difference and – '

'Van,' Elaine corrected him automatically, so shocked she could hardly speak. 'Er . . . it's a camper van.'

Philip looked appalled. 'A camper van?' he echoed. He turned quickly, but it was too late to stop his chauffeur who was accelerating smoothly away.

111

'Damn! If you'd told me sooner I could have stopped Elliot and we could have gone down in my car. Honestly, Elaine, you are impossible. How can you think of such a madness? A camper van. Who are these damned friends of yours, hippies?'

Elaine started to laugh, mainly in relief that Philip hadn't come to stop her going. 'Oh, Phil, you are such a stuffed shirt. Of course they are not hippies. It's Lisa's van – she uses it for her catering business.' Suddenly she flung her arms around her brother. 'Oh, Phil, thank you for being so wonderful. I'm sure the girls will be glad of an extra driver and won't mind a bit. I'm so pleased you are coming. It's going to be such fun.'

There was a sudden wail from inside the taxi. The cabbie was leaning against his cab, rolling a cigarette and discreetly waiting patiently.

'Gosh, that's Sophie.' Elaine laughed, unhooking herself from her brother. 'I'll get her while you get the rest of my stuff out. Oh, Philip, I'm so happy. Could you pay the cabbie for me while I see to Sophie?' She dived into the back of the taxi and swept Sophie out of her car seat and hugged her tightly as she stepped out again.

'Oh, darling, just wait till your daddy sees you. He's going to adore his little surprise,' she cooed.

'And now she's laughing and hugging the brute,' Cathy seethed as she watched, occasionally stretching her neck to get a better sighting of the betrothed couple making it up.

Lisa couldn't bear to look. She leaned her forehead against the warm metal of her van, lamenting the loss of a free holiday. Philip damned Mainwaring – she'd never lament over him ever again! He only wanted to marry Elaine for her position and more money than he already had. *Or* he must really love her after all! And if he did, what a rat for flirting with *her* and raising her hopes that she might have a chance with him. He was no better than Cathy's married boss. A snake!

'Bang goes the holiday, I suppose.' Cathy sighed fretfully. 'Just when I was getting used to the idea. His car has gone, though. I wonder what is going on?'

Lisa couldn't bear to hear any more. She climbed back into the van and washed up the two tea mugs, disappointed as hell for several miserable reasons.

'Hey up! Oh, Lisa, you aren't going to believe this.' Even Cathy was shocked to the core. Elaine had dived into the back of the taxi and come out with . . . nah, she must be seeing things. Now Philip Mainwaring and the taxi driver were unloading more from the cab. Suitcase after suitcase and numerous glossy carriers and . . . and a navy blue polka-dotted travelling baby buggy?

Cathy wasn't easily shocked but this took the biscuit. Elaine was holding a *baby*! Whose, for goodness' sake? she foolishly asked herself and then it all became clear – some of it. From that first sighting of Elaine in the wine bar she had thought how different she looked. More vulnerable, softer, plumper. *The baby she was carrying was her own!*

'Um . . . she's got a baby with her,' she directed through the door to Lisa, keeping her tone light to minimize the shock to her. Lisa would be devastated. What on earth was Elaine up to, she thought angrily, wanting to run away from an arranged marriage when she already had a child by the bridegroom-to-be?

'Don't be silly,' Lisa muttered, putting the mugs

113

away and wiping down the sink. She didn't want to look, didn't want to see Philip with Elaine, hugging and kissing and making up, ruining the holiday she had been looking forward to. She had wanted it so much, to get away and try and forget that Philip Mainwaring had had such an impact on her. Even though they would have been travelling with his fiancée, so thwarting the wedding plans, she had convinced herself that it would have doubled as an exorcism and a swipe of revenge at the man who had treated her so badly.

She'd thought she had covered her feelings so well with Cathy, but the truth was that she still hurt inside. She might tell herself and Cathy that she hated him for ruining her business, hated him for wanting to marry Elaine, but her heart, racing so frantically now, said it all. He was still there, paddling around in her heart, causing ripples and tidal waves that had no right to be there.

'Elaine has seen the van. She's waving. What a minx that girl is,' Cathy seethed. 'She actually looks happy, and after all this trouble we've gone too she's going to sail up to us and tell us the trip is off and she's going ahead with the marriage. Aren't we the mugs to have agreed to all this?'

'You can say that again,' Lisa murmured mournfully. She glanced out of the window to see the queue of cars and vans like their own moving on to the ferry. Lucky devils, she thought.

'Oh, well, nothing for it but to go home,' she muttered, stepping out of the van, hiding her disappointment for all she was worth. Her eyes suddenly widened. 'That *is* a baby she's pushing in that buggy!'

'I told you so. Her own, too. I thought she had

changed and you said she had as well. Elaine Morton is a mother,' Cathy stated flatly.

'And Philip Mainwaring a father,' Lisa groaned, her eyes suddenly filling with tears. Oh, how much worse could it get? This wasn't fair, it just wasn't fair!

Cathy slid an arm around her, but there were no words to comfort her with. What could you say? Lisa's Philip was no better than Charles Bond. A deceiver.

As for Elaine? Cathy wanted to murder her, but then the feeling suddenly passed. Elaine had a baby and, whatever she might think of her, she had to concede that in this day and age you had a choice. Elaine had chosen to have that baby out of wedlock and in the circles she swam in, her father a respected judge, that must have taken some heartfelt soul searching.

'Oh, well,' Cathy sighed, squeezing Lisa's shoulder as they watched Elaine, a baby and a well-loaded-up Philip Mainwaring, struggling with a mountain of luggage, wend their way towards them. 'Put on a brave face and wish them well for the future. That's all we can do.' She frowned suddenly. 'What's with all that luggage anyway?'

'And why did Philip's car leave?' Lisa added faintly. 'What do you think is going on?'

Flummoxed, the girls stood rooted to the spot.

Elaine's smile of happiness that Philip was coming with them suddenly faded. As usual she hadn't been thinking again. Her brother knew nothing of the lie she had told the girls to get them to agree to this trip. The girls knew nothing about Sophie. There was going to be some explaining to do here and where did she start?

'Good Lord!' Philip growled in disbelief. He

dropped the suitcases at his feet. 'It's my little chef!'

Lisa gritted her teeth and lifted her chin and wished she wasn't at a severe mental disadvantage here in skimpy denim shorts and a skimpy vest top and her hair spikier than ever with the heat. No make-up either. How had he ever recognized her? She was angry now. Angry at looking so dishevelled when he looked so chic in designer chinos and a white Lacoste polo shirt, angry for what he had done to her business and bloody mad at him for catching Elaine and making it up with her before they had even got out of the country!

Her anger erupted. 'You bastard, Philip Mainwaring. And I'm not *your* little chef. Thanks to you, I'm not anyone's little chef *any more!*'

'Steady on, Lisa,' Cathy said faintly, shocked at her friend's outburst.

Elaine went pale. 'Philip, Lisa, you know each other?' she squeaked in disbelief.

Philip's grin was as suddenly as wide as an ocean. After the initial shock of recognition, he actually looked delighted to see Lisa now.

'Well, this is a coincidence for the *Guinness Book of Records*,' he laughed. 'I feel better already about this trip. So you are Elaine's friends. Cathy – ' he nodded at Cathy who was gazing at him wide-eyed ' – and Lisa. I should have known when Elaine mentioned you and the catering van, but of course I didn't make the connection.' He shrugged. 'Who would, under the circumstances?' he added, a definite sparkle to his flirty eyes which put Lisa on further alert.

She opened her mouth to give him a further lashing but already he was gathering up the suitcases and taking charge.

116

'We'd better get this lot loaded. They are embarking. I'll drive on. It can be a bit tricky. Honestly, Elaine, do you really need all this stuff? I'm sure the girls aren't as loaded as this.'

Meaning we don't possess so many clothes, Lisa thought idiotically, the first thought his remark had provoked and ludicrous, too, because this was all so terrible and she was in shock. She swallowed hard to try to clear her throat. Cathy had gone completely silent, Elaine was pale and looking shocked that her betrothed knew her and everyone, apart from suave Philip, who looked like the cat with the cream, was looking thoroughly nonplussed.

'Just what do you mean, "I'll drive on"?' Lisa forced out through white lips.

'Um . . . Philip is coming with us,' Elaine managed to croak out. 'Look, I hope you don't mind. I mean, I didn't expect him, it wasn't arranged or anything.'

'No, but I couldn't let Elaine do this without putting up some sort of fight,' Philip interjected as he slid a very expensive suitcase down the middle of the van. 'But if you can't beat 'em, join 'em,' he laughed.

Cathy and Lisa stared aghast at the back of his neck.

'Philip will be able to do some driving,' Elaine said quickly, not comfortable with the look on the girls' faces and wanting to go part way to making it all right with everyone. For some reason Lisa had verbally attacked her brother as if he had done her a personal wrong. She didn't understand what all that was about and for the moment she didn't want to know. She'd come this far in her attempt to be reconciled with Marcus and she wasn't about to let it go.

Suddenly there was a great urgency to get aboard before some other complication reared its ugly head to stop this trip. Elaine heaved the buggy into the last smidgeon of space in the van, urgency to get going giving her the strength to do it unaided.

'I'll explain once we're settled on board,' she whispered to Cathy and Lisa.

The baby yowled. Elaine went red and scrambled inelegantly into the van to comfort her. 'Er, um, this . . . this is Sophie,' she started to explain. 'I should . . . well, I should have told you about her.' Elaine's colour deepened as, wide eyed and practically legless with shock, Cathy and Lisa stared at her blankly through the sliding door of the camper. 'She happened last year . . . it was why I left you so in the lurch. Um, Daddy was furious and Philip was pretty shocked and furious too. I didn't tell you before in case you thought badly of me and wouldn't help me out, but – '

'Come on!' Philip urged, leaping into the driving seat. 'You girls can soul search to your hearts' content once we are on board. Lisa, get inside beside me. I've never driven a vehicle with gears before. I might need some help.'

Like two mindless robots, Cathy and Lisa moved as ordered, Cathy into the back with Elaine, catching her shin on the buggy but feeling no pain because she was anaesthetized from head to toe, Lisa into the the front passenger seat next to Philip, who was grating the gears horribly. Numbly Lisa's hand came out and slid the gear stick into first as she stared blindly out of the windscreen, her mouth still gaping open, trying to snatch in life-giving breath.

It was turning into the trip from hell and back and

they hadn't even set foot on foreign soil yet, Lisa thought dully as she sensed Philip smiling from ear to ear as they lurched forward into the queue of traffic boarding the ferry.

'This is going to be fun,' she heard him breathe, for her ears only. 'I never thought I'd see you again and now the fates have thrown us together again. Life is a marvel, isn't it?'

His hand came out and settled on her bare knee and though Lisa tried to stem the frisson the contact sparked, it was impossible because he had taken her by surprise.

Instinctively she brushed his hand away as if it was a marauding wasp. 'Life's a bitch, as it happens,' she seethed through tight lips, hating him evermore for having the nerve to flirt with her when his wife-to-be was just behind them nursing their child. If she wasn't so shocked by the whole business she would have ordered him out of her van and ditched Elaine too.

Two things stopped her. His adorable innocent daughter who might be left stranded on the quayside and . . . and the man himself.

Lisa bit her lower lip very hard, desperate to quell this dreadful, dreadful rush of hormones threatening to drown her sensibilities altogether. Philip Mainwaring was a rat. She knew it for certain. He was also the only man in the world who had the ability to set her heart tipping and spinning.

Lisa closed her eyes, not believing that she and Cathy had actually obeyed his curt order to get in the van, that they were actually going to go through with this. Worst of all was the sudden doubt about her own self-respect. What sort of a woman was she to allow this damned heart of hers to tip and spin at this very minute? This was a part of her she didn't know and was hugely ashamed of too.

Lisa suddenly felt very nauseous . . . and they were still on dry land.

CHAPTER 6

'Can I buy you a drink?'

Cathy leapt a foot in the air. So deep was she in compassionate misery for Lisa that she was completely unaware of the man leaning on the bar next to her while she waited to order a drink she was badly in need of. She hadn't been able to settle in the cramped cabin so had wandered around till she found a bar.

She and Lisa were still in a state of shock. Lisa's reaction had been to disappear into a world of her own. After entering the small cabin, she had coiled into the foetal position on her bunk, claiming seasickness, but Cathy knew better. The ferry was as calm as an iceberg gliding through the calm sea. Lisa was distraught over Philip Mainwaring's appearance. And to add to the distress of it all, while embarking he had confessed he hadn't booked a cabin and Elaine had offered to share hers, which was further confirmation that all was well with the lovers.

Cathy, like Lisa, could picture them snuggled up together with their adorable baby daughter and planning their future together, a future that the fickle Elaine only days before had declared would be unbearable. Cathy rather wished Elaine had had the guts to admit she had made a mistake and opted to go back to Knightsbridge with her lover instead of going ahead with this trip. Cathy had an uncomfortable feeling that she was only going through it so as not to disappoint them. Somehow they had all been bundled on to the ferry before any sense had been talked about abandoning the trip. It was surely unnecessary now? And very, very painful for Lisa.

Cathy eyed the stranger suspiciously. 'Do I know you?'

The stranger grinned. 'Not yet, but it's going to be a long crossing and I bore easily. You look as if you might be good company through the night. So what sort of a girl are you? A lager topper, a gin and tonicker, or a strait-laced pineapple juicer?'

Cathy smiled slightly. Hardly her type. Men in jeans and trainers didn't turn her on. She preferred the Charles Bond suited type . . . *no, she didn't*! He was good looking, though, had a small scar on his chin that added roguish charm and a teasing sparkle to dark brown eyes that somehow were at odds with the fair, sun-bleached hair. But he looked open and honest and sort of safe and . . . and it was going to be a long, agonizing night.

'So I don't come across as a Moët et Chandoner, then,' Cathy teased him.

He grinned. 'If you are, I can't afford you.'

'On a budget, then?'

'Backpacking,' he told her, glancing down at his feet.

Cathy followed his gaze. A shabby backpack was crumpled on the floor. No, definitely not her type, but . . . it was going to be a long night.

'Allow me to buy the drinks then. Mild and bitter, is it?'

He threw his head back and laughed, showing perfect white teeth without amalgam. Cathy liked a guy who could laugh openly. There was nothing more off-putting than a man who opened his mouth and either neighed like a horse or guffawed like a sea lion. The stranger laughed like a man who had charge of his life, knew what he wanted from it and wasn't afraid to go out and get it. Strangely enough her heart did a little skip.

Smiling, Cathy ordered the drinks from the barman who already looked bored and fagged out at the thought of the long crossing to Santander. 'A Scotch and soda for my friend and a white wine for myself, thank you. And have one yourself.'

The barman's face lit up. 'Thank you. I can't drink on duty, but I'll take one for later,' he grinned.

The stranger was smiling now. 'You have a friend for life,' he murmured, nodding at the barman's back. 'And how did you know I drink Scotch?'

'I didn't, but in preference to a mild and bitter everyone drinks Scotch.'

He laughed again and held out his hand. 'Greg Turner.'

Cathy took his hand. It was warm and strong and didn't linger suggestively, which warmed her to him more. 'Cathy Peterson.'

'Pleased to meet you, Cathy. So where are you heading?'

'Marbella.'

'Ah, the Costa del Crime.'

Cathy raised a dark brow. She wouldn't have thought him the sort to come out with such a hack-neyed cliché.

123

'Yeah, I'm going down for a family reunion. My brother robs banks, my mother works the coast pickpocketing and I'm on the run from the Serious Fraud Squad.'

Greg choked on his drink, which the barman had just served him. Cathy eyed him warily. She'd thought he'd laugh at her joke but he seemed disturbed by it rather than amused. Perhaps she had hit a raw nerve and he was a bit of a crook himself. The scar on the chin? A bit of a rough diamond, was he?

'You shouldn't joke about such things,' he said after recovering.

Cathy reached for her purse to pay for the drinks, slightly disappointed that his sense of humour wasn't quite on her level and convincing herself that she had imagined a raw nerve the reason for him choking. Crooks didn't travel on ferries. Crooks weren't usually backpackers.

'No, let me get these,' Greg insisted, plunging his hand into his jeans pocket.

'No, let me,' came a voice from behind them.

Cathy turned in surprise. Philip Mainwaring smiled at them both. 'And a G & T for me – make it a large one. I'm not *au fait* with babies, I'm afraid. Sophie is howling like a banshee; in a small confined space it's hell on the nerves. I had to get out for a drink. So how are you doing Greg? Got yourself fixed up with a lift to Marbella yet?'

Cathy opened and shut her mouth like a gasping goldfish deprived of oxygen. This man was awful. Talking about his darling little daughter that way. Poor Elaine and misguided Lisa for brooding over such a chauvinist.

And these two seemed to know each other.

'No, not yet, but I'm working on it.' The two men exchanged glances which mystified Cathy.

'So you two know each other,' she broached the subject, sipping her wine and eyeing them curiously. Hardly a match made in heaven. Philip Mainwaring, in spite of casual attire, oozed money and sophistication and Greg oozed backpacker. But if they were blood brothers she wouldn't be surprised. Nothing could match the shock of Elaine being a mother, Elaine trying to flee an arranged marriage and the groom-to-be turning up out of the blue and the couple making it up before their very eyes.

'Er . . . we met on the way down from London,' Philip volunteered. 'Greg was hitchhiking and I stopped to give him a lift. We seemed to hit it off from the start, didn't we, Greg?'

Greg nodded. 'We have birds in common.'

'Well, I knew Philip was a bird fancier,' Cathy interjected sarcastically, giving Philip a dirty meaningful look. The men laughed, but Cathy hadn't mean't it as a joke.

She didn't like Philip Mainwaring and never would after what he had put Lisa through and was still putting her through – he was loathsome. As for Elaine, she could well understand her not wanting to marry him, but what she couldn't understand was the sudden turnabout in her emotions now. Was the girl crazy?

Suddenly she was tired. If Philip hadn't come to the bar, she might not have been. She just might have spent the night chatting to a good-looking guy with an interesting scar on his chin and might have found out more about him. As well as the blip in her heart rate he seemed to be the no-nonsense tonic she needed at the moment after the shocking turn of events this evening.

It was a good sign. Not for a minute did she fancy him, but enjoying his company had been some light relief and showed that there was life where Charles had sucked it dry. She was about to reach down for her bag and bid her goodnights when Greg closed a hand over hers on the bar. His smile was very charismatic.

'I meant the birds that fly in the air, Cathy. Philip and I both belong to the RSPB.'

'Really Slimy Play Boys?' she drawled, directing her insult to a deserving Philip. Cathy's hand was suddenly burning under Greg's.

Philip laughed, albeit hesitantly. Greg's dark eyes were holding Cathy's hypnotically.

'I have a feeling Cathy doesn't like me very much,' Philip commented smoothly.

'How very perceptive of you, Philip. And not without reason.' She withdrew her hand from under Greg's, missing it already, which was idiotic because they had only met minutes ago, but she supposed Philip's evil presence made anyone else appear God's gift. 'None of which I wish to drive home at the moment. There's time enough.' She glared fiercely at Philip. 'Just a word of warning, though. Do what you must with Elaine, but lay off Lisa. She's suffered enough at your hands and I saw the way you leered at her on the quayside and I saw you touch her knee in the van . . .'

Oh, hell, the two men were staring at her as if she'd just shed a few brain cells in front of them. She really was very tired and shouldn't be here propping the bar up and feeding insults to Philip Mainwaring. Time enough to tear him off a strip good and proper at a later date, and without witnesses.

126

'I'm going to bunk down now or whatever you do on ferries. Goodnight. It was nice to meet you, Greg. Pity it was spoiled by the appearance of Casanova's second cousin. I'll leave you to swap stories about the lesser spotted weed warbler and its nesting habits.' She gave Philip a last look to kill and swept off, only just hearing Greg mutter,

'So what was that all about?'

'Damned if I know, old man. You've got your work cut out there and I rather feel I've spoilt it all for you.'

And what was that supposed to mean? Cathy fumed, as she headed back to her cabin through a labyrinth of oppressive passageways. She didn't know because another pressing thought impinged on her. There had been no hitchhiker in Philip Mainwaring's limousine when he had pulled through the entrance gates of the port.

Suddenly she wasn't as tired as she thought she had been. Instead of following the arrows which indicated the cabin numbers, she went up on to the next deck to look for somewhere she could get some fresh air. Everywhere was enclosed in glass, but up there she found a place she could see the moon glistening on the black sea. And it was deserted, free from bodies bedding down where they could and groups of people wiling away the hours playing cards like those in the bar.

It was good of Elaine to arrange cabins for them. It was good of her to arrange a villa for them to stay in. It was good of her to pay back her debts. But it was all a mystery to Cathy why she had done all these things just because of an arranged marriage. And the events of the last couple of hours were an even bigger mystery. Inviting the man she was running away from to join them on their trip?

Well, she always had been a strange one.

'Beautiful sight, isn't it, the moon on the sea? Makes you feel kinda humble.'

Cathy jumped again. The stranger had an uncunning knack of making her leap out of her skin.

'Do you have to creep up on people that way? You frightened the life out of me.'

Greg smiled and dropped his backpack at his feet. 'Yes, you jumped when I spoke to you in the bar. You must have a lot on your mind. Do you want to talk about it?'

'What are you, a social worker?' she flashed back.

'So you have some problems?'

Cathy turned to him. 'Not a single one,' she smiled sweetly. 'But I think you might have. Are you trying to pick me up?'

'Would you object if I was?' he said calmly, his smile very open and honest.

'Possibly not earlier. As you said it's going to be a long night, but then I discover you're buddy-buddy with the man from hell and suddenly you don't appeal any more,' she told him tightly.

He shook his fingers as if he'd been stung but he was grinning as he did it. 'Wow, you're a hard lady,' he teased her and then shrugged. 'We're hardly buddies. Until today, we had never met before.'

'You surprise me,' Cathy said tartly, not to be placated by a winning smile. She turned her gaze back to the moon and the sea. 'You seem to know each other very well: Christian name terms, little asides like "you have your work cut out there". And if you think I believe Philip Mainwaring in his

Rolls Royce picked up a hitchhiker *en route* and you talked about birds, well, you must think I fell off the top of the Christmas tree.'

It surprised Cathy that she had assessed all this and actually come out with it all but sometimes the mind worked in peculiar ways. A few months back she might not have given anything like this a serious thought. But just lately her world had been turned upside down. Charles had undermined her trust in human nature and now she was questioning everyone and everything.

Not very fairly either, she supposed. Greg hadn't asked for that.

'I'm sorry,' she breathed. He hadn't responded to her accusations and was now leaning on the handrail next to her and gazing out of the salt-speckled panoramic windows. 'I'm a bit stressed out,' she told him. 'I rather need this holiday and so far it isn't working out very well.'

'It hasn't started yet. I'm sure it will get better,' he said kindly. 'Is Philip the problem? I thought he was rather a nice guy. He's travelling with you all, isn't he?'

Cathy smiled cynically to herself. Mr Nice Guy obviously had the rapport with men that he didn't have with women. Anyway it wasn't her problem to discuss with a stranger who only had a passing acquaintance with him.

'Not altogether,' she mused but offered nothing more.

'Your friend is sweet,' Greg said, changing the subject. 'Lisa, isn't it?'

Cathy's hands tightened on the handrail. This guy was coming across as rather too curious for his own good. 'You seem to know rather a lot about us.'

'Philip filled me in just now. And before you get on your high horse, I asked. I saw you all driving on and you interested me. I'm a curious sort of a guy.'

'You said it. You're *very* odd.'

Greg laughed. 'I meant that I'm curious about other people. We all are, if we admit it. Haven't you looked around you and wondered about people's lives? I do it all the time. People fascinate me. You fascinate me.'

Startled, Cathy turned to look at him. 'You *are* trying to pick me up!'

'You're very attractive.'

'Apparently, so is my friend Lisa,' Cathy accused him sarcastically.

'Ah, but she is spoken for.'

'Spoken for?'

'Philip.'

'Philip!' Cathy exploded, The heat of indignation rising to steam in her throat. 'Is that what he has told you?' she cried with disbelief. 'Honestly, you men never cease to amaze me. You live in a different world to women.' She shook her head. 'Philip and Lisa, over my dead body! The man is a dedicated womanizer and my friend Lisa is as innocent as the first snowflake of winter. You heard me warn him. I meant it too. If he comes on to her one more time, I'll rip out his heart and drop-kick it sky high!'

'Wow!' Greg laughed. 'You are some feisty lady. I wouldn't like to cross swords with you on a dark night this side of Michaelmas. Your loyalty is to be admired, though. I rather wish you were on my side,' he added mysteriously.

Cathy was onto that remark as quick as a whip. 'And

what is that supposed to mean?' she said sharply.

Greg shrugged. 'I get the distinct feeling you don't like me very much either.'

Cathy gave that one some ponderous thought. She was so uptight lately she was in grave danger of becoming some waspish old maid with a hostile attitude to all men in general. She relaxed her shoulders and took stock of this Greg Turner who had just popped into her life. He was a very attractive man who had certainly done her no harm and here she was giving the impression of being a manhater.

'Sorry,' she uttered wearily. 'It was unfair of me to blast off and give that impression.' She suddenly smiled wickedly. 'But your showing an interest in my *sweet* friend doesn't do my ego much good. Is that why you joined me at the bar and then followed me out here, to get an introduction to Lisa?'

'Hell, is that what you think?' Greg said gravelly. His mouth broke into a wide smile. 'I was making conversation, trying to squirm my way into your good books. I thought I had a chance before Philip joined us, but it kinda went downhill after. Lisa is sweet but not my type.'

'And I might be?' she quizzed him daringly.

'I'm sure you are,' he said deliberately, eyes smouldering. 'You're a beautiful, smart, feisty lady, and I'd rather like to kiss you goodnight . . .' Cathy's eyebrows shot skywards. Greg held his hands up in mock defence '. . . but I'm not going to risk it. I rather value my life too much.'

Yes, I like you, Cathy decided. No funny business, straight down the line.

Shame, because it would be nice to have something to look forward to, bumping into him again in Marbella, where he was heading too, apparently. But seeing as they probably weren't going to get there, anyway, it wasn't going to happen. For Lisa's sake she was going to demand a meeting to discuss this first thing in the morning and suggest that under the circumstances there was no point in the trip now that Elaine and Philip were reunited.

'Goodnight, Greg,' she murmured.

'Goodnight, Cathy,' he countered softly.

And that was it. Cathy left him leaning on the handrail gazing out to sea, which was slightly choppier than it had been a few minutes ago. But Cathy was suddenly all calm inside. Greg and his nice smile had warmed a little of the frost in her heart that Charles had left behind. There were some nice guys in the world and there was always breakfast to look forward to. She *might* see him again.

'Shush,' Elaine breathed as her brother tripped over one of her suitcases when he came back to the cabin. 'I've just got Sophie off to sleep.' She leaned up on one elbow in the narrow bunk and eyed Philip sleepily. 'Where have you been?'

'To the bar and I wish I hadn't bothered,' Philip whispered. 'Your friend Cathy was there and she just blasted my ears for nothing. What's with that girl? If looks could kill, I'd have been prostrate on the floor, gasping my last breath.'

Elaine grinned. 'She can be fearsome when she wants to be, but she's really nice. She doesn't take any nonsense from anyone. You should have heard her ripping into her boss that night I went to their dinner party.'

'What dinner party?'

132

Elaine told him all about it in hushed tones so as not to wake Sophie who was snuggled in the bunk next to her, against the cabin wall so she wouldn't roll out in the night.

'If she can hold her own against Charles Bond, then she's quite a girl,' Philip said admiringly as he struggled out of his clothes and pulled a pair of silk pyjamas out of his holdall 'Tell me, Elaine, what do you know about her and Charles?'

Elaine was surprised Philip was interested. He seemed to be far more interested in Lisa. He'd certainly been giving her the eye and apparently they knew each other but how and where she hadn't asked yet.

'Only that she worked for him and then they fell out and he wanted her back. Lisa told me that, and then, of course, he rang me.'

'Charles Bond rang *you*?'

'Keep your voice down,' Elaine hissed. 'Yes, he rang me, said he wanted me to talk to Cathy because he wanted her back. She must be a very good secretary.'

'Why did she leave?'

'How should I know?' Elaine sighed, wanting to snuggle down and think of Marcus, run through her opening words to him. Should she start with how much she loved him and had missed him? Should she wait to introduce Sophie to him? It really needed to be sorted out in her head before they got there.

'Could you find out? Discreetly, of course.'

Elaine's eyes widened. 'What an earth for? Gosh, you don't fancy her, do you?'

Philip slid into the bunk across from his sister. 'Don't be absurd.'

Elaine grinned knowingly. 'No, of course not, Lisa

is more your sort, isn't she? The sort you can blind with your good looks and seduce with your charm, or so you thought,' she teased. 'She certainly wasn't pleased to see you today. How do you know her?'

'She did an executive lunch for me. It was a total disaster.'

'She used to do sandwiches from baskets round the office. I didn't know she had branched out.' Elaine frowned. 'Anyway, she's out of work now. They both are and it was lucky for me they were. They both jumped at the chance of this trip.'

'Yes, I suppose they would with you footing the bill for everything,' Philip bit out, squirming uncomfortably in the narrow hard bed. 'So how do they feel about you chasing Marcus and springing an illegitimate daughter on him?'

Elaine bit her lip and lay back against her hard pillow. 'I haven't told them yet,' she whispered hoarsely. 'Actually, until we met up on the dock they didn't know I had a baby.'

Philip sat bolt upright and glared at Elaine. 'They didn't know!' he breathed in disbelief.

Elaine rubbed her forehead. 'I didn't know how they would take it, so I didn't tell them before. I suppose I was a bit ashamed. I mean, they are very worldly but, well . . . I thought they might disapprove. You wouldn't help me, and they were the only two friends I thought I could trust and, well . . . I owed them anyway. If you had come as I asked you in the first place, I wouldn't have had to involve them – '

'So they don't know the purpose of this trip! That you want a reunion with Marcus and to introduce him to the daughter he doesn't know about? For goodness' sake, Elaine, what were you thinking? You just offered them a free holiday and – '

'Not exactly.'

'Not exactly,' Philip repeated in exasperation.

'Oh, you might as well know,' Elaine sighed helplessly. 'You might be of some help, actually, because I do sort of owe them an explanation now that you have turned up to complicate matters. I knew I would have some explaining to do when I turned up with Sophie, but so far I haven't come up with a thought – '

'When have you ever come up with a sensible thought in your life, Elaine? You really are exasperating.'

'That's unfair, Philip,' Elaine protested. 'It hasn't been easy for me and I know I'm stupid at times, but at least I'm trying to put my life to rights for Sophie's sake.

'I'm sorry, darling,' Philip relented softly. 'You are an adorable little goose, but you do get yourself into some pickles. So go on, tell me all.'

Elaine took a deep breath. 'I told them I wanted to run away because . . . well, it was almost a truth. Daddy *was* pushing Philip on to me and . . . well, I just elaborated a trifle. I told the girls that Daddy was pressuring me into an arranged marriage that I didn't want. Next week, in fact, hence the urgency. I told Lisa first, said that I hated Philip and I couldn't possibly marry him, but Daddy was very powerful and was forcing me to marry him and – '

'And they believed you?'

'Of course they believed me,' Elaine insisted innocently. 'Why shouldn't they? It happens, arranged marriages and all that. Lisa was with me all the way. She said this Philip sounded an ogre and no one should be made to marry someone they didn't love. I said Philip didn't love me either, was just marrying me because of Daddy's position and I was a good catch. She was horrified. She was only too pleased to help.'

'I bet she was.' Philip laughed. 'Did you by any chance say Philip was Philip Simmons-Blackshaw?'

Frowning, Elaine whispered, 'I can't remember if I mentioned his surname or not. Why, and what is so funny?'

Philip plumped a pillow under his head, the smile fading from his mouth. 'It isn't funny, come to think of it,' he said seriously. 'I'm beginning to see the light a bit now. Remember the time we met in the wine bar when you wanted my help with your plan? It was the day of my disastrous lunch with Lisa, the very day. They were there in the wine bar. You said you had seen two friends you didn't want to face. It was them, Cathy and Lisa, wasn't it? I thought I recognized little Lisa – her spiky blonde hair is very distinctive.'

'What are you getting at, Philip?' Elaine yawned.

'Oh, no, poor kid. I was a bit beastly to her that day,' Philip went on sorrowfully. 'She made a mistake and made me look a bit of a fool although everyone was very good about it. In fact, they thought it a hoot and I got the order from the Japanese anyway. The food was rather special, if over-catered, but at the time I didn't see it that way. I suppose I was rather terse with her and I shouldn't have been as I had flirted with her in the past.

'She was always such a ray of sunshine when she came into the offices with her basket of sandwiches. I did rather lead her on, I suppose, and perhaps I shouldn't have done.'

'Sounds like you,' Elaine mumbled, struggling to stay awake.

'I expect I gave her all the wrong signals, and then when she saw us together in the wine bar . . .' He sighed. 'She doesn't know we are brother and sister, does she?'

'Haven't got round to introducing you properly yet,' Elaine whispered, unable to keep her eyes open a minute longer.

'That accounts for it, then,' Philip mused uncomfortably. 'Her verbal attack on me when I arrived, Cathy's verbal attack on me in the bar just now. You'd told them you are running away from an arranged marriage to a Philip and . . .'

He turned his head to see if Elaine was making any sense out of this, but she was sound asleep. Wearily Philip adjusted his head and stared up at the ceiling and murmured, 'Dear Lisa and stroppy Cathy think I'm the Philip you are supposed to be running away from and they probably think Sophie is my daughter too. Hell, Elaine, you don't do anything by halves, do you?' He sighed. 'I'm here, though, and I wouldn't be if I wasn't concerned for you. Lisa is so adorable – I'll make it up to her somehow. Must be careful, though, she's so vulnerable I could give her the wrong idea all over again. Marbella is usually heaving with beautiful women and I ought to keep my options open. Don't want to get into a relationship I can't get out of quickly. Goodnight, sis.'

Lisa dressed quickly in the shorts she had worn for travelling the previous day and a fresh clean white shirt which she knotted at the waist. She slipped on

137

new white espadrilles and silently let herself out of the cabin as Cathy slept on.

She felt great, physically. No seasickness, but mentally she was all at sea. Philip's sudden appearance had shocked her so deeply she hadn't been able to think properly. Now in the light of day she could. It was going to be impossible travelling with him and Elaine and their lovely baby, so impossible that she had decided it wasn't going to happen.

It was her camper van and she was in command, not Philip Mainwaring who had had the audacity to take over as if he was in charge of this trip now. Cathy would be disappointed when she told her that she had decided they were going to get the first ferry back to England and forget Marbella, but really there was no other option. Lisa couldn't and wouldn't go any further. It would be too unbearable.

Lisa queued up for breakfast in the restaurant and chatted to a family from Watford who were going to camp and tour the eastern coast of Spain. She sat with them to eat and listened to their plans and felt a well of envy filling up inside her. She and Cathy had been so looking forward to this holiday break and now it wasn't going to happen.

A little while later, Lisa kindly wished them a happy holiday and made her way to the enclosed deck to get her first and last glimpse of Spain as they drew closer to the coastline.

She drew in her breath with surprise and sorrow when she saw the lush green coastline and the rolling hills. It was a stunning day, clear and bright, not a cloud in the sky and the land beyond the creamy white beaches so, so green. She longed to be there and was so disappointed she wouldn't be.

'It's a surprise, isn't it? You think of Spain as scorching hot, dry and dusty. A lot of it is, but this part is very reminiscent of Wales.'

Lisa stiffened, but didn't face him. She glared out of the windows, saddened that she wouldn't even be setting foot in this lovely country. And all because of him.

'Never having been to Wales I wouldn't know,' she said thinly.

'Lisa, we've got off to a bad start and I want to – '

Lisa spun round, fixed cold violet eyes on Philip Mainwaring and froze him to the spot. 'You want to what? Apologize for living? Go ahead, but I won't be here to hear it. You disgust me. You see no wrong in your life, do you? You just plough through it, all cool sophistication and arrogant aplomb. You are a rat and if I didn't like Elaine so much I would tell her just what you and – '

'You've got it all wrong and I want to explain – '

'And I don't want to hear any of it because whatever you might have to say means nothing!'

Philip caught her arm as she turned to flee. His grasp was firm and Lisa was stunned by the effect it had on her. Her arm burned at his contact and her heart thudded and she hated herself for allowing herself to have any reaction to that physical touch.

He was the deadliest of males, too damned good-looking and so very sure of his winning ways with women. Oh, how she hated him! She tried hard to squirm out of his grip, but he hung on like a limpet.

'I want to explain about me and Elaine – ' he started.

'I bet you do!' Lisa flared. 'You're no better than Cathy's old boss, that two-timing devious schemer

139

who's been carrying on with Cathy and poor Cathy not knowing he was married till she met the wife. Oh, you high flyers are all the damn same!'

Suddenly she was free, but not by her own attemps. Philip had suddenly let her go as if she was on fire.

'Cathy was having an affair with Charles Bond?' he growled in surprise.

'Oh, you know him too!' Lisa was scathing. 'Well, that doesn't surprise me, you probably went to the same school of deception. As I said, you are the same sort. You flirted with me, yet you must have been involved with Elaine then because you have a baby and . . . and what the hell are you smiling at? This isn't at all funny!'

'No, dear Lisa, it isn't a laughing matter at all,' he smoothed her with a smile,' but I never knew you harboured so much deep feeling for me.'

Hot colour flooded Lisa's cheeks. What an idiot she was for screaming at him so. Now he knew for sure that she must have cared for him a lot to be so mad at him. So there was nothing for it but to own up. She had nothing more to lose. He had Elaine anyway and she wasn't going to lose any more sleep over him.

'Yes, I cared once.' she admitted in a soft whisper. 'When I was doing the sandwich rounds I thought you were wonderful and then you took an interest in me and furthered my career and gave me my first chance at executive lunches and my feelings deepened. I was a fool to think that your flirting meant anything. I was naïve enough to think you actually liked me, but when I made a mistake with that lunch there wasn't room in your heart to forgive me. You laughed at me and I never got a job after that, thanks to you. You spread the word and – '

'Oh, no, Lisa, never. I wouldn't have done that,' Philip protested. 'I might have mentioned it to a few colleagues, only for humour's sake – it was rather funny on reflection – but you are a marvellous chef and it was never my intention to maliciously damage your career.'

Lisa bit her lip. Oh, if it wasn't for everything else she might believe him. But the everything else was too painful to put aside.

'Only the tip of the iceberg, Philip,' she went on. 'I agreed to this trip to help poor Elaine escape you and – '

'And perhaps for revenge on me,' Philip suggested knowingly.

Lisa couldn't meet his eye. She glared down at her espadrilles and then quickly raised her eyes in case he thought she felt guilty.

'It doesn't matter any more,' she told him strongly. 'I've decided that it isn't going any further.'

He raised a teasing dark brow at her. 'I would say that it was my decision to take if we continue our flirtation or not, not yours. I'm old-fashioned about such things,' he mocked her.

'I didn't mean that,' Lisa gasped in exasperation. 'What I meant is that this trip is off!'

His dark eyes widened with surprise. 'What do you mean, off? It's only just started; if you give me time to explain, it could turn out to be a very memorable trip. Now to start with, Elaine and I are – '

'Are an item,' Lisa caustically interjected. 'And as an item the pair of you are on your own from now on.'

'On our own!' Philip spluttered.

'Will you stop repeating everything I say! Yes, on your own. Cathy and I are going home. I'm not even going to offer to take you back with us because the pair of you are loaded enough to make your own return arrangements. The van is mine and I call the shots. Cathy and I are going back and you can do what you like.'

'But . . . but you can't do this!' Philip protested. 'We have no transport! You can't just strand us here. Where are you going?'

'Back to my cabin to pack and tell Cathy my plan,' Lisa threw over her shoulder.

'She won't agree!' It was the determined way he said that that had Lisa stopping dead and spinning on her heel. Philip Mainwaring was just impossible. He thought he had the power to manipulate people to his wishes every time.

Philip caught her up, took her arm again, this time far more tenderly than before.

'Listen, Lisa, it's a bad decision to opt out of this trip. Whatever our differences, other people have to be considered. Cathy wants this trip as much as Elaine wants it. Cathy is your friend and you would want to help her if she was in trouble, wouldn't you?'

Cathy in trouble? What an earth was he talking about? Dumbstruck she stared at him in confusion.

'The engines are slowing down, we'll be docking shortly,' Philip told her urgently. 'Now forget all this nonsense about going back. Elaine and I have Sophie to consider. You can't strand the pair of us with a baby in tow, it isn't fair to the baby. As soon as we land and disembark, we'll drive somewhere for lunch and we'll have a talk. There are things I have to tell you.'

His urgency and sudden seriousness completely took the wind out of Lisa's sails.

'Go back to your cabin, say nothing to Cathy about

142

aborting this trip. We are going through with it. Is that clear?'

Lisa couldn't even flutter an eyelash, let alone agree to all this.

Suddenly Philip's eyes softened and, to her surprise, he lowered his mouth and covered her lips with his own in a very soft sensuous kiss that completely played merry hell with Lisa's senses. For so long she had dreamed of this, Philip taking her in his arms and kissing her – now it was happening.

'Oh, gosh,' she murmured as at last he released her. When she blinked open her heavy eyelids she was surprised to see Philip's expression as dazed as her own. In confused silence they stared at each other, then Philip cleared his throat.

'Good girl. Do as I tell you and all will be well. We'll all meet at the van below deck when it's time to drive off.'

So perplexed and flustered Lisa couldn't remember finding her way back to the cabin. When she arrived back at the cabin door, she didn't burst in, just stood stock-still to get her senses together. She touched her lips and they were swollen and warm and she closed her eyes for a second. Philip had kissed her and . . . and it had been wondrous and if only . . .

Could she cope with this, knowing Philip could never be hers? But if they did go through with this trip, it would at least give her a chance to gain her own self-respect back. Knowing he belonged to Elaine, she had still let her heart race hopefully and that had been very wrong; she ought to pull herself together over that. But putting all that aside, why was Philip even thinking about this trip now that he had Elaine back? What was the point of it?

And what had he meant about Cathy being in trouble? Had it been a throwaway remark to get her to forget the idea of going back home and stranding him and Elaine, and the baby, of course, on foreign soil? The baby would have been enough to change her mind. When she had furiously outlined her plan she hadn't given that darling baby a thought. Of course she couldn't abandon them all – Philip, yes, but Elaine and Sophie, no. Philip was astute enough to have known that she wasn't unkind enough to do that, but to use Cathy as moral blackmail as well, that was strange.

Lisa took a deep breath before going in to haul Cathy out of bed. She couldn't trouble Cathy with her concerns. Cathy had been through enough lately, what with finding out her lover was married, walking out on her job in disgust, all those awful phone calls from Charles, and not forgetting the supposed stalker. Her friend's nerves had been so ravaged by Charles' betrayal that to pile any more on her would break her.

Anyway, suggesting that Cathy might be in trouble was nothing, just an extra pull on her heartstrings from Philip to ensure that they didn't get stranded. Philip didn't even know Cathy before yesterday.

'Come on out of bed, sleepyhead. You've missed breakfast, but I'll make you an omelette in the van once we are off this ferry.'

'Oh, don't mention omelettes,' Cathy groaned. 'I feel utterly seasick.'

'Don't be daft, we've docked. You've just got a hangover! Come on, up and dressed. Spain is gorgeous. Just wait till you see it!'

Cathy groaned and lifted her tousled head.

'Hang on a minute,' she uttered weakly. 'Things

144

have to be sorted. We can't go any further with this business. As far as I'm concerned, this trip is off.'

'Look, I've had a word with Philip,' Lisa told her as she bundled her overnight stuff together and shoved it into a bag. 'I told him the same thing, said you and I were going back on the next ferry, and he said we couldn't just walk away and strand them in Santander and he's right. We might not get all the way to Marbella, but we're going as far as lunch and a talk. Philip seems to think he can persuade us into cooperating, so the least we can do is hear him out. Now get a move on!'

Half an hour later, Lisa and Cathy joined the others in the belly of the ferry where the cars and vans were waiting to drive off into glorious hot sunshine.

Waiting by the white camper van were Elaine and Philip and baby Sophie gurgling happily in her buggy. And someone else.

Lisa frowned.

'Oh, it's Greg,' Cathy whispered to Lisa as they approached, sounding quite pleased. 'I met him last night in the bar. Good looking, what? Nice with it too, not like someone else who shall remain nameless,' she said pointedly, glaring icily at Philip. 'Hi, Greg.'

'Cathy. Hope you slept OK.' He grinned.

'And I hope you don't think this a liberty, Lisa and Cathy,' Philip said, 'but Greg is looking for a lift down to Marbella and I suggested he could join us. If there are any objections – '

Cathy gasped in surprise and Lisa couldn't utter a word. She stared at Greg hard and her skin began to prickle and her insides clenched as if she had been punched. He and Cathy knew each other?

145

'Super.' Elaine grinned. 'The more the merrier. Oh, it's going to be lovely. I can't wait to get going.'

Lisa, suddenly feeling rather faint and woozy, somehow managed to climb into the back of the van with Elaine and Cathy and the baby. Philip was in the driving seat again and the hitchhiker climbed in the passenger seat next to him and suddenly they were moving off.

Sunlight blinded Lisa and she closed her eyes for a second or two, her head spinning. It was all getting worse. Shock after shock seemed to be the order of the day, now this, the one that had her seriously doubting her own sanity.

Could she be mistaken? She opened her eyes and studied the back of the neck of the hitchhiker, praying that she was hallucinating. But, no, she wasn't mistaken. The faceless person who had spent so many hours parked down their Battersea street in a dark blue Rover was now sitting in the passenger seat of her van and they were all off to the funny farm.

Greg, the hitchhiker, was Cathy's stalker.

CHAPTER 7

Elaine tried to stretch her legs but it was impossible. There was luggage piled everywhere. She had greeted Philip's suggestion that they take on board Greg the hitchhiker with approval at first but it didn't seem such a good idea now. He had taken the seat that Lisa ought to have occupied while Philip drove. Her brother could then have made his peace with Lisa, who was obviously still holding a grudge against him for all that business over the lunch she had done for him that had somehow gone wrong. What all that was about she couldn't imagine but there was definitely still an atmosphere between the two.

Elaine didn't like hostile atmospheres and it was going to be bad enough having to explain the real reason for this trip, as she would eventually have to do at some stage, without her brother and Lisa being at odds with each other.

She was still nervous about telling the girls the truth. She could imagine their reaction being similar to Philip's: aghast that she was taking a holiday romance seriously and, after a year apart, preparing to spring her lover's child on him, a baby he knew nothing about. And the more she thought about it, the

more she was beginning to think Philip might be right.
And once the girls started on her she'd feel even worse.
Now there was this Greg travelling with them, and
really it was one too many, what with his grubby
backpack taking up extra space.

'See, Lisa, I'm not the only one in the world who
adds up car number plates.' Cathy laughed, peering
over Greg's shoulder. They had been merrily adding
and subtracting to their heart's content for hours now.

'Look, that Renault ahead has my flat number,'
Greg said excitedly.

'What — six, six, six?' Lisa breathed, unusually
bitchy.

Elaine laughed. 'Isn't that the devil's number?' she
said, trying to sound knowledgeable.

'You said it, Elaine,' Lisa murmured.

'Don't you like him? I think he's rather nice and
Cathy seems to like him too.' The engine in the back
made enough noise to drown out their conversation.
But there wasn't any, because Lisa had clammed up,
her lips thin and her eyes without their usual sparkle.

Elaine watched her worriedly. Lisa wasn't happy at
all and she supposed it was because she was still
uncomfortable with Philip.

'Can't we stop soon, Philip?' she called out. 'We
need to find a hotel with baby facilities and have some
lunch ourselves — we are so cramped in the back here,
we could do with the break.'

'You shouldn't have brought so much junk with
you, Elaine,' Philip called back sharply. 'If you're
cramped, it's your own fault. Live with it.'

Lisa stiffened at the hostile way he spoke to Elaine
and Cathy pulled a face for Lisa's eyes only.

'Philip speaks fluent Spanish,' Elaine told Lisa and

148

Cathy proudly, oblivious to the fact that Philip had been so sharp with her. 'We won't have any trouble travelling with him and he'll find us some nice hotels to stay in.' She bent over the buggy that was jammed in front of her to check on a sleeping Sophie.

Cathy whispered to Lisa, 'There's love for you. Elaine's dafter than I gave her credit for. If my lover spoke to me like that – '

'Your lover was *married*,' Lisa hissed under her breath without thinking.

'Thanks a bunch, *friend*,' Cathy hissed back.

'Right, that's enough!' Philip suddenly bellowed, making them all jump. He did an abrupt right into the driveway of a dubious-looking roadside Cafeteria-cum-bar, nearly throwing the girls into each other, and slammed on the brakes, jolting Sophie awake and into an instant bawl.

'Honestly, Philip,' Elaine cried in concern. 'You've woken Sophie and made her all fretful now.'

Cathy and Lisa looked at each other in alarm as Philip leapt out of the driving seat and came round the side to slide open the door for them. He leaned in and, to Cathy and Lisa's astonishment, whipped baby Sophie out of her buggy and into his arms. Sophie stopped grizzling immediately and gurgled happily.

Philip stood on the dusty driveway of the bar till they had all bundled out of the camper van and then started.

'This baby is not mine,' he told them forcefully as he held Sophie in his arms.

'Of course she's not,' Elaine giggled hesitantly. Whatever was possessing Philip?

'Shut up, Elaine, and let me finish. And I am not the man Elaine is supposed to be marrying.'

Elaine let out a strangled cry of, 'Philip, whatever are you saying!'

Cathy and Lisa both widened their eyes.

'No, Elaine, the truth will out! I've been driving for three hours with a bad atmosphere rebounding around my ears; I'm bored rigid with Cathy and Greg playing number conundrums till I could throttle the pair of them; and if you girls think I can't hear what you are saying in the back of the van, you are wrong. I don't miss a trick. Cathy and Lisa are making snide remarks to each other and very soon we are all going to be at each other's throats if we don't clear the air. And this is all down to you, Elaine. You should have told the truth from the start.'

'Um . . . excuse me, but I have a few phone calls to make and this has nothing to do with me,' Greg said, leaning through the open door to rifle through his backpack, eventually coming out with a mobile phone. He stalked off round the back of the bar to an olive grove, punching out a number.

All eyes were suddenly back on Philip, who seemed to have calmed down and was jiggling Sophie in his arms.

Elaine began to cry softly to herself, sniffing behind her hand. She didn't know what was going on here, but it was something not very nice and she hated rows.

'And will you stop that, Elaine! You're not a child any more.'

'And don't you speak to her like that!' Lisa suddenly cried in defence of Elaine. She put her arms around her to comfort her and directed cold eyes to Philip. 'Poor Elaine, she just doesn't know where she stands with you.'

'She knows exactly where she stands with me

because we know each other better than anyone else does.'

'Huh, that's a good one,' Cathy interjected sarcastically, rallying after the initial shock of his outburst. 'You deny that adorable child, and now you say you are not marrying Elaine after all. I'd say you didn't know her at all, any woman come to that.'

Philip sighed impatiently. 'Cathy, Lisa, listen to me. Elaine and I are not lovers, as you both thought, and this baby isn't mine, as you both thought. I am Elaine's brother.'

'Brother!' Cathy and Lisa squawked in unison, Lisa's arm dropping away from Elaine with shock.

Elaine stopped crying and stared at everyone in turn. She couldn't believe this. The girls thought Philip was her *lover*, and the father of Sophie!

'When Elaine elicited your help,' Philip went on, 'she apparently omitted a few facts that were very relevant, like Philip Simmons-Blackshaw's surname for one.' Suddenly he sighed. 'And don't look at me so blankly, Elaine – don't you remember any of our conversation last night?'

'I . . . I was a bit sleepy,' she admitted. 'You . . . you told me about Lisa and how sweet she was and you had flirted with her – '

'Well, that's beside the point,' he said hurriedly as Lisa went beetroot red with embarrassment. 'Lisa, I'm sorry,' he went on softly. 'I worked things out last night and tried to tell you this morning when we met after breakfast, but you were still very angry with me. Both of you got the impression that I was the Philip Elaine was running away from. She told you about an arranged marriage with a Philip and you just guessed it was me. You saw us together in the wine bar and

151

then I turned up at Portsmouth . . . well, it was an easy enough mistake to make.'

'So, you're not the Philip she is supposed to be marrying next week,' Lisa said weakly. She managed a small smile.

'No, I'm not.' Philip smiled back at her. 'Elaine asked for my help and support before she asked you and I refused. But when I realized she was determined to run away, I relented and turned up to give her some extra support.'

'Oh, how kind of you,' Lisa said in a rush, grinning now fit to burst.

'So, if you are brother and sister,' Cathy spoke up suspiciously and rather sarcastically,' and talking about omitting surnames, how come you two haven't the same ones? You, Elaine, are a Morton and Philip is a Mainwaring.'

'Oh, I never thought of that,' Lisa murmured as if her happiness was about to be snatched away from her.

Elaine got in before Philip, so relieved that the air was clearing now she wanted to add the final breath of fresh air herself. 'My father married Ruth, Philip's mother, after her divorce and then I was born. We have the same mother so we are half-brother and half-sister. Sadly, Mummy died some years ago and Philip and I are very close though Philip and Daddy don't get on very well and – ' she shrugged suddenly ' – well, that's it really.'

Philip frowned at her and Elaine knew he wanted her to go on but surely the girls had been through enough. It was quite funny really, their thinking Philip was her lover. It explained a lot, like how angry and upset Lisa was on the quayside. Now everything was all right. Philip had sensibly cleared the air and they should press on.

'I'll take Sophie inside and get her sorted out and you can order lunch, Philip.' She stepped forward, but Philip stepped back with Sophie.

'No, Elaine. I'll take Sophie inside. Knowing the Spanish and their love of children, I'm sure I'll find a willing hand to change her. You owe Cathy and Lisa some further explanation because I've done my bit.'

'Oh, please, Philip!' Elaine cried helplessly as he turned to go inside the bar. He ignored her.

Elaine couldn't meet the girls' wide-eyed looks of expectation. She looked everywhere but at them. She wrung her hands and shuffled her Manolo Blahnik gold sandals in the dust at her feet. There were white plastic tables and green umbrellas outside the bar and the sun was burning the top of her head. She longed to sit down, but more than anything she longed to run away. Yes, she owed them the truth but what would they think?

Suddenly she felt an arm on her shoulder and was surprised it was Cathy's.

'Come on,' Cathy said soothingly. 'Let's sit down and get some shade and order some drinks and you can tell us all about it. You've got some guts, Elaine. A lot of girls would marry the father of their child, even if they didn't love them. But have you thought about this Simmons-Blackshaw bloke? I mean, he must love Sophie as much as you and – '

Elaine burst into tears again. 'He's not the father either!' she blurted out. 'Marcus is her father and he doesn't even know she exists!'

'Blimey!' Cathy and Lisa muttered in unison.

* * *

153

The three girls sat under the shade of the umbrella. Philip had sent out drinks. Cathy and Lisa sipped San Miguel beers from the bottle and Elaine clutched a glass of orange Fanta. She felt as if a great weight had been lifted from her shoulders.

'You are funny, Elaine. Fancy thinking we would be so censorious,' Cathy said sympathetically after Elaine had hesitantly blurted out the real purpose of this trip. 'I think you're brilliant for going through with the birth in the first place when a lot of girls would have done the other thing. As for your father – well, he was wrong to do what he did, hiding those letters from Marcus. I'd say it was fate that you found them. Destiny, in fact.'

'Do you really think so?' Elaine gushed enthusiastically. 'A sort of sign?'

She was so relieved they were taking it so well. Their faces had been a picture as she had admitted the whole story, sort of shocked at first – well, she had expected that – but only shocked because they probably thought she hadn't got it in her to have got herself in such a mess. But then they had smiled and made sympathetic sounds and given their verbal support when she had thought they might have laughed at her.

'You wouldn't be doing what you're doing now if you hadn't found them, would you?' Lisa offered. 'I think it's terribly romantic,' she sighed, 'and Philip is a very special brother to support you, even though at first he was dead against it. Him being a company director and all that, he must be enormously busy and yet he just dropped everything at the last minute to come with us.'

'Probably didn't trust us to look after Elaine, more like,' Cathy added cynically.

'That's not fair,' Lisa protested.

'No, it's not,' Cathy conceded quickly. 'You're a lucky girl, Elaine, to have such a caring brother.' But she couldn't resist adding, 'Pity he didn't show the same measure of thoughtfulness for Lisa when he scuppered her career.'

'Cathy, will you cut it out?' Lisa insisted. 'He's explained all that to me. It was all unintentional.'

'Oh, I'm sure he'll make it up to you,' Elaine said quickly. 'Once you are all back in the UK.'

'You, not we?' Cathy asked, raising her dark brows quizzically at Elaine.

Elaine twisted the glass of orange in her fingers, her grey eyes thoughtfully watching the fizzy bubbles. 'I hope to be staying down there to live with Marcus,' she admitted softly,' and I know everyone things I'm scatty and naive but I do believe Marcus will still love me and be thrilled to see his baby daughter.' She lifted her gaze to the two girls who were watching her with interest.

'Perhaps it's a blind faith but it's a faith all the same and I'm going to cling on to it for all it's worth because it's all I've got. I've been such a nincompoop all my life, spoilt and indulged as a child, relying on my father so, leaning on Philip, but I hope I've changed since giving birth to Sophie. I love Marcus so much and he really did love me last year and I just hope it's the same this year for him. If it all goes wrong, I'll just have to be very strong and think of it as a learning curve in my life and come out of it an even stronger person.'

She smiled suddenly, her eyes bright. 'But I don't even want to think of failure. I'm full of love and hope and I don't want to think of the worst that could happen. Don't you agree that it is the right way to think, the right way to believe?'

Eyes brimming with tears, Lisa quickly closed her hand over Elaine's and squeezed it hard. 'Oh, Elaine, I think you are wonderful. Not at all naïve. I think you are incredibly brave and strong. I want you to know that I support you all the way with this and it will work out OK, I just know it,' she ended enthusiastically.

Cathy reached out and placed her hand over Lisa's, making a pyramid of hands.

'Sisters all. I'll support you too, Elaine,' she told her sincerely. 'Listening to you has restored my faith in human nature.'

'Gosh, really?'

'Yes, gosh, really,' Cathy laughed. 'Now if you'll excuse me I'll go and find Greg. He must be feeling a bit left out.' She got up and drained the last dreg of her beer and sauntered off round the back of the bar where Greg had gone earlier.

'Phew,' Elaine exhaled. 'I rather guessed I might have your support, Lisa, but I was worried sick about Cathy's.'

'She's had a bad time lately. You must allow for that, Elaine. She has a heart of gold under that sharp exterior. This break is just what she needs.'

'And Greg seems to have softened her a bit. Wouldn't it be wonderful if they fell in love?'

Lisa looked extremely doubtful. 'Knowing Cathy's luck, he's just been phoning his wife,' she said cryptically.

Elaine's eyes widened innocently. 'Oh, he doesn't look as if he's married.'

'But we don't know anything about him, do we?'

156

Lisa said slightly frostily as she got up from the table. 'I'll go inside and see what Philip is up to,' she said keenly. 'I hope there's a decent menu here. I don't much fancy cooking for five in the van.'

'I'll come too. Sophie must be missing me. Lisa . . .' she added quickly before she disappeared inside.

Lisa turned at the plastic strip curtain at the open door of the roadside bar. 'What?' she smiled.

Elaine looked at her slightly pink cheeks and wondered if it was in anticipation of seeing her brother now that he had cleared up their misunderstanding. She didn't want to see Lisa hurt and wondered if she ought to warn her that her brother wasn't exactly the charmer he appeared to women. Philip hadn't come out of his youth altogether unscathed. He'd seen the demise of his parents' marriage; he'd tried to get on with his stepfather and that had hardly worked. He wasn't against marriage, simply wary of it. He'd had girlfriends by the score and broken a lot of hearts. Not cruelly, but he always managed to ease himself out of affairs when the women concerned got too clingy for his liking.

'Thanks for being such a good friend, Lisa,' she said instead of the gentle warning that was on the tip of her tongue.

She'd keep an eye on the two of them and if she saw Lisa getting too involved she might have to warn her then. But first she'd warn her brother not to hurt Lisa but she suspected he might just laugh at her anyway, call her a goose and tell her she was being silly. But the warning might strike home and he'd think twice about leading Lisa on.

Lisa grinned. 'Thanks for involving us in your life,

157

Elaine. It's all going to work out well for you and Sophie. I feel it in my bones.'

Elaine nodded happily. She felt it in her bones too, and everywhere else in her body. Already she was sending telepathic messages down to a cocktail bar in Marbella. *I'm coming, Marcus. I'm on my way. I love you, Marcus.*

'Summit meeting over with?' Greg drawled lazily from under the shade of an olive tree in a grove at the back of the bar. He was leaning against the trunk and reading an SAS thriller.

Cathy slumped down beside him, pulled her floaty cotton skirt up beyond her knees and stretched her long legs out in the sun.

All through Elaine's moving confession she had wanted to bite her knuckles and turn her head away. Instead, she had forced a smile and offered her support in every way while secretly thinking that Elaine might be in for a nasty shock when they reached Marbella.

A year was a long time – an eternity of woman-foraging for a bar owner on the Spanish playboy coast. She didn't doubt this Marcus had loved Elaine last year but, struth, there must have been a million more women in his life since.

'If you don't want to talk about it, you don't have too,' Greg drawled, throwing down his paperback, 'but Philip did fill me in on the reason for this trip, Elaine in hot pursuit of the father of her child. I don't really understand what was going on between you all, but when Philip threw a wobbly just then I guessed there must have been a few misunderstandings.'

'Yeah, we thought he was the lover and the baby was

his and we didn't know about Marcus and I rather think the world has gone mad,' Cathy muttered, closing her eyes.

Greg laughed softly and then Cathy felt his warm lips on her own. She was surprised but let it happen all the same. It was hot and restful under the tree and she wanted life to drift over her and pass her by. She wanted to forget about Charles and being out of work and struggling with her emotions till it had all got a pain in the neck. She wanted to forget that Elaine might be very hurt when she arrived in Marbella and found her lover involved with someone else. She'd been through enough heartache herself without witnessing more. It would break Elaine up and she and Lisa would have to be very strong for her and Cathy wasn't sure if she had much strength left.

She blinked open her eyes and Greg was grinning down at her. 'Well, I didn't really expect white-hot passion so soon in our relationship,' he murmured, 'but I could have done with a bit more feeling on your part.'

She smiled sleepily. 'This ain't the movies, Greg. To be honest, I'm drained of any passion. Besides, I don't know you.'

'Yet,' he smiled. 'So where do we start? Childhood memories, GCSE results, ex-lovers?'

Cathy rolled over on to her elbows to look at him. 'How about wives?'

'Ah, that says a lot,' he mused knowingly. 'Broke your heart when you found out he was married, eh?'

She smiled thinly. Greg Turner was very perceptive. 'My heart's not that easily broken, but my faith in human nature kind of got stretched to its limits. So before this conversation gets too profound, is there a wife, two point four children, a tabby cat with four cute white paws and a golden hamster at home?'

'Ah, you make it all sound blissful. So blissful I rather wish there were.'

Cathy grinned. 'And that's as about as noncommittal as you can get.'

He shook his head. 'No wife, no kids, no fluffy cute pets, but then you aren't going to believe me anyway, are you?'

'Sadly not.' She smiled, enjoying him. 'But I am asking myself what you are doing here, hitchhiking down to Marbella with us lot?'

'Meeting Philip is the answer to that.'

'Ah, yes, I remember. He stopped to give you a lift. Wealthy company directors in Rolls Royces do that sort of thing all the time, don't they?'

'You have a very suspicious mind.'

'I didn't always have.'

'But now you do and you are wary of me? OK, fair dos. I'm on my vacation, destination Marbella – so what else do you want to know?'

Cathy rolled on to her back and stared up at the spiky silvery leaves of the olive tree and the clusters of green olives hanging from the gnarled branches. She was curious more than suspicious. Students opted for hitchhiking because they were usually hard up and Greg was too old to be a student and didn't *look* particularly hard up, anyway. His hair, slightly over-long, was well cut, his clothes, though casual, were of good quality, his trainers pricey Reeboks, and he possessed a mobile phone so planned calls home which would be costly. So why hitchhike when flights to Malaga could be picked up reasonably cheaply?

And why on earth couldn't she accept Greg at face

value instead of reasoning the whys and wherefores of him? She knew that without giving it any more thought. Charles Bond's legacy of mistrust. She closed her eyes, wishing that damned man's name didn't keep popping into her head.

'Cathy, are you asleep?'

No.' She laughed and opened her eyes. 'Tell me about how you come to play the numbers game?' she asked, going for something light and trivial. 'You're the first person I've met who does it. I drive Lisa up the wall with it but when you work with numbers you can't switch off. I've always done it. I count flowers on wallpaper too, and cans on supermarket shelves. I don't buy fruit and veg by the kilo but by numbers. It's a compulsion.' Greg laughed as if he understood. 'Do you work with figures?' she added.

'I have a mathematics degree and I work in the public sector.'

'Civil servant?'

'More or less. And you?'

'Secretary. Out of work at the moment, but I was a financial secretary.'

'How come you're out of work?'

'Personal reasons,' she murmured, not prepared to say more. Greg had already sussed out a lot about her so leave it to him to make of that what he wanted. She didn't want to open up about Charles's betrayal. It was beginning to fade with distance and hopefully by the time they reached Marbella it would be a blank space in her life. 'I think we ought to join the others,' she suggested. 'I'm getting hungry.' She rolled over to get up and saw Greg watching her very intently.

'Why so serious?' she asked as she brushed the dust from her long cotton skirt.

161

'Was I looking so serious?' he asked pensively as he got up himself, reaching down for his book and slotting it into the back pocket of his jeans.

'Yeah, as if you have the world's worries on your shoulders.'

Greg laughed. 'Hardly that. No, I was just thinking I'm very glad I'm travelling with you and not a hairy, greasy lorry driver with no teeth!'

'Huh, am I supposed to take that as a compliment?' she teased him.

'You had your compliment just now when I kissed you. I don't kiss just any girl, you know.'

'No, you just kiss the one that is going spare at the time.'

'Going spare?' He frowned.

Cathy shrugged lightly and grinned and leaned towards him. 'I'm the only one available,' she said meaningfully. 'As you said, Lisa is spoken for and Elaine too. '*I'm* the wallflower of the trio.'

Getting her drift, he suddenly reached out and grasped her hands and pulled him towards her till their noses were almost touching. His voice was very throaty when he growled at her teasingly, 'I don't scoop up spare, Cathy Peterson. I take what I want and *you* I happen to want.'

This kiss was different. It ground unmercifully against her waiting lips and sparked something like passion deep inside her. In fact, her legs went a little wobbly, too, and she found herself leaning against the length of his body for support. He was well built, hard and muscular; as his arms wrapped around her, she knew she should be putting up some sort of resistance, but submission was taking precedence.

So her hormones were intact after Charles. No

162

permanent damage done and it was a relief. But rebound reaction was a strong possibility.

She found herself linking her arms around his neck and drawing on his mouth as equally ardently as he was drawing on hers. Was she on the rebound? Was she testing herself to see if anything was left after Charles had drained her? But no, it was a pleasure to discover this was *pleasure* without any hang-ups.

'Wow,' she gasped when at last he drew back from her. 'That was brilliant!

'I didn't doubt it would be,' he murmured with a confident smile.

'Funny, but if anyone else had come out with such an arrogant remark I would be very wary.'

'So you trust me at last.' He smiled.

Cathy looked deep into his dark eyes and thought perhaps she did, but there again she had trusted Charles, too, and look what had happened there. Unfair, though. She was allowing a bad experience to infrange on a new experience.

'Any reason I shouldn't?' she asked with her head to one side.

'Now, would I tell you if there was?' he teased.

'Oh, you're a tricky one.' Cathy laughed. 'But I'm a risk taker so I'll take you on gut feeling. But double-cross me, sunshine, and you will wish you had hitched a lift with a hairy, greasy, toothless lorry driver.'

He slid an arm around her shoulder as they picked their way through the grove to the bar, so naturally Cathy didn't object. He gave her a light squeeze. 'You are quite a formidable lady, Cathy Peterson, quite a challenge. So tell me about these risks you take. I'm all ears.'

'It was a figure of speech,' she told him lightly. 'But

163

don't think it means I take risks with *men*.'

She stopped suddenly and turned to him. It had suddenly struck her that things were happening rather rapidly between the two of them. They scarcely knew each other and already they had both acknowledged their attraction to each other. These things happened of course, instant chemistry, the wow factor, but all the same . . .

Her eyes, dark and serious, locked on his, which were looking at her quizzically now.

'Greg, you're a really nice guy, but don't let's rush things. I've done some stupid things recently and got involved in something I should have seen coming, but didn't till it was too late. For me it's not quite over yet and I must be very careful. I jumped at the chance of this trip because . . . well . . . it was getting too hot for me at home and – '

'And you're on the run,' he breathed, sounding so disappointed that Cathy almost wished she hadn't started to open up to him.

'Yes, I suppose you could put it like that,' she murmured. On the run to put space between her and Charles and his persistent phone calls and threats. If only he had left her alone she might have coped better, but that constant barrage of calls to get her back in his life had worn her to a frazzle.

But she couldn't talk about her heart and the damage Charles had done to it, not with Greg who was so nice and obviously keen to get to know her better.

She shrugged it away with a light lift of her shoulders. 'It will be sorted once we get to Marbella and I unload some of my excess baggage.'

Suddenly he gripped her shoulders earnestly. 'I can

help, Cathy. Your involvement in all this wasn't your fault, I'm sure. I'm in a position to help and we can nail this bastard – '

'Cathy! The food is ready!' Lisa called from the rear of the bar.

Greg let her go as if Lisa had fired bullets at them and narrowly missed and he ought to run for cover.

Cathy, frowning slightly, watched as Greg strode off without her, mobile phone jutting out of one jean pocket, Andy McNab the other. She noticed that the slight gap between his hair and the crumpled collar of his shirt was flushed as if he was blushing. What had she said to cause that? But perhaps it wasn't what she had said but what *he* had said so vehemently. It wasn't her fault – he was in a position to help – we can nail this bastard!

With a sigh Cathy followed him. He was astute. Already he had sussed she had some emotional problems and was keen to help. It showed he had sincere feelings for her already and she didn't know if that was a good thing or not.

Suddenly the feeling was good, she decided. He was now embarrassed at showing his feelings so heatedly and that was rather endearing. She liked Greg Turner. He was safe and trustworthy and . . . and very sexy. Her blood was beginning to sing as it once had for Charles, and that was a relief and rather exciting too.

'I think two overnight stops are essential,' Philip commanded, in the driving seat again.

This time Lisa had leapt into the passenger seat next to him before anyone else had gone for it. Lunch at the roadside cafeteria-cum-bar had been a delight for her. The Spanish husband-and-wife owners had produced a wonderful feast for them, a traditional paella, fluffy yellow saffron rice heaped with chicken and pork and mussels and prawns, so good she had come away with the recipe. And they had been so attentive to baby Sophie, leaving the adults free to eat outside, all crowded round the plastic-topped table, and getting to know each other better.

Philip had sat across from her, giving her long looks and once his foot had come out and tapped her ankle and he had smiled meaningfully at her.

Lisa was in seventh heaven. Philip was Elaine's brother, not her lover, and Christmas had come in July.

'Oh, Philip, don't be so mean,' Elaine whined. 'One stop will be enough – in fact, with all these drivers we could carry on through the night. You know I can't wait to get there.'

'After a year, one more night isn't going to make any difference,' Philip reasoned with her shortly.

And because Philip was Elaine's brother and brothers usually talked to their sisters like that, Lisa didn't stiffen at his shortness with her.

'He's right, Elaine,' Lisa said. 'Two overnights are sensible. It's the van I'm worried about more than anything. It's not getting any younger and I don't want to push it too hard.'

The thought of two nights staying in hotels, which Philip had insisted on, would lengthen their time together before they got there. They'd had a pow-wow over the route they were taking, down to Madrid then a curve down to Cordoba as Philip had never been there and wanted to see the Roman bridge, then dropping down into Marbella.

She didn't know what was going to happen then.

166

The villa Philip had arranged, Elaine had told them, was somewhere in the hills at the back of Marbella. She didn't know if Philip was staying with them or not, that hadn't been discussed, but she hoped he would be. It was sure to have every luxury, a pool too, and the thought of spending more time with him was making her heart race even now.

'I suppose you're right.' Elaine sighed in resignation and stared blindly out of the window.

Lisa turned and smiled reassuringly at Elaine in the back, seeing her disappointment. 'He's worth waiting for,' she offered. Elaine just nodded miserably.

Poor darling, Lisa thought, gazing ahead at the beautiful countryside, browning more now that they were speedily heading south. She prayed everything would work out for her but she and Cathy would be there for her if it didn't. Usually an optimist, she was feeling a bit shaky on this one though. Elaine was taking a helluva chance, but when you were in love you only saw your goal and nothing anyone said or did could put you off. She guessed if she was in Elaine's shoes she'd probably do the same. Wise or not she'd give it her all. When you were in love you weren't open to negative reasoning.

Her heart was doing somersaults just sitting next to Philip as he drove, so she was well aware of how Elaine must feel. She and Marcus had already had an affair; if she and Philip got as far as having an affair, Lisa knew she would fight tooth and nail to keep him and if people voiced the thought that had once occurred to her – that sandwich girls didn't swan off into the sunset with their company-director lovers – she'd pooh-pooh them.

Philip turned slightly and gave her a warm smile

and she smiled back and her heart raced more. She leaned back in her seat and thought she'd never been happier, until she heard Greg say something to Cathy sitting next to him and she laughed, the way she used to laugh when she was speaking to Charles on the phone, in the days when everything was so good between them.

Lisa's happiness stalled for a moment or too. No problems with Elaine and Philip now, but life never bowled along without further complications. Cathy and Greg were getting close in a very short space of time and Lisa wasn't comfortable with that one bit.

Should she tell her that she had recognized him as the stalker in the blue Rover? Of course, it could all be very innocent. He might have seen her somewhere, in the pub maybe, fancied her and just followed her for a while. But stalking someone wasn't a healthy way of getting to know them. She had seen him speaking to John and Gerry, laughing and going into their flat with them, then, hours later, Greg had turned up on the ferry, seeming to know Philip already, and apparently having met Cathy the night before in the bar. Now he was travelling down to Marbella with them.

It was all a bit of a mystery, but Cathy seemed bowled over by him. But then she had been bowled over by Charles and look where that had led. Nothing but misery.

She had an idea, though, something that might put her mind at rest. As soon as they got booked into a hotel, she would phone John and Gerry and find out about Greg Turner and just what he was about.

'Hey, why are you looking so worried?' Philip asked softly.

Lisa grinned. 'Just wondering what to wear tonight in Madrid.'

Philip laughed out loud. 'Now I know why you and Elaine are such good friends.'

'I heard that,' Elaine called out and everyone laughed.

'Oh, gawd,' Lisa groaned in the foyer of the most luxurious hotel she had ever set foot in. 'The blinking Madrid Ritz with five hundred *estrellas* to its name and me in mucky shorts and downtrodden espadrilles.'

'The Grand with only five *estrellas*.' Cathy laughed as they waited while Philip and Elaine, both immaculately dressed, did the booking in formalities. 'What is it with rich folk? They have just tumbled out of the camper after hours and endless hours on the road and they look the bees' knees, whereas we look the pits.'

Lisa giggled. 'I think it's a case of chainstore-wear versus French designer chic. Even Sophie wears Chanel frocks and her blessed talcum powder is Dior.'

They were clutching each other in fits of giggles when Philip came back to them.

'I've booked a double room for you two, a double room for Elaine and Sophie, a double for myself and Greg. They are only de-luxe rooms, no suites left, so we have to rough it for the night.' He handed them a weighty gold key.

'Blimey, if you call that roughing it,' Cathy whispered to Lisa under her breath. It was all they could do to stop themselves going into further fits of laughter.

'Grow up, Cathy,' Philip ordered thickly.

Which wiped the smile off her face for a second. Lisa hadn't got such a warning, but that was understandable. Philip was treating Lisa like precious porcelain, but she was getting the dishrag treatment, tolerated when needed, cast to the bottom of the tea-leaf-stained sink when finished with.

Philip Mainwaring didn't like her, that was obvious by the suspicious looks he kept casting in her direction. So she was outspoken. Hadn't he ever met a woman who was? In his world, obviously not. Compared to his dreamy sister and a permanantly pink-cheeked Lisa, she supposed she must come over as a bit brazen. Well, he might be Elaine's brother and not her lover as they had presumed, but all the same he had done the dirty on Lisa over her catering business; though Lisa had soft-heartedly forgiven him, she wasn't so forgiving. And he knew that. No flies on Cathy Peterson.

'Where's Greg?' Philip asked, looking around the oyster-coloured marble and gilt foyer.

'Getting ready in the van,' Cathy volunteered, with Greg all the way on this one. 'He's taking me out to dinner tonight. We're going to hit the Madrid night-spots and – '

'Oh, Cathy, you can't,' Lisa protested. She flushed suddenly. 'I mean, I'll be alone and – '

'It's all right, Lisa, you'll be dining with me anyway,' Philip butted in, which put a smile on Lisa's face. 'Elaine is too tired to do anything tonight and she wants to get some decent sleep with Sophie before we press on tomorrow. But there is no need for Greg to get ready in the van. He's sharing a room with me.'

'He prefers not to,' Cathy rather proudly told him. She respected Greg for making this decision and it was one in the eye for pompous Philip, who was throwing his money around on this hotel business as if they were

grateful peasants who should be gibbering in grati-
tude at the thought of staying in a glitzy hotel. She and
Lisa weren't about to look a gift horse in the mouth,
but Greg had a pride that was admirable. 'His budget
doesn't allow for this place and he said he'd rather
spend the night in the van. You don't mind, do you,
Lisa?'

'Not at all – in fact, I prefer it. I mean, security and
all that. Most of our stuff is still in the van.'

'Oh, yes, of course,' Philip murmured. 'Yes, I see
his point now.'

The wrong point, Cathy thought. She was sure
Greg hadn't given security a thought; he was just
covering his embarrassment at having charity
thrown at him from a great height by Philip.

'Right, then,' Philip breathed authoritively. 'Is two
hours long enough for you to get ready, Lisa?'

'Make it thirty minutes and I'm all yours,' Lisa
promised keenly.

'Fine, then. We're all on the same floor, so I'll give
you a knock up in half an hour. Apparently there is a
very good restaurant here.' With a smile for Lisa only,
he went back to reception to give Elaine a hand,
though already she was surrounded by a crowd of
young nubile porters eager to metaphorically throw
rose petals at her feet in exchange for the heavy tip
which she looked as if she could afford.

'I hope he doesn't mean that literally. "Knock up",
my foot – arrogant swine!'

'Oh, Cathy, he's wonderful. Don't be so harsh on
him.'

'And don't you throw yourself at him so obviously.
He only has to look at you and you're grovelling.'

'Look who's talking! Greg is Mr Flipping Universe

171

all of a sudden. Just you remember the earth is flat and you are very adept at falling over the edge.'

Bursting into laughter again, they lifted their chins and headed for the lifts, Cathy noticing that the hoards of young nubile porters didn't rush to metaphorically strew rose petals in their paths.

Cathy was ready first. She could do it in twenty minutes – shower, shampoo, blow dry, make up and dress – and she told Lisa so, teasing her for taking so much time over her hair which was minuscule in comparison to Cathy's long bob.

'How do I look?' She twirled in a simple white cotton sundress with a back that was non-existent above the waistline.

'OK, just right for the back streets of Madrid, sangria and chips and outdoor disco,' Lisa teased goodnaturedly.

'You're just jealous because you're dining here, skimpy nouvelle cuisine and pangs of hunger at three in the morning. I'll bring you some chips home.'

'Glad to hear you're planning on coming home,' Lisa said cryptically as she ran her fingers through her spiky hair yet again as she sat at the dressing-table.

'Is that a warning?' Cathy laughed, taking a last look at herself in the full-length mirror. 'Give me credit for some sanity, Lisa. I've only just met Greg and, though I like him very much, I'm not about to bunk down with him on our first date, not in the back of a camper van anyway.'

'Cathy, be careful,' Lisa said with feeling.

Cathy looked at her in surprise. They always looked out for each other, but Lisa sounded so serious this time. Lisa gave her a hesitant smile. 'You hardly know him,' she added.

172

She'd heard that before, from her own inner counsel. She went to Lisa and gave her a hug. 'I made a grave mistake with Charles and I'm not about to do it again. You be careful too,' she warned with a grin. 'Have fun.'

She swept out of the door and Lisa waited till it closed after her before sighing and lifting the phone. She should have made this call before Cathy left but there had been no opportunity. At least Cathy was being sensible and thinking rationally. A night out in Madrid with Greg Turner could do no harm, but if she heard anything adverse from John and Gerry she'd have to mention it to Cathy.

A few minutes later Lisa put down the phone, none the wiser. The boys weren't in. She would try again tomorrow. Meanwhile she was going to enjoy herself with Philip tonight. She was bubbling with excitement as she fixed pearl studs to her ears and adjusted her red silk dress over her narrow hips. She looked a million dollars and felt it in this lovely glitzy hotel that she could easily get used to more often, even for the rest of her life!

CHAPTER 8

'Are you enjoying yourself?' Greg asked, leaning
across a pavement café table and squeezing her hand
after a waiter had dispensed with their empty plates.
They'd gorged on seafood till they couldn't eat
another shrimp, drank lots of Rioja wine with it,
and talked and laughed as if they had known each
other for ever

'The best,' Cathy laughed. 'Fabulous food and
this.' She raised a large brandy, then sipped it and
gazed around her.

The square was bursting with young people
having fun and it was two o'clock in the morning
and looking as if it was set to go on till dawn. A
discoteca across the orange-tree-lined square was
belting out rock music, lights were flashing everywhere, car horns blared. The noise was huge, the
billowing sound of a city alive and raring to go. The
hot air smelt foreign, a heady mixture of jasmine,
Fortuna cigarettes, which all the young girls seemed
to smoke, and chargrilling food from the restaurants. Cathy loved it all.

'So the food and wine is the best – anything else?'
Greg asked.

'The company too,' Cathy told him, raising her brandy glass, again to clink against his.

In fact, she couldn't imagine being here with anyone else. She spared a fraction of a thought, only a fraction, thinking that Charles wouldn't and couldn't ever fit into this blaring, skidding, raucous cacophony of teeming nightlife. Not in a million light years. He was stuffy and pompous . . . and not worth thinking about!

But Greg was definitely worth thinking about. She gazed at him across the table and felt her pulses racing. He was such good company, so sexy, so bloody nice.

God, it was a great feeling to realize that she wanted him.

'Cathy,' Greg suddenly breathed urgently. 'I want to tell you something.'

Cathy shook her head, her slinky hair swishing against her cheeks. 'No, you don't, Greg,' she laughed.

She didn't want him to tell her that he felt the same way, and she knew he did because he had clutched her hand tightly as they had wandered away from the hotel, round the back streets looking for the real Madrid. Clutched her hand, nuzzled her neck when they had stopped to peer into bars and shops that never closed, slid his arm around her to pull her in close when the crowds got too oppressive.

She could feel it in his touch, see it in his eyes, smell it in his musky, male scent and he didn't need to say a word, because to verbalize it would spoil it.

'Go with the flow, Greg,' she told him, her eyes bright and teasing.

'You have no idea what I was going to say,' he said, still not relaxing enough for Cathy's liking.

175

'No, but you look serious suddenly and I don't want to be, not tonight. I'm enjoying myself too much. Come on, let's pay the bill and walk and stare at people.'

Cathy offered to pay half but Greg insisted he'd pay and she let him. It wasn't as expensive as she had expected it to be, so she didn't feel guilty about letting him pay.

He took her hand and entwined her fingers with his and in silence they wended their way through the back streets in the vague direction of the hotel.

'I hope you know where you're going,' she said at last.

'I don't care where we're going,' Greg said softly. 'I could walk all night with you . . . though I'd rather tumble around a bed with you.'

'That's better.' Cathy laughed. 'You have your humour back.'

'Did I say something funny?' Greg said in a voice heavy with mock hurt.

Cathy leaned against him and laughed.

'If you suggest me coming back to the van with you and tumbling around in your sleeping bag, then that would be funnier.'

'I should have taken up Philip's offer of a hotel room since sleeping bags don't turn you on. So, you have extravagant tastes for seduction, do you?'

'Oh, yes, rather. It's all or nothing for me,' she teased flippantly. 'It's why I didn't turn down Philip's offer of a glitzy hotel as you did. I have no pride where dosh is concerned.'

'So you'd do anything for money?'

Cathy didn't like the way he said that, sort of accusingly. She stopped and pulled her hand out of his. The narrow street they had been strolling along was relatively quiet compared to the others before it. Dimly lit, too, but enough light to see that Greg looked different, far more serious than he had been all evening.

'I was only joking. Why did you say a thing like that?' she asked, serious herself now. Had he been offended because she had offered to pay half the bill in the restaurant? Some men and their pride!

Greg looked concerned now and shrugged his shoulders. 'I didn't mean it to come out the way you are obviously taking it. It's just my way of getting to know you better.'

Cathy shook her head. 'I'm not taking that, Greg. We've had a brilliant night getting to know each other. Now you are getting serious and accusing me of being money-orientated and where the hell you get that assumption from, I don't know. If it's because of the restaurant bill, for goodness' sake get into the real world. Where I come from it's par for the course on a date and – '

'It's nothing to do with that,' Greg interrupted heatedly. Suddenly his hand came up and kneaded his brow. 'Can we leave it alone for now?' he mumbled and started off down the street again.

Cathy caught his arm. 'No, we can't leave it alone,' she insisted. 'What the hell has got into you? We were having such a good time and now it's all ruined and *I* didn't ruin it. Why are you acting this way?'

His eyes darkened suddenly. 'I'm acting this way because you, Cathy Peterson, are getting to me and I don't need this.'

'Need what?' Cathy cried in exasperation.

'Need to bloody well fall in love with you, that's what!' he rapped out.

Stunned, Cathy nearly staggered back against a stone wall. Greg, falling in love with her? Not *needing* it in his life?

And then he was holding his hands up in the air, staring down at the cobble-stoned roadway in exasperation with himself. 'Forget I said that. Forget the money bit, forget everything I've said since leaving the restaurant. A thousand pardons and – '

'And to hell with you!' Cathy cried in a fury, sensibility flooding her now that she realized where this was leading. Suddenly Greg had a guilty conscience and she knew why. 'You think I can wipe out what you have just implied? I have you sussed out now. I know just what your game is.'

His head shot up and he glared at her, waiting for her to go on.

Cathy stepped towards him and stopped in front of him, very close. Her eyes were narrowed with anger. 'How dare you think, even consider, that I could forget anything you've just said. Recently I got in too deep with someone just like yourself and I'm still paying the consequences. I know what is really bugging you. You were testing me just now, suggesting I was money-orientated in case this was going to cost you more than you bargained for.'

'What an earth are you going on about?'

'My last lover could afford a mistress but you are a civil servant, hitchhiking to save on air fares, sleeping in a van rather than cough up for a decent bed for the night – '

'Cathy, please, I don't know what you are trying to say.'

He reached for her but Cathy stepped back out of

178

his way, lurching back and nearly falling as she stepped on an uneven cobble.

'Don't you dare touch me! What I'm trying to say is that I know what you are about. I'm getting used to it now and should have learnt my lesson, but obviously I'm a slow learner. You're getting worried now that we might be getting too serious. Panicking because this lone holiday of yours might cost you too much in money and emotional turmoil. Well, you're off the hook now, Greg. Once bitten, twice shy and all that. I don't have affairs with *married* men!'

In a fury of disappointment she swung around and stalked off down the dimly lit street, hoping that when she turned the next corner she would know where she was, because the last thing she needed in the early hours of the morning was to be lost in a foreign city.

'Oh, Cathy, darling.' Greg was laughing with relief as he ran after her. He caught her on the corner and swung her around into a doorway.

He held her very firmly by her shoulders to entrap her. He was shaking his head and smiling at her.

'I told you I wasn't married,' he insisted.

Cathy lifted her chin. 'You would say that, wouldn't you?' she accused him vehemently. 'Of course you would. But at least it's one up on my last lover! He couldn't deny his wife because she was in my face, so he tried to convince me it was an unsound marriage anyway.' She looked skyward and went on, 'And I can't believe I'm saying this, but that is now beginning to sound more honourable than what you have done, denied a wife in the first place!'

Greg wasn't laughing any more. His grip on her tightened. 'Cathy, darling, I have no wife, I promise you. I am not married and never have been.

179

How can I convince you of the truth?'

'Huh, you can't! Because everything you have said so far indicates the very fact that you *are* married. You were going to tell me something back there and I was slow on the uptake. You were going to tell me then you were married but you lost your nerve. Then you said you didn't need this, us. You are panicking because you are afraid to fall in love with me and that smacks of a guilty conscience because you have a wife waiting at home!'

His voice was low and sympathetic as he responded to her outburst. 'You must have loved that guy very much for him to have hurt you so deeply.'

'Huh, love?' Cathy almost screeched, her eyes welling up now. 'Love had nothing to do with it. It was a matter of trust and his betrayal of my trust in him. He took me for a ride and then tipped me out halfway through. I trusted him, did things for him I wouldn't have dreamt of doing for anyone else – '

'And that is why you are on the run?'

'God, you make it sound as if I'm some sort of criminal!' she objected.

'I don't think for a minute you are,' Greg said earnestly. 'I think you just got so deeply involved you couldn't get out and ran for your life. But it's never the right way. You should have stayed and battled this out instead of implicating yourself by running.'

'What are you, some amateur pyschologist, Greg Turner? Don't try and interfere in something you know nothing about. This is my life and my choice to do what I think best. Yes, I'm running away, doing it my way because to stay would have been more harmful for me.'

180

She tore herself out of his grip and glared at him angrily, biting back her tears.

'And you might think you are being very smart in turning this argument around, accusing me of not handling my affairs in the right way, but I know what you are trying to do. Very skilfully you have diverted attention away from yourself and brought up my past. Nice try, Greg, but nil points for effort. I still believe you to be a married man!'

She went to push past him to get out of the doorway but he blocked her way with the hard bulk of his body. He pressed her hard against the solid wooden door behind them. Cathy was assailed by the weight of him, the urgency of his entrapment, the sheer power of his sexuality as he held her tightly.

'Cathy, I'm not married,' he breathed hotly against her flushed cheek.' There is nothing I can say or do to prove that I'm not. You just have to take me on face value which you were doing just fine till now. Trust me, Cathy. Drop this accusation because it is spoiling everything. I want to help you and I will, but more than anything else I want to make love to you to prove that I care.'

His mouth crushed over hers so fervently that Cathy's head reeled and her pulses stung. His sexuality rose so powerfully against her groin it aroused all her own dormant sexuality till there was a need so strong she thought she might lose all sense of propriety, here in some dark doorway in a Madrid backstreet.

Instead of pushing him hard away she was drawing him hard to her, wanting him to grind himself unmercifully against her, wanting to feel his whole body possessing her. His hands were on the naked skin of her back, his fingers massaging her flaming flesh in a parody of penetration.

Cathy's fingers dug deep into his hair; her mouth, hot and swollen, ground against his. Her naked breasts under the thin cotton were aching to be caressed. There was no thought of past or future, only the very urgent present of wanting him so very much.

Rage and anger and fear of being betrayed again had balled into a holocaust of sexuality and she was wanting to blast it all away with possession. And she knew it was wrong and it shouldn't be like this but it was compulsive. Greg was compulsive.

His hand moved to the front of her dress as the kiss endured, grew evermore out of control, moist and deep, his tongue probing. He moved her skirt above her knees and his hand on her naked thigh brought a small moan of submission from her throat. He caressed her between her legs, breaking the contact of their lips to groan against her throat in despair, as his fingers stroked her tiny silk briefs.

Wild with need, Cathy ran her trembling hands down his back, clawing at the fabric of his shirt, wanting to feel his naked flesh. Her hands slid around to the front of him and she felt his hardness, traced the contours of its length and breadth till he was shaking and moaning against her.

'Oh, no, don't, Cathy,' he cried. 'This is breaking me.'

Suddenly Cathy was sobbing as she held him in both hands, free from all encumberances, hard and silken and urgent. In haste he tore at her briefs and for a very swift second she felt him press hard into her and she gasped and cried out and then it seemed the whole world went black.

She opened her eyes and in the dimness saw him draw back from her and then guilt and shame rocked her. She sobbed quietly as Greg, breathing very hard and much more in control than her own shameful self, adjusted her clothes and his own. Then he was holding her face and kissing her hungrily, small devouring kisses, wiping away her tears with his soft sensuous mouth.

'You deserve better, my darling,' he breathed hotly and then he clasped her tightly to him, his arms enfolding her, crushing her whole body to his. 'Not some bleak, dark doorway.'

With one arm tightly binding her to the side of his body, he urged her out of the doorway and into the street. They staggered at first, both still shaken very deeply at the experience of near coupling, hardly able to speak with the frustration that choked in their throats.

At last, long minutes later, Cathy was able to form words on her dry swollen lips. 'I . . . I'm sorry,' she uttered helplessly. And she was helpless, completely rocked by what had nearly happened. She was thinking more clearly now and the thought that overwhelmed her wasn't one of shame or regret as she ought to be thinking, it was that Greg had aroused more deep emotion in her than anyone before – namely Charles. The passion she had experienced with him had been milk and water to what she had put herself through with Greg just now.

Her whole body – every pulse, every sense, every last nerve ending – was still raging at what he had aroused in her. Blinding white-hot passion that had almost culminated in making love in a doorway. The

183

thought of it happening in a bed behind closed doors was . . . staggering.

'Hey, I think we've had too much to drink.' Greg laughed softly and held her steady as she nearly fell against him. 'And your apology wasn't needed, Cathy,' he whispered in her tousled hair. Cathy clung to him as they walked on slowly, both arms locked around his waist as far as she could reach. 'And I'm not going to apologize either, but I'm going to make you a promise. When we do get it together, it's going to change both our lives.'

Cathy's life was already changed, she mused to herself. She did believe he wasn't married, she did believe he really cared because he had been the one to stop when she had been too far gone to have cared. When it came down to it, her first judgement of him had been spot on – Greg was to be trusted. And it was a good feeling to know that she had come through the débâcle with Charles unscathed.

She was crazy about Greg. He was a good man, a sexy man, the sexiest man she had ever met! He wouldn't hurt her. His restraint this evening proved it all. She felt so happy, so free of all doubt and more than anything she was sorry she had ever accused him of having a wife and that was what her weak apology had been about just now. Why apologize for seemingly to be a shameless, brazen sex bomb in that doorway when it had been the most exhilarating, risky experience of her life. Gosh, she was still tingling with excitement over it. And when it really did happen with Greg, as he said, it would change both their lives.

'So, to the experienced eye, any criticism of the menu?' Philip asked as Lisa perused the menu.

As her eyes were rose-tinted at the moment, Lisa restrained from making a gushing comment in case he thought the menu wasn't up to much and was testing her. No doubt he had dined in the best restaurants around the world and knew good from bad and she didn't want to appear gauche.

'The menu is only the written word,' she told him with a smile. 'As ever, the proof is in the tasting.'

'How diplomatic of you,' he said admiringly.

She handed him back the leather-bound menu. 'You choose. It's all in Spanish and you understand it better than I do. I'm not a vegetarian or a vegan and I have no food allergies or particular likes and dislikes, so feel free to order what you please.'

Philip laughed lightly. 'And I get to choose the wine too, do I? I think you are my kind of woman, Lisa,' he teased her.

A yes woman, eh? she pondered, but made no comment to the contrary. It was very nice being his yes woman for a while. She leaned back against plush dusky blue velvet in a secluded corner and clasped her hands in her lap while Philip's skilful eye ran down the menu.

Every woman in the room had turned to look at Philip when they had walked in the seductively lit restaurant. She had felt ten feet tall, tripping along beside him, his hand gently at her elbow. All those elegant women staring at him in admiration had swelled her pride and teased her hope buds that this was just the beginning of a very lovely relationship. He was so elegant and handsome in narrow black trousers and a sizzling white evening jacket, and he had chosen to dine with her.

He had no other choice, she thought briefly, though

he could have invited Cathy, but that was hardly a possibility as they only ever glowered at each other. Or he could have opted to dine in his room, or with his sister in hers. But no, here he was with her.

Smiling happily, she watched him order from the hovering waiter, and then order champagne from the wine waiter.

'Do you mind champagne?' he asked her. 'I always think it safe when I don't know my guest's preferences.'

'Suits me,' Lisa nodded, rather wishing he had sounded more romantic and murmured something hopeful like, she was special enough for champagne. Early days yet, though.

And then there was silence and Lisa was surprised he wasn't making any attempt at further conversation. Philip was gazing around at the other guests dining and occasionally giving her a tentative glance and a small smile. She shifted her feet uncomfortably under the table. This wasn't the Philip she had expected. He had always been so up front in the offices when she had been delivering her sandwiches. All those exciting innuendoes and sexy glances.

Her heart sank. He wasn't at ease with her in this environment. The sort of environment he was well used to. She was but a sandwich girl after all.

'Philip,' she forced out, 'you didn't have to ask me to dine with you tonight. If you'd rather – '

He smiled at her warmly, giving her his full attention now. 'Lisa, I'm delighted to be dining with you. Besides, I couldn't let you sit in your room all alone.'

Lisa's face dropped.

Philip groaned. 'That was a silly thing to say.' He

186

shrugged helplessly. 'I don't know why I said it because I would have asked you to dine with me even if Cathy hadn't been going out with Greg.'

Lisa tried not to look doubtful. She tried to smile, but that didn't quite come off either.

'And now I've offended you,' Philip uttered with concern, 'and it's the last thing I intended. Ah, the champagne.' He leaned back to let the wine waiter serve them. When the waiter had retreated after placing the bottle in the ice bucket next to him, Philip lifted his glass to her. 'Here's to a very successful trip for all concerned and here's to you Lisa. I'll make a promise to you before anything goes any further. I'll do everything in my power to make your business a success when we return to the UK. Here's to Lisa's executive lunches.'

Miserably Lisa lifted her glass to her lips. She'd rather he had toasted *their* future and not hers alone. Her instincts were right. Sandwich girls and executives were hardly a partnership made in heaven. She had been so thrilled to find him Elaine's brother and not her lover and her heart had sprung with eternal hope when he had looked at her so lovingly and touched her ankle under the table when they had stopped at the roadside bar. And all those other interested looks he had warmed her with . . . was she imagining it all? She hadn't imagined the kiss on the ferry, though. That had been real, but then he had drawn back from her in surprise as if he had shocked himself.

Cathy had said she took flirting as a lifetime commitment and perhaps she was right. She wasn't half so streetwise as Cathy. She did let her heart rather rule her head, but when she came to think of it, Philip was the only one she had thought seriously about. Without even knowing him properly she had feelings she'd never had before.

'Have you a boyfriend?' Philip suddenly asked.

Lisa shook her head. It would be nice to think he was enquiring because he didn't want to tread on anyone's toes, but she knew it was just conversation. The worst sort too. The idle making-conversation-for-the-sake-of-it to fill in the silences on an unfortunate ill-matched date that was looking as if it would stretch interminably.

'No, I don't,' she told him shortly. 'I've been concentrating on my career lately rather than men. For all the good it's done me,' she added cryptically.

Philip sighed. 'I'm really sorry about that, Lisa. It was all my fault, but it was never intentional.'

'I know. You said. I believe you,' she bit out, not sounding thoroughly convinced, though.

'I meant it. I will do everything to put it to rights when we get back.'

Lisa lifted her head to look him in the eye. 'I think I can do without your help, Philip,' she told him tautly. 'I'm quite capable of pulling myself up by my own boot straps, thank you.'

'And now I've offended you even more.' Philip sighed yet again.

Lisa riled quickly and learned across the table to him, her lovely violet eyes narrowed. 'If you sigh one more time I shall get up and leave this table,' she breathed warningly. 'You obviously think it was a grave mistake to have asked me to dinner but we are both here now and we might as well suffer each other as long as it takes to get through this meal. But, of course, if you wish to abort the evening now I'll go along with that because I will not be patronized one second longer.'

Philip's mouth dropped open.

Lisa felt a blush infuse her cheeks. She wished she had kept quiet now, because she was making it worse. Now he would think she really cared and was disappointed this evening was all going wrong. But neither of them could disguise that fact that it was.

Lisa stood up. 'Actually, I'll save you the trouble. I free you from all obligation. Suddenly I'm not hungry and – '

'For chrissakes, sit down,' Philip hissed. 'People are looking at us. Lisa, please sit down!'

Lisa hesitated. She glanced around and people were staring and suddenly she felt as if she was in one of those ghastly dreams when you get up on stage in front of thousands to sing the aria from *La Bohème* when you are really tone deaf, *and* you are stark naked to boot!

She slumped down into her seat and grabbed at her champagne, her face flushed, her fingers trembling nervously.

'Lisa, darling, I'm sorry,' Philip whispered urgently. 'It's all going wrong and I know why. I'm as nervous as hell with you and saying the most ridiculous things. This isn't like me at all and it is thoroughly flummoxing me. I never thought I would see you again and suddenly we are thrown together again and my heart is doing three thousand revs to the second.'

Lisa's eyes widened till they were nearly popping. She managed to get her glass to her lips and took an enormous gulp which nearly choked her.

'I've never met anyone like you before,' he went on

189

quietly. 'My other girlfriends are sort of . . . well . . . well, none of them has ever wanted to walk out on me before the first course has arrived.'

Hope sprang eternal. Lisa felt the champagne bubbles warming her insides.

'They generally wait till after the second course, do they?' she murmured.

A small grin touched the corners of his lovely mouth. 'Not even then,' he replied.

Lisa laughed lightly. 'Some daft women you've been out with, then,' she teased him.

Philip smiled ruefully. 'I think you have a very valid point there. On reflection, they do all seem rather vacant and fey. But you seem to have focused my life in a very short time.'

Given the chance, Lisa would rather like to focus it forever. She sighed, though – not out of the woods yet. It was obvious Philip had a past with women.

'So there have been many?' she ventured.

He shrugged and looked down at his glass of bubbling wine. 'A few too many, I guess. I drive Elaine to distraction. She thinks I'm the world's most prolific flirt.'

'And as you said, you both know each other better than anyone else,' she offered knowingly.

He lifted his dark eyes to meet hers. 'And you, knowing Elaine, should realize that she isn't always spot on with her judgements.'

Lisa laughed and twirled the stem of her glass in fingers that weren't trembling any more. 'I could take that several ways – that you are implying that you are not the champion flirt she believes you to be, or that her judgement on picking Cathy and me to accompany her on her venture wasn't a particularly good idea.'

'Ah, you have me backed into a tight corner now,' he laughed. 'Whatever I say could have me at a distinct disadvantage.'

'Say nothing, then,' Lisa said, light-heartedly enjoying having put him on the spot.

'That's what got us this far.' His eyes softened to deep fathomless pools of sincerity. 'Earlier I was feeling very awkward with you. A first for me. I'm over my reticence now, so how are you feeling?'

'Apart from a little tipsy already, just fine.' She smiled and lifted her glass to him.

'Don't get too tipsy, Lisa,' he warned teasingly. 'I rather like you sober because then you will have no cause to doubt my sincerity afterwards.'

'That is a very daring thing to say, Philip, so perhaps *you* had better stop drinking in case you do and say something you don't mean.'

'Sober or otherwise, I could never say anything I didn't mean to you.'

'So we have no worries. Let's get *very* tipsy, then.'

Philip laughed in surprise and topped up her champagne and Lisa accepted. She knew just how much she could drink without making a fool of herself and she certainly didn't want to make a fool of herself tonight.

They were very relaxed with each other now and she was mightily relieved. For a while she had thought it was all going downhill. But no – Philip, she had been surprised to find, was quite a shy guy. Nice to think it had only affected him with her . . . if all was to be believed.

The first course Philip had ordered was a selection of hors d'oeuvres; as Lisa helped herself from the silver salver which had been placed before them,

Philip asked, 'So how do you feel about Elaine's mission?'

'It's not for me to say.'

'You must have an opinion that you can voice to me, though. I have severe reservations,' he went on. 'But I had to come and offer my support, though as I said before I was against it in the first place.'

'I guess women have a different viewpoint,' Lisa said thoughtfully. 'I think it very romantic, but I'm terrified for her. I don't want to see her hurt and she might be, but she has a very positive attitude about it which is to be admired. Is your stepfather such a terrible ogre?'

Lisa listened pensively as Philip told her of his and Elaine's past. She supposed that John Morton only wanted the best for her and his over-protectiveness was only born out of love for Elaine. She also supposed that whatever happened down in Marbella, good or bad, Philip would just have to resolve his differences with his stepfather afterwards and that must be good at the very least.

Later she told him about her uncomplicated family and her successful model sister who worked in Paris. It was a very nice evening, talking and exchanging life histories. The steak Philip had ordered, cooked in a rich red wine sauce, was very good and Lisa was tempted to ask for the recipe but didn't because she knew how secretive chefs were about their culinary talents.

They both declined a sweet and ordered coffee and Lisa didn't want the evening to end, though she was feeling fatigue dragging at her bones.

'You must be tired,' she suggested to Philip. 'You did all the driving today.'

'Greg can take over tomorrow.'

'What about me? If you and Greg hadn't arrived, I would have been doing most of the driving anyway.' Her eyes sparkled mischievously. 'Don't you trust my driving skills?'

'If they match your cooking skills, I fear you not,' Philip laughed.

'Once we get to the villa, I'll do all the cooking.'

'I look forward to that,' he smiled.

Lisa's heart leapt. He would be staying with them because he'd had the ideal opportunity to say otherwise if he wasn't. So she had something more wonderful to look forward too.

'So what about Greg?' Lisa asked, wondering if when she got back to her room it would be too late to phone the boys back home.

'What about him?

Lisa noticed Philip's eyes narrow and wondered if he was jealous that she had asked about him. She felt a little glow inside.

Lisa shrugged her narrow shoulders. 'Cathy is out with him tonight and he is a stranger to us. You seem to know him.'

'Never met him before this trip,' Philip said quickly and poured more coffee.

'Yes, but you are both men and you seem to get on with him well and I'm quite curious about him.'

'Why?' Philip replied sharply.

Gosh, he *was* jealous. Lisa smiled to reassure him. 'Because he is out with Cathy, as I said, and we worry about each other.'

Philip looked relieved, which made Lisa's insides glow some more.

'And do you think she is worrying about you?'

193

'I'm sure she must have given me a thought or two. After all, she doesn't know much about you either.'

'So I'm not trustworthy either.'

'I didn't say Greg was untrustworthy,' Lisa was quick to jump to her own defence. 'But as you brought it up, what do you *think* of him?'

Suddenly she was feeling a bit concerned. Here she was, having a lovely time with Philip and she'd almost forgotten that Cathy was out with Greg, who had followed her for days before they had left home. He seemed OK, but what did they know about him? Hopefully Cathy would return and have all the answers, but as Cathy didn't know he had been stalking her in the first place, she probably wouldn't be any the wiser to why he had done such a thing.

'Greg is a very nice guy,' Philip told her. 'I usually have good judgement of character and if he had asked Elaine out instead of Cathy, I would have been very happy to let her go.'

Lisa looked at him pensively because she wasn't sure whether to believe that or not. Elaine was very precious to Philip and, after all, Greg was a hitchhiker who they had only just met. But perhaps Philip had chatted to him more, found out where he came from and most things about him. Perhaps she was being oversensitive, but it was a strange business.

'Yes, I suppose you're right,' she murmured. All the same, she was going to make that call to the boys. It might be all innocent, John and Gerry had laughed with him and they had all gone into the house together so she was probably worrying needlessly, but she was very curious to know what they might have had to talk about.

194

'When you're ready, I'll escort you back to your room,' Philip said.

Lisa smiled. Elaine might think her brother a prolific flirt, but if he was he would surely have asked her to his room for a nightcap. She had mixed feelings about the fact that he hadn't, which was very contrary of her.

'It's OK. I have to go to the van to get something for the morning. It's such a muddle in there with everyone's stuff I forgot to get a clean T-shirt for tomorrow. I gave Greg the spare key, but I've got mine.'

'Greg might be sleeping.'

'At midnight?' Lisa laughed, glancing at her watch. 'If I know Cathy, they will be out till dawn.'

'I'll come with you anyway,' Philip said, getting up from his seat and beckoning to the waiter to sign the bill. 'Can't have you wandering around the carpark on your own.'

'Do you think the hotel mind him sleeping out there in the hotel carpark?'

'This is Spain, anything goes – besides they don't know.'

The heat washed over them as they stepped outside the hotel and wandered around the amber-lit façade to the rear of the building.

'Thank you for a lovely evening, Philip. I have really enjoyed it.'

'Good, we'll do it again. Cordoba must have some nice restaurants, Marbella, too. I look forward to it.'

He took her hand as they walked and Lisa was ten feet tall again. Philip took the keys off her to open the side door of the van which was parked in a corner under a tree.

'Is there a light in here?' he asked.

'No, but there's a torch on the shelf.' She climbed in and Philip stood by the door. 'If I can find it,' she giggled.

Philip climbed in after her.

'Here it is. Hold it for me while I delve for my T-shirt under the seat.' She lifted the padded bench seat and Philip held the torch in the right direction. 'Someone's been in here,' she gasped, 'my stuff is all over the place.'

'Er, well, we have rather packed our gear clumsily,' Philip said quickly.

'Yes, but *our* gear was all packed neatly and – ' She frowned suddenly. Greg had been getting ready in here. Had he gone rummaging in their things? Her insides went cold at the thought.

Suddenly the light went out and Lisa squealed. Philip laughed and caught her as she stumbled and before she knew what had happened they were both sprawled on the other bench seat in a heap.

Philips's mouth locked over hers, stemming the gasp of surprise in her throat. She was quickly over her shock, though, as his arms moved around her and held her so urgently her heart somersaulted. The kiss didn't compare to the earlier one. This was pure passion, hot and so desperate, firing her skin till it flamed with desire.

'Oh, Philip,' she sighed as he swivelled them both to a more comfortable position. His mouth sought hers again, parting her lips urgently. His breathing was deep and laboured and quite shocked Lisa. For a prolific flirt, he sure was taking this seriously.

And she was acting pretty dramatically, she realized – already her arms were around him possessively, her wanton body with a will of its own, pressing hard

196

against his, her lips warm and willing. Months and months of wanting him were suddenly coming to fruition.

His mouth on hers was rampant, while a hand moved over the front of her dress to caress her breast through the silky fabric. The combination of the silk rubbing against her nipple, his tongue probing her inner mouth so erotically made her senses swim perilously.

'You're fantastic,' he breathed hard, loosening the black silk tie at his throat.

'So are you,' Lisa gasped, helping him, tearing the tie from his neck and casting it aside. She pressed her hot lips to the flesh of his throat and he groaned helplessly.

He was pressing so hard against her that there was no doubt of his arousal. His sexuality and urgency and her response to it shocked her. But never in her life had there been such a sexy charismatic man. She was lost, hopelessly abandoned on wave after wave of new sensation.

He released her dress by the zipper at the back and Lisa cried out in torment as his mouth sought her breast, seeking her swollen nipple and drawing on it deeply. He was throbbing against her, moving against her, and she was losing all control.

'I want you so much,' Philip grated, moving her skirt up and over her knees, his hand on her inner thigh, stroking her sensitive skin till she writhed beneath him.

She didn't want him to stop. But then she did, because she was afraid. Afraid for the corniest of reasons.

'I can't, Philip,' she moaned miserably. 'Not like

this. You'll hate me tomorrow, think I'm no better than those other women who never say no to you. I do want you, I really do, but not on the seat of my old camper van.'

Philip jerked as if he'd been shot. In the dim light from some far-off hotel lamp she could see him looking around him as if he wasn't quite sure where he was.

And she couldn't help it, she really couldn't – she started to giggle. Perhaps it was the champagne or just that Philip looked so aghast at his surroundings, but suddenly the passion was gone and it was all so funny.

'Oh, my darling, I'm so sorry,' Philip whispered at last. 'I got rather carried away. Oh, this is unforgivable.' He stood up and bumped his head on the roof and suddenly they were both laughing helplessly.

Outside the van Philip gathered her to him and nuzzled her neck and rumpled a hand in her spiky blonde hair. 'Forgive me, darling. I never want to take advantage of you again like that. Philip Mainwaring, making love in a van. Oh, it's unforgivable.'

Laughing, Lisa pushed him away. 'Oh, Philip, you are so sweet and pompous.'

He grinned and gathered her to his side as they walked slowly back to the hotel. 'I think that is the loveliest thing anyone as ever said to me.'

Lisa walked ten feet tall beside him. She loved him. It was as simple as that. And she hadn't found her T-shirt for tomorrow after all. What she had found was the sexiest, funniest man in the world. Never would she forget his shocked expression when he realised he had nearly seduced her in a battered old van. Must have been a first for executive Philip Mainwaring.

* * *

'Hello, hello, hello! What have we here – intruders?'
Greg picked up the torch and a black silk bow tie as he
leaned into the van.

Cathy giggled. 'You sound like Dixon of Dock
Green. "Hello, hello, hello,"' she mimicked in a
deep voice and rocked on her heels with her knees
bent.

'Seriously, someone's been in here.'

Cathy leaned past him and sniffed. 'Lisa – she wears
Arpège perfume.'

'You should be a detective.'

'And that must be Philip's tie because Lisa doesn't
wear one. Mystery solved. Philip and Lisa have been
bonking in the van.'

They fell against each other, laughing, because it
was so unlikely it was funny.

Greg gathered her into his arms as they stood by the
van. 'Do you realize we had our first row this evening?'

'I rather liked the consequences of it,' she teased
him.

'I look forward to the next one, then, but hopefully
the location will be more suited to the occasion.' He
kissed her warmly on the mouth, not too passionately
as they knew the consequences of that. 'Come on, I'll
walk you back to the hotel. There might be stalkers
about and you look so stunning.'

Cathy repressed a shiver at the thought. Thank
goodness that was all behind her now. If it was ever
there in the first place. Being here in Madrid with
Greg, so distanced from Battersea, was making her
feel she must have imagined it all.

'See you in the morning,' Greg whispered at the
foyer of the hotel. 'I don't think I'll sleep a wink
tonight,' he added meaningfully.

'Me neither,' Cathy murmured as she kissed his lips.

He waited till she was safely inside before turning away after a last small wave which Cathy delivered with a wide grin on her face. She guessed she was falling in love if she hadn't already fallen. It was a good feeling, better than anything before. The best.

CHAPTER 9

'Do we have to overnight in Cordoba?' Elaine pleaded yet again with Philip, who was sitting in the passenger seat next to Greg who was driving. 'The further south we are getting the hotter it is and I've had enough of this already.'

She stared gloomily out of the side window at the landscape which was incredibly boring, scrubby dry and mountainous, with not a green tree or flower in sight.

She ached to see Marcus again – the nearer they got the worse was the tension, and another overnight stop would be too much to bear. It was all right for them wining and dining the night away, but she had been stuck in a hotel room with Sophie who had been extremely fretful.

'This is for your benefit, don't forget, Elaine,' Philip said tightly.

'Yes, and I'm truly grateful to you all, but you don't realize how hard it is for me. Sophie needs feeding and changing so often and we are all cramped in this van and it's getting on my nerves. The quicker we get there the better it will be for us all.'

'She has a point, Philip,' Lisa volunteered, giving

Elaine a warm smile, understanding the underlying frustration for her. "This travelling is getting wearing and the sooner we get there the better. This isn't easy for Elaine.'

'It isn't easy for any of us,' Philip snapped back.

Everyone sighed in agreement. Cooped up in a van in this heat and staring at monotonous landscape was frazzling everyone's nerves. They all had to climb out of the van every time Sophie needed changing, which was horribly often, because there wasn't room to move, what with the buggy and all the extra gear they were carrying.

'Is it possible?' Cathy asked, leaning forward so the boys up front could hear her properly. 'It's a helluva way, but we could all take a spell at driving – '

'I can't,' Elaine interjected morosely, wishing she could drive because she would put her foot down and get there ten times quicker if it was up to her.

'You have enough to do with looking after Sophie,' Cathy said as an aside. 'How about giving it a go, Philip? If it gets too tiring we'll have to make another stop, but we can give it our best shot.'

Philip glanced at Greg. 'What do you think?'

Greg shrugged, keeping his eyes on the road ahead which was trusting and curving this way and that. 'We'll give it a try. The sooner I get down there the better as well. You realize it will be dark, possibly the early hours of the morning, when we arrive – do you know exactly where this villa is we're staying at?'

'Are you staying with us as well?' Elaine asked Greg.

Cathy and Lisa exchanged glances, Cathy's hopeful expectation, Lisa's dismayed.

'I've invited Greg and he's accepted as he hasn't planned on where to stay yet,' Philip told them quickly. 'Apparently it's a large villa with plenty of room so it shouldn't be a problem.'

'Tough if it was,' Lisa murmured under her breath.

'Of course it's not a problem,' Elaine enthused, seeing herself getting her own way and pressing on and not wanting to rock any more boats. Besides, that should make Cathy very happy as those two were getting on so well. Lisa didn't look too happy, though, and Elaine wondered why. She hoped it wasn't to do with Philip. No one had said anything about the night before, but everyone had seemed happy this morning; not that she had taken too much notice of anyone but Sophie and she was worrying about her own hair, which hadn't been responding very well to the hotel's air-conditioning.

She was beginning to realize just how much Karen had done for Sophie as a nanny. Though Elaine loved being a mother, it had really come home to her on this trip just how much work was involved. She couldn't have done it without Cathy and Lisa's help. They were marvellous at giving Sophie cuddles and Lisa always made sure the water in the van was boiled properly for her bottles and her food was taken care of.

'If we are going to press on, then it's a good job I went shopping before we left Madrid,' Lisa said. 'I bought loads of bread rolls and salad and cold meats and drinks and stuff, so we can eat *en route* and not waste time in cafés.'

'Oh, Lisa, you are wonderful,' Elaine breathed gratefully.

'She's one in a million,' Philip agreed.

Lisa grinned with happiness at the compliments.

'So do you know exactly where this villa is, Phil?' Greg reminded him.

Lisa's smile evaporated. 'Hear that?' she whispered to Cathy. 'It's Phil now. Talk about well and truly getting your feet under the table.'

'Shut up before I whip *Phil's* bow tie out of my pocket and tell everyone where I found it,' she hissed under her breath.

Lisa went as red as the sweet pepper she had bought that morning.

Philip delved into the back pocket of his chinos and took out a wallet and shuffled through a pack of gold and platinum credit cards till he found what he wanted, a card with something scrawled on it.

'*Finca* Esmeralda,' he read. 'Mijas. I believe it's somewhere up the back of Marbella.'

Greg roared out laughing. 'Is that it? All you've got to go on? What about the key? Have you got one?'

Philip snapped the wallet shut and stuck it back into his pocket very quickly.

'Apparently it's under a pot of geraniums round the back of the villa,' he said shortly.

'Oh, Phil, you're priceless!' Greg laughed.

'What's so funny?' Elaine asked, looking worried.

Cathy and Lisa exchanged further glances, both equally perturbed this time.

'I know Mijas and people don't leave keys under geraniums pots round there. Some of the villas are worth millions, with millions of pesetas worth of security to go with it.'

'What exactly are you getting at, Greg?' Philip rasped.

Greg shrugged. 'How well do you know this friend of yours who owns it?'

204

'Well enough. Why?'

'Enjoys the good things of life, does he?'

'Get to the point, Greg,' Cathy urged with a hesitant laugh.' You've got us all worried out of our lives now.'

'Sorry, didn't mean to put the wind up you all, but don't think it's going to be a plush marbled villa with Olympic-sized pool, hot and cold running water, and electricity.'

Elaine nearly exploded with shock. 'Oh, no, Philip, what have you done?' she howled. She couldn't live without all mod cons! A five-star hotel in Madrid had been bad enough. She'd had to do her and Sophie's laundry in a terrible rush the night before and there had been nowhere but the balcony to properly air the clothes after. Hadn't the hotel thought of airing cupboards?

'Don't be bloody ridiculous, Greg!' Philip bit out. 'I wouldn't put myself or Elaine anywhere that wasn't right.'

'*We* can slum it, though,' Cathy retorted sarcastically.

Lisa dug her in the ribs. 'Why are you doing this, Greg?' Lisa blurted out angrily. 'Philip isn't an idiot and what do you know about anything anyway?'

Greg said no more and simply shrugged in resignation.

Philip cleared his throat. 'Come on, Greg, give. If you have anything more to say, say it. If you think we are walking into trouble, have the decency to let us know now so we can make other arrangements.'

'Wish I hadn't said anything now,' he muttered. 'But whatever it's like, it will have to do. It's the height of the season down there and you'd be hard pressed to

205

find standing-room only in the hotels.'

A horrible silence fell upon everyone. Elaine glanced nervously at them all in turn. The back of Philip's neck was red, which meant he was angry, Greg was all stiff, obviously wishing he'd never opened his mouth, Lisa looked suddenly pale, cross with Greg, fearing that her beloved Philip might have made a fool of himself over this villa and Cathy, well, Cathy looked rather smug at the thought that it was very likely Philip *had* made a fool of himself and she was glad because she didn't like him.

And it was all going wrong and it was all her fault. She had involved far too many people in her mission and tempers were getting short; furthermore, it looked as if they might not have anywhere to stay when they got there anyway.

'Er, what does *finca* mean anyway?' she asked, miserably contemplating it might mean dump. Dump Esmeralda, that was all she needed.

'Go on, Phil,' Cathy jibed. 'You're the linguist, translate for us.'

'It means an estate, a property,' he muttered.

'There you are, then, it will be marvellous.' Elaine grinned with relief. 'Philip has an estate in Suffolk and it's beautiful with tennis courts and stables and a sauna.'

'Gosh, have you really, Philip?' Lisa gushed, hugely impressed. 'Crumbs, a sauna for the horses, that must be something.'

The tension was broken as they all burst out laughing, though Lisa looked a little bemused at what she had said to make everyone laugh.

'Andalucia isn't Suffolk, though,' Greg laughed, 'so don't set your sights too high.'

206

'Oh, stop messing around, Greg,' Cathy chuckled. 'It sounds like we're going to have to make the best of it anyway so tell us what you know. Better prepared than not.'

'Before Marbella and the outlying districts were developed, Marbella was a fishing village and beyond that the *campo*, where the poorer people farmed. Tourism came and the farmers sold their land and their rustic farmhouses for development. There was no electricity or running water in the *campo* and there still isn't in some parts. Hopefully Phil's friend has converted his and there is electricity and civilization, but I don't like the sound of the key under the geranium pot.'

'You idiot.' Cathy laughed again. 'My mum does it all the time and in London, too.'

'She shouldn't,' Greg reprimanded rather stiffly. 'Someone could be watching and, once you'd gone, let themselves into the property and strip the place down.'

'Oh, and you know all about that – ' Lisa stopped herself before she said something she might regret. 'Look, shall we take a break soon?' she went on hurriedly. 'I'll rustle up some rolls and make coffee and we can all stretch our legs.'

'Brilliant idea,' Elaine enthused as Sophie began to stir, kicking out her chubby legs and gurgling as she sleepily opened her eyes. 'And it's all going to be wonderful once we get there because Philip wouldn't have a friend who wanted to holiday in a *finca* without all the services. Who would, for goodness' sake? And we are all getting on so famously now nothing can possibly go wrong.'

* * *

Greg drove down a rough track off the main road so they could relax for a while in peace. There had been a lot of holiday traffic most of the time and everyone had agreed on getting away from thundering lorries and tooting cars for five minutes of silence.

Philip and Greg wandered off towards an outcrop of craggy, savage rocks to stretch their legs and bird spot. Elaine, after changing Sophie yet again and feeding her mashed banana and warm milk, had taken her in the buggy for a walk down a beaten track to a poor solitary gnarled olive tree, the only one for miles. Cathy and Lisa stayed in the van to prepare lunch, all the doors and windows wide open to let in the air.

'I wish you'd lay off Greg, Lisa. You're biting at him all the time.'

'Same goes for you and Philip,' Lisa retorted, as she buttered crispy white rolls that were still warm and feathery inside. 'I know you think he ruined my career, but he didn't. It was all a misunderstanding.'

'Maybe, but he gets my back up and I don't want to see you hurt.' She put out five mugs and spooned coffee into each while the water heated in a pan on the hissing gas ring.

'And I don't want to see you hurt either and we know nothing about Greg.' Lisa paused for a moment. 'Cathy, do you get the feeling Philip and Greg know each other? They seem very friendly.'

'What, before Philip picked him up?'

'Yes. I mean I know they are worlds apart, Philip an executive and Greg just an odd bod hitchhiker – '

'He's a civil servant.'

'Oh, is he?'

Cathy grinned at her. 'Lisa, he's a lovely guy. We had a super time last night. He makes me laugh and

208

he's very sexy and think I'm already in love with him.'

Lisa looked astounded though she shouldn't be. Already she was crazy about Philip and all in all she'd probably had about the same private time with Philip as Cathy had with Greg, just one evening. But she knew more about Philip because of the sandwich rounds and the disastrous lunch she'd done for him and Philip wasn't a stalker either, though now she was beginning to think she really had made an identity mistake. Everyone but her was getting along famously with Greg and Philip had reassured her last night. Nevertheless . . .

'He's not married, is he?' Lisa asked worriedly.

'Now that's a dumb question. Do you want these tomatoes sliced?''

Lisa nodded and unwrapped the cold meats, which were getting a bit sweaty even though they had been in the fridge.

'Why is that a dumb question when Charles deceived you for so long?'

'Exactly because Charles *did* deceive me. I'm ultra-cautious now and made sure from the start. I asked him and he denied a wife. Of course, I have no proof, but I trust Greg.'

'You trusted Charles.'

'Greg's different, I just know it. He's as open as a book. Anyway, why should a married guy be hitch-hiking alone?'

'Yes, why hitchhiking with *us*?' Lisa persisted, wishing she had rung John and Gerry as she had planned the night before. Instead, she had got up early and dashed out to find a shop to buy food for everyone.

'Drop it, Lisa.' Cathy sighed. 'For some reason you

209

don't like Greg and I'm not over-fond of Philip, so let's call it quits. We've been friends too long to spoil it over men.' She grinned suddenly. 'So what were you up to in the van last night? We found Philip's tie on the floor and when I went to get something out from under the seat this morning all my clothes were muddled. Haven't you enough sexy underwear of your own?'

Lisa bit her lip. So Cathy had seen the muddle under the bench seat too. But then Elaine had stuff in there as well – mainly Sophie's diapers, jars of baby food and packets of cereal – and she wasn't renowned for tidiness; she had staff at home to pander to her needs.

Yes, she had to stop this, suspecting Greg of every misdemeanour in the book. Cathy was obviously over the moon with him and – 'Lisa, you didn't,' Cathy gasped, seeing Lisa's silence as guilt. 'Not with Philip, here, where I'm slicing the tomatoes!'

'No, I didn't!' Lisa squealed. 'Philip wouldn't . . . I mean . . . I didn't want him to and he wouldn't anyway. Oh, hell, you've embarrassed me now!'

'Who's embarrassed?' Philip asked from the door-way of the van.

'I am. I forgot to bring salt and pepper,' Lisa said quickly, giving Cathy a sidelong glance warning her not to say anything more to embarrass her, or Philip.

'Well, I won't hold that against you, Lisa,' Philip laughed. 'You've been a marvel so far. Those rolls look absolutely delicious. I'll call the others.'

'Blimey, he makes all this sound like Enid Blyton's latest Famous Five adventure,' Cathy said once his back was turned. 'All we need is some ginger pop and for Uncle Quentin to appear round some rock.'

Lisa laughed. But then she frowned as she looked through the window behind Cathy and saw Greg punching at his mobile phone in frustration. Who on earth could he be trying to call so determinedly in the middle of nowhere? The wife he had denied, perhaps? Oh, please don't let Cathy be hurt again, she prayed inwardly.

Cathy roused herself and tried to stretch, but Lisa's legs were over hers. She blinked sleepily and her head throbbed with the heat and the constant whine of the engine. She shifted Lisa's legs and managed to sit up.

Elaine was curled on the opposite seat, a cushion under her head, sound asleep. Sophie in her buggy in the well between the seats was sleeping peacefully. Philip was driving; Greg was next to him, his head lolling against the door frame.

It was dark and had been before she had dozed off herself. White lights dotted around the landscape twinkled and the terrain looked hilly again.

All but Elaine had taken a spell at driving. Cathy and Lisa had done the motorway driving when there was one, but when the roads became narrower the two men had taken over.

Cathy leaned forward and managed to get the small fridge door open after pushing aside Greg's backpack and a pile of Elaine's carriers. She took out two cans of Coke and opened them, handing one each to the men, nudging Greg awake to hand him his. She took out another for herself and drank thirstily before asking Philip where they were.

'Greg, do you know where we are?' Philip asked with concern.

Greg shone a pencil torch on the map on his lap and

peered at it. 'We're in the right region but that's all I know. I think it best to stop at the nearest civilization and ask.'

'There isn't any bloody civilization,' Philip snapped exhaustedly. 'We should have done this in daylight, stopped over as I suggested. Too many Indians and not enough chiefs,' he added cynically.

'OK, Philip, we're all tired and snidey remarks won't get us to the *Finca* Esmeralda!' Cathy snapped. 'Oh, look there's a traffic warden! Stop and ask the way!' she added sarcastically.

'Not funny, Cathy,' Philip rasped under his breath, glaring out of the windscreen at nothing but blackness.

'Only trying to make you laugh. Though I might as well attempt swimming the Channel underwater with lead weights round my ankles.'

Philip slammed on the brakes and wrenched on the hand brake furiously.

'OK, Miss know-it-all, you drive if you've nothing better to do than grate on my nerves!' He leapt out of the driving seat and slammed the door shut so fiercely Lisa and Elaine jerked awake and Sophie let out a fearful wail.

'Temper, temper,' Cathy sighed as she climbed over Sophie's buggy to get out of the side door.

'What's going on?' Elaine muttered sleepily. 'Are we there yet?'

'Yes, we are, actually, Elaine,' Cathy called out as she wandered round the side of the van.

Philip, who was standing in the headlights from the van, turned on her in a blaze of fury.

'Will you quit winding everyone up, Cathy? It's bad enough we are lost in the middle of nowhere in the

212

pitch dark in this bloody heat without you making inane remarks.'

Cathy, hands on hips, grinned at him. 'I'll have you thanking me for those inane remarks in time, Philip Mainwaring. If I hadn't wound you up enough to have you slamming the brakes on in a temper, we would have missed it.'

'What the hell are you going on about now?' He came towards her as if he was sorely tempted to put his hands around her throat and throttle her.

'Open your eyes, Philip.' She nodded her tousled head to the side of the road where a makeshift wooden signpost was nailed to an olive tree by the side of a dirt track.

'*Finca* Esmeralda!' he yelled at the top of his voice and grabbed Cathy around the waist and swung her around till she screamed for mercy.

'Oh, well done, Cathy.' Greg laughed as he steadied her after Philip had dropped her. He gave her a squeeze himself and a quick peck on the cheek.

They all piled back into the van and Philip reversed a bit to get into the driveway and spirits were soaring as they bumped and bounced up a long, long drive flanked by olive and orange trees.

Philip finally pulled up in front of *Finca* Esmeralda and everyone's euphoria sank like a sack of pebbles in a pond.

'You were right, Greg,' Philip muttered as he gazed at the sprawling white building with narrow shuttered windows that compared more to a rambling cowshed than the villa they'd optimistically prayed for. 'I'll leave the van lights on so we can see to unload, at the very least.'

'Oh, God, it's awful,' Elaine moaned, her eyes

filling with tears as they all tumbled out of the van.

Cathy gave her a hug of comfort. 'I'm sure it's not as bad as it seems. It's dark and we're all tired and in the light of day it will look different. It smells lovely here anyway, all herby and sweet. Listen to the cicadas buzzing, and that sounds like a bullfrog croaking so there must be water around.'

She looked apprehensively at Greg, who just gave her a small shrug.

Elaine hugged a whimpering Sophie to her breast as she stared miserably at the rustic old building that offered no promise of comfort whatsoever. Poor Philip, he must be feeling wretched at having let everyone down. And she felt very wretched herself. She was tired and, after the long hours in the van, dirty and unkempt, her hair just awful. She felt as if she'd never be able to get herself right for Marcus, not here in this miserable place.

Suddenly she was swamped with depression and apprehension. Supposing Philip was right and Marcus had someone else? Supposing he wasn't even here at all? He could have sold up and moved on. She bit her lip hard and hugged Sophie tighter, not wanting to break down and cry in front of everyone.

What had once seemed a good idea, to come here to her lover and pick up where they had left off over a year ago, now seemed utterly hopeless. To have to return to England, unfulfilled, heartbroken, alone but for Sophie, was a heartrending thought, but one she might have to face, she thought despondently.

And on top of everything else she was beginning to worry about her father too. He would have returned and found her and Sophie gone and a panic-stricken nanny moaning that it wasn't her fault. Even now he might have involved the police, maybe even Interpol, because surely he would guess where she had gone? There could already be a search in progress. Oh, Marcus, please be there for me, she inwardly prayed, save me from the wrath of my father, take me in your arms and love me forever, because I can't bear the thought of life without you.

'Found the key,' Philip told them jubilantly, coming round the side of the old white house with Lisa's torch lighting the way for him. 'Tried the back door, but the key doesn't fit.'

The others were grouped by the van with its lights still on, waiting in silence. There was a bright moon and each in turn had looked around at the building and the surrounding land. It was isolated, with no sparkling white lights to indicate that there were neighbours.

Greg whispered to Cathy that he couldn't see any electricity wires or poles. She whispered to him that they could be underground to which he whispered back that pigs might fly.

'Shut up, you two,' Lisa said under her breath. 'This must be very embarrassing for Philip. He's done his best so it's up to us to make it better for him.'

And Elaine in her misery heard it all and wished she hadn't involved them and had been strong enough to go it alone. Given another chance she would have flown down on her own, making sure she booked a first-class hotel in advance.

Eventually Philip, with some muscular help from Greg who had stepped forward quickly, managed to heave open a very solid oak door.

'Any light switches?' Elaine whimpered hopefully.

'Doesn't look like it,' Greg called back.

'Huh, he sounds delighted,' Lisa muttered as she promptly dived back into the van. 'I've another torch here and a box of candles and matches,' she shouted to Philip.

'You're an angel,' Philip breathed in relief as she handed them to him.

'Come on, Elaine,' Cathy urged. 'Give me Sophie and let's go inside. I bet it's a palace inside.'

'Yes,' Lisa breathed enthusiastically. 'Look at the National Theatre on the Embankment, all that concrete looks hideous from outside but inside it's – '

'Hideous!' Elaine uttered hopelessly as she handed Sophie over to Cathy.

Philip had lit several candles before the girls entered and, with the torch, was halfway up a flight of stone steps that led up from the main room, eager to see if there were any decent beds to sleep in.

'Oh, it's lovely,' Lisa enthused as she stepped across the long room that seemed to take up the whole floor space of the building.

Elaine wasn't sure. The floor was polished terracotta with a few Moroccan-type rugs strewn on it, the walls roughly hewn grey stone; a huge stone fireplace was set back in one wall with a black cast-iron stove sitting in it. The large wooden furniture was old and rustic and dark, huge chests and sideboards. But the sprawling black leather sofas and deep matching leather chairs looked expensive and gave Elaine hope that Philip's friend wasn't some sort of environmental freak who was trying to get back to nature occasionally in a high-tech world of business.

'What's it like upstairs?' she asked her brother hopefully.

'The place is huge,' Philip told her from the top of

the stairs where there was a landing galleried over the room below, 'it's far bigger than it appears from outside.'

'I didn't ask how big it was, Philip,' Elaine retorted. 'Are there bathrooms with hot and cold water, preferably en-suite? Are the mattresses sprung? Are there fitted carpets? I can't get out of bed if I haven't something warm and springy under my feet. Oh, God, it's awful up there, isn't it? We'll all get eaten alive. We'll die in our beds. Oh, I can't bear it and it's all my fault!' She covered her face with her hands and burst into tears.

Philip leapt down the stone steps two at a time and he and Lisa both put their arms around her and comfortingly led her across the room and up the steps to see for herself.

'As far as I can see, there is no bedlinen on the beds,' Philip told Lisa over the back of Elaine's heaving shoulders. Elaine let out a wail reminiscent of her daughter's.

'It's all right.' Lisa grinned, already anticipating Philips glowing compliment. 'I brought loads of linen with us, just in case.'

'Lisa, darling, you're a marvel,' Philip murmured.

Greg came up behind Cathy as she stood on a thick rug, gently rocking baby Sophie in her arms. He slid his arms around her waist and pulled her back against him and nuzzled the back of her neck.

'I've hardly spoken to you all day and now we are alone, you have someone else's baby in your arms,' he murmured. 'Wish it was mine,' he added.

Cathy laughed softly so as not to disturb Sophie, who was dozing off to sleep again. Though surely her thudding heart would wake the little one?

'Meaning you fancy Elaine?' she said provokingly.

'Meaning I fancy *you* and I should have said I wish it was *ours*,' he corrected.

'If I wasn't so exhausted I might take that seriously.'

'You're just the sort of woman I would want to have my children.'

'Oh, not *the* one but the *sort* of woman,' she teased him, forcing herself to turn around because his hard body pressing into hers from the rear was making her legs weak.

Greg enfolded her and baby Sophie into his arms. Smiling, he said, 'And because I'm tired, too, I don't seem able to say the right thing. How does this sound though? Share my bed tonight.'

'You might not have one.' Cathy grinned.

'Can I share yours, then?'

'I might not have one either.'

'Hell, Cathy Peterson, you make life really hard for a guy!'

'Yes, I can feel just how hard I'm making your life,' she murmured knowingly as he hugged her tightly to him. 'But not in front of the children, Greg,' she warned him lightly.

'Oh, you're going to be that sort of prudish mother, are you?'

'At the moment I've no intention of becoming any sort of mother.' Cathy laughed.

Greg leaned over Sophie's sleeping form and took Cathy's mouth hungrily in a kiss that aroused the thought of what preceded motherhood and how staggering it would be with Greg. Tired and tousled as she was, Greg was capable of making her feel that sleep was the last thing she wanted at that moment.

'Oh, don't,' she groaned, reluctantly drawing back from him, her head swimming, her legs weak, her arms aching with the weight of Sophie. 'We have things to do: finding the well and drawing up a few buckets of water, rubbing sticks together to build a fire to boil it, gather straw to sleep on . . .'

'Sweep out the cockroaches and put up the mosquito nets,' added Greg, laughing as he cupped her face in his hands. 'And I'd love doing it all with you, too, which goes to show how demented with exhaustion I am as well.'

Yes, she was in love, Cathy decided as Greg took a candle and, putting his arm around her, guided her towards the stairs. And she guessed tomorrow she would be more in love because, after all was said and done, this place wasn't the hell they had all anticipated. It was old and rustic with heaps of charm and she bet outside was magical, hot and scented with jasmine and bougainvillaea scrambling over walls alongside grape vines. It was the perfect place to be in love in, away from the rat race of life in London. It was tranquil and romantic and ten times better than any five-star hotel with a four-poster bed and chocolates on the pillow.

Happily Cathy closed the door on memories of Charles Bond. Charles was gone and Greg filled her heart now.

An hour later Cathy and Greg hugged a glass of wine each and sat perched on a terrace wall and breathed the night-scented air. The light was a solitary candle, but enough to see that there was a long terrace at the back of the old house with all the bougainvillaea and grape

219

vines and jasmine that Cathy had imagined.

Lisa had worked miracles in that hurried hour. Everyone had their own bedroom, everyone had clean warm linen on the beds, both bathrooms were piled with springy towels, all produced by Lisa from the storage compartments of the van like white rabbits out of a magician's hat.

Philip, relieved that Lisa had rescued the situation when he looked as if he was going to come out of all this looking a bit of a fool, had praised her glowingly till she was scarlet with pleasure, and then gushed on, promising her the earth in the form of the best meal in the best restaurant he could find down on the *costa*.

Cathy, who had found a very decent-sized kitchen at the back of the *finca*, albeit without a working fridge or a cooker that raised a flame – though both, she hoped, would look promising once daylight dawned and she could see what she was doing properly – had managed a brew-up on another of Lisa's miraculous provisions, a camping stove. Also a bottle of warm milk for Sophie, and the rest of the rolls filled to brimming point with all the leftover salad, slightly limp, goat's cheese, slightly smelly but creamily satisfying, and a bag of sweet sponge madeleines which they had all pounced on for dessert.

Philip had humbly thanked Cathy for her efforts, but the compliment had paled into insignificance against Lisa's glowing testimonials. She and Greg were laughing about it now that everyone but themselves had fallen into their own beds in exhaustion.

'Do you get the impression Philip doesn't like me?' she grinned.

'I get the impression you get on his nerves, but any woman who answers Phil back would.'

Cathy frowned. 'So you did know him before this trip?'

Greg raised a brow. 'What gives you that idea?'

'Lisa put it forward, said you were getting on so well with each other it appeared you had a past together.'

'I make assessments of people very quickly,' Greg told her, cradling his glass of wine and looking down at it. 'Philip takes no nonsense from his sister and arrogant men like him usually find sharp women like yourself too much of a challenge and back off. He's the sort to want complete and utter submission from his women. He gets it from Lisa, but not from you, so you are out of the running.'

'And treated like dirt beneath his chariot wheels,' Cathy mused. She shook her head and then pushed the errant strands behind her ears. 'Well, if he does think Lisa weak and submissive, he is in for a nasty shock. She's adorable but she's nobody's fool. But if she does let her head rule her heart and he messes her around, he'll have me to contend with.'

'I'd better give him a stern warning, then, but I have a feeling it won't be needed.'

'Why?'

Greg leaned towards her and kissed her lightly on the lips. 'Because a man can read another just as a woman can read another. Philip is besotted with her.'

'Besotted doesn't read faithful, Greg. Philip Mainwaring smacks of womanizer to me. A man as successful and as good-looking as Philip isn't single for nothing. He can get what he wants from a woman without making a commitment himself.'

'So Lisa is hungry for marriage, is she?'

Cathy laughed. 'Not hungry as in "must eat now",

but like most women she wants security in the end. Someone to love and give love back.'

'Is that what you want too?'

'Do you?' Cathy countered, grinning over the rim of the glass.

'I guess it's what we all want in the end. It's what we are put on this earth for, no more, no less.'

'Sounds profound,' Cathy murmured, tilting her head slightly.

'Sounds too heavy at this time of night,' Greg chuckled. 'Let's get down to something lighter, like . . . your room or mine.'

'I don't think that a light question at all,' Cathy retorted. 'Sounds like a very weighty question demanding an even weightier response.'

'I'll give you three seconds to think about it, then.'

Exploding with laughter, Cathy, with her free hand, gave him a nudge which proved to be more of a shove and with a yelp Greg fell back over the wall.

'Oh, crikey, Greg. I didn't mean it. Are you all right?' She grabbed at the candle and hung over the wall and breathed a sigh of relief that the drop wasn't very much. 'Hey, what's that?'

Greg was already on his feet and brushing himself down. His grin was as wide as the ocean as he stepped forward in the light from the candle. 'It's a swimming pool!' he shouted in triumph, already tearing at his clothes.

'Greg, don't be crazy!' she yelled in warning. 'It's dark and it might be infested with all sorts of horrible things. It might be stagnant and – '

She heard a splash, then another cry of triumph. 'It's great, warm too. Get down here, Cathy.'

She needed no further bidding. Snuffing the candle

and putting down her wine glass, she leaped over the wall and landed on springy grass. She wondered why they hadn't seen the glint of moon on water before. It was a swimming pool, not exactly Olympic-sized, but big enough to stretch the limbs with a length or two. She'd stripped off her own clothes hurriedly before she realized what she was doing, about to skinny dip with Greg.

What the hell? It was dark and Greg was obviously naked too and no one else was around.

'Oh, sweet heaven,' she breathed as she slid into the silky water and struck out for the other side, her eyes quickly adapting to the darkness. She didn't care if it was heaving with frogs and little water creatures, it was sheer bliss, the warm water caressing away the aches and strains of their long journey. She grasped the rail at the other side and breathed hard.

Greg swam up behind her and grabbed her round the waist. She laughed as she felt his naked skin against her own. 'Wow, I thought water would have the opposite effect, sort of deflationary.'

'Tell that to the dolphins,' he muttered against the back of her neck and then he was turning her around in the water to face him and she had to hang on to him to keep herself afloat.

His mouth, wet and warm, was on hers and a cry of pleasure caught in her throat as she clung to him. They were locked together, hot, wet bodies melded. With one hand Greg held on to the rail behind her neck and ran the other across her taut breasts, the peaks already hardened by the effect of the water. It was the most erotic of feelings Cathy had ever experienced. His mouth kissing her so passionately, his hand sensuously caressing her breast, the water lapping

223

their heated bodies, was almost too much to bear. Instinctively her legs came up and locked around him and Greg tore his mouth from hers to let out a groan of need and then he had lifted her slightly to lower his mouth to her breast and draw on the aroused nub till she wanted to scream. And then his mouth came back to hers and ground hard with desire till she thought she couldn't stand it a second longer. He used his free hand, guided himself between her legs as they were wrapped around him and his penetration was deep and thorough, throwing her pulses into action till she was moving as urgently as he was, thrashing the water around them.

But whoever said making love under water was easy must have been a dolphin, Cathy thought ludicrously as suddenly Greg withdrew from her before they both went under the water. Driven by some unknown force, Greg heaved her up out of the water and suddenly they were both lying by the pool, and the damp, warm, springy grass was being flattened under Cathy's naked back.

Greg's mouth sought hers again fiercely, neither having lost the urgency of need that had powered their coupling in the water. He ran his hands over her wet body, touching every part of her till her skin was flaming, exploring her deeply, his fingers working her into a frenzy. Then he slid into her again, his mouth drawing on her lips, his tongue probing the soft flesh of her inner mouth as he moved rhythmically inside her, his length and deepness of penetration so thorough she arched every muscle in her body against him.

He was fire inside her and she tore her mouth from his to breathe and to cry out with the intensity of her pleasure. Nothing could stop the rise of her climax, which washed over her like a flood of molten gold. She cried out and Greg closed his mouth over hers and moved faster till she thought the world must end. And then she was coming and Greg cried out, too, and shook violently, his breath rasping in his throat as his own climax broke free.

Deep, deep throbbing engulfed them both as fused together, they rode to the stars till there was no higher to go and they sank down and down in a cushioning billowing warmth of completion.

Breathing hard and still clinging together, they lay wet and naked against each other, slowly, slowly, becoming aware of the night sounds around them – the cicadas' ceaseless buzz, the rustle of spiky olive leaves in the trees nearby as a hot Sahara breeze worried them.

Greg's kisses on her damp cheeks were warm and loving now and she murmured small incoherent sounds that meant nothing but said it all. She had never known such completeness, such oneness. Greg was the best lover, the only lover that existed for her now.

She blinked open her eyes and saw Greg watching her in the moonlight that was suddenly so bright everything around them was clear. He said nothing, but she wasn't prepared to say anything either. A great tranquillity was enveloping her and she wanted to sleep because when she awoke she knew the world would be a different place for her from now on.

In silence they gathered up their strewn clothes and groped their way into the dark house and Greg lit a candle to light their way upstairs. They broke their silence at Cathy's bedroom door, soft murmurings of goodnight and warm kisses on each other's lips. Then Cathy closed the door behind him and fell into bed and her last thought was that Greg had been right. Once it happened, their lives would change for ever.

CHAPTER 10

Lisa had worked since the crack of dawn. She'd woken up to hear Sophie gurgling in the next room. When she'd knocked on Elaine's door and got no response, she'd gone in and lifted Sophie out of her cot, the cot Philip had found in a storage cupboard on the landing the night before, much to Elaine's relief.

She'd taken Sophie downstairs with her as Elaine was deeply asleep. She'd changed the baby, warmed some bottled water and washed her, then fed her some cereal and made up a bottle of powdered milk for her. Cool, happy and well-fed, Sophie had settled contentedly in her buggy as Lisa wheeled her around with her as she had set about exploring the rustic house.

She'd flung open windows and shutters to let the warm air and light in, dusted everywhere because it had obviously been left for months with no one inhabiting it, picked bunchs of wild French lavender and rosemary from outside and dotted them around the place and swept the back terrace, which was strewn with old olive leaves and debris that had fallen from the cane shades above it.

It was beginning to look lovely, though Lisa was worried about water and electricity. There wasn't any, yet there were taps and appliances and wall lights.

'You've been busy,' Philip yawned as he stepped into the large kitchen behind the sitting-room. He was wearing white tennis shorts and a white T-shirt and was amazingly barefoot. Lisa thought he looked so sporty and macho her heart leapt.

'I'm boiling the last of our bottled water for coffee,' she told him brightly.

'Great, I could murder a cup.' He bent down and jiggled Sophie's toys that were strung across the buggy and murmured, 'Hello, sweetheart, enjoying yourself, are you?'

Lisa smiled. He loved his little niece. He'd make a wonderful father.

'I'd better take a look around and see what goes on here.'

'There's a pool beyond the terrace,' Lisa told him enthusiastically, 'so there must be water, but don't take a dip yet – ' she laughed – 'it looks lethal, leaves and debris floating around in it and there's a frog up the shallow end and a few plastic bottles bobbing around and I found an old sock by the side of it and a sticky wine glass. Goodness knows what goes on here when there is no one around. Maybe the locals come here for raves when the place is empty.'

'A swimming pool, eh, can't be so bad after all,' he muttered as he went to the kitchen door which was wide open to the terrace.

Lisa went and stood next to him on the terrace as he gazed out over the pool and a very overgrown garden beyond.

'It's a lovely place, Philip,' she murmured, 'you mustn't feel bad about it. I know it's not up to Elaine's standards, but it has a wonderful rustic charm. And look in the distance, down beyond the green hills – you can see the Mediterranean.'

'But not Marbella,' Philip groaned.

'I expect that's it.' Lisa pointed to the right of the horizon where there was a misty blur of what looked like civilization. But the shimmering heat and a few green hills almost obscured it.

'We're a helluva long way away,' Philip mused. 'I wouldn't have dreamt of taking this place if I'd known it was so far out. Elaine isn't going to be pleased. I'll have to hire a car to get her down there.'

'We have the van,' Lisa volunteered.

''Struth, I hope I've seen the back of that thing for the last time.'

Lisa was hurt and suddenly annoyed too. 'Yes, well, it hardly compares to a Rolls Royce but it got us all safely here,' she retorted stiffly and turned her back on him to go back inside the kitchen where the water on the camping stove was boiling as fiercely as her blood. Her catering van was her pride and joy; if anyone insulted it, they insulted her.

Philip's hand got to the primus first and switched off the jet. He put his hands on her shoulders and gently drew her round to face him. 'And now I've offended you,' he murmured with a smile of apology. 'You're right, your faithful little van got us all safely here and I shouldn't have sounded so disparaging.'

'And now you are sounding patronizing,' Lisa snapped back, not as easily placated as he thought she might be.

229

He lightly kissed the tip of her nose. 'If I am, it's because you humble me and I'm not used to being humbled. You're a treasure. I can imagine how difficult life would have been without you on board. And here you are, up bright and early, and making the place as nice as you can for us all.' He grinned. 'You are going to make some man a wonderful wife. I envy him already. Come now, Sophie is asleep and safe here, so show me around.' He slipped his arm around Lisa's stiff shoulders, and led her to the door again.

Damn you, Philip Mainwaring, Lisa inwardly cursed. He had the ability of raising her hopes one minute and dashing them to the ground the next. Make some man a wonderful wife, eh? Did he realize how hurtful that had sounded? Oh, dear, she was off on one of her fantasies again, imagining a life with him and him already anticipating her life with someone else. Someone he might envy sounded hopeful, though.

Philip found another room at the side of the old *finca*, a room that couldn't be approached from inside the house. Lisa stood in the doorway and watched him step inside. There was some strange-looking machinery inside there. She asked what it was.

'Generator and pumps. Marvellous.' He stepped outside and looked around at the garden. There was a rise of ground across the yard outside the room and Philip strode towards it and leapt up the rough rock steps to the top of the hillock. 'Marvellous,' he echoed again, 'solar panels.'

'What does that mean?' Lisa called out.

'It means hot water and electricity.'

'Do you know how it works?' she asked when he was

back down the hillock and peering into the dark room again.

'Of course. So how about that coffee while I work? I'll have this place civilized in next to no time and we can all have hot showers before we start the day.'

Lisa left him to it, happy for him that today he had the chance to put to rights what had appeared to be a big mistake on his part yesterday. He couldn't have known the villa his friend had offered him for them to stay at was so uncivilized, but at least now he had a chance to salvage his pride.

'Oh, thank you for seeing to Sophie this morning,' Elaine said gratefully, pulling the cord of her peach-coloured silk robe around her waist as Lisa stepped back into the kitchen. 'I feel awful this morning. I don't know what we are going to do,' she went on anxiously.' You did your best to make us all comfortable last night, Lisa, but it isn't enough, you know. No water or electricity, it's going to be – '

'All right,' Lisa interjected with a laugh. 'Philip is fixing it all. There are solar panels and a generator and Philip has promised us all hot showers.'

'Oh, he's so clever.' Elaine sighed with relief as she plopped into a wicker and wood chair that creaked ominously under her weight. 'I can't bear feeling so dishevelled. I must look ghastly and I want to look my best for Marcus. Lisa, can I ask you a further favour? After breakfast and when I'm ready, could you drive me to Marbella, wherever it is – we can ask on the way and – '

'Hold on, Elaine,' Lisa exclaimed, going quite hot all over. She understood Elaine's urgency but travelling to Marbella after breakfast was pushing it a bit.

231

'There is no breakfast and we need to get our bearings before anything else. Find a village, find some shops, get ourselves organized. I know this trip is for your benefit, but let us get straight before we do anything else.'

Elaine's look of disappointment was so poignant that Lisa sighed and went to her and gave her a hug. 'I know you can't wait to see Marcus again, but let's take it a step at a time.'

Elaine rubbed her forehead fretfully. 'I guess you're right, but I'm terrified, Lisa,' she whispered hoarsely. 'All my optimism has evaporated. I'm afraid that it isn't going to work and I suppose that is why I want to get it over with quickly. Get down there to his bar and find out where I stand with him. I think I would die if he didn't want me.'

'Of course he'll want you,' Lisa reassured her quickly, crossing her fingers behind Elaine's shoulder. 'He'll take one look at you and throw his arms around you and forget that you've been apart for a year. Then when he sees little Sophie, well – need I say more? She's so adorable and he'll be so proud of her.'

'Oh, Lisa, you say all the right things, but everything is so awful here and I'm so depressed and there's another thing,' she admitted, head bowed.

What now? Lisa thought, waiting for her to go on. Was there something else Elaine hadn't told them?

'It's Daddy,' she croaked. 'I do love him, you know, but he is such a difficult man and I'm terrified he will do something ghastly to stop me seeing Marcus.'

Lisa fell into a chair across from Elaine. 'What do you mean?' she queried nervously. Elaine bit her lip,

232

her eyelashes fluttering nervously. 'He'll be home now and found me gone and have searched my things and found my passport missing and know I've left the country. I'm even beginning to think he might have anticipated this before he went off to Chester. I was in a terribly nervous state, he must have thought I was up to something. I'm not very clever at hiding my feelings. He might even have had me followed – you know, put a private detective on to me before he left. We might have been followed all the way here.'

'A private detective!' Lisa uttered in shock.

Elaine was breathless with anxiety now. 'He'd do that because he is so against Marcus, though he hasn't even met him. Daddy might even know I am here at this old *finca* this very minute. Interpol might be waiting at Marcus's bar, waiting to snatch me and Sophie and haul us back to England before I even get a chance to speak to Marcus Daddy might even have made Sophie a ward of court in my absence.' Elaine suddenly let out a small sob of anguish. 'Oh, Lisa, there might be a helicopter on its way already, hovering over us and ready to snatch me and Sophie before we even get down to Marbella!'

Lisa felt her blood drain from her face as she suddenly heard a whirring sound that could very well be a helicopter hovering. It was getting louder and louder and Lisa's head started to spin with realization. Greg! Greg Turner was the private detective Elaine's father had hired to follow his daughter and find out what she was up to and where she was going.

He wasn't Cathy's stalker at all, but Elaine's!

It all fitted. Lisa's mind raced. John Morton the

judge was no fool and had access to information other people weren't allowed. Somehow he had found out what Elaine was up to – very easily no doubt, knowing Elaine – and had arranged for Greg to follow them, Cathy, actually, rather than Elaine herself. And was Philip in on this as well? Her mind sped on feverishly. He was very friendly with Greg and had claimed he had picked him up as a hitchhiker and then invited him to join them, but now Lisa was sure they had known each other before. *And* there was his mobile phone! Greg had made a lot of calls *en route*. Had he been reporting back to John Morton on his daughter's progress?

Elaine suddenly let out a strangled cry as she, too, heard the whirring of helicopter blades. She gave an anguished panic-stricken look at Lisa and then leapt to her feet, snatched Sophie from her buggy and dashed out of the room. Lisa, stunned numb, heard the click of her satin mules on the stone stairs as she clattered up them at the speed of light, sobbing in panic.

Quickly coming to her senses, Lisa ran to the front door, which was wide open. She stopped dead on the dusty drive outside and blinked her eyes in the sudden sunlight. Her heart was hammering so wildly she clutched her chest. Then all her fear rushed down to her ankles and she sighed in relief – there was no helicopter hovering threateningly, but a fleet of three diesel-driven cars throbbing to a halt in the driveway. Greg got out of the first one, a battered white Fiat Panda of indeterminate years, as Philip came padding round the side of the *finca*.

'You found a car-rental company, then, excellent!' Philip said to Greg. 'Couldn't bear the thought of

234

another turn in that bloody van. I hope that one isn't mine.' He nodded to the car Greg had just stepped out of.

Greg smiled ruefully. 'No, mine, yours is the yellow Mercedes.'

Two Spanish men got out of the following cars, the yellow Mercedes and a red Uno taking up the rear, and came towards Philip, who spoke to them in Spanish. They all shook hands and the two Spaniards got into the Uno and backed off down the driveway.

'Best I could do,' Greg told Philip apologetically, 'height of the season and all that.' He leaned back into the Panda and hauled out bags of groceries. Seeing Lisa frozen to the spot outside the front door, he grinned at her. 'Shopping for you, Lisa.'

Slightly bemused, Lisa stepped towards him and helped with the plastic carriers. She felt slightly foolish, too, for allowing Elaine to hype her up to believe three diesel-driven cars coming up the ill-made driveway were a police helicopter hovering overhead.

'Kind of you, Greg,' she muttered. 'I didn't know anyone was up before me this morning. Is the village far?'

'A kilometre or so. Walkable if you leave early enough to avoid the heat. It's a charming place. You'll like it.'

'How would *you* know what I would like?' Lisa snapped back before she could stop herself. Yes, he was a detective, she was sure. He might not have arranged a helicopter to abduct Elaine back to England, but the other suggestion of Elaine's rang very true. It all fitted and, though he hadn't done anything yet to jeopardize Elaine's plans, there was still time.

She'd keep an even closer eye on him from now on.

Greg sighed as he handed her one of the smaller carriers. 'I don't know what I've done to offend you, Lisa, but there was no need for that remark.'

Lisa bit her lip. No, there wasn't. Not if she was to keep what she knew about him to herself. Now her allegiance to Cathy had switched to Elaine though it made little difference. She hadn't wanted Cathy to be hurt and now she didn't want any harm to come to Elaine. But if Greg had been hired by John Morton to report back to him, simply to report back but not interfere, it might be all right. But if he tried to prevent Elaine from getting any further in her quest to be reunited with Marcus, then there would be trouble. Though Lisa was concerned about Elaine, she wouldn't do anything to stop her. It might work out for her after all, but at least give her the chance. And Lisa was going to be there for her whatever happened.

She lifted her chin and slightly raised her voice so Philip could hear this too. He was taking no notice of what was going on between her and Greg, but was too engrossed in suspiciously circling the Mercedes and checking to see if it had a full set of wheels.

'Sorry if I was a bit snappy, but as I seem to be the dogsbody around here I'd like to make things a bit clearer from now on. Thank you for doing the shopping, Greg, though why hand the groceries to me – why not Philip?'

Philip jerked his head up and looked at her in surprise. Lisa jutted out her small chin even further. She was cross with Philip for yet again making a disparaging remark about her van. 'In a weak moment I offered to do the cooking for us all, but on second thoughts I've considered that this trip is my holiday too, so why *should* I do it all? I'll work out a rota so that I get some time off. All of you are able bodied enough to do a bit of cooking and cleaning and washing.'

Philip's eyes widened like saucers. The corners of Greg's mouth twitched slightly at the astounded expression on Philip's face.

'And don't you look so smug, Greg. You can start by cleaning out that disgusting scummy swimming pool before we all go down with the plague.'

Greg's face lengthened in dismay and he went quite pale.

'Right, those are my terms. Take them or leave them. I'll take this lot inside and cook the breakfast, but someone else can do the bloody washing up. I'm here for a suntan, not choring!'

With that she turned on her heels and stormed off inside the *finca*.

'Did she say whoring or choring?' Greg said, the colour coming back to his face.

'I heard that!' Lisa cried out.

'That's quite enough, Greg. That was a very offensive remark,' Philip rebuked him. 'Lisa is a darling and she has a point. We've all been taking her for granted and it has to stop.'

And Lisa heard that too, but it didn't give her the warm glow inside it might have done yesterday. Twice this morning Philip had made disparaging references to her beloved catering van and twice was two times too many! Besides, she now nurtured suspicions that Philip knew exactly who and what Greg Turner was about and that didn't bode well for how she had felt about Philip. She was more than halfway in love with him – probably all the wretched way, if she cared to ponder it more deeply, which she hadn't time for at the moment as she had a heaving great breakfast to cook.

In a desultory fashion she unpacked the shopping. Why wasn't life a decisive black and white instead of indeterminate grey and hazy with misgivings? She wanted to love Philip unconditionally, but the more she got to know him the more complicated he was becoming. If he was involved with Greg and they were here to stop Elaine seeing Marcus, then he wasn't to be trusted. It was a cruel deception and marred her feelings for him.

'Wow, what a heavenly day!' Cathy said breezily as she stepped into the kitchen all glowing with vitality in a skimpy red bikini with a matching scarlet sarong knotted around her waist. 'Where did all that shopping come from? Crumbs, you haven't done a supermarket sweep already? Did you know there's a pool here? I can't wait to dive in.'

'Yes, I've seen it, but have a tetanus jab before you risk it,' Lisa said tightly. 'Only a mad rabid dog would dive in there without a thought!'

Practically foaming at the mouth, Cathy gulped weakly. 'Is it that bad? Anyway, anything rabid has a *fear* of water.'

'Not if it's mad as well,' Lisa muttered, still feeling pretty mad herself as Cathy belted outside, leaving her to cope on her own.

She sighed suddenly and lifted her head from a pile of fat knobbly tomatoes and kilos of artichokes. Their first day here in this lovely climate and sweet-smelling air and she was feeling bitchy because of Philip's crass remarks about her van and her suspicions about him.

238

She grinned suddenly. Well, she wasn't going to be. She was going to give everyone the benefit of the doubt until it was proved otherwise. They were all going to have a lovely time and Elaine was going to be reunited with Marcus even if Greg was a private detective and Philip was in on the deception and . . . and . . . oh, hell, Elaine was probably hiding in a cupboard upstairs thinking that the helicopter had landed!

Lisa dropped what she was doing and fled upstairs. She had better put her out of her misery before anything else.

Cathy found a sombre Greg already at the poolside armed with a long pole with a net affair at the end of it. He was scooping out leaves and wine corks and tipping them on the side. One of his socks was flattened on the tile surround steaming in the hot sun; a fat bull frog croaked its protestation from under a shrub as Greg worked.

'Oh, it's not as bad as Lisa painted it,' Cathy observed, peering into the water, which was mercifully quite clear and not sludge brown as she had anticipated. Her head had reeled at the thought of her and Greg just plunging in there last night, without a thought that it might be a soup of viral bacteria.

'Yes, she put the frighteners on me too.' Greg grinned. 'Once Philip gets the pumps going it'll be fine.'

Cathy slipped her hand into his and stood very close to him, gazing down into the rippling water where it had all happened last night.

'We didn't speak after,' she said softly, hoping he

239

would know what she was referring too and not make it difficult for her.

'We could hardly indulge in pillow talk when there wasn't one.' He smiled. 'Besides, I think silence says more. In such a situation it's easy to come out with the wrong thing and spoil a beautiful moment.'

Cathy nodded. 'I guess so,' she murmured, though wondering if his noncommittal silence was indeed better than a stereotyped exclamation that the earth had moved, her body was that of a goddess, and it was the best sex he had ever had in his life.

'You don't sound convinced.'

Cathy sighed and looked into his brown eyes, not particularly looking for something deep and mean-ingful this morning after the night before, but looking for just a hint that he hadn't regretted it. She didn't, but it had been rather a hasty coupling with little thought of the consequences.

'I suppose it's a woman's thing,' she told him softly. 'We are very insecure creatures and need coddling all the time.'

'And you think it's any different for men?'

Cathy shrugged and looked away. 'So do you want *me* to say something post-coital that will swell your ego?'

He laughed and swung her around to face him, the net dropping from his hand to clatter on the tiles and send the frog hopping off in alarm. Tenderly he took her by her shoulders. 'You swelled my ego last night, Cathy, in more ways than one. But both our guards were down last night.'

Cathy stiffened.

'I felt that,' he said gently. 'Now will you stop being

240

all female? You of all people I would expect to handle this in a more adult way.'

Cathy widened her eyes. 'You mean in a manly way? Shrug it off as if it was just another bonk? Hell, Greg, you sure do have a way with words, pity you didn't spout them last night, *before* we both let our guards down!'

Hurt and embarrassed, she went to draw away from him but he didn't let her. His fingers on her bare flesh clung on. 'You see, talking about it is fraught with dangers. Someone always gets hurt.'

'If you are implying that I am hurt, think again. I have a safety valve on hurt, but one thing that makes me hellishly mad is being *used*, Greg!'

'Ditto,' he uttered.

'Ditto?' Cathy echoed incredulously. 'You think *I* used you last night?'

He shrugged. 'Why not? You've been through a hard time with a married man. Your ego is at an all-time low. What better way to get your confidence back than to seduce me and lay back and await showers of compliments on your performance?'

Aghast, Cathy stepped back and this time Greg let her go. Her hands came palms up to ward him off if he thought of entrapping her once again. She hadn't expected this: his outrageously accusing attitude, his hard cold reasoning on something that to her had been a voyage of joy and wonder. More fool her for fishing for something that obviously wasn't there for him.

'There's nothing I can say to that,' she told him levelly, 'nothing that wouldn't sound decidedly *fe-male*. Let's leave it at that, shall we?'

'Cathy,' he sighed, suddenly looking sheepish. 'It

was only a suggestion, not a statement of fact. You want to talk about it and I'm obliging you, giving you the in-depth discussion you seemed to need this morning. Personally I don't want to talk about it because I believe actions speak louder than words.' He shrugged. 'I'm sorry, it's the way I am.'

Cathy steeled herself. He made sense, but not her sort of sense. She was a woman, wasn't she? She wanted to hear the damned compliments, the flattery and the rest. What she didn't want to hear was his indifference, as if the whole experience was something inconsequential that happened between lights out and lights on.

'You are so spot on, Greg,' she seethed through her teeth. 'Thank you very kindly for putting me straight and I accept your apology that you are the way you are, though I abhor the hidden undertones of "if you don't like it, tough". Well, I'm a quick learner suddenly. You've converted me to believing actions speak louder than words.' She stepped towards him and, with one great heave, shoved him as hard as she could.

Greg lost his balance and, with a look of short sharp shock, could do nothing to stop himself toppling backwards into the pool with a great splash. He surfaced almost immediately with the same expression of disbelief he had gone under with.

Cathy picked up the net he had been clearing the pool with and flung it in after him and smiled thinly. 'Might as well do the job properly, Greg, while you're down there – have a rake around for your feelings, though I guess you'll never find them. They are obviously well suited to the depths of a stagnant, stinking, heaving mass of bilge. I hope you catch

242

something down there too. Bloody bubonic plague would be too good for you!'

She heard him laugh behind her as she stormed to the terrace steps and took them in one great leap at freedom. He thought it a huge joke, damn him! And she was the flaming joker!

'Oh, Cathy, I heard that,' Lisa bleated worriedly at the kitchen door. 'You were a bit strong there. Poor Greg, is he all right?'

'Well, you've changed your tune suddenly,' Cathy cried in temper. 'Flavour of the month for you, is he? Well, he's all yours. I never want to see him again in this life or the next! He's a rat!'

She left Lisa beating eggs and stormed upstairs to her room and slammed the door after her.

Lisa closed her eyes and willed good humour for everyone. A nourishing breakfast would do it. Food always did.

Later Lisa called a meeting. Philip had found white plastic garden furniture and a big shady, green-and-white umbrella and set them up down by the poolside. The pool was shimmering as the pump worked through the water, filtering it and chlorinating it. The fridge worked, the cooker worked; there was hot running water, though it was so hot and humid anyway that cold showers seemed preferable for everyone – Elaine didn't dare say anything to the contrary since she'd made such a fuss about having all mod cons at the villa. Philip had strutted around proud as a peacock that he had brought civilization to their world and so absolved himself from any blame for the misfortune of finding the old *finca* wasn't the glamorous villa they had all expected.

In a utility room beyond the kitchen there was a washing machine, and already there was a string of baby clothes and underwear and shorts and T-shirts drying in the yard by the pump room.

In a couple of hours civilization had arrived but no one except Lisa looked happy about it. They all sat around the white plastic table, morosely waiting for Philip to appear with the beers. Greg had thoughtfully bought a couple of crates of San Miguel at the shops along with the masses of groceries he'd purchased earlier.

'Cheer up, you horrible lot,' she goaded, fed up of the sight of long faces. 'This is a summer holiday in paradise and look what it did for Adam and Eve!'

Elaine sniffed and examined her polished nails at close range, Greg afforded Lisa a small grimace, Cathy afforded him a mutinous look, Sophie under a French broderie anglaise parasol rigged up over the buggy blissfully slept, a cute flowery bonnet set at a rakish angle over her eyes.

'Ah, here's Philip. Now we can get down to business.' Lisa pulled her list towards her and, as Philip cracked open bottles of cold beer and handed them around, started to read out her conditions.

'I thought it best to do it in days so we can all have plenty of free time, instead of allocating each breakfast, lunch or dinner,' she started enthusiastically. 'It will be nice to know that when we wake up in the morning and it's our free day we don't have to do a single thing. I've duplicated these so we all have a list we can pin up in our own rooms. If it's your day to cook you do the lot, washing up and all. Your bedrooms are your own responsibility. Laundry and cleaning is down to us girls while you guys can look after the general maintenance of the place, the pool, the generator and the gardens, which look as if they could do with some attention.'

'If you think I'm laundering *anyone's* undergarments but my own, you can think again,' Cathy said meaningfully, looking particularly at Greg as she spoke. 'And that list of yours, Lisa, smacks of sexism. The women getting the menial household tasks the men getting the fun tasks like the garden and the pool.'

'Well, you could suck the pool clean for starters with that overloaded mouth of yours,' Greg ground out.

Elaine giggled nervously. Philip slammed his bottle down on the table as if he was in charge of the boardroom.

'If you two have fallen out, have the grace to fight your battles in private,' he directed pointedly at Cathy and Greg. 'Listen to Lisa because she is the only one with any sense here, apart from myself, of course. I will support her every inch of the way because if it wasn't for her heroic efforts, her sturdy camping van that got us safely here, her marvellous organizational skills, *and* her wonderful good nature, we'd all be in a sorrowful state.'

Lisa blushed and smiled thankfully at Philip, who beamed back at her and gave her the thumbs up. Cathy mimed the sticking-the-finger-down-the-throat-and-throwing-up routine, over the side of her chair, at which Greg threw back his head and roared with laughter. Elaine jerked her head up to see what she had missed.

'Thank you for that vote of confidence, Philip,' Lisa

happily murmured. 'It's easy to see why you are the successful business man you are – '

'Can I interrupt the mutual admiration society for a minute, please?' Greg interjected. 'This rota business is all very well, but aren't you forgetting that Elaine has a mission to accomplish?'

That was all the proof Lisa needed that Greg was very deeply embroiled in this. That he was indeed the private detective that Elaine, probably in her innocence, had suggested. Suddenly he was taking her plight on board when, if he was but an ordinary bird-watching hitchhiker, it was none of his business.

'I know you think I am probably speaking out of turn and it's none of my business – '

Mind reader too, Lisa surmised, vowing to bird-watch him within an inch of his life.

'But in the short time I have got to know each of you, I have begun to care about you all.'

Cathy let out a disbelieving guffaw which Greg ignored as he went on. 'You have made no provision in this list of yours for Elaine's absence, Lisa. Mine, too, come to that. I have things I want to do in Marbella myself and there are going to be days when I'm not here either.'

I bet there are, Lisa thought, stalking Elaine and reporting back to the judge, no doubt, and waiting for further instructions like, *Keep them apart at all costs*.

'Greg has a point,' Elaine put in, obviously not having come to the conclusion that Lisa had: Greg wasn't her friend but her mortal enemy, hired by her father. 'I realize that today is lost, but certainly tomorrow I must go and find Marcus.'

'And I'm offering myself as your escort, Elaine,' Greg suggested, which suggestion had Lisa frowning in dismay. 'I'm going down to Marbella myself so it will be no trouble.'

'That's most kind of you, Greg,' Philip responded, 'and I will come too because she is *my* sister.'

Lisa's frown deepened. Oh, lord, what were they up to? What did they hope to achieve by both of them sticking to Elaine like glue? It wasn't fair to Elaine. She loved Marcus and perhaps he might not be a suitable lover for her, but how dare anyone judge him without meeting him? There was a chance that both men were simply concerned for her safety, but Philip had already admitted he didn't want Elaine to do this and Elaine's father was so dead against it he had apparently hired Greg to stalk her. Elaine was so naïve and innocent and the men knew that, but would they be cruel enough to let her come this far and then snatch her and Sophie away just as all her dreams might come true? Greg was just doing his job, however despicable that might be, Lisa sadly thought, but much as she adored Philip, he might just do anything to stop Elaine. He was a man of integrity and an unsuitable marriage for his sister wasn't a welcome proposition. They were a respected wealthy family and Marcus was just a bar owner who had fathered Elaine's illegitimate baby. Which was a thought that suddenly depressed Lisa. *She* was just a sandwich girl, at best an executive lunch chef, hardly suitable marriage fare for Philip Mainwaring.

'Thank you both for offering,' Elaine said firmly, 'but if anyone comes with me I'd like it to be the girls, if they wouldn't mind. I've got it all worked out, you see. I've decided to play it cool, so to speak. Philip, you can look after Sophie while we are away. I don't think it wise to spring her on him just yet. I thought an

247

informal lunch at Marcus's bar, sizing everything up, seeing how the land lies. See-seeing if . . . if . . . he's sti-still free.' Her voice started to give and everyone stared at her in dismay, all suddenly uncomfortable. Elaine took a deep breath and went on in a hushed whisper, 'I'd like the girls with me because it's a girl thing and they understand me and will be there for me if . . . if it goes badly.'

Cathy gulped and reached out for Elaine's hand and squeezed it hard. 'We'd be happy to come with you, Elaine,' she murmured. 'And you are very wise to plan it so sensibly. Lisa and I will be discreet and back off if you want to talk to Marcus alone, but till then we will be by your side every inch of the way.'

'Yes we will, every inch of the way,' Lisa generously reiterated.

'So it seems we will have to reschedule your rota, Lisa,' Philip said quietly. 'I think perhaps we have all overlooked the point of this trip, Elaine's happiness. This isn't Club Med and we aren't all here for the sun, sea and sangria.'

His statement, obvious now to all, sobered them. Lisa lowered her eyes to glare at her hands clasped in her lap. She felt guilty now for trying to put some order in everyone's lives so they could all have a good time. A good time wasn't on the agenda. Elaine's future was.

'Yes, it was a silly idea,' she conceded, reaching for her list and crumbling it hard in her fist. 'Don't worry. I'll see to everything.'

'No, you won't,' Philip told her firmly, taking the crumpled paper from her hand and smoothing it out on the table. 'We'll rearrange it and I'll start by offering to take you all into Mijas tonight for a

248

meal. Sophie, too, because we know the Spanish love children and will make her more than welcome.'

'Oh, you are a brick,' Elaine enthused, looking at her brother lovingly, brightened by everyone's support. 'I'm truly glad you came, Phil. You'll love Marcus once you meet him, you all will. I feel so much more optimistic now. You're all so wonderful and I'm so proud you are all my friends. I'm a very lucky girl.' She stood up and went round the table giving all of them, even Greg, a big kiss on the cheek and a hug.' I love you all,' she laughed, 'and now I'd better find something to wear tonight and something special for tomorrow and then I'm going to lie down with a hot wax treatment on my hair because it's such a frightful mess.'

She hurried off and in the long silence that followed four sets of fingers and thumbs came up and kneaded four sets of feverish brows.

Lisa swam several lengths of the pool on her own. Everyone had disappeared and she understood why. The heat was almost unbearable and after a light lunch of salad and crusty bread topped with a tuna and mayonnaise concoction she had made up as she worked – adding bits of this and that till it was a creamy mound that melted in the mouth – everyone had melted away.

Elaine had given them all food for thought too. Her sudden effusion of warmth and love towards everyone had affected them all. Elaine might come across airy-fairy and only worrying about what she was going to wear and how her hair looked, but underneath she was panicking. She switched from moroseness to bubbling effusion and it was all to mask a very deep concern that Marcus might not feel the same way as she did after a year – and everyone knew it.

Her own heart bled for Elaine's predicament. But a small part of her heart bled for herself. Like Elaine, she was switching her emotions this way and that, insecure as to how Philip might feel about her. She and Philip were worlds apart, just like Elaine and her bar-owner lover. Last year they had indulged in an affair, a holiday affair, and this was a sort of holiday and Philip was flirting with her and it could very well turn into an affair, so perhaps she ought to be putting the brakes on now before it went any further.

'I found your sun cream in the kitchen. I hope you put plenty on before swimming. Your arms and face could catch the sun.'

Lisa clung to the rail round the pool and blinked up to see Philip hovering over her. He was wearing black swimming shorts and the rest of his naked body was stomach-tighteningly gorgeous. He was already bronzed from a previous soirée with the sun – the Caribbean in the spring, she remembered, poignantly remembering too that she had missed him badly the three weeks he had been away. The sandwich round hadn't been the same without his gentle flirting that always brightened her day.

'It's OK, I swamped myself in it.' She went to lever herself out, but he put a hand down and grasped her wrist and flicked her up beside him as easily as if reeling in a fish.

He reached down for her towel on the tiles and looped it round her shoulders, holding her close and patting her dry. Lisa let him because her brakes were suddenly a little lax.

'Where've you been?' she asked. 'You all disappeared after lunch.'

'I can't speak for the others, but I went into the town to make your life a little easier.'

Lisa grinned ruefully. 'Disappearing before the washing up doesn't make my life any easier.'

'I've hired a maid to come in every day and do the cleaning, a gardener and pool-maintenance man to keep everything shipshape outside, and a dishwasher is coming first thing in the morning so there won't be any more washing up to worry your pretty little head over.'

Lisa's lips parted with pleasant surprise. What a hero!

The hero bent his dark head and took her parted lips in a kiss made in heaven. Then he slid a hand under the towel and cupped her bikini-covered breast in a caress that was made in a tormenting hell. It flamed through her till she thought she might frizzle.

'Philip!' she gasped in shock, but did nothing physical to stop him.

'I rather wish we were dining alone tonight,' he whispered at her throat as he nibbled her cool wet skin. 'In fact, I'd go as far as to say I wish we were alone here forever instead of holed up with the rest of them.'

Lisa stepped back from him, clutching the towel tightly around her. Now was the time to put the brakes on though her heart was willing her to pedal towards him for all she was worth. He must care because he had done such nice things for her, obviously regretting making disparaging remarks about her precious van and showing such concern for her now. But the sun was beating down and the air was heady with foreign scents and sounds and they were a million miles away from the real world and that real world had to be returned to some time.

'Thank you for being so thoughtful, Philip,' she murmured, 'and it would be nice to be here alone together but . . . but we're not, are we? We are all here for a purpose, to support Elaine and that should be our top priority. *Our* feelings don't matter.'

'Lisa,' Philip murmured worriedly. He pulled her towards him again and looked deep into her eyes. 'Our feelings matter very much as well. Whatever comes about with Elaine shouldn't stop us having a wonderful time while we are here.'

'But don't you see, Philip?' she breathed anxiously. 'That's what happened to Elaine last year – she had a wonderful time and then look what happened. She had a baby and – '

'Good lord. I wouldn't be so careless! You have no worries there.'

'Oh, Philip!' Lisa wailed, stepping back out of his reach. 'You don't get the point, do you? I'm not talking about contraception here. I'm talking holiday romances. Elaine had one and it might or might not work out for her, but it doesn't alter the fact that she is hopelessly in love with the man and has suffered a great deal. I don't want to get to the stage when the suffering starts. I came to support Elaine on this and I will, but I did want a break too, and in a way this is a holiday for me.'

'I understand that,' Philip said, but didn't sound convinced or even as if he had the vaguest idea of what she was getting at.

'You don't!' Lisa insisted. 'You are flirting with me, like you used to do but more intensely now because we

252

are here, here in a holiday environment. You're saying things like you wish we were alone, you kiss me and you dried me off so tenderly just now and it's all leading up to you wanting me in your bed.'

'And what's wrong with that between two consenting adults?' he muttered, still looking confused. 'I thought you felt the same way, felt the same attraction as I felt for you.'

'Attraction isn't enough for me, Philip,' she blurted out, knowing she was probably making a huge fool of herself now, but at least she was trying to be honest. 'I don't want to get hurt and you are very capable of hurting me, Philip. I'm not a prude, but I'm not a candidate for a ephemeral holiday affair either.'

'You . . . you don't want me?' Philip gasped, his expression so astounded that she was turning him down that Lisa felt quite a thrill of power course through her veins. It was a totally new feeling for her. Little Lisa the sandwich girl, turning the business tycoon down.

'No, I don't want you, Philip,' she said determinedly, meaning that she didn't want a holiday affair, but as soon as the words were out the power play slackened off leaving her decidedly weak around the knees.

His expression astonished and confused her because Philip wasn't gazing at her, affronted that she had turned him down, he was gazing at her with such deep hurt her whole insides bunched with regret at what she had said. Philip Mainwaring was hurt, a hurt not caused by damaged pride or losing a potential conquest so soon, but in agonizing pain as if she had struck him hard in the ribs with a blunt object.

In confusion Lisa stepped back, her violet eyes wide

253

and bewildered. Oh, what had she done? With a cry of remorse she turned and ran, unable to bear the weight of that painful look of anguish on his face. She'd hurt the one man she'd ever truly cared about and for him to have shown such agony of emotion meant that *he* had truly cared for her, too. And she'd ruined it all before it had really begun!

CHAPTER 11

'Good of Philip to lend us the Mercedes,' Cathy remarked, trying to make conversation. Lisa, sitting stiffly next to her, drove. Elaine was equally silent in the back, twisting a Dior silk scarf between her fingers till she had reduced it to the consistency of a well wrung-out dishcloth.

The roads were clearly signposted to Marbella and they were now driving down a winding road to the coast, the windows tightly shut because the car was blessed with air-conditioning.

'I'm surprised he was so generous this morning after that débâcle of a meal last night in Mijas,' she tried again.

'There was nothing wrong with the food,' Lisa offered tightly, 'it was just the company that was off.'

Cathy forced a laugh. 'So you've fallen out with Philip and me with Greg, so it bodes well for you, Elaine,' she directed to the back of the car. 'One out of three must be a distinct possibility.'

'Don't be so crass,' Lisa whispered. 'Can't you see she is sick with worry?' Lisa glanced in the rear-view mirror to see if Elaine was still with them. Bodily she was, but her heart and mind were obviously in another stratosphere.

'She looks lovely,' Cathy said quietly, confident that Elaine couldn't hear. She'd already enthused about Elaine's outfit before they left – lovely cream silk palazzo pants and a cool floaty peach-coloured top that enhanced the Titian highlights in her hair. Cathy had helped conceal the shadows of worry under the other girls eyes with some tinted cream and done her very best to lift Elaine's spirits. Greg and Philip had showed equal enthusiasm in trying to boost her moral, but Cathy feared that nothing but Marcus flinging his arms around Elaine and proclaiming undying love would have any affect on her mood.

Her own troubles with Greg paled into insignificance compared to Elaine's trauma. She was sorry now she had spoiled it all between herself and Greg. Her only excuse was insecurity, the wretched legacy Charles had saddled her with even though she had vowed to put him out of her mind. She was an idiot for now objecting to Greg's honest openness when it was what had first attracted him to her. She liked a guy who spoke his mind, yet when Greg had been totally honest with her by the poolside yesterday she had flown at him like a mad thing. She could well understand why men didn't understand women! She wasn't sure she knew her own species any better.

'So what's to do with you and Greg?' Lisa asked.

As usual the girls were sensitive to each other's moods and what might be troubling them. Though Lisa had witnessed her dumping Greg in the pool yesterday morning she didn't know what had been the cause of it. They usually told each other everything, but Cathy had held back on this one. She wasn't proud of herself for what had happened, before, during and after their lovemaking. 'Too much too soon' was an old adage she should give sensible thought to in future. 'Diving in at the deep end' another, in more sense than one!

Cathy shrugged. 'All and nothing,' she said as casually as if Lisa had enquired about the weather.

'Come on, Cath, the only time you spoke to each other over the meal last night was to snap at each other. The atmosphere was thicker than the soup.'

'And you and Philip were hardly as dreamy-creamy as the dessert. He looked as if he'd taken a nibble at your earlobe only to find it was a lemon. If it wasn't for Sophie and the crowd of admirers she had drawn, the evening would have been a washout.'

'The evening *was* a washout,' Lisa emphasized. 'We were all back at *Finca*-blinking-Esmeralda by eleven, just as everything in the town was warming up.'

'Yes, I was miffed at that.' Cathy sighed. 'I was stone-cold sober with nowhere to go, a champagne cork short of being deliriously witty and making Greg laugh enough to break him down.'

'He laughed when you pretended to be sick when Philip was complimenting me round the pool yesterday afternoon, and that was after your row so there has got to be hope. What were you rowing about anyway?'

'I'll tell you some time, when it doesn't hurt so much,' Cathy murmured. 'Anyway, I thought it was all going famously with you and Philip. What happened?'

'I'll tell you some time, when it doesn't hurt so much,' Lisa echoed with a wry smile.

257

Cathy wished hurt could be obliterated from the world. No one was immune to it and there ought to be a cure. Most of it stemmed from love. Love hurts – whoever penned that knew what it was about. She was hurting, Lisa too, Elaine as well. But their men? You couldn't hurt Greg if you bulldozed him with a JCB, Philip hadn't a heart thudding in his arrogant chest to be hurt, and Marcus . . .? Cathy was curious to see this man who had stolen Elaine's heart and given her so much angst, though it seemed he wasn't directly responsible for that. The ball lay in her father's court for the distress he must have caused her in withholding those letters from her. If only she had found them sooner. Hell, a year was a long time.

'What do you keep looking in the rear-view mirror for?' Cathy asked to get on to another subject.

'I thought we were being followed.'

Cathy laughed. 'Don't you start! You're getting as paranoid as I was back in England. Funny thing, but I've almost forgotten about Charles. You know, at one stage I thought Charles might have hired that stalker – '

'Shut up,' Lisa hissed under her breath, taking another glance at Elaine in the mirror and giving Cathy a warning frown.

Cathy turned her head and saw that Elaine had nodded off.

'Elaine thinks her father might have put a private detective on to her,' Lisa whispered.

'And you think he might be following now?' Cathy laughed softly. 'That's absurd. He doesn't know where she is.'

'She thinks he might have anticipated this and put a

258

detective on her even while she was in England, preparing for the trip. The more I come to think of it, the more I think she's right and we've been tracked every leg of the journey. In fact you might as well know that I think G – '

'Don't be absurd, Lisa,' Cathy interrupted, keeping her voice low. 'Whatever is the point in doing that? Her father doesn't want her to have anything to do with Marcus any more. If he knew she was coming here, he would have swooped on her at Portsmouth, if not before. Why let her go this far? We're practically there already.'

Lisa ground at her bottom lip, doubtful now. 'Yes, I suppose, but – '

'Look, right here at the roundabout,' Cathy directed, raising her voice. 'Heavens, it's busy down here and so built up. Hard to believe, if what Greg said was true, that this was once a fishing village. Wow, look at all those flashy cars. Do you reckon they're all bank robbers? They call this the Costa del Crime, you know.'

'That's what my father thinks,' Elaine muttered dismally as she leaned forward to see where they were. 'He's convinced Marcus must be a criminal.'

'He's not, is he?' Cathy queried, thinking that if he was, Elaine had hidden depths they didn't know about.

'Of course not.' Elaine grinned.

'It put a smile on your face though,' Cathy lightly teased.

'Yes, I'm wearing my brave face now, to hide a multitude of terrors,' she admitted. 'Do you think we could find a small church that I could say a quick prayer in before we get there?'

'Blimey, it's too late for the patron saint of lost causes to offer you any hope, girl!' Cathy joked and they all burst out laughing.

Fifteen minutes later they were still driving around looking for somewhere to park, Lisa keeping her cool because she was used to London traffic and parking problems and this was very reminiscent of Piccadilly Circus, but with palm trees. Cathy leaned out of the window and was asking parked drivers if they were going or not and Elaine was looking this way and that, trying to familiarize herself with her surroundings.

'Over there!' Cathy shrieked. 'Where that pink Pontiac is pulling out from under a palm tree. *Grazie*, babe,' she acknowledged as the Pontiac driver thoughtfully blocked the road so they could pull into the space he had left.

'This is Spain, not Italy,' Lisa laughed, 'it's *gracias*, not *grazie*.'

'He was a member of the mafia. The Godfather himself, I'm sure.'

'Looked more like Sean Connery to me.'

Cathy's head nearly did a double turn as Lisa yanked on the handbrake. 'It could be. He's got a place down here hasn't he? I'll die if it was. I love him to death.'

'Wow,' Lisa breathed as she locked up the car and looked around her. They were parked under palm trees that edged a small exotic garden that fronted a gorgeous-looking French restaurant. Beyond you could see the sea and further along the crowded esplanade were more bars and restaurants. Across the road there were hotels and more bars, all heaving with beautiful people. 'It's all so lovely.'

'If you like that sort of thing,' Cathy murmured as a

crowd of youths wearing back-to-front baseball caps and baggy shorts and peeling red chests reeled along the road, whistling at everything in a skirt.

Elaine was oblivious to everything but searching for something she recognized. 'I didn't realize a year was such a long time,' she murmured worriedly, looking this way and that. 'It looks so different.'

'What's Marcus's bar called?' Cathy asked.

'Marcus's Bar.'

'Yes, Marcus's bar,' Lisa said. 'What's it called?'

'That's what it's called, Marcus's Bar, unless of course he's changed it.'

'Oh,' Cathy and Lisa uttered together, both wondering if Elaine had the foggiest idea where she was and what she was looking for.

'But that's the hotel I stayed at,' she said, pointing excitedly across the road. 'Yes, I'm sure that's it. Well, his bar is on the same side, down a bit, over by the pink pavement.' She laughed suddenly. 'I remember the pink pavement because my nose came pretty close to it a couple of times. Honestly, I was so tipsy the first night I met Marcus. It was all he could do to support me. Oh, he was so wonderful. He could so easily have taken advantage of me that night, but he didn't . . .'

'Didn't take long, though,' Cathy breathed to herself.

'He was such a gentleman, such a poppet and . . .' Suddenly her eyes brimmed with tears and she leaned back against the yellow Mercedes and covered her face with her hands. Cathy and Lisa were instantly at her side, glancing at each other nervously.

'I can't do it! I can't!,' she cried in anguish.

'You can,' Cathy soothed, drawing her hands down

261

from her face. 'Pull yourself together, Elaine,' she added gently. 'If you don't go through with this, you'll never know, will you? You can't chicken out now, now that we are here. Think of Sophie, she needs a father, her own.' She bit her lip, wondering if that was a bit over the top. If Marcus did reject her . . . but no . . . he wouldn't.

'Elaine, come on, stop crying, your mascara will run and your eyes will be red and he won't recognize you.'

'He might not anyway!' Elaine howled. 'Look at me, fat after having Sophie, all my clothes crumpled, my hair an absolute mess. I shouldn't have come. I must be crazy!'

Cathy was sorely tempted to give her three short sharp slaps around the face to calm her, but that would make matters worse. Instead she linked her arm around Elaine's heaving shoulders and steered her, with Lisa the other side of her clasping her around the waist, to the nearest bar.

'You're not fat and your hair isn't a mess and you look stunning. You're just fishing for compliments. What you need, my girl, is what got you into this mess in the first place,' she seethed.

'Cathy, take it easy,' Lisa warned.

'Easy isn't what Elaine needs at the moment. Don't you think I don't know just how terrified she is?' Cathy argued. 'I'm as bloody nervous as her and what we need is Dutch courage. Three very large brandies and I mean mega ones,' she snapped at a waiter as they eased Elaine down into a chair on the pavement outside a bar.

'All our drinks are big 'uns,' grunted the waiter with a thick Liverpool accent and tattoos up to his armpits.

'That's not Marcus, is it?' Cathy nodded her head to his retreating back.

Lisa looked appalled at Cathy's insensitivity, but Elaine smiled through her tears. 'Cathy, you are awful – ' she laughed nervously ' – but just the tonic I need.'

Lisa looked relieved. Cathy grinned and gave her hand a squeeze and silently breathed a sigh of relief. Left to sweet Lisa, the pair of them would be snivelling in the car by now, heading back to the sanctity of the *finca*, mission unaccomplished.

A little while later, fortified and just a little giggly, except for Lisa who had abstained from the brandy as she was driving, pouring hers into Elaine's glass, they paid for the drinks and headed across the road to the hotel Elaine had stayed at the previous year.

'Now was it to the left or the right?' She giggled. 'Only joking. I know exactly where I am now. This way.' Arm-in-arm they strolled along a wide boulevard, determined not to be broken up by the crowds of people spilling in and out of glamorous-looking boutiques. 'That brandy has cleared my head. Thanks, Cathy, it was just what I needed. Aren't the shops lovely here? When this is all over with I'm going to treat you both. We'll go on a wild spending spree. Versace, here we come.'

She stiffened suddenly, gripping the girls' arms tightly. 'There it is, the one with the garden entrance and all the pots with ferns and geraniums and the green canopy. His apartment is over the canopy – look, you can see the window boxes with all the flowers trailing from them.'

Cathy was impressed; it certainly wasn't any old

bar, more like one of those swish restaurants in Chelsea where the rich and famous hung out.

Elaine gulped. 'Marcus was so proud of his pots. There's masses inside too. It's all gleaming chrome and green foliage and sparkling lights and – '

'And closed by the look of it,' Lisa muttered in disappointment as they came to a stop in front of it.

In silence the three girls stared at the ornate wrought-iron gates closed over the shiny chrome double doors of the entrance. The windows each side of the doors were shuttered too. The windows of the apartment above were also shuttered.

Cathy closed her eyes for a second in disbelief. The whole town was swinging and this was the only bar closed and that could only mean one thing. It wasn't a bar any more. Marcus had gone.

'Oh, God,' Elaine moaned and leaned heavily on Lisa, who was biting her lip hard, her eyes searching Cathy's, looking for guidance what to do. 'He's not here any more,' Elaine sobbed.

'Hold on, Elaine,' Cathy said brightly, looking up. 'It still says Marcus's Bar on the canopy.'

'Does it?' Elaine cried, looking up. She smiled with relief. 'Oh, yes, yes, yes, yes.'

'And there's a notice on the door. I expect it's closed for redecoration or something. I doubt he'd go away in the middle of the season, so if it is being done up it shouldn't be closed for long.'

Cathy stepped forward to read the notice, which was printed in five languages, and then reeled back with shock. She turned quickly to stop Elaine reading the notice, but it was too late, Elaine was on her heels.

'What does it say?'

Cathy widened her eyes to appeal to Lisa for help,

but all in vain. Elaine turned blindly away after reading the notice, her lovely face suddenly pale and ravaged with distress.

She didn't see the girls, she didn't see anything. Stiff-backed, she started to run back along the boulevard, weaving from side to side till she bumped into someone who steadied her and then went on their way. Brought to a sudden halt, she looked up and, as if suddenly coming out of a trance, barged through the swing doors of a small hotel slotted in between a boutique and another bar and disappeared from sight.

'Quick, after her,' Cathy urged, grabbing Lisa's arm.

'What an earth did that notice say?' Lisa cried as they hurried after her.

'Closed for Owner's Wedding,' Cathy bit out.

'Oh, God, no!' Lisa sobbed.

Elaine was already at a small bar to the left of a small reception area when the girls burst in. She was seated on a chrome bar-stool, a glass and a whole bottle of brandy in front of her, her head bowed over the glass, a bemused young barman eyeing her curiously.

Cathy quickly got her bearings as she looked around the hotel. It looked extremely exclusive, small but expensive. Already people were glancing at Elaine nervously. She must have just reeled in like some common tourist and slumped down at the bar like an alcoholic, not the sort of person you would expect to see in such a fashionable place.

Elaine already had the brimming glass to her lips and was sobbing and gulping furiously at the brandy as Cathy came up behind her, Lisa, trembling with concern following close behind.

'That's enough, Elaine,' Cathy warned softly,

265

reaching for the glass and trying to get it out of Elaine's iron grip without looking as if she was wrenching it out of her hand. People were staring in haughty disapproval. Cathy wasn't easily embarrassed, but Elaine was in great danger of making a spectacle of herself and this exclusive-looking hotel wasn't the place to do it.

Elaine turned to her, her face tearstained and so distraught that Cathy nearly burst into floods of tears with her. 'Oh, Cathy, Cathy,' she moaned, 'I'm too late . . . it's all too late!' She flung her arms around Cathy and sobbed hysterically. Then, as suddenly as she had flung herself at Cathy, she went slack in her arms.

'Oh, Gawd,' Cathy bleated. 'Lisa, help, she's passed out and I can't hold her!'

Lisa let out a strangled yelp of panic as both Elaine and Cathy slid to the floor, Elaine's bar-stool, suddenly released from under her, ricocheted against the chrome bar and slid across the highly polished marble floor, bringing every member of staff down on them all like a ton of bricks.

'Move aside!' someone in authority shouted.

Cathy, who was on the floor with Elaine, supporting her head with one hand and trying to adjust her own flimsy short dress which had ridden up to her thighs in the fall, looked up to see a gaunt-faced man peering down at them with concern. She just had time to register that, in spite of his pale, lean features, he was strikingly beautiful with stunning long black hair hanging in ringlets around his face as he leaned down over them. He wore a pure white Armani suit, an open-necked silk shirt and smelt like the men's cologne department of Harvey Nichols.

266

No, this wasn't the time to be drooling over a gorgeous guy!

'My friend isn't well,' she uttered helplessly.

Suddenly Lisa was kneeling beside them, pink-faced and blubbering, 'She's had a dreadful shock and what with the heat and – '

'And the drink,' he finished for her with a hint of contempt which made Lisa's colour deepen. 'Move aside,' the man repeated, calling something out in Spanish to several bar staff who were hovering near-by. One reached for a white telephone on the bar and the others dissolved the gaping crowds who were watching in awed silence.

The man bent over Elaine and, with surprising strength for such a slim man, effortlessly scooped her up from the floor and into his arms.

Cathy scrambled to her feet, hugely embarrassed for Elaine now and thinking it was a good job she was well out of it, because if she came round now she'd die a thousand deaths.

'Where are you taking her?' Lisa bleated to him as Cathy adjusted her dress.

'To my apartment at the back of the hotel,' the man snapped. 'Get your bags and follow.'

Cathy and Lisa didn't need to be told twice. Lisa scooped up all their belongings and together they tripped after the man, Cathy reaching out and supporting Elaine's head, which was lolling over his arm like a rag doll's, her luscious hair billowing in the tornado he'd evoked with the speed he was using to get Elaine out of sight.

Lisa leapt ahead to open doors every time he nodded his head, Cathy moved aside to let him and Elaine through, thinking that the man must be the manager and must be furious with them for making an exhibition of themselves and hoping that the owner didn't put in a sudden appearance.

The apartment was stunning, Cathy was quick to observe as Lisa pushed open the last door. It was all white, chrome and glass, stylish like a film star's Beverley Hills home. She amended her thoughts. He wasn't a mere manager, he must be the owner!

'The bedroom door,' he snapped and Lisa leapt forward.

'Gosh!' she gasped at the sight of an enormous frothy white bed with a frothy white canopy over it, suspended from the ceiling.

The man was gently laying Elaine down on the top of the frothy bed and Cathy started to panic. Even in a drink-induced stupor Elaine looked stunningly beautiful lying there, her hair fanned out around her head, her face serene if slightly flushed, her lovely silky clothes falling into delicate folds around her body, leaving no one in any doubt that apart from a few extra pounds she was carrying, she was very shapely, very sexy. If the hotel owner dismissed them, Cathy would start to scream. Anything could happen to Elaine at the hands of this man whose brow had suddenly broken out into a sweat.

'Good God,' he exclaimed as for the first time he took a hard look at the prostrate form of the woman he'd carried into his apartment.

'Look, is this really necessary, your bedroom? Couldn't you have put her down on a sofa or something?' Cathy blurted out, rushing to Elaine's side.

The man's arm shot out to stop her getting near Elaine. His face was paler than ever, his dark eyes wide, his hand trembling as he restrained Cathy. 'Good God!' he repeated.

'Well, God won't help you if you touch her,' Cathy snapped furiously as she cast his restraining arm aside. 'Can't you see she is helpless? Lay one finger on her and I'll knock you . . .'

Elaine started to come round. Her eyelids fluttered, she mumbled something incoherent, tiny little murmurings of distress which sounded very much like, Marcus, Marcus, Marcus.

'Oh, my God,' the man groaned helplessly and fell over Elaine and gathered her hard into his arms.

'Help, Lisa! Call the police!' Cathy screamed.

Elaine was fully awake now, struggling in the man's arms and then she went all limp again as her eyes widened in disbelief. Suddenly she was clinging to the man and he was raining kisses on her face and they were both incoherent now.

'Marcus . . . Marcus.' – 'Elaine . . . Elaine.' – 'My darling.' – 'My love.'

'My God,' Cathy and Lisa breathed in unison.

Elaine lay back on the downy pillows with an ice pack on her head and thought she'd gone to heaven and back. If it wasn't for her throbbing head all would be perfect in her life. But what was a headache after all she had been through?

Slowly she opened her eyes to make sure she wasn't floating on a cloud, strumming a golden harp.

'Marcus,' she breathed.

He turned from the window where he had been standing gazing out at the pots of ferns and geraniums on the patio beyond and was at her side in an instant, clasping her hand and kissing her delicate fingers profusely.

'Tell me again,' she whispered. 'I want to hear it all again.'

Marcus beamed down at her and softly repeated what he had told her already. 'I sold the bar at the beginning of the year because I couldn't bear it any longer. It held such bittersweet memories for me. The new owner didn't want to change the name as it was so successful. It's he that is getting married today, not me. I opened this place instead, just a few metres along the boulevard so that I wouldn't be far away if you ever came back.'

'Oh, Marcus,' Elaine breathed. 'This is all music to my ears. I saw the notice, thought it was you getting married and – '

'And got very drunk and plopped back into my life just as you did that very first time we met.' He smiled down at her. 'If that isn't providence, I don't know what is.'

'Oh, darling, I can't believe this has happened. I can't believe I have found you at last.'

The smile of happiness slowly slid from his pale face and concern took it's place. 'What happened, darling? You used to phone me all the time when you first got back to England and then nothing. I phoned your house in Battersea and some screaming girl said you didn't live there any more and slammed the phone down on me. Then through some contacts down here I got your Knightsbridge address – I remembered you telling me your family home was Knightsbridge – and I wrote, even phoned, but some awful barbarian bawled my head off and told me to bugger off.' Marcus sighed deeply before going on. 'I thought you didn't want to know me any more.'

'Oh, you shouldn't have given up, Marcus,' Elaine cried, thinking that if he hadn't she might have been spared so much distress.

'I didn't give up, darling, not till the day I came to find you.'

'You came to England to find me?' Elaine breathed quickly.

He nodded, his dark eyes filled with pain. 'I was distraught when your maid said you had left for America to get married to a lawyer. I gave up then and I shouldn't have done.' He frowned suddenly. 'Did you get married? Did you leave him to come back to me?'

Elaine laughed and winced at the same time. 'Of course not. How could I think of marriage to anyone after loving you? It was a lie – my father must have instructed the staff to get rid of you.'

'But, why, Elaine, baby, why didn't you answer my letters?'

The use of his endearment, baby, had Elaine's head throbbing even more. Sophie. Should she tell him now? She gazed in rapt yet worried adoration at his thin pale face. He had changed so in a year, grown thinner and sort of fragile-looking, though he was still gloriously beautiful. Had absence from her done this to him? Had he pined away for her? Maybe his business commitments were worrying him. She only had a fleeting recollection of the hotel they were in before she had passed out at the bar. Luxurious and probably very expensive and expensive in Marbella was far more expensive than anywhere else. It must cost a fortune to run.

'My father kept them from me, Marcus,' she whispered fretfully, deciding not to overburden him too soon with the news that he had a baby daughter. It was enough for the time being that they had found each other again. 'I only discovered them a short while back and when I did I knew I had to find you again.'

Marcus was still frowning. 'But, darling, why should your father hold letters back from you? Why didn't he want you to see me again?'

Elaine bit her lip. 'I . . . he . . . he didn't think you suitable for me,' she went on quickly. 'He's over-protective with me because I'm all he's got left. I . . . I told him all about you and your bar and he didn't like it and . . . and the fact that you lived here, here in Marbella. I mean, he's a judge and – well, you know, criminals and all that.'

Marcus grinned and shook his head. 'There are some funny characters down here and it's sad it has such a reputation, but your father has nothing to fear. I'm not a criminal and that's all that matters.'

Elaine sighed happily. Marcus reached up and took the ice bag from her forehead and pressed his warm lips on her brow. 'You rest some more, darling, and I'll go and get you some more black coffee. I sent the doctor away and – '

'The doctor,' Elaine murmured.

'I called for one before I realized who you were. I just thought you were some drunken tourist . . .'

'Oh, crumbs,' Elaine cried and sat bolt upright, sending her head spinning. 'My friends, Lisa and Cathy! They were with me and – '

Marcus laughed. 'I sent them away too. The dark one was all for calling the police when I fell across you

272

in rapture as I realized that it was you! The other one, the blonde, is sweet, though – '

'Where did you send them?' Elaine cried, trying to swing her legs over the side of the bed but failing dismally because suddenly they were lead-weighted. Her stomach somersaulted. Had they said anything about Sophie before Marcus had dismissed them? It needed to come from her when it did, not from two strangers Marcus had never met before.

Gently Marcus eased her back against the pillows. 'I only sent them to the hotel restaurant with instructions for my staff to pander to their needs as expensively as possible,' he told her caringly. 'The poor darlings were in quite a state, shocked at first and then hysterically relieved. I'll go and tell them you are just fine.'

'Th-they didn't say anything, did they?' she asked as he got up from the bed.

'Like what?'

'Oh . . . oh, nothing,' Elaine sighed, willing her body into relaxed mode but feeling the tension winning. No, the girls would be sensible enough not to say a word about Sophie. All the same, she would rather like to speak to them before they left to go back to the *finca*.

Oh, dear. Her hand shot to her brow. What should she do now? She had found Marcus and couldn't bear to leave him just yet. He still felt the same way, adored her as she adored him. The relief was enormous, only clouded by what she knew and Marcus didn't, that she had conceived his darling child and born her and that Sophie was at this very minute being looked after by Philip up in the hills behind Marbella.

She needed time, time to be with Marcus. They had

both had a shock this afternoon and needed to settle their emotions before she told him everything. He would understand and would still love her, she had no fear of that, but not yet. She was still feeling woozy and Marcus was doing so much for her and had been very generous to the girls and she didn't want to crash Sophie on him yet. She badly needed to see Cathy and Lisa, to plead with them to look after Sophie for her till she got herself sorted out. But already she was missing her daughter.

'Marcus,' she breathed faintly as he grasped her hand to kiss it one more time before he left. 'Do . . . do you want me to stay?'

'Oh, my darling, of course I want you to stay. The girls told me what you had been through and now that we have found each other, do you think I would let you go again?'

Elaine smiled weakly. 'I do love you so, Marcus.'

'And I love you too,' he said warmly and kissed her hand yet again. 'I'll send your friends in to you later, when you've had more time to rest. You've been terribly brave to fly down here to find me. But from now on I'm never going to let you out of my sight. I'm fully booked here and would have liked your friends to stay here, too, but the girls said they are quite happy at the Don Carlos anyway. We'll have a nice dinner together one evening when we get ourselves sorted out. You have two very good friends, Elaine. They really care about you. I'll be back soon.'

'Fly here? The Don Carlos?' Elaine whimpered after Marcus had closed the door after him. What an earth had they said to him when she had been out cold?

* * *

274

'I had to think on my feet, Elaine,' Cathy berated her after the hugs and kisses and congratulations were over with and after Elaine had quickly told them that all was wonderful between her and Marcus. They were all coiled on the bed with a stronger-looking Elaine, sipping her three-hundredth black coffee to sort out her throbbing head and she'd just asked what the flying down bit was about. 'What was I to say, that we had bumped our way down here in a decrepit old camping van – '

'It isn't decrepit,' Lisa protested, but no one took any notice of her.

'With your mad brother, the hitchhiker from hell and the baby – '

'Keep your voice down,' Elaine hissed, looking urgently at the door in case Marcus came back into the bedroom.

'And that we are all bunked down in a funny old *finca* out in the campo?' Cathy ranted on in a hoarse whisper. 'Did you take a look around here before you hit the bottle, kicked the furniture around and went out cold, Elaine?'

'Steady on,' Lisa breathed in exasperation at Cathy's brashness, but no one took any notice.

'Your Marcus owns a damned exclusive establishment here. It's out of this world and he must be rolling in money. I didn't want him to think that you had hit bad times – '

'But I haven't,' Elaine protested.

'But it might have *looked* as if you had if I'd told the truth. I said we'd flown down together, yesterday, and that we were staying at the Don Carlos, which I'd heard of as being one of the best hotels on the Costa. I did it for you, Elaine, because I didn't know what else

275

to say. He was asking all sorts of questions when he took us to the restaurant.'

'The food was wonderful,' Lisa murmured appreciatively, but no one took any notice.

'My head was spinning, Elaine. I didn't want to tell him we had driven down here because we were on the run from your father. I didn't want to come across badly for you. I was terrified of mentioning Sophie – '

'You didn't, did you?' Elaine gasped.

'Of course I didn't!' It's for you to tell him, not us.' Cathy's eyes suddenly widened. 'And you haven't told him yet, have you?'

'Give me a chance, Cathy,' Elaine pouted. 'One step at a time.'

Cathy and Lisa stared at her.

Elaine put her coffee down on a glass-topped table by the bed and held her head in her hands. 'I can't tell him yet,' she reasoned weakly. 'I've been a shock to him. I've been shocked too, thinking he was getting married and then passing out and waking up in his arms. I thought I'd died and Marcus was the last person I was seeing before going down the long tunnel to the light at the end. It's all been too much. I can't cope with all this emotion.'

Cathy patted her silk-clad knee. 'Yes, I understand,' she whispered. 'I wish I hadn't come out with all that junk now, it's only complicated matters, but you can sort it out with Marcus when you feel ready to tell him everything. But you're not the only one who can't cope, Elaine. I'm almost at breaking point myself. We've grown close and have taken on your troubles too. I only lied thinking I was doing my best for you.'

'Yes, I know.' Elaine smiled as she lifted her head

out of her hands. She took a deep breath. 'You've both been wonderful.' She licked her dry lips. 'Could I ask you to be a little more wonderful for a little while longer?'

Cathy's heart sank. What now?

'Of course,' Lisa enthused. 'We'll do anything.'

'I'm not out of the woods yet. So far it has all been wonderful, like a fairy story really, but before we live happily ever after I have to tell him about Sophie and it isn't going to be easy. You've seen the state of Marcus – '

'He's gorgeous,' Lisa said enviously, 'like some French film star – you know, that Delon bloke and Distel – sort of macho but pretty, if you know what I mean. Well, I don't mean pretty exactly,' she added quickly, feeling herself going pink.

Elaine smiled at her. 'I know what you mean, Lisa. Marcus is beautiful and he was beautiful last year but he has changed. He's lost weight and looks rather gaunt and I fear I must have done that to him. Or perhaps he has money troubles taking this place on. It is rather lovely and exclusive and he must work terribly hard to keep it that way. Anyway, we need time together and I must pick my moment to tell him about Sophie. I miss her dreadfully already, but I know she will be safe and loved by you two for a couple of days. I need those couple of days,' Elaine implored. 'You do understand, don't you?'

Cathy and Lisa nodded together.

'Of course, Elaine,' Lisa told her. 'Don't worry about Sophie. She's young enough not to miss you too much, I hope, and it won't be a problem. But what about Philip? Shall we tell him everything?'

'Why not? Elaine grinned happily. 'Marcus and I

are reunited and even if my father arrived now there is nothing anyone can do about it. I'm staying with Marcus. He wants me and I want him.'

The girls nodded again. 'All's well that ends well,' Cathy said with a smile of relief as she got up from the bed. 'We're very happy for you, Elaine.'

'Better get back then,' Lisa suggested, leaning across to peck at Elaine's cheek before she got up.

'Yes, we'll give you a couple of days with Marcus and then come back to see how things are going,' Cathy suggested.

'If I don't see you first.' Elaine laughed. 'If all goes well and the shock isn't too much for Marcus, I guess he'll not be able to wait to see his daughter. So expect us up at the *finca* any time.'

'OK,' the girls murmured and left her languishing on the frothy white bed where all her dreams had come true.

'I wouldn't like to be in her shoes,' Cathy muttered after they had left the sumptuous apartment and were making their way to the front of the hotel. 'Marcus has had one shock and Sophie might be one too many.'

'He'll be over the moon. He's already in raptures with Elaine.'

'Take a look around, Lisa,' Cathy said flatly. 'Can you see a Sophie crashing around this place in one of those wheely jobs kids learn to walk in, sticky fingers all over the chrome and glass, teething problems and howling all night, waking all these rich guests who've paid a fortune to stay in the smartest place in town? No, I can't see an Armani-clad beautiful person such as Marcus taking too kindly to the baby game.'

'You're nothing but an old cynic, Cath,' Lisa snapped. 'He adores Elaine and – '

'I don't doubt that. They are admirably suited, but not the sort to have children. Let's face it, last year when we knew Elaine the last thing we imagined was her having a baby.'

'But she had one.'

'Not by choice. It was landed on her.' Cathy stopped before the last door that led into the luxurious reception area. She looked at Lisa worriedly. 'Don't you see, Lisa, Marcus has the choice. He can walk away.'

Lisa went pale. 'You mean he could yet dump her, because of Sophie?'

'Exactly!'

'But he loves her!' Lisa protested.

'But does he love her *enough*?' Cathy concluded as she swept through the door, Lisa following quickly after her, a worried expression on her face now.

'We'll just say goodbye to Marcus before we leave,' Cathy suggested, glancing across to the reception desk to see if he was around. 'He's been very good and – oh, there he is. Marcus!' she called softly, not wanting to draw too much attention in case some of the guests who had witnessed Elaine's collapse were still around to heap more disapproving looks on them.

'Cathy!'

Cathy spun around as if she had been shot at. Her face whitened, her body froze. Lisa let out a small mewing sound as she bumped into her.

'Cathy, darling, how *wonderful* to see you.'

'Ah, Mr Bond, I've been paging you,' Marcus said as he strode towards them. 'Some faxes for you. Ah, Cathy and Lisa, are you leaving?'

At the speed of light, Cathy inwardly screeched as she stared at Charles in shocked disbelief. Charles

Bond, of all people? Staying here, of all places? Here in Marbella? It was impossible!

'Er . . . er . . . yes, Marcus. Er . . . thanks a bundle for the meal and . . . and, er . . . see you again.' She snatched at Lisa and fairly hurtled her through the doorway without giving a bemused Charles a second look.

'Cathy!' he bawled at her, just as he used to bawl at her when he needed her in his office. 'I didn't come all this way to have you walk out on me again! Get back here!'

Dragging a whimpering Lisa behind her, Cathy ran for her life, parting crowds of holidaymakers as easily as Moses parted the red sea.

Lungs fit to collapse, breath coming in short bursts, Cathy threw herself across the bonnet of the Mercedes and pounded it furiously as Lisa fumbled with the key in the lock.

'I don't believe it!' she croaked as she slumped in the passenger seat while Lisa reversed like a bat out of hell and, with a scream of rubber on tarmac, hurtled along the road.

'Cool it. It was a coincidence running into him, Cath,' Lisa tried to reassure her.

'Coincidence my foot!' Cathy exploded. 'You heard him, he hadn't come all this way to have me walk out on him again. The man is a maniac! He followed me here! That bloody stalker *was* working for him. You said you thought someone was following us – well, you thought wrong in thinking it was Elaine's private detective. It was Charles's detective. He's been with us all the way!'

Lisa blanched and shifted uncomfortable.

'But why, Lisa? Why should he do that?'

Lisa shrugged and bit her lip.

'Hah!' Cathy suddenly grinned and settled back in her seat. 'No problem, no problem at all.'

'Wh-what do you mean?'

'He's found me now, so the heat is off.'

'What do you mean?' Lisa almost screamed.

'He's staying at Marcus's hotel. It was obvious that we knew Marcus and he knew us. He probably knows where we are staying by now and he'll call off his detective and I'm home and dry.'

Lisa sighed, reluctant to ask yet again, what did she mean?

'You see, a few white lies come in very handy at times,' Cathy laughed, relaxing back in her seat. 'If Charles asks Marcus about me, Marcus will say we are staying at the Don Carlos as I told him and we're not, are we, we're staying at the *Finca* Esmeralda and no one but we know that?'

'Elaine does,' Lisa reluctantly volunteered.

'Huh, Elaine. If I know her, she'll be on the Planet Marcus for a good while yet and we'll be forgotten. They haven't seen each other for over a year so they probably won't surface to the real world for days. By then Charles will have given up.'

Without Lisa seeing, Cathy crossed her fingers in her lap. She closed her eyes, humming a tune so as not to allow her real thoughts of concern show to her friend. Truth was, she was shocked beyond belief, her heart racing like a piston engine, her insides churning like butter. Just when she was beginning to forget his very existence, Charles was there in her face again.

And his appearance had nothing to do with feelings for her. Charles had never been that caring and his behaviour after her walking out on him had been bizarre to say the least. The man had followed her to Marbella for another reason, a reason that was becoming ever more sinister. What in heaven's name was he up to?

CHAPTER 12

Lisa needed a hug. A big, fat, all-comforting hug.
She wished with all her heart she hadn't cast Philip
aside, like a Kleenex before she had even used it.

She pulled up the dusty uneven track of *Finca*
Esmeralda and hoped Philip would be waiting. After
telling him Elaine's wonderful news and waiting for
him to digest it, she wanted to throw herself in his
arms and beg for forgiveness. And then she wanted to
unload on him all her fears and worries, a million
questions that needed to be answered because she was
so confused. Who was Greg? Was he a private detective? If so, did he work for Philip's stepfather or work
for Charles Bond, whom everyone in the world
seemed to know? And what was Cathy's involvement
in all this? Her very best friend who didn't fool her for
a minute. Even now she was feigning sleep after
making light of Charles's shocking appearance at
Marcus's hotel. Cathy was worried sick.

'We're back,' she told her, pulling up outside the
finca and switching off the engine. Lisa didn't move,
though. She sat back and closed her eyes, exhausted
with driving, exhausted with thinking.

'You'd better tell Philip everything,' Cathy uttered

as she wearily got out of the car. 'I'm going for a shower and a siesta.'

They were hardly out of the car before Philip descended on them, hot and flustered, not in a good mood. The girls groaned.

'Where is she?' he bawled.

'Where's Greg?' Cathy countered.

'Out! He's been gone all day, leaving me to cope on my own. Sophie has been a little devil all day. Do you two know what time it is? Gone five! I've been distraught with worry. Where the hell is Elaine?'

Of course he would be concerned for his sister, but a small thought for them wouldn't go amiss, Lisa thought despondently.

'Don't be so dramatic, Philip,' Cathy cut back at him. 'How can a four-month-old baby be a little devil? And if you think Elaine's future can be sorted out in five minutes flat, you are an even bigger nerd than I took you for! I'll go and see to Sophie while you whip Lisa to within an inch of her life for supporting *your* sister through a trauma you wouldn't have had a clue how to cope with!' She stormed off inside the *Finca*.

Lisa ran her fingers through her cropped hair. 'She's had a hard day, her nerves are frazzled,' she told Philip by way of an apology for Cathy's vitriol.

Philip's shoulders sagged wearily. 'Join the club,' he muttered under his breath and then gave her a weak smile. 'I'm sorry. You must be tired too. It's been a long day without you.'

Lisa's heart did a spin and she smiled weakly.

Philip stepped towards her and enfolded her in his arms and Lisa got the big, fat, blessedly comforting hug she so badly needed.

'Go and stretch out by the pool,' he murmured in her ear, 'and I'll mix you a long cool drink and you can tell me all about it.'

Lisa did as she was bid, slowly sauntering around the *finca* to the pool, which looked so coolly inviting she was tempted to plunge in fully clothed. But she didn't. She slumped into a long padded lounger that she hadn't seen before and stretched out and closed her eyes. All manner of thoughts tumbled around in her head but at least she was relieved of worry over Elaine. *She* was in safe hands.

She heard Philip approach and blinked open her eyes to see him place a tray of iced drinks on a nearby low table which she hadn't seen before either Philip perched himself on another lounger and handed her a tall glass with a slice of lemon in it.

'Where did all this new furniture come from?' she asked, more to make conversation than anything else. She had a lot to tell him, about Elaine and then hopefully about how she was feeling about him; that she was very sorry she had told him where to go when, in her heart, she knew she wouldn't be able to bear it if she never saw him again after this holiday.

'The place is very sadly lacking in creature comforts and I bought these yesterday when I ordered the dish washer. I also found out the place was up for sale and thought I might like to buy it. What do you think?'

Did her opinion matter? Lisa thought wearily. Nice if it did.

'Wouldn't you rather hear about Elaine's fate?' she asked.

'Cathy was in the kitchen boiling water for Sophie's feed, she's taking her up to her room with her. She actually apologized for her outburst just now and said

I wasn't to worry, Elaine was on cloud nine and you would tell me all about it.'

Lisa sipped her drink and pulled a face.

Philip laughed softly. 'Gin and tonic, loads of tonic so don't think I'm trying to pull your defences down. Cathy said you might need something reviving as you did all the driving and didn't have a drink on the coast. She added, rather wryly, that Elaine had made up for it. What's that all about?'

Slowly Lisa told him all about it, from beginning to end. She didn't leave anything out because everything was relevant – everything that was relevant to Elaine, that was. Charles Bond she would leave till later, because Philip's only concern for the moment was his sister.

To his credit Philip listened without interrupting, occasionally nodding, occasionally rubbing his brow with concern. Eventually he let out a long sigh when Lisa came to a finish.

'So what did you think of this Marcus?' he asked.

'Personally I thought him wonderful. He's very caring and obviously adores Elaine and his hotel is out of this world so he must be pretty secure financially.'

'But?'

'But what?

'You sound a little hesitant.'

Lisa sipped some more of her drink which was nearly finished now. It had relaxed her and cooled her down. She felt a little languid though.

'It was something Cathy said to me as we were leaving,' she told him, pushing aside what else had happened as they were leaving. 'Elaine hadn't told him about Sophie, she said that she needed time.

Cathy was doubtful that Elaine was home and dry yet.'

'What did she mean?' Philip asked anxiously.

'That perhaps Marcus wasn't the sort to be baby-orientated and the shock might be too much for him. There is no doubt in my mind the he loves Elaine, but Cathy thought it might not be enough when he finds out he has a daughter.'

Philip nodded sagely. 'I did try and warn her.'

'So you agree with Cathy,' Lisa murmured dismally. If Philip thought that too, from a man's point of view, there might be some substance to it. 'But surely if he loves her, he'll want a family at some stage? It follows.'

Philip shook his head this time. 'Not necessarily.'

Lisa squirmed in her seat. It sounded as if Philip was with Cathy all the way on this. Nice to think they agreed on something, but that *something* was all important. Philip couldn't be the devoted uncle she had wanted him to be. He had just called Sophie a little devil because today she hadn't been the sweet little thing she normally was. Parenting was all about taking the rough with the smooth. If he couldn't accept that, he wouldn't make a good father himself.

'Is there another drink?' she asked, holding out her empty glass, not wanting to think that she was leaping off into the wide blue yonder again and imagining Philip fathering her children.

Philip poured her another drink from a tall jug clinking with ice.

'I warned her about holiday romances,' he went on gravely. 'I've had a few myself and they mean nothing . . .' Lisa gulped her drink. 'It appears this one has gone further than I suspected it might, but Sophie might be over the top for Marcus. I think Cathy has a very valid point.'

'I think you and Cathy have more in common than either of you ever dreamed,' Lisa told him tightly. 'You are both cynics. She wasn't born with her cynicism, but has had it bestowed on her by man's betrayal. What's your excuse?' she added thinly.

He looked at her for a good long minute, a minute in which Lisa wished a sunbeam would come down and whisk her off to somewhere else.

'I don't have an *excuse* for being the way I am,' he told her stiffly, 'but I have numerous *reasons* for not living in the romantic dream world that you and Elaine obviously inhabit. I don't know about you, but Elaine's has been cosseted in cotton wool all her life. She might have lost her mother in tragic circumstances, which is not to be belittled, but that is the sum total of the tragedy in her life. I have seen enough adultery, betrayal, pain and hurt inflicted by my father on my mother before and after their divorce to last me a lifetime; because of that I don't get too seriously involved with women. Yes, I have reason to be cynical about love and about how men treat women, but it is not an *excuse*.'

'And I'm not even going to say I'm sorry for suggesting such a thing,' Lisa suddenly blurted out and slammed her unfinished drink down on the table and swung her legs over the side of her lounger. 'Because you, Philip Mainwaring, are a flirt and a womanizer, you use women but refuse to involve your heart. You believe that, confronted with a baby, Marcus will run for his life because that is exactly what *you* would do because *you* are too *selfish* to commit yourself to any woman.'

She stood up and glared down at him. 'You might have convinced yourself that you are doing women a favour by dropping them like hot bricks after you have used them; your warped sense of reasoning might tell you that you have your father's genes so therefore "love 'em and leave 'em before it's too late" is a damned good philosophy to live by, but you don't fool me. You are simply selfish. You forget that your father once loved your mother deeply enough to marry her. How can you judge what went on in their relationship when it wasn't *your* heart involved? Get a life of your own, Philip, don't live in the shadows of what you believe your father was and the side of his nature you fear you might have inherited!'

She left him with not a look of hurt as before, when she had lashed out at him, but more a look of utter astonishment.

Upstairs, she threw herself in a heap on her bed and lay there, equally astonished. What demon had possessed her to come out with all that? All that amateur psychology? She didn't have it in her, surely? She *was* right, she sensed, but the feeling held no satisfaction. She shouldn't have thrown his past in his face like that, but her only excuse was that she loved him and was despondent that he could never love her.

He didn't have the love gene in him, only the lust gene, which might be fun for five minutes but wasn't lasting enough for life. Suddenly she felt inexplicably sorry for him. He had a helluva lot of emotional baggage to carry around with him and not all his own. What an uncomplicated life she had led. Her parents adored each other, not a single hiccup in their married life to give her any grievances in her own love life. Except she had one now. She loved a man who didn't know the meaning of the word; not for himself would he contemplate it, nor for anyone else, like Marcus, whom he didn't even know. It wasn't fair to impose his own thinking on what someone else might do. Marcus would *not* run a mile when he heard about his baby daughter. He would take Elaine in his arms and hug her and kiss her and say all manner of wonderful things and yes, they jolly well would live happily ever after!

'Lisa, I've made you coffee,' came from the doorway.

She rolled over to see Philip standing there sheepishly. And sheepish didn't suit Philip – why should he be looking that way anyway? She was the one who had rammed into his emotions, headbutting him with her silly amateur psychology.

'Oh, hell, Philip, I'm sorry,' she said quickly, sitting up and running her fingers through her hair. 'I didn't mean to offend you and drag your past up and fling it in your face.'

'I brought my past up and flung it in your lovely face, Lisa. It's for me to apologize, not you. As I believe I've said before, you humble me.'

'And being humble you don't like,' Lisa reminded him with a twinkle in her eye. She shifted so he could sit on the edge of her bed and took the mug of coffee he handed her.

'Bloody dismal room this,' he commented, looking around at the narrow window, which started at the floor rather than midway up the wall and let in the minimum of light.

'You commandeered the best in the house,' she laughed, 'the one with the double bed.'

He looked down at his hands. 'I had immoral intentions,' he said softly.

'Oh,' Lisa murmured, her heart again doing that funny Highland fling thing.

He looked up and his eyes were softly tempting her, sort of slumberous and yet at the same time teasing. 'Is "oh" all you can say?'

'What do you expect of me?'

'Something like another tirade that I might be more prepared for this time.'

'Did I shock you with my accusations?'

'Surprised might be closer to it – they were an endorsement of what I think of myself at times, a selfish bastard. Also surprised that you could have assessed me so quickly in our relationship.'

'I'm not as dumb as I look, Philip.'

'Dumb I never thought you were,' he laughed softly.

'Good,' she said. 'Now, what is this tirade you expect me to give you and which you are well prepared for now? Might it have anything to do with that immoral intention of yours?'

'Come to my bed now, Lisa,' he murmured and took the coffee mug from her fingers as if he expected her to leap up and with a cry of 'Wahey!' hurtle out of the room before him, straight to his room across the hallway.

Lisa lay back on her pillows and thought how delicious power felt when you were in control. This whole trip was a learning curve for her. A while back she might have gratefully leapt into his bed and thought herself the luckiest girl alive. Not that she was promiscuous, not that she had ever . . . But she badly wanted Philip, always had done and always would. But all of them were teaching her lessons in life, in their own different ways. She felt sure that Cathy and Greg must have had good reason to have rowed; because Cathy had avoided telling her anything, she suspected that what she was keeping from her wasn't something she was proud of. They had been alone that first night here, Cathy was already halfway to being in love with Greg and could have fallen into Greg's bed on the rebound from Charles. And now they were at loggerheads with each other.

Elaine's affair last year had turned out well this year, but only by fluke. It could very easily have gone the wrong way and left her heart broken. It might still if Cathy and Philip were right and Lisa was wrong.

Lisa couldn't take any chances with her heart. It would hurt too badly if Philip used her. Much as she wanted him, it had to be on her terms, not his. So she would have to turn him down yet again.

Suddenly the powerful feeling evaporated out of her. She had no power over Philip, but if she tally-ho'ed into his bed he would have all the power in the world over her and her heart.

'I think we've been down this route before, Philip,' she told him softly. 'I might be like Elaine in many ways, but there is no cotton wool over my eyes. Your bed, with you beside me, would be nice, but I'm not going to be another of your statistics.'

He leaned across her and took her lips under his and kissed her so dreamily she wondered if she was spouting rubbish and what she really wanted was the caveman treatment, over his shoulder and tossed down on his bed and ravaged to heaven.

But at the very least he hadn't tried to reassure her that she wouldn't be just another statistic.

But suddenly she was lost in paradise as he manoeuvred himself to lie beside her. Her skin was suddenly burning, senses spinning. His arms enfolded her and her heart missed a few more vital beats till she thought she might faint. She felt his hand move across her breast and it was like before, so deeply arousing it hurt. She ached unmercifully for him, her breasts, her loins, every muscle in her body wanted to envelop him and draw him down into her being. She just wanted him, bodily, spiritually – she wanted it all. But Philip could only give her short measure with his attitude to love.

'I want you more than I have ever wanted any woman in my life,' he murmured heatedly into her throat. 'I'm prepared to sell my soul to the devil for you. I want you, Lisa, and I know you want me. You're driving me crazy.'

No doubt, Lisa thought as he ground against her, parting her lips, moving against her so sexily she was almost tempted to give in, to let him into her, to satisfy this hunger that gnawed at her. His hand on her inner thigh nearly spun her out of control. She clung to him, fingers clawing into the back of his silk shirt, her body taut against his, his responding in short rhythmic thrusts against her pelvis.

It was too much, she was losing her grip, the tide of sexual response to him threatening to sweep away all negative thought.

And then he drew back from her, shocking her body till it trembled with rejection and her eyes widened painfully.

He stood up quickly. She wondered what was happening because it was obvious that his arousal was still potent and yet he had stopped himself.

'I can't do this,' he muttered, refusing to look her in

the eye. He raked both hands through his hair and went for the door and then he turned, more composed. 'The ball is in your court, so to speak, Lisa. I don't want this on my conscience. Christ,' he added as he went out the door, 'I didn't know I had one!'

Lisa coiled into a ball and bit hard on her pillow. She didn't know whether to laugh or cry. Her body ached with rejection and lack of fulfilment and she could well cry with frustration, but at the same time she felt well . . . jubilant. Philip did have feelings after all. Somehow she had brought his conscience to the fore. He had rejected her just when it seemed his intentions towards her were about to come to fruition. A man who could do that must have a heart, to say nothing of an iron-like will. Her own body was still trembling with desire.

She heard his bedroom door slam shut and she closed her eyes in sufferance, but to put the ball in her court, *so to speak*, was very unfair. She would have to go to him and that wasn't really the intention. She, being a woman, wanted it all, him to make the commitment, him to make the running, him to make her feel she was the only girl in the world for him.

But she'd gone wrong somewhere. She sighed into her pillow, exhaustion sapping her thinking. This was supposed to be a relaxing holiday, but it was stress on top of more stress from morning to night.

And she hadn't even had a chance to unburden her other worries on to Philip's shoulders. Cathy and Greg and Charles Bond. Oh, it was too much. She buried her face in the pillow till her breathing evened out and she felt herself slipping out of it all and into a deep sleep.

* * *

Cathy jolted awake at a door slamming and turned over to see if the noise had woken Sophie, who was parked by her bed in her buggy sleeping peacefully.

The baby was the image of Marcus now that she had seen him. In another few months, the baby's hair would be hanging in dark ringlets just like her father's.

How could Philip call her a little devil when she was such an angel? Mind you, she was a female and obviously already had the talent to twirl Philip around her tiny chubby fingers and wind him up. Let's hope she had the same talent to win over her father Marcus.

Rotten of her to think so cynically. She would never have admitted that to Elaine herself – the poor love had been through enough – but she couldn't help not taking everything as optimistically as Elaine and Lisa did.

Because of that traitor Charles. Cathy started twirling her hair. Why an earth was he pursuing her so relentlessly? If she had just bumped into him on the Marbella esplanade, she might have put it down to coincidence, a squeaky coincidence, maybe, but not beyond the realms of possibility. But in Marcus's hotel and with that remark about having come this far and she wasn't running out on him again, it suggested that he had followed her down here. And the stalker back in Battersea – had Charles instructed him? Had they been followed down here all the way by some nasty little nerd who earned a living by spying on other people?

Cathy sighed deeply. She would never make a Miss Marple or a Hercule Poirot. It was all a mystery to her.

She heard a car throbbing to a halt on the driveway and got up from the bed to look out. It was Greg and her heart turned over. She wished they hadn't fallen out. She wished she could run downstairs and throw herself into his arms and for him to give her a good hard hug and make her feel that all was well with the world. But a verbal slap in the face she wouldn't be able to bear.

She'd go and make him a drink, though. He looked as bedraggled as they had when they had got back from Marbella. His hair was damp at the collar of his checked short-sleeved shirt; the back of the shirt itself was damp and his white chinos were badly creased. The car he had hired obviously didn't have the benefit of air-conditioning as the Mercedes had.

She wheeled a still-sleeping Sophie into the kitchen with her to see him already helping himself to a cold drink from the fridge.

'I was going to do that for you. You look bushed.'

'Hard day,' he muttered, not looking at her.

'Yeah, bird-watching must be exhausting,' she tried to joke.

He came and stood in front of her, very close; his eyes were dark and ringed, and very cold.

'Yeah, depends on the species of birds you are watching,' he said in a tone that chilled Cathy's bone marrow because it implied he wasn't talking about the feathered variety. He turned away and went outside to drink his drink under the shades on the terrace.

Cathy poured herself a drink, a lemonade with a dash of gin to give it some oomph. She might come away from this trip with a drink-dependency problem if she wasn't careful, but it was turning out to be one of those holidays from hell. Stress, stress, stress, instead of sun, sun, sun.

'So, you've been out all day, chatting up birds and

one turned you down. Tough, but don't take it out on me,' she told him, plopping into a wicker chair across from him.

He drank thirstily before speaking, ignoring her remark and asking about Elaine.

Cathy told him, as briefly and concisely as she could, leaving out the Elaine drunk and falling on the floor fiasco, for the sake of Elaine's pride.

'So how come you just happened to walk into that particular hotel and Marcus was just there?'

Cathy thought it an odd question but didn't give it much thought. She shrugged. 'It was the first one we came to after finding his old bar closed down. We all needed a drink,'

'And what else did you do while you were down there?'

Cathy looked at him warily. Anyone would think they'd had time to shop till they dropped and to play every gaming machine in every bar along the coast.

'The point of the trip was to reunite Elaine with Marcus, Greg. There wasn't time for anything else. We left Elaine with Marcus and came home.'

'And that's it, is it?' he ground out, gazing into the distance.

'Yes, that's it,' Cathy repeated, her dark eyes narrowing. 'And what's with the inquisition? What's it to do with you what I do with my time?'

This time he turned and gave her his full attention, but not the sort of attention she craved. His eyes were still cold and hostile, now with added suspicion to boot.

'It's everything to do with me!' he snapped. 'I thought we had something special going and – '

Cathy exploded at that. A 'huh!' that halted him in

mid-sentence. If he was coming the old possession bit on her, he could think again.

'According to you yesterday morning, we have nothing going, Greg Turner! What an earth has brought this on? Do you think I've been down in Marbella scouting for a replacement for you?' She got to her feet and was sorely tempted to tip the remaining contents of her glass over him. 'I'm not even flattered that you might be jealous, Greg. You can't come up with the goods yourself, but you obviously object if anyone else is in the running. That doesn't warm my heart, it hardens it. Jealousy is healthy, possession ain't.'

She was about to sweep back into the kitchen when Greg caught her and swung her round into his arms, pressing her hard up against the door jamb. He was angry, very angry. Cathy stiffened in his grip.

'Damn you! I told you from the start I didn't need this, but you have got under my skin. I find my thoughts going soft on me where you are concerned and I don't need that either. I need my wits about me with you, but I am failing. What really burns me up is that there are two sides to you, apparently. One warm and giving, the other so bloody tricky I think you quite capable of deceiving me and winning in the end.'

'For goodness' sake, Greg, what's got into you?' Cathy blurted out in astonishment, too weak and confused now to struggle under his grip. She might be crazy about this man, but for sure she didn't understand him.

Suddenly his grip on her slackened. She physically felt the strength drain out of him. His head dropped forward and he couldn't look at her.

'I'm sorry,' he uttered helplessly. 'I'm going completely crazy with all this.'

'All what?' Cathy murmured. Couldn't he cope with her? Was she what he thought, double-edged, warm and giving one minute, tricky the next? She guessed she might have confused him, as she could easily swing from warm to abrasive, but it was the way she was. But perhaps that was the wrong way to be with him. For all she knew, he had a sad past with women, had been hurt and couldn't show how he really felt towards her. *Something special going*? She knew they had and now he had said it but neither of them was handling it very well.

She lifted her hands and linked them around his neck and pulled him towards her. 'Greg,' she whispered, 'what on earth is happening between us? It started out so good and now it's downhill all the way.'

She leaned her head back to look into his face. She smiled. The hard warmth of his body against hers, pinning her to the door frame, was all she needed to know that he was worth fighting for. She loved the feel of him, his touch, his smell, his very being. She didn't want to lose him and he had given her enough fuel to feed her with the thought that there *was* something special between them and he didn't want to lose it either.

'Yesterday was a nightmare,' she confessed in a hushed whisper, 'me glowering at you, you glowering at me. Today was fraught with Elaine's troubles and then I'm back here and Philip is glowering at me and I find myself shouting at him. I fell asleep feeling wretched and then I woke up and heard your car. My heart flipped and I suddenly realized how much I had missed you all day and I realized that the one thing I

299

wanted was you to give me a big hug and make it all go away.'

'Oh, Cathy,' he moaned, burying his face in her hair. 'We don't need all this – Elaine and her troubles, all this outside interference. I just want to take you away somewhere where no one can find us. Just us together.'

'Go on the run and leave the others to it?' Cathy laughed softly. 'I wish we could. Oh, Greg, let's start again. Let's forget everything: our awful rows, me pushing you in the pool, you and your hang-ups, me and mine. I came on this trip to escape, but it isn't exactly working out that way. I'm still stressed out. I want to forget it all.'

Greg stiffened in her arms and Cathy wondered what she had said that was wrong. She'd thought she was coming over loud and clear that she was willing to start over again.

She hugged him tighter. 'Please, Greg, give me the chance to make it all right. I'm not a tricky lady, just a little confused at times. I do and say the silliest things and get myself into all sorts of messes.'

'Yes, you can say that again,' he murmured, responding to her warmth and clinging to her. 'But I can help and I will. Someone along the way has got their wires crossed.'

She laughed softly. 'That's a funny thing to say when it's us who've got our wires crossed.'

'So how about us getting our bodies crossed over each other's then?' he suggested softly, breathing kisses across her throat till he reached her mouth and claimed it, demanding an answer.

She gave him her answer in the depth of her kiss, a kiss that swept all doubts and past reasoning out of the

300

way, leaving nothing but clear water ahead. He ran his hands down her body to her hips and pulled her hard against him.

'Now,' he murmured, 'let's block it all out, forget who we are and why we are here. Let me get inside you and we'll take off together. And afterwards we'll indulge in the pillow talk we didn't indulge in before. Afterwards you can confide in me. It's the only way, Cathy. Clear your conscience and let me help you.'

If it wasn't for the fact that Greg was lulling her into madness here in the doorway of the kitchen, his hand caressing her so erotically under her flimsy skirt, his heated kisses along her throat, blazing her skin with reckless abandon, she might question that peculiar suggestion. Her conscience was clear but . . .

'Oh, 'struth,' she moaned as he slid his hand under the lace of her briefs. 'Oh, Greg, not another doorway,' she groaned helplessly.

He laughed softly, nipped her earlobe and was about to sweep her up into his arms when a small fretful wail brought them both to a stiffened halt.

'Oh, no, Sophie is awake.'

'And she isn't even ours,' Greg bit out in frustration. Before Cathy could turn to attend to the baby Greg grasped her hard to him and pressed his mouth over hers and then released her. 'Come up to my room when you've finished,' he whispered. 'I'll be waiting.'

He left her to deal with Sophie and Cathy sighed and gazed down at the baby, who was now gurgling and smiling up at her. 'You are a little devil after all, Sophie Morton, but don't try tricks like that on your daddy. Best behaviour for him or you could land your mummy in another fine mess.'

She had just put the kettle on and had a clean

disposable nappy in her hand when Philip walked into the kitchen. His brow was furrowed and he was looking as if he'd successfully predicted the winning line of the lottery, but his local newsagents' computer had broken down on the ticket before his.

'Never mind, Philip, tomorrow is another day. This should cheer you up though, the little devil's nappy needs changing.' She smiled sweetly and plonked the disposable in his hand. 'And it's for yoo-hoo,' she cooed, pointing an index finger at him.

He looked at her as if she was mad. 'And where are you going?'

'Don't ask!' She swept out of the kitchen and leapt the stone steps two at a time.

She fell on Greg, who was sprawled out on his bed still fully clothed and almost dropping off to sleep.

'Gotcha,' she laughed, 'you were nearly gone then.'

'Not anymore,' he breathed as he pulled at her clothes.

It took the record for stripteases, four seconds with no extra time for injuries. They were suddenly naked in each other's arms and their pace slowing rapidly, wanting to relish every touch, every kiss, every heartbeat.

'You have the body of a goddess,' Greg murmured over her.

'Don't stop,' Cathy uttered weakly, running her tongue over the line of his mouth till he groaned helplessly. And he didn't stop, he increased the seductive pressure on her breasts till she squirmed with desire. 'I meant the compliments. More, more.'

'OK, you win, though it goes against my nature as you well know. You have the body of a goddess, and um . . . er . . . and er . . .'

302

'Oh, forget it.' Cathy sighed happily as his hands ran over her hips and between her legs, raising her pulsing senses to astounding heights. 'Silence is golden with you. Wow, platinum when push comes to shove.'

Greg moaned as he moved over her goddess-like body. 'You sure have a way with words yourself.'

'Oh, shut up, Greg,' Cathy cried as she wrapped her legs around him to draw him fully into her. And not another word was spoken as they moved together, bonded in perfect rhythm, tuned into each other's needs as completely as if they were made for each other.

A good while later Cathy stirred herself. She shifted her position to look down on a sleeping Greg. He ought to be looking completely relaxed after their wonderful lovemaking, but there were lines of tension around his eyes and mouth that hadn't been there when she had first met him on the ferry. Over the few days they had been together it appeared his tension had grown; it was a small disturbing thought that marred her complete happiness.

She ran a finger very lightly over the small scar on his chin and she realized how little she knew about him. Odd, but he was a very open sort of guy and yet when she thought about it he seemed a closed book as well. He was a bit of an enigma, she thought, fascinating because of it but at the same time it left her with a feeling that she wasn't making him happy. And that wasn't a good feeling.

She bent and kissed his brow and stroked his sunbleached hair back from his face and then left him undisturbed.

She showered and slipped on a cool sarong skirt and vest top and went downstairs to look for Lisa. She found her in the kitchen, cooking, which was comforting because it reminded her of home.

'Where's Sophie?'

'Philip has taken her for a wander around the garden in the hope she will sleep well tonight. I've offered to have her tonight and you can have her tomorrow night.'

Lisa poured a couple of glasses of wine and pushed one across the tiled work surface to Cathy.

'Seems this holiday is turning out to be a babysitting marathon,' Cathy said ruefully. 'I hope Elaine gets herself sorted out before long.'

Lisa sighed and nodded in the direction of the terrace. 'I'm cooking something light, artichokes and pork in wine sauce. It can wait. Let's go outside.' She sighed as she sat down. 'We're not getting much of a break, are we? I know Elaine has footed the bill for all this, but I did hope for some time to enjoy ourselves.' She turned her head to look at Cathy and smiled ruefully. 'But we're not, are we?'

'You too,' Cathy muttered, then she let out a long sigh. 'It's not good with you and Philip, is it?'

'Could be better. What about you and Greg?'

Cathy stared down at her glass of wine. 'I've just left him, he's sleeping now.'

'Oh, 'struth,' Lisa uttered. 'It's got that far, then?'

Cathy shrugged and gulped at her wine. She could imagine what Lisa was thinking. Too much too soon wasn't very smart.

'After all that business down on the coast with Elaine and Marcus and then that dreadful encounter with Charles, well, I just needed him, Lisa,' she confessed. 'I'm in love with him and – '

'You don't even know him,' Lisa said sharply.

'I do and I don't,' Cathy admitted, 'but it doesn't alter my feelings for him. I've searched my soul and put up all the reasons against: rebound from Charles, stressed out because I've no job, but it doesn't make any difference. I care very deeply for him and I think he cares very deeply for me, but . . .'

'But what?' Lisa urged when Cathy faltered.

Cathy shrugged. 'Something is holding him back. I don't know what, but something about me is troubling him. It's as if he expects me to be someone I'm not; I know that sounds peculiar, but I just feel it.'

Lisa rubbed her forehead. 'Cath, I need to tell you something,' she said softly. 'I don't understand it myself. I've tried to reason it out, but as soon as I think I'm getting there it all falls apart. I know you are close to Greg now, but there is something I know that you don't.'

'About Greg?' Cathy asked. 'Has Philip said something about him?' She laughed shortly. 'Take whatever Philip says with a pinch of salt. He can't stand the sight of me and has seen me and Greg grow closer and he's probably as jealous as hell.'

'Philip doesn't fancy you,' Lisa objected.

'No, but he fancies *you* and is not getting very far by the look on both your faces.'

'That's not fair!'

'Sorry,' Cathy mumbled, 'No, it wasn't fair.'

There was a long silence before Lisa admitted, 'No, it isn't going well with me and Philip, but I'm more concerned for you at the moment. Greg isn't what he seems and I'm deeply suspicious of him and Philip hasn't said anything, it's just me.'

'What do you mean, suspicious?'

'Well, don't you think it peculiar? Him being here with us all?'

'I haven't a clue what you're getting at.'

Lisa sighed. 'I haven't a clue what I'm getting at, actually. I've been thinking that Philip is in on this as well, because he and Greg seem so familiar with each other.'

'Greg is that sort of a person, I suppose. He gets on well with everyone – everyone except you, because you are looking out for my interests since we are friends. Anyway, what do you mean, Philip is in on this as well?'

Lisa took a deep breath. 'I think all this was pre-arranged, Greg being with us. Look how he has smarmed his way in. Got a lift down with us, Philip inviting him to stay here. And . . . well, Elaine got me to thinking he might have been following her. You know what I said on the way down to Marbella about a private detective? You scotched that one for me by saying if Elaine's father was against her and Marcus he would have stopped her before we got here. No, I don't think Elaine and Marcus have anything to do with Greg. But . . . well . . . I think he is here for a purpose. You.'

Cathy gazed at her in awe and then she burst out laughing. 'Are you mad or what? Are you suggesting Greg has been following *me?*' Suddenly a huge dawning thought wiped the laughter from her lips. Her eyes widened to saucers. She glared at Lisa, her mind racing back to what Lisa had said before. 'What the bloody hell did you mean, you know something I don't?'

Lisa shakily reached for her wine glass and drank

thirstily. 'OK, I know I should have told you sooner. I was going to check with the boys first, John and Gerry, but they were out when I called and since then I haven't really had a chance to try again. And Greg seemed all right and you and he were getting on fine,' she went on in a rush. 'And Philip obviously thought him OK and I wasn't too worried. And then everything has been so hectic here and – '

'And will you get to the point, Lisa!' Cathy insisted.

'I . . . the day we left, – you know, when the boys were seeing us off – I looked back in the mirror. Someone got out of the blue Rover and went and spoke to them. It . . . it was Greg, Cathy. I recognized him on the ferry. I think Greg is your Battersea stalker,' she admitted in a hoarse whisper.

Stunned, Cathy wasn't sure if she had heard right, then suddenly a horrible reasoning rushed her senses till she felt quite sick. A huge tangled web of mind-blowing thoughts hit her. If it wasn't for one overwhelming thought, she would laugh this off as one of Lisa's crazy fantasies. And that one over-whelming thought loomed in the shape of someone she had thought she would never seen again – Charles Bond.

Cathy got to her feet, unsteady because of the blow Lisa had just dealt her. She didn't know what was happening here, not yet, but soon she would know.

'Where are you going?' Lisa asked faintly as Cathy turned to go back into the house.

'I need some space and time to think about this,' she murmured tightly. Then she turned to Lisa and said quickly. 'Lisa, don't mention this to anyone, will you? Not to Philip or Greg, no one. Say nothing, nothing about your suspicions. Promise me you won't?'

'Of course I promise, but where are on earth are you going?'

'For a walk.'

'Well, don't be long then. I'm cooking supper.'

Cathy snatched up the keys to the Mercedes from a table by the big oak front door and flew out into the night. She wouldn't be back for supper. She might not even get back for breakfast because what she had to thrash out with Charles Bond was going to take a long time.

She was piecing it all together now, like working with an upside-down jigsaw puzzle, the picture face down. It was hard but not impossible. Charles knew the scenario and she knew just where to find him as he had known just where to find her.

The bastard. And as for that other bastard Greg Turner! It was obvious he was in this with Charles, hired to keep an eye on her in case she ran off with the money. She wondered if it was still in her bank account, the million sodding quid Charles had planted on her for safekeeping till a later date, the money he had embezzled out of the company they had both worked for. No wonder he had been so persistent in trying to get her back. No wonder his accomplice, scar-faced Turner, had stuck to her like glue and seduced her to keep her within his sights.

Oh, yes, so much fitted into place, she fumed as she sped down the narrow mountain road that led to Marbella. And when she got hold of Charles embezzler Bond, he would wish he had never been born.

CHAPTER 13

'Happy, darling?' Marcus asked warmly.

Elaine squeezed his hand as he opened the door of
the apartment after a tour of his lovely hotel. Wearing
the same clothes, but refreshed after a shower, she
guessed some of his guests had recognized her as the
mad woman who had fainted at the bar. But with
Marcus beside her she was able to volley back those
curious looks with the haughty air of one who knew
that Marcus adored her and she could do that every
night of the week if she so wished.

But she'd never touch a drop again. She had no
need. All her dreams had come true.

'Oh, Marcus, I'm so proud of you. Your old bar was
lovely, but this place is something else.'

'And all down to you, of course. I was so distraught
at losing you that it fired me to achieve all this. I have
the best chefs on the *costa*, the finest staff, the finest
guests and now I have you back in my life and I
couldn't be happier.'

He drew her into his arms in the gleaming white-
and-gold sitting-room. As his mouth closed over hers,
Elaine knew that when she told him about Sophie he
couldn't fail to be even more happy. But not yet. She

309

wanted him just for herself a little while longer.

'Has your headache gone, darling?' he asked softly as he drew back from her at last and gazed into her slumberous eyes. 'I don't think I can wait much longer,' he grinned, holding her fast against his lithe body so she would know what he meant.

Elaine coloured slightly. It had been so long and she had wanted him for so long she was just a little afraid that she wouldn't know what to do or say any more. He had been the only man in her life and had taught her so many magical things about her body but . . . but Sophie had happened.

'I feel wonderful now, Marcus, and I'll never have another headache for you, darling. But – '

'But what?' he laughed.

Elaine fluttered her eyelashes shyly and could barely look him in the eye. 'I . . . feel suddenly nervous,' she admitted. 'There hasn't been anyone else and . . . and it's been so long.'

'For me too, darling. I couldn't even bear to look at another woman,' he told her sincerely. 'But I guess it'll all come back to us.'

'Like riding a bike, I guess,' she giggled.

Marcus frowned, but the corners of his eyes were crinkled with humour. 'That's not the sort of remark I would have heard from you a year ago.'

'Yes, well, water under the bridge and all that. I guess I've spent too much time lately with Cathy and Lisa. They are a scream.'

'But you're the cream,' he smiled as he bent his head to kiss her lips again.

He scooped her up into his arms and carried her through to his frothy bedroom and lay her on the bed. 'I couldn't believe my eyes when I put you down here earlier,' he told her as he peeled off his jacket and joined her. 'You were like a miracle beamed into my life. Oh, darling, I've missed you so much. The year without you was a nightmare I worked through torturously, every day a long haul, trying to forget you, but finding it impossible. I'll never let you go again, never,' he breathed hotly against her cheek.

Elaine clung to him, as he removed their clothes in that slow sensuous way he used to, the disrobing ritual he had made into an art form. But when he saw her naked body he must surely know and it frightened her. She hadn't a mark on her silky skin to show she had been through childbirth, there was just more of it and he would know, surely?

But then his strokes and caresses relaxed her, yet aroused her deeply, and she put aside her worrying thoughts because it was just her conscience that was the trouble, not her body.

'Oh, Marcus,' she murmured as she writhed under him as he stroked her breasts. 'It's all coming back to me, all the marvellous feelings you aroused in me.'

His mouth suckled her breasts and she bit hard on her lips and though she was pleased she wasn't still breastfeeding, she suddenly thought of her beloved child. Oh, Sophie – how she missed her. She was sure the girls would take good care of her but it wasn't like having her real mother beside her. Oh, dear, she remembered she hadn't written down the formula for her feeds, though Lisa seemed to know what she was doing and had made up her bottles before. But what if she awoke in the night and they weren't there for her? Supposing Sophie wailed for her mummy and she wasn't there . . .

'Darling, what's wrong? You're not with me?'

'Oh, Marcus,' she breathed, grasping him to her. 'Make love to me now, quickly, it's been so long and I can't wait any longer.' She wanted Marcus to make her forget because she felt so bad now, so terribly guilty for leaving her daughter. She should have told him before now. She was being selfish, putting her own needs before all else and it was wrong, and it was too late . . .

He pressed into her and Elaine let out a gasp of pleasure and anguish. He moved inside her and she cried out and clung to him and he moved faster. And then she was sobbing and feeling the rush of her climax and it was a shock that it was happening so quickly. And then Marcus was coming with her, not able to hold back and for one blissful moment in time she was able to black out everything but the fever of eruption, the molten flow of their love, so fast and furious and glorious.

They lay in each other's arms, trembling, moist and feverish and Marcus was saying something and she couldn't hear for the blood rushing in her head.

'Darling, why are you crying? It was wonderful, quick but wonderful. You're different somehow, far more sensitive, incredible, in fact.'

'Oh, Marcus,' she sobbed, clinging to his neck, 'I should have told you before. I shouldn't have done that, let you make love to me before I told you. I'm so ashamed now. You'll think me a tart for coming so quickly and putting sex before telling you – '

'Telling me what, darling? I don't understand you. There is nothing to be ashamed of in coming quickly. I couldn't stop either. It's been so long. You're not a tart at all. Where have you been getting your ideas from?

312

lately?' He hugged her tightly. 'Those friends of yours again?'

'Oh, my friends,' Elaine moaned in his silky long hair. 'My friends are doing what I should be doing now.' Suddenly she gathered her strength together and gulped hard. It had to be now because she couldn't go through this again, making love to Marcus and him not knowing. Already he had noticed the difference in her – she was more sensitive, he'd said. Her whole body was different, she was different. 'I'm a mother,' she wailed and closed her eyes shut to bolt back the tears.

She heard Marcus laugh nervously. 'Darling, what do you mean, a mother?'

And she braved herself to look at him now and was even more afraid than ever. Her wonderful elegant Marcus might not like the idea of being a father. He already had the massive responsibility of this business, a hotel that was impressively exclusive. Would one more burden in his busy life be too much for him?

'I . . . I don't know how . . . how to tell you this but . . . but I have a child, Marcus, a beauty – '

'A *child*!' he suddenly thundered and leapt off the bed as if she had pronounced she had some ghastly communicable virus.

'A baby daughter, Marcus.'

'A daughter!' he repeated, aghast. 'You said there had been no one else, no other man in your life!' he spluttered, his black eyes wide. 'How could you, Elaine? How could you tell me a pack of lies? You've just made love to me knowing you've had a baby with someone else!'

Elaine was on her knees, naked and embarrassed now, grasping at a pillow to cover herself. 'There

313

hasn't been anyone else, Marcus,' she whimpered. 'It's our baby, ours! Last year, I found I was pregnant when I got home and – '

'Ours?' he bawled, perspiration breaking out on his brow. His whole body was shaking from head to toe. 'That's impossible! I can't have children! Why do you think I didn't bother with contraception when we first made love?' he stormed on. 'I'm bloody sterile. I fire blanks. I had mumps as a child! How dare you suggest such a thing, that I am the father of your child? Your friends put you up to this, didn't they? Slam a paternity suit on the rich guy down in Marbella, he won't contest it for fear of scandal. I bet you all looked round this place and thought, he's a patsy, he'll fall for it. Well, think again, Elaine. Now get out before I throw you out!'

Elaine, sobbing hysterically now, went to clutch at him but he stepped back and started piling his clothes on and it wasn't an art form any more.

'Please, Marcus, don't be so cruel. It's true, Sophie is yours, she looks like you, she *is* the fruit of your loins, our loins. There was never . . . no, never anyone else!'

He leaned down over her as he adjusted his Armani jacket over his shoulders, eyes glazed with rage. 'How dare you come here after so long, claiming your child is mine when it can't possibly be? And anyway, why wait so long? Did all the others turn you down? Was I the last resort?'

'It was my father!' Elaine blurted out hotly. 'He wouldn't let me come, said you were a holiday romance. I didn't know where to turn, he looked after me – '

'Well, he can look after you some more,' Marcus

314

raged, burgundy with anger, 'because your child isn't mine, it can't possibly be. I don't give babies!'

'Marcus, don't leave me,' she implored as he stormed towards the door. 'I couldn't bear it, I just couldn't. Sophie is – '

The door slammed after him. Elaine uttered a plaintive, ' – yours,' but he didn't hear it.

Never, never had she foreseen this, how could she have done? She had imagined he might have been shocked, but to cruelly deny the child as his? Never, never that. It had never crossed her mind that he might not believe her. But Sophie *was* his! There hadn't been anyone else for her, Marcus was her only lover!

She knawed at her knuckles in anguish, tears coursing down her face, hurting so deeply inside that all she had been through before now appeared to be minuscule in comparison. Marcus had rejected her in the worst possible way, casting insults and aspersions like confetti. Oh, God, what was happening to her life and how could she convince him that he was wrong? He couldn't possibly be sterile! What had he meant, he fired blanks, and what had mumps got to do with anything?

Oh, she needed the girls, Cathy and Lisa, they would know what to do and say to convince him of the truth. But they weren't here and her daughter wasn't here either. One look at her dark eyes and dark hair that promised ringlets like her father's would surely convince him?

In a stupor of grief Elaine hauled herself off the bed and put on the same clothes that she felt as if she had lived in since the beginning of time. And what would her brother say when she crawled back to the *Finca*

Esmeralda with her tail between her legs – 'I told you so,' sounded very likely.

Sniffing miserably, hands shaking, white with anxiety, she looked in her purse to see if she had enough money to get a taxi back up the mountain. She started to sob again as she pulled twenty-pound notes out of her bag. She hadn't even had the sense to exchange her currency to pesetas. She was useless, a total wimp, no good to man nor beast! And she was alone again and it was too much to bear. She sobbed hysterically.

'I'd like to see Mr Charles Bond,' Cathy stated at the reception desk of the Ailene Hotel. She hadn't noticed the name of the place before. Now she did because it was a small diversion to steel herself before facing Charles. It was an anagram of Elaine. Marcus must have named it after her and that proved that a good, loving, decent man had been born and Elaine had him, the only one in existence.

'I will ring for him,' the receptionist told her and picked up the phone.

'I'd rather have his room number if you don't mind.'

'We don't allow that,' the girl told her stiffly and waited while the phone rang. 'And who shall I say?'

'Cathy Peterson,' Cathy told her, matching her severity with a look that had the girl averting her eyes.

It took Charles Bond a mere fifteen seconds to appear in the reception area, just as Marcus appeared out of an office behind the reception desk, looking gaunt. Marcus glared fiercely at Cathy.

'What are you doing here?' he barked. Cathy widened her eyes in surprise. 'She's gone and if you

316

think you can argue her case, think again. No one takes me for a fool, least of all a rich tart!'

'What was that about?' Charles asked, breathless behind her as Marcus glared at them both before striding off to the restaurant.

Cathy looked at him, bemused by Marcus's strange turnabout since earlier when he had been charm personified and blissfully happy, and at the same time wondering what went on in her former boss's head to make a banal comment like that when she held his past, his present, his future in the palm of her hand.

'Crumbs, you take the biscuit at times, Charles. You're not even fazed out that I'm here, are you?'

He grinned at her. 'I expected you. I knew you would come to your senses at some stage, though I was a bit miffed at not finding you at the Don Carlos. Playing hard to get, eh? You little tease.' He went to gather her into his arms but Cathy sidestepped and he grasped at air.

'Pull yourself together, Charles,' she hissed and looked around her to see where they could go to talk. 'This isn't a social call. I've just realized what you are up to. Where can we discuss your *scheming* in peace?' she said pointedly, glancing at the receptionist who was making out she wasn't listening, but her ears were twitching like a rabbit's.

Charles's neck went red and he took her arm and led her out to the lift area. 'My suite,' he grunted, 'and keep your voice down.'

Cathy said no more; she didn't even argue that neutral ground would be preferable, but what she had to thrash out with him was extremely confidential, not for anyone else's ears.

'Nice suite,' she said once inside the second-floor

317

apartment that screamed out quality and style. She was happy to note patio doors open to a small balcony and lights twinkling outside, close enough for anyone to hear if she had to scream for help. 'Expensive, too – using a company cheque to pay for it, are you?'

'I don't know what you mean.'

'Cut it out, Charles. I have it all sussed out now,' she told him coldly. She had long cooled down after her drive down to the coast. She had left the *finca* in a rage but now she had it all in hand. She was coldly motivated now, icy with disgust and loathing for how he had involved her in his dastardly deeds and her heart was frozen for ever more where Greg Turner was concerned.

'A drink, darling,' Charles flustered, taking jerky movements around the sitting area of the suite. He offered her a seat on a low white leather sofa, picked up a bottle of vodka from a glass-topped sideboard and waved it at her as if she would fall for its temptation. She saw him for what he was, a desperate man, needing her more now than he had ever done before.

Cathy shook her head. 'You have the drink, you need it more than I do and I don't need to sit to tell you just what I think of you. But I guess you know that already. No one can be that thick-skinned.'

'I . . . I don't know what you mean, Cathy, darling.' He looked thoroughly affronted. It didn't stop him pouring himself a large vodka, though, and throwing it down his throat like yesterday's slops down the waste-disposal unit.

'I mean a million pounds, Charles. The million you stole from the company we both worked for and floated in my bank account before you could launder it elsewhere. And I'm beginning to wonder if that is only the tip of the iceberg,' she accused him tightly. 'A million quid is sesame seed on the top of the burger bun these days, especially to you and your expensive wife. You never did question the fact that I'd deleted the Belgian metal account from the computers before I left. I guess it suited you down to the ground because that was probably another of your scams. When I think of all the discrepancies you have talked me out of over the months, I could spit for my own naïvity. And you and your persistence – trying to get me back in the office, needing my signature on cheques and in the same breath pleading that you cared about me, offering me a *pied-à*-bloody-*terre*, diamonds and blinking roses – '

'I love you, Cathy,' he suddenly blurted out, shaking now. 'It was all for us, you and me. I was going to leave my wife for you – everything I did was for *you*.' He slammed his empty glass down on the sideboard and came towards her. 'Darling, don't you understand? That money was for us. A new life for us – '

'I don't need a new life, Charles!' she cried, stepping back from him, not wanting him to touch her because if he did she would kill him. His scams and treachery were beastly but there was worse, something she would indeed need a new life to get over – his wretched, scheming, damned, damned accomplice who had done more harm to her heart than fifty Charles Bonds could have done to it.

'Not with you, Charles, not with any man after what you and he have done to me. The pair of you have implicated me in something I had no knowledge of. You have used me, put me at grave risk, turned me into a criminal, made me the scapegoat for your embezzling deeds, your company frauds. You bastard, Charles. You didn't have me followed down here because you care about me, you just wanted me in sight in case I ran off with your rotten million quid!'

'What are you talking about, had you followed?' Charles squeaked uncharacteristically. His eyes were huge pools of panic, a nerve was twitching frantically at the corner of his mouth, his whole face looked as if it was going to metamorphosize into a gargoyle. And once she had thought him good-looking.

'Too late for blind innocence, Charles. I know what you are both up to and the pity of it all is that I didn't realize it sooner. I should have reported the Battersea stalker before I left, I should have put two and two together and realized that the hitchhiker was down to you. He even worked it so that he's been living with us, eating with us, sleeping with us . . .'

Her eyes suddenly filled with tears. Oh, Greg, you bastard, doing that to worm your way into my heart and my confidence, just as Charles had done before you! What kind of fool am I for letting it happen not once, but *twice*!

Suddenly he moved so quickly she had no chance to take evasive action. His grip on her shoulders as he practically shook her with rage had her teeth chattering and the tears spilling from her brimming eyes.

'What bloody stalker, what hitchhiker, what are you damned well talking about?' he raged.

'Your bloody accomplice!' Cathy cried back, her tears gone now, her fury at being manhandled this way firing her to shake herself out of his grasp. 'Your partner in crime, sticking to me like superglue since I walked out on you. You know exactly who I'm talking about, Greg Turner, that bird-watching, slimy creep of a civil servant!'

320

Charles's hands went to his head and he clawed at his scalp; then he reached for the bottle again. In the instant it took him to slop the contents into a tall glass, Cathy came to her senses with a serious jolt. This was foolhardy madness. What was she doing here, exposing herself to him this way, showing how much *she* knew about his nefarious deeds, his criminal activities? She should have kept her mouth closed. She shouldn't even have come here. She was in mortal danger because, against two crooks, what chance had she?

As he gulped down the vodka, Cathy's eyes darted nervously around the room. There was a phone on the table, no doubt one in the bedroom, even the bathroom in a sumptuous hotel like this. The door had a gold key with a gold tassle hanging from it in the lock. Had he locked the door when they had come in? Could she make a bolt for it? Hah! She could dive on the phone once he went to the loo, which must be shortly because he'd drunk so much vodka . . .

'You stupid bitch,' Charles ground out as he stared into his glass. He was sort of hunched over, by the sideboard where the drinks lived, side on to her, not even looking at her. Then slowly his head turned and he was a gargoyle. Twisted and ugly and stone-faced, his mouth a wide grinning leer. 'You think I have an accomplice, do you? You think I would actually share what I've worked so hard for? This one was the big one, the rest was chicken feed compared to this coup.'

'You . . . you've done this before?' Cathy uttered weakly.

'Not on this scale, but I've been pushed to take a bigger risk this time,' he grated at her. 'Julia doesn't know I've been bleeding her dry over the years. I had to get it all back and more. My wife is an expensive lady, an influential lady – '

'You horrible rat,' Cathy breathed, clenching her fists at her side and glancing around again for ways of getting out. He was rambling now, in a drunken haze, rambling it all out and she didn't want to hear it. The less she knew the safer she was, but she knew enough already and . . .

He moved across to her. Cathy moved around a little; he got closer. She felt the back of the sofa against her bottom. She gripped it behind her, shuffled some more. He was breathing in her face. She had nowhere to go.

'No, Cathy, sweetheart, no accomplice and you know what that means. You're going down, not me, not Charles Bond. I'm too smart, but you are a fool.'

'I *don't* know what you mean,' Cathy whimpered like a small trapped animal.

'It means that you are the one with a million in your account, Cathy,' he boasted smarmily. 'They are *your* signatures on all the company cheques. It's all down to you – nothing to do with me. You were the one that walked out on me and the job and went on the run down here, the Costa del Crime. Your very actions scream guilt and they are on to you.'

'On to me? Who?' she croaked.

He laughed then, the maniacal cry of an animal of the jungle. 'The law, sweetheart. Your Greg Turner isn't my accomplice, isn't anyone I want to know, thank you very much. Turner is one of the highest ranking officers in the Serious Fraud Squad. If he's been stalking you, sticking to you like glue, sleeping with you, you are in it up to your pretty little neck You are doomed, Cathy Peterson, bloody doomed!'

Fire, ice, tornado, hurricane, all suddenly descended on her from a great height. Appalled, Cathy opened her mouth to scream that it couldn't be true, it couldn't be!

Charles had hold of her throat now and she feared for her life. But then he lowered his mouth to hers as if to kiss her for the last time before they threw her in jail and tossed away the key. And a kiss from him was worse than the thought of being banged up for life.

She spun away from him at the same time, pushing at his chest till he reeled back against the sofa with a grunt. In a shocked daze she moved the wrong way and found herself backing through the open patio doors and out on to the balcony. Her head was reeling, her whole body shaking and then she heard a sound behind her – water, the ripple of water as if someone was cleaving their way through it. Charles was in the doorway now, still laughing at her, still reeling, his intention obvious as he edged through the door towards her.

Cathy turned quickly, saw the gleam of a swimming pool two floors down below, underwater lights beckoning her down. She took a huge breath, adjusted her shoulder bag over her shoulder, clambered over the wrought-iron balcony and leapt for her life. Her last prayer was, please let it be the deep end.

Cathy came round on the big frothy bed and thought she had come back into the world as Elaine. She sat bolt upright, the blood whooshing to her head. She was naked. Her hands clawed at her body, trying to find a scrap of clothing she could cling on to, but there was only a thin crisp sheet to gather to her naked breasts.

Marcus was sitting on the edge of the bed in a white towelling robe. His hair was as wet as hers was. She remembered leaping into the pool.

'Gosh, were you swimming in the pool?' she gasped.

'No, mercifully no one was,' he said gravely, 'but I saw you come flying past the window of the garden room and dived in to haul you out.' He leaned towards her, eyes dark and broody. 'Just what are you girls trying to do to me? Ruin my hotel with your drunken soirées, trying to hang a paternity suit on me, leaping off balconies and terrifying my guests. Just what the hell are you all up to?'

Cathy closed her eyes and a hand went to her wet head to ease the tension. 'Leave it out, Marcus, I've had a really bad hair day.' She blinked open her eyes. 'Paternity suit, what the devil is that supposed to mean?' Suddenly she looked around her. No Elaine. Earlier he had said she had gone. Too much had happened since for her to give it any more thought. Now she did.

She looked at Marcus properly. He looked even more gaunt and fragile than ever. And he might have saved her life by dragging her out of the pool and bringing her to his apartment, but he was looking at her as if he'd rather wished he'd left her floundering.

'You know exactly what I mean,' he said tightly and got up from the bed. 'Now are you going to give me your reasons for diving fully clothed from a second-floor balcony into my pool, or would you rather wait and explain to the men in white coats when I ring them to ask for a collect service?'

'I'm not the mad one around here,' she snapped back at him, thinking that perhaps an explanation along the lines of a drunken embezzler guesting in

324

his posh hotel and threatening to leave her – his erstwhile ex-secretary with a million quid in her current account – to take the rap for his misdemeanars might not go down to well as an excuse for the moment.

'I found myself in a compromising position,' she muttered, 'and the only escape was a nose dive. Sorry if it put your guests off their Singapore Slings, but it was a better alternative than a murder on your premises.'

'He was going to murder you!'

'Oh, 'struth, Marcus, I was trying to humour you,' she sighed. She smiled suddenly. 'Hey, thanks for pulling me out of the pool. You're a hero. Now if you can give me back my clothes.' She swung her legs over the edge of the bed and sat there with the sheet around her, waiting for him to move. Her clothes would be wet, but she needed to leave rather quickly. Suddenly it was all crashing down on her again, hellfire and brimstone. She needed to get help, though who she could turn to she couldn't think for the minute.

'Your clothes are drying off so you are going nowhere till this is sorted out and you tell me the truth of what went on in Suite Five half an hour ago.'

Cathy shook her head. 'You don't want to know, Marcus. Take my word for it and forget I was here.' Suddenly she looked up at him, eyes bright with concern. 'Half an hour ago? Have I been unconscious all that time?'

'You weren't unconscious when I pulled you out of the pool, just a little confused and crying out for a Greg, whoever he is. I brought you here and my receptionist undressed you – '

'I *must* have been unconscious,' Cathy protested

325

wildly. 'I wouldn't allow that! What sort of a girl do you think I am?'

Marcus suddenly looked world weary and sighed impatiently. 'Unconscious, delirious, drunk, whatever – frankly, I don't give a damn. All I want from you is information about your friend Charles Bond, because by the time I got up to the suite he had vanished without paying his bill. I don't like being ripped off, not moneywise, heartwise, or any other-bloody-wise. Now you are not leaving here till you tell me where I can find him. You lot have brought chaos into my life since arriving here and I'm all for a quiet life so get your act together and give me the information I want before I call the *guardia*.'

'Is . . . is that the police?' Cathy moaned.

Marcus said something under his breath which Cathy didn't quite catch, but it sounded like something not very pleasant so she refrained from asking him to repeat it. Instead she rather plaintively asked for a drink of water. Her mouth felt as if it had been through the white cycle of a washing machine with a full quota of something biologically efficient.

'I'll get you some water and some coffee,' he said rather more warmly now and added, 'Rest. I guess whatever happened up there, you had no choice but to do what you did. Perhaps I've been a bit harsh on you.' He gave her a watery smile. 'But you rather ask for it,' he added.

Cathy smiled back at him. 'It's been one of those days you just don't wish to repeat,' she murmured wearily.

'I know what you mean,' he muttered as he went out the door.

Cathy lay back on the bed and closed her eyes.

wishing she could block everything out, but it was impossible. She was in a hell-hole of trouble, none of it her own doing. But there again she had been a stupid fool for not have seen all this coming. Charles had seduced her for one reason only, to blind her with love so that she wouldn't see what he was up to in the office. She remembered the first time he had kissed her, when they were arguing figures over one of the accounts – she convinced she was right, him and his kiss persuading her otherwise. Now she could see that she had been right and already he had been up to his deceptive tricks. How many millions had he embezzled out of the company with her, lovesick and blind, giving him support and making it easy for him?

But somehow it all paled against what Greg had done to her. Very much the same as Charles, seduced her for gain. She shivered and pulled the sheet up around her cold, cold body. Everyone thought her so smart, so streetwise, up-front Cathy who took no nonsense from anyone, man, beast or child. But she had been taken for one of the biggest rides in history. Charles had used her to gain money, and Greg had used her to lower her resistance far enough for her to incriminate herself and he could make the arrest of his career. Serious Fraud Squad? Oh, how he had fooled her and, oh, how very badly it hurt. Charles's deception merely angered her because now she knew her heart had tricked her where he was concerned. But her heart hadn't tricked her over Greg. What she had felt for him had been true and positive and she knew it for sure because the pain of his betrayal was excruciatingly worse than anything she had experienced before.

'Hey, why the tears?' Marcus asked softly as he sat

on the edge of the bed with a glass of iced water in one hand.

'Life is a bitch,' Cathy sobbed and tried to pull herself together. She wiped her face on the edge of the sheet and tried to smile for him. 'I'll amend that,' she sniffled, 'love is a bitch.'

He smiled wryly. 'I'll endorse that,' he murmured. 'Do you want to talk about it?'

Suddenly Cathy did. She so badly needed someone to talk to and there was no one else available. She looked at Marcus sitting on the edge of the bed, looking forlorn and gaunt. Very true, they had put him through the ringer today. The girls on the run had turned his lovely hotel upside down, turned him upside down along with it. Elaine had gone – why, she couldn't imagine, because earlier it had seemed as if the heavens had been smiling on them both.

'On condition you tell me what's gone wrong between you and Elaine,' she suggested softly. 'You said she had gone – where?'

Marcus shrugged. 'Back to the Don Carlos, I suppose.'

Cathy bit her lip. Poor Elaine. She was probably back at the *finca* by now, tearful and clutching at her brother and him telling her, 'I told you so,' with that all-knowing pompous arrogance of his.

'So what happened?' she asked with concern.

He looked at her, eyes brimming. 'I can't talk about it. It hurts too much.' He forced a smile. 'I warm to your concern for us though. It appears you have all the troubles of the world upon your shoulders and yet you are worried about Elaine. I guess I misjudged you.

'I don't think I understand that,' she murmured, sipping her water.

'You don't need to. So give, tell me all about you and Charles Bond and how he broke your heart.'

Cathy shook her head. 'Sure I'm suffering a broken heart, but *he* didn't break it.' She sighed. 'Are you sure you want to hear all this, Marcus?' She grinned ruefully. 'It could take a long time.'

He smiled back at her and nodded to the bedside table. 'I brought a large pot of coffee and the night is young.'

Cathy patted the bed next to her, knowing that Marcus would take it as a friendly gesture rather than a come-on. 'I guess you'd better be relaxed when I tell you this because it isn't going to be music to your ears. In a way you might be drawn into all this, but I don't want to frighten you yet. Suffice it to say that I'm totally innocent in all this and when the mire hits the fan I'll do my very best to keep you and Elaine out of it all.'

'I'm intrigued,' he murmured, pouring two large cups of coffee and swinging his legs up on to the bed beside her.

'Not for long, I suspect, but if you are still on this bed when I've finished and resisting the urge to have me flung in irons then you might be able to give me some advice as to what to do. Do you have friends in this *guardia* of yours?'

'What sort of a question is that?' Marcus laughed.

And because he laughed and didn't leap off the bed with fright she knew she could trust him, but a reassurance that his father was in fact the chief of police for the state of Andalucia would have been music to *her* ears; the chief of police for the whole of Spain would have been a symphony.

She started, right from the very beginning. She told

329

him everything. And it took a long, long time because she had Marcus well and truly intrigued, intrigued enough for him to interrupt with questions which heartened her to answer honestly.

By the time she had finished her throat was raw, the coffee pot was empty except for grounds and Marcus was pacing the room as if preparing her line of defence in a court of law.

'You are totally innocent in all of this, Cathy,' he was saying. 'You have been used. It's outrageous.' He stopped pacing. 'You must go to your lover immediately and tell him all you have told me. He must know that the woman he has been making love to is not a crook, not a deceiver. He must know how you feel about him and – '

'Of course he knows how I feel about him, Marcus,' Cathy butted in hoarsely, 'but he has no feelings for *me*. He used me like Charles did, for his own ends. His lovemaking was all about sex and control, power over me to get what he wanted – me behind bars. Men are like that, they can make love and not mean it. It's different for women. They give their heart first and ask questions after, more bloody fool us.'

'You've had a bad experience with men. It's clouded your reasoning. Elaine and I were never . . .' His hand went to his forehead and he kneaded it wearily. 'What am I saying?'

'Yes, what are you saying, Marcus?'

He bumped down on the edge of the bed and rubbed his forehead again. 'Like your Greg, she has deceived me,' he admitted in a low voice.

Cathy reached out and patted his shoulder lightly. 'You'd better tell me all about it,' she encouraged him softly. 'You've heard my ghastly tale of woe, now yo lighten up. I don't wish to trivialize your problems with Elaine, but I doubt either of you are facing a prison sentence through it.'

Marcus smiled wryly. 'No, but a life sentence without bars is a strong possibility. Anyway, you are not going to prison. True, you are in a mess, but it's a mess that can be sorted out. Mine can't.' He turned his dark head towards her. 'Did you know Elaine's child is not mine?'

Cathy stared at him in shocked horror. What horror was this on top of everything else?

'She . . . she told you that?' Cathy croaked. What an earth was Elaine up to now? The girl was beyond belief.

'She didn't have to admit it, I know it.'

'What do you mean, you know it? You had an affair last year, a holiday romance! Elaine has a beautiful baby daughter as a result.'

Marcus shook his head. His hair was bone dry now and the tight ringlets were so endearing Cathy wanted to cry for him. He was doubting Elaine's sincerity when she had confessed to bearing his child . . . the shock had been too much for him. All the same, Cathy was astounded that he couldn't accept it. She'd had her doubts at first, after seeing his lifestyle, reasoned with Lisa that Elaine wasn't home and dry yet and that springing the baby on him might be too much, but after spending half the night with him, talking and talking, she knew him to be a kind and caring man, a man with a big heart.

'The baby isn't mine, Cathy,' he said gravely. 'If she led you to believe that, it was it was despicable of her.'

'Elaine doesn't know the meaning of the word

despicable, let alone be it,' Cathy reasoned in mounting horror.

'You don't understand, Cathy. The baby can't be mine. I can't have children. I'm sterile.'

'*Sterile*!' Cathy shrieked, the shock to her spine propelling her up from the pillows.

'It isn't a crime,' he shot back at her. 'It happens to a lot of men. It's nothing to be ashamed off. I didn't choose to be this way. Mumps is a cruel illness to young boys and – '

'Mumps!' Cathy cried again. 'You are sterile because of mumps? Who told you that?'

He flushed deeply with anger. 'My mother, of course. She said there are worse things in life than not being able to father children – like being penniless, for one. My father left her and me without a *sou* to our name when I was small. I vowed then to give her the very best. All my life I've worked to give her everything she didn't get from him. She likes nice things and . . . and what the hell are you laughing at? This isn't at all funny.'

Cathy swallowed hard and struggled to keep the grin of her face. Actually, it wasn't funny at all. Poor Marcus. What a bitch of a mother he had.

'Tell me, Marcus,' she asked, gulping back a trickle of mirth, 'are you the only child?'

'Yes, how could I have brothers or sisters when my mother was alone in the world but for me?'

'And she loves you very much, right?'

'Of course, I'm all she's got.'

'And I bet she has always discouraged your girl-friends.'

'Sort of, only in my best interests. She knew I had no time for serious relationships. The bar took all m'

332

time and now this hotel, and though there were a few girlfriends no relationships that I encouraged to go too far.'

'Thank goodness for that,' Cathy breathed in relief, thinking that Marcus casting his supposedly sterile seeds around all over the place had been a frightening thought for a minute. She smiled at him, not laughing now, though, because he got all hot and bothered when she tried to make light of his situation.

'Oh, Marcus, you are daft. I can now see how well-suited you and Elaine are. I mean, I thought so this afternoon, but now you have well and truly confirmed it. You were made for each other.'

'What do you mean?'

He was frowning at her, all boyish and sort of pretty, and so very vulnerable because he was such a nice guy. She leaned across the bed and put her arms around him to give him a big hug.

'You might know everything to know about running a successful business but you ain't very bright in ways of the world.' She let him go to look into his wide black eyes and she spoke softly and meaningfully. 'Marcus, I have two brothers and they both had mumps as kids. My eldest brother has two sons and another on the way, my other brother's wife is expecting her first.'

He shrugged. 'Statistics. 'Some are OK, others fall by the wayside like the grain on stony ground.'

Cathy shook her head. 'Have you had any tests?'

'Tests? Oh, Oh, that.' He coloured slightly, understanding what she meant. 'I don't remember. I was only five when I was ill.'

'Tests around puberty?' she suggested. Marcus shook his head.

Suddenly Cathy realized she was up against a tricky one here. It wasn't for her to put his mother down. Let him work that out for himself that the woman had only self-interest at heart in convincing her only adored son that he was incapable of having children. She didn't know her, though; she might be a sad old girl, clinging to all she had, a son she adored, or she could be the other type, a convincing old bat, hellbent on savouring the luxuries Marcus obviously bestowed on her and not wanting some she-devil in the form of a daughter-in-law to take him away from her.

'Marcus,' she implored sincerely, 'I know Elaine and I know where her heart lies – with you. She's been to hell and back with what she's had to cope with since last year. Her father is a tyrant and rules her life, her half-brother is a pr – . . . forget about him. She loves you and you are the only man in the world for her. You both know it and as for Sophie not being your child . . . Marcus, Elaine doesn't sleep around, she wouldn't know how to. I'd put money on it that you were her first.'

Marcus lowered his thick dark lashes and nodded.

'And her last, Marcus, because she was pregnant when she came back last year, pregnant with your baby, no one else's, your child. I've spent the last few days of my life with that darling baby and when I met you I knew for sure you were her father. She has your eyes, big black eyes, her hair is dark and she'll have ringlets soon and if you don't come to your senses you won't ever see them.'

Marcus shakily got to his feet and rubbed at his hair and Cathy could see the tears welling in his eyes. 'And I told her to get out,' he moaned in despair. 'I didn'

334

believe my darling Elaine. I cast her out with only my abuse for company. Oh, what have I done?' Suddenly he looked up at the ceiling in sufferance. 'Oh, God, I need a drink.' Shoulders sagging with emotion, he went to the bedroom door and turned to face her when he got there. 'I think we both need a drink. I'll get a bottle of brandy from the bar. Thank you, Cathy, you're wonderful, a heroine.'

Cathy gave him the thumbs-up. 'Think nothing of it, hero,' she grinned at him.

She lay back thinking that at the very least she had brought some measure of happiness to someone. The phone suddenly shrilled in her ear and she reached for it because Marcus wasn't here, noting that it was four o'clock in the morning and it was probably his mother checking to see he had no prospective daughters-in-law in his bed.

'Hello.'

'Who's that?' Elaine cried.

'Elaine, it's Cathy. Marcus and I were just talking about you. Where are you calling from?'

There was a small silence. 'The *finca*, Greg's mobile,' Elaine responded weakly.

'Gosh, you sound terrible. I must sound rough too,' she laughed hoarsely. 'It's been one helluva night. You ain't going to believe this, but I'm lying on your frothy bed and Marcus has gone for a bottle because, boy, do we both need it – '

There was a strangled cry from the *finca* end of the phone, quickly followed by, 'You bitch, Cathy. I thought you were my friend, you absolute bitch. I've been distraught all night, unable to sleep, distraught and you . . . you pig. I never want to see you or Marcus ever again!'

Cathy winced as the phone crackled in her ear. Mortified, she lay there in a stupor of remorse. 'Nice one, Cathy,' she bleated to herself, 'another mess you have created with your big mouth. Won't you ever learn?'

CHAPTER 14

'Philip, will you stop pacing? You're getting on my nerves,' Lisa told him. 'Here, eat this, you've had nothing this morning and too much coffee is bad for you. You've drunk at least ten cups through the night. None of us have had any sleep and we all need feeding.'

She placed a plate of fluffy scrambled eggs and crispy bacon down on the terrace table. She went to him, gently took his arm and guided him to the table where he sat down with a bump and stared blankly at the plate before him.

'How can I eat? How can you sound so normal this morning after what has been happening through the night?' He pushed the plate away and sank his head into his hands.

Lisa sat across from him and gazed around at the lovely shades dripping with bougainvillaea and grape vines, the bright blue sky beyond and a huge white hot sun dappling shadows over them both. The scent of rosemary and jasmine filled the hot air and the buzzing cicadas were doing their business in force this glorious morning. And yet everything that human life was offering to the day was ugly and dark.

337

'I guess I sound normal because I'm the only one around here that is,' she told him gently. 'Besides, one of us needs to stay sane. You lot are letting yourselves down with your hysterics.'

He lifted his dark head. 'We all have good reason to be hysterical. Cathy disappearing with *my* car last night, Greg flying off in a panic in *his* car, so panicked he forgot his mobile. Poor Elaine last night, returning in a taxi with a driver who couldn't speak a word of English – good job I was here to sort her out and pay him. That bastard Marcus rejecting poor Elaine, denying the baby is his.' He shook his head in disbelief that so much had happened. 'Then the crunch: to add more horrors to the night, Elaine finding out Cathy is shacked up with him down in Marbella and – '

'Will you shut up, Philip!' Lisa seethed, her lovely violet eyes narrowed with exhaustion. 'Cathy would never do such a thing, never. If she was with him, there had to be a reason and we won't find that out till she gets back.'

He laughed ruefully. 'And you think she's coming back, do you? Hasn't anything I've told you sunk in, Lisa, sweet one? Your trouble is you only see good in the world. It's a tricky old world out there, dog eat dog. Face the fact that your precious Cathy is a crook. She and her boss, Charles Bond, ripped off their company and arranged to meet down here. You saw him yourself, in the hotel. She's dumped him and taken up with Marcus now and they are probably on their way to Gibraltar this very minute, to stuff her bags with embezzled money drawn out from phony bank accounts she'd already set up down there. Next stop South America. She's not coming back, Lisa,' h added wryly. 'Face it, she's fooled the lot of us, even Greg, who let his heart rule his head over her, and it's why she got away last night. This will ruin his career, seducing a prime suspect and letting her get away.'

Lisa sighed in despair. They'd gone over it all again and again through the night. She didn't believe a word of it. This was Philip's side of the story, what *he* believed, with the help of the treacherous Greg. He might be the law, not some silly private eye as she had thought, but treacherous he was all the same. Cathy had really loved him and he had used her. But what none of them knew but her was that Cathy *would* come back because she wasn't a crook – this was all some horrible mistake.

'Don't try and make out you are innocent in all this, Philip,' she murmured. 'You knew all along who Greg was and why he was trailing her. The pair of you had it all worked out between you – he would seduce her, you would seduce me, all to get to the bottom of this.'

Philip sighed deeply and reached for her hand across the table. His eyes had that hurt look about them but Lisa wasn't fooled, not again. 'Darling, Lisa, it was never my intention to seduce you to help Greg nail Cathy. It's hurtful to me to hear that. I've lost my heart to you, completely and utterly. I love you and, even with all this turmoil going on around us, I want to marry you and look after you for the rest of our lives.'

Oh, how she had longed to hear those golden words, but what timing. Instead of her heart singing with joy it was humming with despair. Slowly she pulled her hand out from under his and clasped it in her lap so he couldn't reach her again.

Her lovely eyes were wide and determined now as she gazed at him.

'Philip, if you had said that to me yesterday you would have made me the happiest girl in the world, but it isn't yesterday. Today you aren't the man I fell in love with. You are a cold hard man who has accused my friend of dreadful things and my love and allegiance is with her, not you.'

'Lisa, darling, what are you saying? That you put your friend before our love?' he said plaintively.

Lisa bit her lower lip and her eyes welled with tears, but she wouldn't allow herself to shed them, not in front of Philip. Later she would cry for all that was lost because it *was* a huge loss. She loved him and wanted to go on loving him, but it was impossible now.

He was letting her down so badly by not having faith in Cathy. True, they had all got off to a bad start and those two had been at each other's throats from day one of this trip, but Cathy had her reasons, believing him to have ruined Lisa's catering career, believing him to be Elaine's lover and the father of her child. All those misunderstandings had been ironed out; because Lisa was in love with Philip, her heart had been open to forgiveness. Cathy's heart hadn't been so affected. She was abrasive with Philip because she hadn't wanted to see her friend hurt. Cathy knew about hurt. Charles's betrayal had hurt her; when she found out about Greg's betrayal, she'd be even more devastated. She'd never trust a man ever again.

'Cathy needs my friendship more than you need my love, Philip,' she told him strongly. 'I know her and you only know the part of her you choose to see. You've never liked her, probably because Greg had already tainted everything by confiding in you back in the UK. Before even meeting Cathy you had branded her a thief. Last night you told me you and Greg were at school together, Harrow. Your friendship goes back as far as Cathy's and mine. We were at school together too, not yuppie Harrow, just a good old standard state comprehensive, but it's all the same in the playground. You have given your allegiance to Greg because of your past together; well, I have the same allegiance to Cathy. You should understand that, Philip, not belittle it and look hurt that I have made the same choice as yourself: friendship.'

He looked at her for a very long time, so long Lisa had to avert her eyes before she let go and blubbered in front of him.

At last she said, 'I'd better go up and see how Elaine is. She'll suffocate that baby with love and cuddles if she's not careful.'

'And I want to suffocate you with love and cuddles,' Philip uttered helplessly. His eyes locked with hers, mesmerizing her. 'Lisa, you humble me again and I'm getting to like the feeling more and more. I can't bear to lose you over something that is not our own doing. I do understand how you feel about Cathy,' he said sincerely. 'I was beginning to warm towards her, you know, getting to understand her a little more. For your information, Greg was convinced of her innocence in all this. Not from the start because he had a job to do, but gradually he began to have doubts that she was involved in all this. But what she has done now – '

Lisa was on her feet suddenly, angry with him for still accusing Cathy. 'You don't know what she has done *now*, Philip,' she said heatedly. 'None of us knows, but already you have her halfway to South America with her bags stuffed with money!'

Philip was suddenly on his feet too, matching her

anger with steel in his eyes. 'She went to Marbella, we know that. Elaine called Marcus to try and reason with him and Cathy answered the phone and told Elaine she was in his bed. Isn't the circumstantial evidence enough?'

Lisa leaned towards him over the table, her lips thinned. 'I hope your judge stepfather doesn't use the same reasoning in his courts of law. The judicial system would go down the pan if supposed criminals were convicted on such flimsy evidence. Charles Bond is staying in that same hotel, Philip – if she was the heister shyster you think her to be, she'd be in his bed, not Marcus's!'

'Well, perhaps he is in on this as well,' Philip argued as Lisa turned away, not wanting to hear any more wild conjectures. 'It's his hotel after all!'

Lisa turned then, hands on her hips, and faced him with an engaging smile on her face. 'You know something, Philip,' she said sugar-sweetly, 'in a screwed-up way I'd enjoy you proving me wrong in all this, but it isn't going to happen. In my dreams I'd like to see Marcus involved, the three of them on their way to South America with the swag bag, because I would love to see your face when the media exposes the lot of them.' She lifted a finger and pointed it at Philip. 'Just you remember who Sophie is: your niece, the High Court judge's granddaughter, the daughter of the man who allowed his hotel to be used as a pick-up point for millions of pounds embezzled out of the country and who then joined the gang and skipped the country. In that respect I wish you right and me wrong, but dreams rarely come true.

'Egg on your face?' she added brutally as his face indeed paled to the colour of egg white. She reached down and picked up his breakfast plate and flicked the lot at his chest. 'That's just for starters. You'd better prepare yourself for the next course because, if you *are* right, it won't smell as sweet when all this gets out!'

She spun on her heel and he spluttered after her,' B- but Marcus isn't the father . . . he . . . he denied her.'

She stopped at the kitchen door and turned to him. 'Trouble with you, Philip, is you believe everything you hear. I've seen the evidence before my very eyes – Marcus. Sophie's the living, breathing image of him. She's her father's daughter!'

With that she left him spluttering even more and went to the cooker to make a decent breakfast and take it up to Elaine. She shook her head as she worked. They were all mad. Cathy was innocent and, like Arnold Schwarzenegger, she'd be back.

'Come on, Elaine, you'll feel better for eating.' Lisa put the tray down by the side of the bed, then pushed open the shuttered windows to let air and light in.

Elaine sat crossed-legged on the bed, rocking Sophie in her arms as the baby slept soundly.

'Give her to me, she needs some fresh air by the window,' Lisa suggested as she leaned over the bed to take her from Elaine.

'Not too close. I don't want her to catch a chill.'

Lisa laughed. 'It's in the nineties out there and you are missing it all, shut away up here.' She lay Sophie down in her cot and shifted it near the window. Satisfied she was still sleeping contentedly, Lisa turned her attention to Elaine.

'You look ghastly,' she told her honestly. 'Not the lovely Elaine I used to know.'

She took a silver-backed hairbrush from the dressing-table and went to sit on the bed with Elaine and started to brush her hair for her.

'You always were one for keeping up appearances; now is more important than ever. Don't let any of this get you down, Elaine. We got all this sorted out in the night. We both know it's going to be all right. There, you look better already.' She grinned at her. 'Now you need to eat because we don't want you getting all thin like you used to be.'

Elaine managed a small smile. 'I'm starving, actually, but I might be sick if I do eat.'

'You're not pregnant again already, are you?' Lisa joked lightly, though it wasn't funny really, not after Elaine had told her everything that had happened between her and Marcus down in Marbella.

Elaine's eyes filled with tears. 'Could be, if what you told me is true. If I wasn't so tired I'd ask you to repeat it all again. I could hardly believe it the first time around. Philip's had mumps too, and I bet he doesn't fire blanks. Gosh, you might be pregnant yourself.'

Lisa laughed. 'I haven't slept with your brother yet, so it's hardly a possibility.'

'Then it must be love. Philip doesn't usually waste much time.' She looked at Lisa to see if she had hurt her feelings, but Lisa was grinning knowingly.

'I still find it difficult to understand Marcus refusing to acknowledge his daughter, Lisa,' Elaine said plaintively. 'I've tried so hard to work it out. I didn't understand all that mumps business till you told me all about it, but Marcus obviously believes it to be true. I can't believe anyone could be so thick about it.' She laughed suddenly and reached for the plate of eggs and bacon Lisa had brought her. 'That says it all, really. I didn't know till you told me so I'm as daft.'

'You are getting smarter by the minute, Elaine.'

'Yes, it's being around you two so much lately.' She took a mouthful of bacon and closed her eyes in rapture. 'Mmm, this is good. You make the most mundane food taste ambrosial.'

Lisa watched her eat. Elaine'd been through more hell than all of them lately and was coming out of it stronger and stronger. Though she had arrived back at the *finca* last night in a terrible state, she had calmed down enough to make a call to Marcus in the early hours; though she had got herself into a terrible state over that as well, she had calmed down enough to reason with Lisa that Cathy wasn't capable of doing such a thing as sleeping with her lover.

It had lifted Lisa's spirits to hear Elaine support Cathy, even argue with her brother that Cathy wasn't the crook he believed her to be when he told them all about it. She had even called him an offensive name beginning with a *p* and ending with a *t* at which Philip had gone white-faced and shuffled out of the sitting-room to brew up yet another pot of coffee.

'Here, drink your tea now. We've all had enough coffee to last us a lifetime.'

'We needed to stay awake, though, in case she came back. And no sign of anyone yet?'

Lisa shook her head. 'Not Cathy or Greg.'

'What's that?' Elaine lifted her head from her mug of tea and looked towards the window. They both heard a sound, a putt-putt.

Lisa was up like a shot and then her shoulders sagged and she came back to the bed. 'Only the maid on her moped. She'll have a fit when she sees all those coffee mugs.'

'Oh, Lisa, it's this waiting that is so awful,' Elaine

groaned. 'I should have called Marcus back, but perhaps you were right, we should let sleeping dogs lie for the time being. She will come back, won't she?'

'Of course she will. And when she does she's going to need our support because she sure isn't getting it elsewhere.'

'Philip has been a pig over this,' Elaine muttered bitterly. 'He's backing Greg all the way. I wish we knew what was happening to her now. I mean I'd really be panicking if we didn't know that she was with Marcus. I know that phone call was a shock at first, but one good thing is that we definitely know Cathy was with Marcus at four this morning. I so regret screaming at her like that, but it was the first thought that came into my head. I think I must have been delirious with grief over Marcus and not thinking clearly. Anyway, she was with him, but that beastly Bond man is in the same hotel. Who knows what is going on now?'

'Yes, it's a worry, isn't it?'

'Wait a minute,' Elaine suddenly cried. 'Greg hasn't come back either. I mean, if all that Philip told us is true, then Greg must have gone down to Marbella after her. Perhaps he's found her and Charles, perhaps they are both under arrest at this very minute. I know that sounds scary but at least Cathy will be able to state her case and prove her innocence – '

'Elaine, hold it, you forget that Cathy was with Marcus at four and that was hours and hours and hours after they all left here. Greg couldn't have arrested her, he would have done it sooner and we would have heard because for all Greg is a rat-faced fink for deceiving Cathy, he's still a man of the law and does things by the book. Anyway, he has no evidence, none whatsoever. You can't arrest anyone without evidence. You must know the law, your father being a judge.'

'Huh, what do I know? He's the judge, not me. I'm just some daft girl who got herself pregnant during a holiday romance and . . .' Elaine suddenly gasped and her hand flew to her mouth. 'Oh, God, Lisa, do you realize this is all my fault? If I hadn't persuaded you all to come down here, none of this would have happened.'

Wearily Lisa patted her on the knee. 'Elaine, Elaine, you can't blame yourself, that's crazy. All this would have happened back in the UK anyway.'

'Yes, I guess,' Elaine murmured, easily placated, 'but all the rest wouldn't have happened,' she said with a sudden sparkle to her eye. 'You and my brother wouldn't be in love, Cathy and Greg wouldn't have fallen for each other, and once I explain the mumps thingy to Marcus we'll be together again.'

'Gawd, Elaine,' Lisa breathed exhaustedly as she got up from the bed, 'have you been on the bottle this morning?'

'Oh, I'll never touch a drop again, only champagne at my wedding, yours too, and Cathy's.'

Lisa stared down at her as she snuggled down the bed. 'You know, Elaine, I was beginning to think you were getting smarter, more like Cathy, but you are beginning to sound like the person I once was, some silly, rose-tinted, idealistic romantic. Nothing is going to be the same any more, can't you see that?'

'Nope,' Elaine said matter of factly. 'I have faith, you see. It's wavered a few times recently, but I still have hold of it.' She nodded towards her daughter's cot. 'She gives me strength and faith. And don't you give me that nothing-can-be-the-same business. You said a very tiny word just now that gave me even more reason to think positively.'

'Oh, yes, and what word was that?' Lisa asked.

'Yet.'

'Yet, what?'

'You said you haven't slept with my brother *yet*, which means that you haven't given up hope either,' she said triumphantly. 'That was a Freudian slip, if ever I heard one,' she added and then closed her eyes and was instantly asleep.

Lisa shook her head in amazement. Elaine was a fast learner or perhaps she always had been brighter than she appeared. Pure genius was like that sometimes. Look at her Marcus, brilliant business head on his ringletted shoulders, nil points where mumps was concerned.

Lisa went straight to her own bed. She needed sleep very badly too. She had a little of Elaine's faith, only as far as Cathy was concerned, though. Cathy would be back. As for Philip and Greg and even Marcus, they all needed a good shaking to bring them to their senses.

Cathy led the way up the mountain road from the coast, driving the yellow Mercedes, Marcus following in a silver Porsche. He had been wonderful, letting her sleep in his lovely frothy bed while he snatched a few hours himself on the sofa. He had brought her breakfast around ten, looking immaculate in cream silk and linen, but nothing could disguise the shadows of worry around his eyes. Nothing could disguise hers either. She looked and felt ghastly this sun-drenched day.

She'd told Marcus about the phone call from Elain

348